WHERE LIGHT MEETS WATER

SUSAN PATERSON

**SIMON &
SCHUSTER**

London · New York · Sydney · Toronto · New Delhi

WHERE LIGHT MEETS WATER
First published in Australia in 2023 by
Simon & Schuster (Australia) Pty Limited
Suite 19A, Level 1, Building C, 450 Miller Street, Cammeray, NSW 2062

10 9 8 7 6 5 4 3 2 1

Sydney New York London Toronto New Delhi
Visit our website at www.simonandschuster.com.au

 A catalogue record for this
book is available from the
National Library of Australia

ISBN: 9781761102240

Cover design: Christabella Designs
Cover images: DigitalVision Vectors/Getty Images, Asar Studios/Alamy Stock Photo
Typeset by Midland Typesetters, Australia
Printed and bound in Australia by Griffin Press

 The paper this book is printed on is certified against the
Forest Stewardship Council® Standards. Griffin Press holds
chain of custody certification SCS–COC–001185. FSC®
promotes environmentally responsible, socially beneficial
and economically viable management of the world's forests.

To my family

The greatest brightness, short of dazzling, acts near the greatest darkness.

Johann Wolfgang von Goethe,
Theory of Colours

What a great heap of grief lay hid in me,
And how the red wild sparkles dimly burn
Through the ashen greyness.

Elizabeth Barrett Browning,
Sonnets from the Portuguese

11 June 1871
Pacific Ocean
N 4° 15' E 178° 53'

On deck the men are listless. The heat swells until the air is viscous with humidity. Sweat runs at their necks and temples. There is no wind, and they cannot stand it. Rough hands, iron stomachs, mouths filthy with fury and words as dark as starless midnight. Men of the sea. I share their passion, their dedication to the secure borders of this tough hull. A sheltered world, in the end.

Our sails now lie slack, like a woman's petticoats pegged loosely from the towering masts.

Five bells.

I practise my confession, but can see no clear point at which to begin.

I was born in a small village in West Lothian, Scotland, in 1819.

I stop myself here, for what fact of birth can describe the fact of being? Except perhaps for the damp. The winter flooding. The wet and sullen earth beneath my simple cradle. I remember the touch of cold, mossy stone; and such dark, a deep dark, a deep unbreathing dark that you could feel against your skin and inside your lungs. My constitution was made between the walls of that cottage, its humble door facing the sea. Water would become my solid ground, but it was the sky that I sought to hold.

Since then I've seen many seas and many lands, and now it is a final port I seek. This image you've gifted me guides my passage: a woodblock print, you call it. It shows a single, almost childlike barrel of an indigo-blue and white-clawed sea, curled atop with energy and about to release. I've known something of that. You chose it well, and with speed I could tell you so. But the absent wind has abandoned us to a deflated sea and feverish imaginings. My men show signs of disturbance. There are stories of what becomes of this.

Each night I am arrested by dreams. Emerging to take breath in the already-stifling morning stillness, what do I find? After all these years. Ghosts. There, in the hallucinatory rise and curl, press and fold, valleys and mountains of a vast silver aqueous motion.

Ghosts I must reconcile with the living.

PART ONE

London, 1847

1

A wailing gale riled the North Atlantic. One towering peak after another, marbled white and capped with foam. No horizon, just a grey wall of sea as the *Majestic* dropped into each wave's dark evacuated hollow.

High upon the mainmast, Tom bore the pounding of a savage spill, saltwater that hit as hard as granite. Many times the sea rose ahead only to twist itself and charge along their side. Strong sailors made slight by nature balanced on the yards. How small their bodies looked as they took in the sail.

The helmsman responded to the pull of the wheel, his body a curving counterweight, and the clipper was scooped up by another glassy crest. A boy gaped as his feet were swept from the ratlines, and Tom snatched at the lad's belted waist, quick enough to curtail his fall. Clawing them both to the rigging, he could almost hear the young heart screaming inside, indistinguishable from the storm. Terror taut at the lad's silent mouth as his hands groped for purchase. A face too tender and those eyes, so wide. One hundred feet and more they could fall from here, and there was a hard, fathomless depth beneath that.

Another crashing wave. Tom did not blink and the boy did not cry out. Already he was learning what every mariner came to know: death is ever a slip away.

'We'll see Gravesend soon,' Tom shouted close to the boy's ear. 'Climb down now.' Such certainty almost a thousand miles out from land was a lie, but it was the sole measure a mind could take to fortify the body's strength.

One hand over another, each foothold staking the body's weight, Tom descended to a gushing deck. The mast pitched and the prow dropped precipitously into another trough. Captain Martin roared from the quarterdeck; the chief mate echoed from the forecastle. As second mate, Tom followed every command. Even the cook had been ordered from his galley to add weight to the battle, his salt-beef supper saved from the teak by the sailors' well-honed stomachs.

Up to his knees, Tom fought an icy surge, and suddenly a man cried out from above, hitting the shrouds as he plummeted. The rigging broke his fall, saving his life, but his outstretched arm shattered beneath him as he landed.

Through it all Tom moved on instinct. His actions were swift and efficient. Beneath this assured activity lay a calm in which his eye discerned the hue of violet-threaded clouds dropped upon the mainmast and the glimmer of a lamp across its distinctive wood grain. In the worst of the gale he knew that if he were to lose his life to the ungovernable sea, if he were to bend his head into the crook of an elbow one final time, he would accept his fate but for the regret he'd never have the chance to paint that terrible beauty.

The battered *Majestic* and an exhausted crew limped the last stretch of their crossing from Port Phillip Bay. Finally the mouth of the Thames was a single night away.

Three and a half months. Fair weather and foul. Whenever his duties allowed, Tom re-created it all in pigment – the foaming of an Atlantic storm, the inky Southern Ocean stretching beneath a long lip of lemon, and the exact orange of the sun that seared at the oarsmen's backs in Rio. All of it locked in memory and swept from wet brush to paper while so many rounds of the bells marked time and miles in between.

The clipper was Tom's home, the crew his only family. His sketchbooks were personal logs that recorded voyages in shaded charcoal and bleeding watercolour.

He slept like he was falling, woke renewed with expectation, and made his last climb to the mainyard as they eased into Gravesend. A brawny steamer came to haul the clipper upriver to the London Docks.

Now he was on the other side: twenty-eight years old and set to be promoted to chief mate on their next run. No longer would he haul and heave the way he'd done since he was a boy. His work would be with stars and sky, wind and compass point; his word would be second only to the captain's.

Wapping was more fetid than he'd remembered, the Thames a slow-moving sewer of murk and waste.

That first morning brought hard news: the *Majestic* was to be dry-docked and the crew given leave. The rudder they'd patched up at sea would need replacing, along with its fittings. They'd need a new mizzen and rigging, and the sternpost repaired.

Tom braced himself with folded arms at Captain Martin's announcement. The shipwright was behind schedule, which would only add to their delay. A ship had caught fire during refitting that week, requiring significant repairs ahead of them. It could be three weeks before they were ready to load for the East. It could be a month.

Captain Martin clapped him on the shoulder in mutual consolation as he went below. 'Soon, Mr Rutherford. Soon.'

Tom simply nodded.

Setting his feet down on the docks after so long, he felt himself waiting for the roll and lean, the falling away. Stilled now, he reset his balance against firm ground.

'You joining us, Tom Rutherford?' The watchmen spat into their palms and smoothed their salt-thickened hair. Faces bright with thirst.

He shook his head and let them turn away to the taverns, almost as one in a wave. 'Later gentlemen, perhaps.'

Beyond the high walls of the docks, the streets closed in. Already the orange light in Rio was a far-off imagining. The sky here a lid on an airless box. He walked until he found a sign for an artists' colourman, from whom he purchased a new sketchbook, and from there followed directions to an affordable tailor, who measured him up. His old shore suit had worn thin and he wanted something befitting his new rank. Retracing his steps, he continued past the taverns, having settled upon a different escape.

By mid-morning, Tom was packing his paintbox, sketchbooks and brushes. Seamus Regan, the ship's surgeon and Tom's good friend, leaned in at the cabin door.

'It'll be good to focus some of your frustration, Tom, but Richmond? I thought you incapable of being three miles from sea.'

It was true Tom rarely slept without the lap of water at his ears, but if he could not go downriver, he would go up.

'We're further than that now, Seamus.' He shrugged. 'The colour-man recommended it for a picturesque study of the river, and I'd do well to find some distraction.'

Once before he'd discovered something unexpected inland. He was reminded of the terracotta gleam that had washed over him in

Siena when he was not yet twenty. Entrusted with the delivery of a valuable parcel from port, Tom had found colour was his reward, worth the isolated days on the road away from the coast. He had never forgotten its power, the way it momentarily relieved him of himself.

'You're sure you wouldn't fancy some country air rather than this cesspit they call the capital?' he added, pulling the cord tight on his bag.

'Indeed, but I need to replenish supplies for our next run – damned fever fleeced me of every drop of quinine – and there's a surgeon in Oxford I wish to consult with.'

'I don't think you could have saved the arm, Seamus.' Tom measured his words, holding his friend's gaze.

'At the time I was certain the infection would kill him.' The doctor's easy-natured face strained with renewed calculations. 'But there's no joy in taking a limb.'

'He was in a hellish mess. You did your best.'

Seamus smiled, quickly resolved. 'I'm sorry you have to wait for your promotion.'

'With luck, the shipwright has overestimated.' Tom hoisted his bag to his shoulder. 'As soon as we get the word, I'll be ready.'

When the next passenger steamboat headed upriver, Tom was on its deck, watching the Thames riverbank loose itself from the city's claw and regain its natural state. Richmond was some sixty miles upstream from the sea by his reckoning but the water was tidal.

Disembarking near an arching stone bridge, he continued on foot from the landing, following the riverbank a short distance until the air grew quieter. At the base of the grassy hill, he dropped his bag and sat to look out at the various launches plying the Thames, automatically estimating beam, capacity and tonnage. He followed the riggings of cream-coloured sailcloth barely filling in the calm afternoon. The passage of skiffs under oar. Canopies of bright parasols. He sketched a quick study in pencil, marking the slower cut of the river craft through the water, but felt he rushed to capture something he didn't yet understand. After a while he simply let the unfamiliar quality of the grass and the river soak into his bones, wondering at how he could ever stay still for so long, watching the wake roll itself to the riverbank. Recede, and roll in again.

Fifteen years at sea had made Tom expert at navigating swell: standing perpendicular to the deck one moment, judging a wrenching shove from the ocean the next, stepping up against the bulwark as the ship leaned to its side. The ground became whatever was under his feet at the time. Here, the earth beneath him was steadfast. It didn't sway or tilt, this grassy English riverbank, lush with summer sunshine. The sea possessed many greens but this, this colour, was something else. He wanted to stretch out along it, rub his bare feet among the silky blades. This wonderful rarity.

A light slap across his face. Tom awoke, batting away the imagined offender, and sat up. A bird? A hand? The wind had got up and played upon the river. He reached for his hat but it had scuffled several feet down the bank and was close to drowning.

Standing, he discovered the culprit. A solitary lace glove on the grass at his feet, its fingers motioning in the breeze. As it lifted again into the air, he caught it and scanned along the river path.

Down by the landing: two men holding their hats in place at the brim. A couple of young girls in crumpled calico dresses and an older boy scrambling along the water's edge.

He couldn't see any obvious origins.

The lace was brilliantly white, with a diamond motif along each finger and a pair of irregular pearls for buttons. A delicate thing, entirely impractical. It lay without weight, queer and exceptional in his hand.

He raised it to his face and was startled by the unexpected scent. How familiar it was.

Turpentine.

2

Retracing his path along the river the following morning, Tom turned this time and climbed Richmond Hill. Near to the top he spread his jacket with its tattered lining face down on the grass. Below him, a patchwork of generous picnic blankets. Amblers on the slopes. A man swaying with his barrel organ, too distant to be heard. The air up here seemed to emanate from dry earth, fragrant and foreign.

As a boy Tom had watched the silent haar slip over the Forth each summer, a fog that reminded him of the cold North Sea even when the sky was wide and azure. It was never far away, the sea that would become breath and blood. He'd lived in its arms since his da was lost to it.

Now he rolled his shirtsleeves to the elbow, opened his tin of watercolours and arranged his brushes. With the new sketchbook open against his knee, he anticipated that first mark, looked out, and felt himself falter. The midsummer green stretched away for miles, rising and falling in light and shadow, and the river was lazy and clear, slipping past leafy islets. Trees, grass, hillsides. Little buds, branches and blades. He could imitate these shapes, but the depths of them would take longer to learn.

He sat and absorbed the alterations in light and the differences in colour between sea and river, noting the cumulus formations that clumped and drifted across the sky and the shadows that followed them across the land. An hour went by. There were the numerous greens of the hillside he'd have to try to mix; the paler tones of the willows on the islets; the shade of the earth along the path, darker than sand, paler than wood. The slower-moving river lacked the sheen of the glittering Pacific, and yet he began to open to its resonant qualities, to shed all circumstance. He'd been drawn in.

'Excuse me, sir. I believe as we passed by just now—'

Tom had been lost in his painting, or rather, as he always felt, he'd found himself freed of time and place, with his whole world narrowed to fit just his thoughts and this impulse, the movement of his hand and eyes.

'Sir? I am sorry to interrupt, but I am certain I recognised in your possession—'

This time the voice pulled him from his brushwork.

Two women stood above him in voluminous outline against the sky. When one stepped nearer still, Tom saw her first as an exuberant spill of gold against the blue and green.

He felt for his hat, pushing to his feet with a quick reflex. As his eyes adjusted, the young woman sharpened in detail. He followed the pale line of her neck, half in shadow beneath a flamboyant straw hat. The shift of collarbones like driftwood under cool white sand. A dark loop of hair at each ear. When she tipped her head back with a repeat of her enquiry, he saw a handsome mouth, and a smile that rushed free and broke over him.

They happened to be crossing the grass close to where he sat, she said. The design was distinctive.

Tom scrambled to make sense of her explanation, looking down at where he had been sitting. The white lace glove was waving its diamond fingers from the pages of his sketchbook.

Dressing in the almost-blue darkness of dawn that morning, he had found the glove in his pocket and held it again to his nose. Such a harsh smell for such a pretty thing. It was a curiosity, a symbol of a different earth, and as the sun cut through at the window, he'd pressed it without thought into the back of his sketchbook. An idle souvenir.

Now the attention was upon him. His words came strange and unpractised. 'It would be a mistake to wear it near a flame,' he said, holding the glove out to her. 'It is ruined with solvent and would ignite in a second.'

'Ah, so you have found me out.' Her voice came low.

The impression of gold belonged to her creamy dress, which was shot through with vertical yellow stripes. He was surprised when she slipped the glove into a hidden pocket in the side of her skirt without any particular inspection.

'Found you out?'

She remained facing him, her smile deep with amusement, while her companion, steps from her side, turned an elegant bonneted head away to the hill.

'I think it is I who is caught,' Tom added finally.

He rubbed his neck below his ear, aware as he did so of drawing the woman's eye to fall on the skin there; his exposed forearm, which he had never inked, unlike so many of his shipmates. He was, for the first time, grateful for the fact.

But her sight had fixed on his open sketchbook and the bright watercolour, almost completed, of a small twin-masted vessel rounding the bend in the Thames below.

'How wonderful it is.'

'Aye.' He nodded, uncertain.

'Might I?' She offered her upturned palm in readiness.

Up close she was certain to see the flaws, his lack of training. He hesitated. Little more than a beat. Long enough to decide he was pleased with the attempt, even if she should find it crude.

With her head bowed over his painting, he caught the flare of a precious stone set in a pin fixing her hat in place – a deep shade of emerald, bluer than the grass. When she lifted her eyes, he discovered a more distinctive blue-green. For a brief moment she allowed him to consider them.

Then she turned away, calling to the other woman. 'Aunt? Cecilia, you must look at this.'

Her companion had been focused on the hill above, perhaps watching out for someone. 'I am sure it is lovely, but we ought not linger, Catherine.'

'I did not paint it for show,' Tom said in defence. 'You will easily find better.'

'I have not seen the hill portrayed in this way before,' she murmured.

'It is inaccurate?'

'It is fresh.'

This time as she smiled he was sure she was trying to fathom him. He imagined his own strange reflection of a sailor misplaced on land, made almost naive because of it. He was disappointed when her attention was suddenly drawn away, her head snapping around as if she had heard a command. Looking up, Tom saw a dark-suited figure observing them from the top of the hill.

Her companion was urgent at her elbow now. 'I apologise, sir.' Brisk in her address. 'We must make haste.'

The young woman nodded her acknowledgement, returning Tom's sketchbook with a lift of her chin. 'I would thank you, but I do not know your name.'

'Thomas Rutherford.'

'Miss Catherine Ogilvie – and my aunt, Miss Cecilia Broughton.'

Setting off, Catherine Ogilvie called over her shoulder, hitching her skirts a little to turn in her stride. 'Perhaps we shall meet you on the hill another day, Mr Rutherford. I should like to see more of what you make of it.'

Shading his eyes, he followed their trajectory across the grass and onto the path. Catherine Ogilvie's striped dress gave way to shadow.

She had discovered her glove in the possession of a stranger. When Catherine first called out to him, he did not turn his head, did not even hear her question. Instead, he continued to paint, draping and blotting and swizzling his brush in the tray, immersed in his work. His hat was off and his hair caught the sun like rose gold. His eyes were barely on the paper before they were soaking in the view again.

He had rolled his shirtsleeves to his elbows and she could see the tensile strength in his arms as he painted. Veins that ran like rope beneath the skin. An unnecessary musculature for an artist. She noted the colouring on his forearms and face – a man whose freckled skin had seen more sunlight than it ever would if he spent his summers in this tepid country, as she herself did. But if certain details suggested a life of labour someplace far from here, his form spoke of a dancer. Fluid when he leapt to his feet. An instinctive physical poise. In all, she was fascinated by the possibilities and had lingered too long. There would be stern words at supper about her improper approach – her *impetuosity* – but she was used to negotiating a narrow path and frequently grazed herself against the limits of her freedom.

She had watched as Thomas Rutherford both disappeared from the world and became one with it. When she had caught his attention finally, it was neither judgement nor embarrassment she had received but an exacting expression of the scene, which had revived her with its clarity, like a dousing in fresh, cold water.

3

The green grass of Richmond took on a different kind of interest for Tom. Time gained a new marker, the horizon a new landmark. It would help to pass the days, keeping a lookout across the sea of summer holiday-makers and well-heeled families that washed across the hill. He sketched and lazed in the sun, and retreated at nightfall to his modest lodging, full of images and sensations: the relentless thrum of crickets, the dappling of sunlight on tree trunks, the way the grass became chilled and the earth felt hard underfoot once the sun went down.

For two days he found himself conjuring Catherine Ogilvie back to the hill, recalling the shape of her hand and its echo, the empty lace glove. The strange force of that first encounter had imprinted on him like an insignia in hot wax. She had complimented his watercolour as if she knew about such things, and he worked up two new paintings, the second notably improved in its colouring of the Thames and the less imposing rigging of the smaller riverboats. Time fell away again as he swirled colours in his tray, and a folding in space occurred, the living landscape before him melding with the reflection of it on his page.

Until, late on the third afternoon, there she was, set up at a prominent spot on the hilltop with a portable easel, a stool and a small folding table. Cecilia Broughton sat next to her, angling a parasol to shade them from the sun striking low at their side, as Catherine Ogilvie concentrated on her painting.

It would soon be sundown. Tom didn't deliberate.

Catherine's steady wrist paused mid-gesture as if she sensed some peripheral movement. Her eyes flicked up.

Tom lifted his hat, polite with apology. Glad he'd trimmed his beard that morning but rueing the week's wait for his new suit from the tailor. He'd spent most of his bonus on it, a foolish fancy. But here he was now, so far from the sea.

She relaxed as he drew fully into view, smiling. 'It is you!'

'Fortune has returned you to us, Mr Rutherford.' Cecilia tipped her parasol further to see him.

'Fortune is what you make of things, Miss Broughton,' Tom replied easily.

'And so here is where it all began. I had a spill, you see.' Catherine gestured at the turpentine on her table. 'And when I set the gloves out to air, the wind caught one up, and air it did.'

'But you were not painting in such a pair, surely?'

She held up her hands, apparently amused. They were clothed in dark kid, stained with oil and varieties of pigment. 'Since I must wear something when painting outdoors, I favour these old things. I am forbidden to leave the house in them. So I obey that instruction and change at my easel. Immediately I am put into the best frame of mind for it.'

'Feminine attire is an unfair impediment,' Cecilia put in.

'I suppose that is the point,' Catherine said quietly.

Tom saw she had been raising her brush with an eye to the hill and its constant wanderers, but it was not the conventional subject matter that made him step in and narrow his eyes to peer more closely. The palette she used was vivid; she had not muted her colours to mirror the natural state around her as he had done. It caused a perplexing and dreamlike effect.

'Tell us, Mr Rutherford,' Cecilia said. 'Where do you hail from?'

Tom drew back from Catherine's shoulder, wondering if he'd been impolite. He threaded a hand through his hair and replaced his hat.

'Born in Scotland, as I'm sure you can hear, but that is no longer my home. I'm a man of the sea. Chief mate on the merchant ship *Majestic*, docked in London at present.' Soon his title would be true, and he enjoyed the way it sounded.

'It must be extraordinary to travel to faraway shores.' Catherine turned and brought him back to her. 'To live on the horizon. Does land hold any interest for you?'

'It never much has.'

'Ah.' She returned to her palette and lifted her brush with a dab of pale orange-gold she had mixed for the sun.

'Aye, until recently, that is.'

Tom ran a palm against his bristled cheek, regretting his honesty.

He knew what the details added up to: her richly coloured skirts beneath the clean cotton painting smock; the large ribbon-embellished hat and its pin with a precious stone. Even her practical gloves were of the highest quality. He clasped his hands behind his back, and was reminded of their calluses. In his apprentice days as a boy on the *Aurora*, he'd flayed them on winching, coiling, climbing and reefing. The cuts then had been lined with tar – the only paint known to a young seaman learning from the bottom up. He'd scrubbed them whenever he could, willed them to be more than the sum of grime, oil and coal dust.

'How long will you spend ashore?' Cecilia pressed.

'Perhaps thirty days.'

'So long as that?'

'We await repairs that can't be hurried.'

What had seemed a kind of purgatory now felt full of possibility. How quickly a day could spill from his grasp. How quickly things could change.

Catherine appeared fixed upon her brushstrokes, yet he sensed something alert in her posture.

'I hope you will make good use of your time,' she said. 'We are in Richmond until the end of the week, and I shall paint in this spot each day.'

'It is a scenic aspect.'

She laughed. 'Each summer is the same: the dress might change but in essence, the people are identical, and I have come to know the sweep of this hill and its trees and the bend in the river so well as to grow bored with its beauty many times over.'

He smiled, astonished. 'It's not boredom I see in your painting.'

'What is it you see?'

'I do not know yet.'

Her shoulders dropped. 'I'm trying to find new vision for this scene, to see things differently. I never paint it the same way twice.'

She returned her attention to what he recognised as the barrel organ player, who worked his silent keys in bright lines and dashes under her brush.

As she painted, Tom was struck by the angles she made against the falling sun. Her erect posture seemed to him a disguise for rebellion. A bluff by which she could blend in and conform when everything else about her shouted against it.

It was not just about shapes and lines, but what was contained and suggested by each surface. What it was that pulsed and breathed, formless and free underneath.

4

He took her words as an invitation and was not disappointed. They slipped into an unspoken arrangement, Tom seeking Catherine at the same spot each afternoon after his midday meal, Cecilia setting herself up an easy distance away, neat beneath her parasol with a pocket-sized book held out in front of her.

Over the next few days, Tom resumed his watercolours while Catherine applied herself nearby at the easel, newly framing the Thames beneath leaves that looked like stars.

She asked to see his sketchbooks and sank down next to him on the grass. He described the tempest they'd survived on their crossing to London, his excitement at his impending promotion. Showed her the great cone-shaped mountain in Rio and the orange sun that burned behind it. He watched as her head bent low to inspect the detail of ships at anchor in broad harbours; ships heavy with sail; ships besieged by the monsoon's catastrophic flare. A life so easily summed up in washes and charcoal.

Sometimes he would take a break from his watercolours, abandoning his spot on the grass to stand at her shoulder and quietly watch her at work. Whenever Catherine sat back to study what she had created, he would move in closer. Conscious as his body came into her view that he might be scrutinised not for his deftness or strength but for his restraint. If he were standing too close, she did not imply it.

He thought she expressed the meandering quality of the river well, showing its variations in depth as it narrowed into the distance, but her brushstrokes were loaded with that same vivid colour: thick, visible and unblended.

'The colours you choose, the way you apply them – it seems bold to me . . .' He trailed off, embarrassed by his lack of understanding.

Catherine cast her eyes to the river before replying. 'Perhaps texture and gesture might convey the very same scene that you paint so precisely.' She paused, glancing at him. 'There is energy in this earth, in that water. There is energy in me. A painting is a translation between the two, so it ought not be static.'

'Aye, your last point is true enough.'

She had begun fresh on an unblemished canvas, already stretched, which she stained in thinned raw umber after first mixing her colours. Her paint was squeezed out of tin tubes, the pigment emerging pre-mixed with linseed oil to a thick consistency. It was so much more convenient, she said, than working with powdered pigment en plein air.

'Do you like to work in oils, Mr Rutherford?'

'I rarely have the opportunity.'

'Come now. What was it you said about shaping your own fortune?'

He watched her flickering face. 'Do I sense mischief in you, Miss Ogilvie?'

'Oh, I must use all my talents in life if I am to build with tiny bricks.'

Tom felt the two of them contained by Catherine's painting, sheltered from the gaze of the buzzing hill. It seemed the sky existed for her to translate into buttery oils. The light too, and the clouds, each blade of grass came to life when she looked at them and moved her brush. Without the motion of her hand he might have forgotten he was on the hill at all.

'I think it is wonderful, here,' he said, as her layering revealed the shape and depth of its subject matter. He was transfixed by the unexpected way the hill unfolded for her. 'And here.'

'I genuinely wonder if it is brilliant or abhorrent. Perhaps it is no better than an experiment.'

Tom could not judge, and did not wish to. She seemed knowledgeable in a way he was not, and he would say nothing to dampen her spirit.

'My father says it is "modern". My brother calls it "abominable".'

'I find it fascinating.'

He observed her twisting the squat pearl earring that hung beneath a plaited loop of hair, turning it around and back again in her fingers. Loading a brush with a tint of ultramarine. Then reconsidering, wiping the brush clean.

'In truth, I am often told my eye is awful,' she confessed one afternoon, leaving her easel to again sit with Tom on the grass. 'That I am no artist. You are kind not to say so too.'

What made a person an artist? Now that she pressed him, he discovered he had no evidence beyond sensation and an intuitive urge.

'It is not kindness. You seem set on developing your own style.'

'I have ideas. Too many to be good for me, I am told. Young ladies ought to be accomplished in all the arts, of course, and not the least of those painting. We ought to be talented, in a particular, unchallenging way. Exceptionality is discouraged. We are seen as children. And if we break out, dangerous radicals.'

'Are you a radical?' He was tempted to laugh.

'A woman with her own mind is always a radical. It cannot be helped.' Watching his face, she was the one to laugh, then she quietened abruptly.

'Do I unsettle you, Mr Rutherford? I would not blame you if it were so.'

'No, Miss Ogilvie,' Tom replied, deliberate and firm. 'I'm not easily unsettled.'

'I could engage you.' Her words were bright again as she dabbed a gleam of cadmium yellow into place.

'Engage me?' Standing near her shoulder, he almost coughed his reply. 'What do you mean?'

'I could engage you as a tutor.' She twisted on her stool. 'For the time you are here. Your eye is particular and from what I have seen your hand is very good – precise, delicate, yet confident. You allow the viewer entry. There is something in your use of light, the way you mix your colours perhaps, the softness of your palette.' Her voice fell, gentle he thought. 'It is quite special.'

'A tutor?' He scratched at his beard. 'Miss Ogilvie, I am a sailor—'

'You have shown me you are also an artist. It does not matter what name we give the arrangement.'

He puzzled at this while she added a final flourish with her brush. Clouds hung in punctuated formations, permitting a wash of amber light. She had caught the right colour there, he thought. She had lit the scene from one side, highlighting the stone path that stepped down towards the winding Thames.

As she turned again for a response, Tom felt his breath catch, as it did on occasion at sea when the wind pressed at him too fiercely. Catherine answered for him. 'It will be easier to arrange this way. If you would visit me at Ogilvie House, we might continue to paint together.'

'Ogilvie House?' He glanced out across the hill to the river, which led to the sea, and gave a small laugh. 'So easy as that?'

This would come to an end. He would depart for the East as chief mate and his world would be righted. She was humouring him, she must be, but he took pleasure in what felt like tender persuasion.

'I am an amateur, as you well know, Miss Ogilvie. What could you possibly learn from me?'

'That is for me to judge, do you not think?'

'Your father wouldn't approve,' Tom guessed. He rubbed his fingers against his palms, keeping his hands behind his back.

'My father? Oh, no, Papa will be no problem.'

'I too am confident he might be persuaded.' The voice was Cecilia's. She softened the unexpected intrusion with a touch at her niece's shoulder, then consulted a small silver watch pinned at the waist of her light-blue dress. 'It is almost time we went in,' she said.

Beneath her hat, Catherine seemed in a storm. She pushed to her feet and began to untie her smock. Tom feared he had been too reticent.

'In the meantime, perhaps Mr Rutherford might accompany us on a visit to the National Gallery? We return tomorrow morning to London, sir, and although we have already viewed the Exhibition this year, I believe there are one or two pieces otherwise on display that may prove of particular interest to a mariner.'

'Yes, Aunt. You are clever.' Catherine's eyes brightened. The emerald hatpin flared. The sun had dipped low on them and Tom had not noticed.

Catherine looked at him. 'Are we agreed? Do say you will come, Mr Rutherford?'

Night would soon fall upon the hill.

'It would be my pleasure.'

*

The quiet each morning was disconcerting. A kind of haunting.

Tom lay unmoving in his bed in Richmond, straining to hear the world. It was all so still, free of the familiar vocalisations of the sea and the insistent shipboard protestations that together made their own silence. Sounds here came in bursts, irregular and short-lived: the sudden complaint of floorboards along the hallway, a closing of the front door, the brief commune of birds as they resettled in the trees outside.

Although he had grown used to his private cabin since he'd been a mate, it was still strange to close his eyes and not hear the breathing of other men. He found it impossible to sleep through the night. He'd wake after four hours, his muscles primed for activity, his ears ready for the bells that did not ring out.

Kept in constant employ since his apprenticeship, he had become trusted. Sought after. He'd worked his way up. Tom held to his ambitions: to run his own ship, to gather his own crew, to teach as he'd been taught.

His childhood in Bo'ness had faded, his family was long gone. His home had been rebuilt on the water. The quarterdeck was all he required and he'd fought hard for it.

He smoothed a hand across his chest as if to explore what had enlivened there. It was too early to judge its nature. He brought his arms to rest behind his head, craving touch. In Port Phillip he had spent a single night with a woman, who had run her hands over his skin as if she knew him. A simple illusion of intimacy, convenient to them both. You have a strong body, she'd flattered him. So lean and muscular. A sailor's body, he had corrected her, the specifics somehow mattering. It was only his surface she touched, and she asked for nothing more in return. Tom had left her afterwards, free of any regret. His privacy unbroken.

It had never been any different.

Now he assured himself nothing had changed; when the *Majestic* next weighed anchor it would not take long until the rhythms of the sea moved him again. He would learn to forget this too.

Reeled back from sleep as the light broke through beneath the curtains, he had seen in the shadows what he took to be a face. Dreams filled in the rest, and he gasped at the flickering moment of confusion between unconscious and conscious, memory and imagination. It was Catherine's image that had slipped in and lingered, tender-fingered. She offered him the skin at the back of her neck, which flushed in the warmth as she worked. Slowly lifted her head so that he was swept into the dip at her throat.

Strange what came to you when you were still.

Summer would fade; this much was certain. The Ogilvies had packed up their belongings and departed by carriage for London that morning. Tom had been instructed by message to meet Catherine and Cecilia before the gallery steps at noon in Trafalgar Square the following day.

And so he would take the small iron steamboat again and chug his way back down the Thames towards the docks and the sour, overcrowded city, its sewers overflowing into the pitted streets and its chimneys blanketing soot over even the grandest stone facades.

5

Tom made himself obscure. It wasn't hard. He was used to small spaces, low ceilings, airlessness, the darkest confines. He was used to a certain stench and to a ship's unsanitary states, but the city's foulness was acrid: effluence, both human and animal, baking in the sun.

The vast meeting point of Trafalgar Square was a convergence of commotion. Open-topped carriages, roaming dogs, women with carts, children with cunning faces, cabs to London Bridge. He noted it all and pressed himself against the base of a stone plinth, a column as tall as a mainmast towering above him in the sky.

Around him the crowd became a stream of tall hats, gloved hands and suited arms bent at the elbow. Enormous skirts navigated the curb. There was hierarchy signified by this finery; a person of rank would observe at once who was of a level, and who was not. But to Tom it meant nothing more than a striking palette of dyed fabric swinging through the light.

Freed from occupation and routine, his mind was wandering. His own observations caught him by surprise. The day was conveyed to him so clearly in a flash of colour.

He adjusted his necktie and checked the lapels of his new suit, his skin already sticky beneath the wool. An irregular clip of hooves passing too close broke his reverie and he set off again across the square to its northern edge.

From a distance he caught sight of them. A black-clad footman swung open the carriage door and Catherine stepped down in a rush of cobalt, briefly accepting the fellow's hand before leaving it to hang in the air. Cecilia, more restrained, a smudge of apricot close behind. Tom crossed to meet them on the steps below the pillared heft of the National Gallery.

'Mr Rutherford.' Catherine was quick to call when she saw him. 'So pleased you could make it.'

'Miss Ogilvie, Miss Broughton.' He glanced from one to the other, wondering what came next.

Catherine paused too, as if considering him against the different backdrop, then wound an arm around her aunt's with a reassuring smile. 'Well, shall we?'

Tom followed the line of her closed parasol, the handle raised before her, pointing them in the direction they should take.

With the doors closed against the rush of the square, a tremendous, cavernous silence hit, as if they had sunk beneath the surface. He shook his head, thinking to clear his ears of water. The ceilings soared. He held his breath. And then small sounds came to him: sharp, reticent, clipped. The tips of women's heels, a parasol or perhaps a stick tapping at wood, at marble. Whispers like zephyrs through the studious atmosphere.

All he had to compare to the scene before him were those early watches when the water gleamed like a vast reflective surface around the ship, and stealthy waves of mist swelled and scaled the bulwark. A moment slowed, saturated with feeling. But even then, even at its quietest, the constancy of rope, iron, wood, all chafing and groaning; the wind like a siren calling; the slap of sailcloth; the cough of a man. A voice cutting through with an order.

And the bells. Decisive markers regulating the watches, breaking the day into perfectly measured blocks. The more voyages Tom had completed, the more the regularity of the ringing bells came to demarcate a passage not just through the day at sea but through his life. With sail set and a swift course being cut, the shipboard world contained everything in existence – a heaving hull of exhilaration and hardship, mateship and loneliness, drunkenness and deprivation, satisfying effort and harsh lessons. Out on the water, beneath the cloth of sky and the pinpoints of constellations, the rest of the world ceased to exist.

'It is extraordinarily wild, is it not?' Catherine whispered at his shoulder. 'I wanted to show it to you in particular.'

Tom read the attribution etched into the gilt frame: JMW Turner. *Snow Storm – Steam-Boat off a Harbour's Mouth.*

'At the Exhibition this year the critics have been outraged by Turner's obscure depiction of the Duke of Wellington atop what could be a giraffe. They are asking what on earth has come over him. And this, painted a few years ago. They all seem to loathe it, except Mr Ruskin. I think it is moving and so modern. Do you not feel, when looking at this painting, that you are abducted by it? I am inside that scene, experiencing the storm, feeling it on my skin. I can hear the roar. There is an abandon in his style, a great freedom.'

Tom didn't know who this fellow Ruskin was, but Catherine was right. The painting was wild, unlike anything he'd seen before, unlike anything he'd ever paint himself. This Turner, was he too a salt? But how did he see this? Tom rebelled, physically, by taking a step back, and then another. And as he did so, it was as if the atmosphere conjured by the smudged sky and peaked waves became more powerful in their evocation. Yet it was all so imprecise. How was this possible?

Tom stared at the painting. It was madness.

In his world, control was everything. It was how a ship held together and mutinies were avoided. It was how a person kept themselves whole after loss. On the canvas when he took up his brush: fine lines, precision rendering, a representation of the world as he saw it. All the detail and observation of a mariner expressed accurately, down to the very last part of the ship's rigging, in a recognisable form. Authoritative. Not this. This chaos. This forgetting of form. This wondrous swirl of colour and suggestion, which tugged him in the gut, drew him in.

With his paintbrush he would always lead a straightforward, guileless depiction: ship, sea, sky, insignia. But when he stood before this painting his vision seared with something more abstract. Here lay danger, greater danger than the tempest that had hit them across the Atlantic, greater than a snapped mast even, or a gash in the hull. It hinted at a more serious risk of sinking. A slip into a sublime loss of consciousness, a willing surrender, a suicide.

He was pulled back to the water through emotion and inference, and used his experience to fill in the gaps. Out of the boxy patch of umber paint he could see the linear bulk of the mast, as if he viewed it straight up from the deck; saw the nimbus swelling in brooding gusts; felt the whole-bodied sickness that he'd fought against during a heavy storm back then, aloft on his first voyage. He was a boy again, thirteen, at the mercy of this world. Buffeted. Seeing everything in a daze, a messy imprecision, unfocused by grief, confusion and newness.

And then he turned. He was a man again, looking out across the floor of the gallery room, adjusting his focus against the sun filtering in from the skylights. And then he understood that he saw her, Catherine, in that way too. She was an expression of courageous relinquishment, a loss of control. He could feel himself sinking next to her. He was, he realised, terrified.

.

6

His path had shifted before in sudden and unanticipated ways. By God's glorious design, as his ma explained it. Privately Tom wondered how she could be so accepting, so full of faith. She had lost three other children in the womb after he was born, had come to know poverty and the sea's ambivalence too well through the life she had shared with his da. Tom understood she wanted something else for her son. She had tried to give it to him through books and poetry and small gifts of ink and paper. Through teaching him his letters, to read and write, to express himself well – just as she, the daughter of a schoolmaster, had been taught. And yet here he was. A sailor like his father. A man entirely of the sea.

The morning of his da's funeral had greeted Tom in subdued shading: a grey and sombre sky, brown earth. The black suits of men, the black dresses of women. The whites of his mother's eyes beneath reddened lids. Even then he saw it like this. He watched his ma sweep her hair into a knot and catch it beneath her bonnet, securing the ribbon at her chin. Her narrow waist did not yet hint of the change but her hand softened there as if to soothe the unborn child.

'We mustn't hope, Tom. No one could survive this long.'

Tom had spent a night by the shore at Bo'ness, keeping watch for the frozen body of James Rutherford in case it should be delivered so late and so far up the Forth. The rest of the crew had been washed up unceremoniously by the North Sea two days prior, down near the mouth, off Fidra. He'd heard the reports: the fishing boat's hull must have been carved by rock as the northeasterly gale snuffed light from the sky and pressed them off course on their return home. A forlorn debris, limbs blue and bent into odd postures, no different from the shattered planks and scattered screws around them.

Tom had remained seeking in the dark, well beyond sightlessness, terrified of finding what he was looking for. Would the stony beach gash his father's bloated cheek as it had done the other men? Would his da have shut his eyes at the last, or died with them open?

'He has been taken back out to sea where he belongs, Tom.' His ma struggled for breath at the door of the church. 'Keep him in your memory as he was.'

How could she be so sure?

'You look so much alike,' she said, smoothing his cheek.

He didn't know whether to feel proud or guilty. He waited at her side while she dabbed her eyes with a handkerchief, then took her arm as they entered the church. Light spread like jaundice across the stone altar.

It was the longest walk Tom had ever taken. It was as if in walking the length of the aisle he walked through his entire life, knew age and melancholy and unrealised dreams, and he imagined that by the time they reached their pew at the front of the church it would be over for him, too.

Yet he made it through the eulogy and the prayers that followed, and insisted on bearing one of the five caskets with the other men, though at thirteen he was barely tall enough to shoulder the weight.

Over the sodden ground beyond the church they filed, slow with cautious steps, to lay to rest those shipmen of the wreck who had been returned to them.

As the last of the earth was shovelled over the graves and the mourners began to disperse, Tom lingered, wondering why it didn't feel real. His mother was at the cemetery gates with the minister, who patted his bible with a flat hand. Tom found it hard to turn his back on the men hidden in the dark earth, their arms now crossed in a peacefulness he could not believe in, their mouths quiet with the unspoken fate of his da. He crouched, awaiting their secret. Their wives had wept at the graves and clutched lockets of hair against their hearts. Without a body, Tom and his ma had stood back, struggling with their own unfastened grief.

Finally pushing to his feet, Tom sensed a corporeal presence across the disturbed earth. A broad-shouldered man enveloped in a heavy coat. He felt the stranger look at him as if they might have met some time ago.

His mother touched Tom on the arm, and the man was gone.

They had not long returned to their cottage before a cart drew up along the rutted road. Closer up, the man in the coat was clearly a salt, betrayed by his wide-set gait.

'Captain Richard Sweet.' He removed his hat at the door, nodding to Tom's mother.

'Marion Rutherford, sir.'

Tom felt his father observing them from an ink drawing on the dresser. He had created it himself on a piece of flour-bag cloth just a week earlier and tacked it onto wood. It was as if Tom had known, his ma grieved; she was grateful for the image. But Tom had no such premonition, no special communication with a higher power, just an impulse to make meaning from the lines of their small existence. The ink had bled and it couldn't capture the colour of his father's blazing red hair, but the likeness was good enough.

'You are clearly James's son,' Sweet said.

'Tom, sir.' He sat on the end of his bed.

The captain did not object when Tom's mother offered to ease the coat from his shoulders, though his breath was visible on the air.

Tom followed Sweet's gaze around the single room of their home, across the low-burning hearth to the cook pot and the scrappy kindling he would need to replenish before nightfall, to the sideboard his ma had arranged with the faded cloth spines of her remaining books and a jewel box that he knew to be empty. His ma with her pinched face, arms folded like wings.

'How old are you, lad?'

'Thirteen, Captain Sweet.'

'That's a good age.' The captain nodded.

Tom didn't know for what.

'Where do you stay, sir?' Tom's mother gestured to a chair, its back to the wash basin where she and Tom had readied themselves for the funeral.

'My ship, the *Aurora*, is docked at Leith, and I shall return by sundown.' Sweet did not sit immediately but seemed to be deliberating.

'You knew my husband?'

'Aye, and once well. Over the years I have often wondered what became of James Rutherford. We lost touch – it must be sixteen years ago – when I rose from able seaman to second mate under a new captain. I was saddened to hear his name among those lost when I docked yesterday.'

Sweet set his eyes on Tom as he spoke, and Tom was eased by the familiar mix of firmness and softness there.

'He was hardworking, your father. Loyal. Stubbornly brave.'

'You sailed with him, sir? On a tall ship?'

'Aye, lad, we faced storm and wind and the rumblings of mutiny together, James Rutherford and I.'

Captain Sweet drew himself up now at the table as Tom's ma poured their tea.

'Tell me, sir?'

Sweet took a sip from his cup and spoke with lowered voice. 'The truth is, I would never have survived if it had not been for your father.'

Tom sat forward as the captain described being caught out as a young seaman once, deep in the night, as he ascended the foremast during their watch. Within seconds of securing the fore topsail, a vast wave rose and dumped itself across the bow, knocking him from the mast, flinging him down towards the deck, then sucking him with unnatural strength over the bulwark. James Rutherford had clutched at his friend as Sweet's body went over the side, holding fast to one arm. Sweet was a competent seaman, experienced, strong. But that weighed nothing against the graceless force of the elements. They were headed far into the fierceness of the fifties, rounding Cape Horn, that treacherous conjunction of Atlantic and Pacific where winds speared vessels on the rocks as if they were prey.

'I was bellowing,' Sweet confessed. 'A fully grown man of more than twenty. To my shame I told him to let me go. But James Rutherford's hands were as strong as iron clamps. He shouldn't have been any match against that swell as it hollowed out and rounded with even more power, breaking across us time and time over.'

The room swirled with the image of Tom's father raging against the sea, refusing to relinquish Sweet; the captain as a younger man, his body dangling and slight against the side of the ship. Tom felt a spasm under his own ribs, a longing for his da he tried to keep down. His mother's eyes shone.

'To this day I can recall the pain surging up my spine, and the shout of the sea as it dragged at my body. I was sure I was broken.'

Tom waited for more. His father had never spoken of this.

'I swear as I stood by those graves this morning I could taste the bile and saltwater that I retched up afterwards in the sick bay, shivering but mercifully intact. In truth I owe him a debt.'

When Tom looked up, Sweet was staring straight at him.

'I gather you can swim, take orders?'

'Aye, sir, been out on the water with my da since I was a wee lad.'

His mother wiped her eyes and nodded too, a strained gesture, both proud and reluctant. 'And read, sir. He's been schooled. And you'll see he can draw.' She turned her head towards the image of her husband.

'Neither skill necessary for a ship's hand.' Sweet's reply came as swift as an order.

Tom looked away.

'Of course, both could serve him well in the end.'

7

Tom imagined when it was over and the world had returned to its expected order, he would recall this feeling of anticipation: the sound of a door opening, the signal of aged timber and the cushioned tread as Catherine hastened down the stairs, her determined figure lost to him momentarily in the blaze of early afternoon then rediscovered as she arrived to greet him. Everything was intense in form and colour. The soft-looking carpeting ran in an ultramarine strip along the staircase beneath her. A cascade of Mediterranean blue. He wanted to crouch at her feet and run his fingers through it.

Tom had been ushered in by a servant and left expectant in the front hall. Ogilvie House sat around his shoulders like an unfamiliar greatcoat. Weighted by its beauty and strangeness, he found himself held in place upon marble flooring; captured by the sweep of banisters, the eyes of round mirrors, and framed paintings that both studied him from afar and urged him closer. He had stepped around the unexpected body of a deer, its skin removed and flattened on the floor, and discovered its antlered head pinned separately to the wall.

As he waited for Catherine, he was back at the National Gallery, viewing everything with respectful distance, from the outside, as an object of wonder. In his mind he stretched out, examined this piece and that. Ran his hands along each surface. Stood with his face so close to each painting he could see where the oils had aged and cracked. But his material form remained composed and contained, his arms secured at his back, fingers curled.

How long would it take a person to polish all that burnished wood and gleaming metal? Who did this work? Invisible men and women, unseen behind doors and hidden below. Hierarchy didn't faze him. He was comfortable within its rules and definitions. But such wealth was more than he had ever presumed. Even in the hall the servants moved wraithlike in black and white among fragile objects that he knew to be from foreign shores. They dusted translucent porcelain vases and arranged orchid stems. Lifted and replaced a black lacquer tea canister inlaid with mother-of-pearl.

He had been instructed to wait beside a statuette on a small plinth, just a head with no torso looking out to a broad-shouldered vessel that writhed with the inky body of a dragon.

Less than a fortnight ago his strong hands had grasped the mainyard on the *Majestic* as they arrived into Gravesend, his body his most reliable tool, every muscle engaged and responsive. Here he would not be required to exert force to make something topple. Delicate surrounds required delicate people, carefully held bodies that gestured with soft limbs.

So this was Catherine's world. Yet in her he sensed something tensile, a deliberate sinewy force he thought he understood.

It had taken him longer than expected to navigate the four miles west across town to the address she had given. With the congestion of carts and carriages and the confusing layout of lanes and streets he'd found himself running late, and sweating from the rush and stress of it all. He cursed himself for his lapse. Time had caught him out, ticking by in minutes and hours, unpunctuated by the imperious bells.

He was drawn by a scent. Woody crushed herbs. Citrus oil. Frankincense, perhaps. Catherine, standing before him, her head angled to one side, smiling as she pulled on her gloves. 'You found us, Mr Rutherford.' Taking in the heat and pulse of him.

In her trail, Cecilia arrived with a generous greeting, patting a bonnet into place. Two manservants manifested as if on cue. Immediately Tom was handed a mahogany box with a brass handle – larger than the one Catherine had used at Richmond – which he guessed to hold her paints and brushes. He readied himself to carry the remaining equipment they would need but nothing more was offered.

'I'm sorry if I've set you out of time.' Tom grasped the paintbox to his side, feeling his face flush.

'Not at all, there is nothing to apologise for. But let us go now.' And then: 'Papa!'

Her call was unrestrained, surprisingly full-voiced.

'*Papa!*' She paused. 'I am going for my lesson. You shall have to meet Mr Rutherford another time.'

Her second summoning brought a figure into view upon the first-floor gallery. Lord Ogilvie approached the banister and hailed the group with a sheath of papers that he waved before him in one hand like a white flag, not unlike a master on deck. Tom found himself anticipating what would emerge from behind the paper shield, waiting for the scene to conclude with a revelation: a voice, a face. A father. Her father.

'Right you are, Catherine.' The man was revealed. Papers lowered, he removed his eyeglasses and spoke with an unflustered smile. 'Mr Rutherford, is that it? Well, I suppose we ought to take a minute first.'

It was an aged face that met Tom, but one unbeaten by storm, unmarked by incident of the violent kind.

'Really, Papa.' Catherine sighed, turning to Tom. 'You ought to go up then.'

Lord Ogilvie had already disappeared along the gallery.

Climbing to the first floor, Tom followed the man's voice, disembodied now, lost in shadow. He heard it instruct him. 'I do hope you can detour my daughter off the path of the artist. She is full of opinions about great art but they are not at all matched by what emerges from her brush.'

A detour was hardly the aim of Tom's instruction. He looked down at Catherine, waiting in the hall below with Cecilia. It occurred to him for the first time that perhaps he had known his own kind of privilege: he had been encouraged in his drawing as a young child, by his ma at least, no matter that the practising of it was limited and humble in means. He'd had no dreams attached to it, no ambition beyond the way it made him feel both calm and joyous. Tom's da had called painting an idle man's dalliance. He believed in labour, in the value of hard work. And Tom had inherited those beliefs, too.

'Do not listen to my father,' Catherine called out. 'He has never grown accustomed to having a daughter with a mind of her own.' This last she added with emphasis.

'No, indeed. And I have the world on my side.'

Tom followed the reply. At an open door he halted, knocked and looked in.

Lord Ogilvie had already resettled at his desk and was arranging his papers before him. Inkwell at hand, nib poised, he gestured for Tom to enter.

If Tom could have opened a small hatch into the man's head, this was how he supposed it might be to observe its interior. A single book-lined wall, orderly with leather spines and stamped gold lettering, faced off against a dizzying patchwork of drawings and paintings closely hung on each of the other three. Gilt frames and wooden, embellished and plain. Portraits, landscapes, large and small. It was a beautiful mess.

He closed the door after him, assuming it was expected.

'In truth I have little to say on the matter.' Lord Ogilvie did not look up.

Tom stood before the desk, an interloper among painted scenes of tranquil rivers with drooping willows; Venice with its narrow gondolas and still waters in dark indigo; torsos in terrible contortions – one pierced by numerous arrows, another with a gash in its side; and women with serene faces and pale breasts exposed from flowing drapery.

On the wall behind Catherine's father, a nocturnal marine painting in darkest green and gold. Two humble boats, fishermen within, and moonlight illuminating their journey across a surging sea that Tom sensed would shift in an instant to overpower them. The painting conveyed so well a fragility he recognised from experience, and from what he had imagined many times over. This was what it looked like before the precipitous balance between humankind and nature was upset, before the wind rose up, blustered and lashed at the fishermen's defenceless bodies; before the slap of its rage, the bite of the salt and ice, and the terror at being lost to the sea's careless power.

'You enjoy that particular piece. Turner's fishers?'

Tom felt exposed, roused from reverie. The man's eyes were on him now. 'Aye, it is moving.' The artist's name rang with familiarity and he peered up at it again.

'It was his first oil piece to be exhibited at the Royal Academy. And a far cry from his latest creations.'

Lord Ogilvie leaned back in his chair and tapped two fingers against the edge of the desk.

'My daughter appreciates it also.'

'Your daughter – Miss Ogilvie – appears to know a great deal about art.'

'Indeed she does. And you see if she were not a daughter then I would not be required to voice reservations about these lessons, which I cannot bring myself to deny.'

Tom sensed a stream of required collusion. He wanted to win the man's confidence.

'Yet, Mr Rutherford, since she is . . .'

Tom puzzled a moment longer, and took a leap. 'I assure you, my lord, I'll do my best to teach a dull lesson in which your daughter will learn nothing of further value about art.'

He didn't want to betray Catherine, but neither did he wish to be turned away. It did not require him to lie.

'Mr Rutherford, I am very relieved to hear it.'

'In any case our lessons shall be short-lived.'

'Yes, good.'

'And I am a sailor.'

'Not even a member of the Academy,' Lord Ogilvie added with a nod.

'No, my lord. So you see, you have nothing to worry about.'

'I agree.' Catherine's father betrayed a faint smile. 'Nothing to worry about at all, Mr Rutherford.'

Catherine led the way out into the large private garden at the rear of the house, with Tom and Cecilia – and the servants, laden with art supplies – trailing behind her like loosed ribbons.

'Did he tell you I should have been a boy?' Catherine called to him as they cut across the lawn. Her movements were strong and fluid: a deliberate flow of ruby cotton with a narrow shadow following close behind her.

Tom's response was just as candid, confessional. He felt his stride matching hers. The wind, cool at his neck, revived him.

'You don't think it would suit you?'

Her hands swung, brushing her skirt as she walked, and she stretched into the breeze, her fingers like constellations.

'Everything would be so easy. Perhaps I should be bored.'

With the easel set up for them in the garden, Tom stood to one side for Catherine to take her place, but she looked at him and shook her head.

'Is something wrong, Miss Ogilvie?'

'Not at all.' Her mouth curved. She was teasing him. This much he could tell. Cecilia offered no clue, already lost in her book and barely within earshot.

'You wanted me to teach you?' It sounded ludicrous spoken out loud. It should be her teaching him. He heard his words from a distance, as if spoken by someone else. He saw each word in abstract too, and read them like labels on a map: emboldened letters that stood out from the landscape. He was trying to identify something he couldn't see, wondering what it was. What she was.

'I wish to observe you as you paint, as you have observed me,' she said. 'Show me how you use colour and line. Show me all that you have seen.'

Tom soon realised the flaw in their plan.

He raised his brush and the gaping expanse of canvas stalled him.

He didn't know how to paint.

He didn't know *how* he painted. Everything he did was by instinct, so how could he demonstrate it for her?

'I'm not sure I can describe . . .' He wasn't even sure how to confess.

'I understand,' Catherine said. 'Your art is unfettered by rule and school and classification. We two are outsiders in the creative world.'

'Well, at least I'll not disobey your father by encouraging you with my great artistic knowledge.' He searched for an acknowledgement of their bind and found in the shifting of her brow that she had understood.

'Pretend I am not here. I will watch for this first example.'

An impossibility, he thought, as an artist, as a man. But soon he relaxed, moving into the assured part of himself that led not with thought but feeling.

He would work with the oils she provided, translating one of his watercolour sketches onto the far larger canvas. He made a light sketch of his composition in pencil and then began. A background wash of pale blue came first, building to a sky of indigo and eggshell white with a hint of lemon breaking through; the Pacific post-storm, still churning and thick with foam. In the foreground, a calming in degrees towards a flat sea, which held the future of the picture.

And then, the particulars that showed himself as a mariner. He knew without fault the length and line of the rigging, could perfectly re-create the pull of the sails in the wind, some furled, others catching. He depicted it all from the distant observer's eye though he had spent so much of his life up close, upon and below the mast.

'And you, Mr Rutherford? Are you in this scene?' Her fingers splayed now at a hip. 'Where are all the people? Is anyone working the sails?'

Tom saw a ship emerging through storm with an invisible crew. He'd never considered who was on board before.

And so he decided, taking a direction that felt true. 'I am in the longboat, here.'

He painted the dark blue jacket on a small figure in the prow of a longboat, distinguishing himself from the other sailors by the addition of a crimson scarf at his neck. He watched Catherine's expression build with a smile he was coming to trust. 'We are coming into shore.'

8

What was it like to lose sight of land and face the sea's darkest nature? Catherine longed to know. Since their visit to the gallery, she wondered how Tom's experience of Turner's painting might differ from her own forceful intuiting, which she had thrilled to describe to him. She had searched him for signs of an embodied response, an especial nod of knowing. He had been made quiet, powerfully so. His body seemed almost to vibrate with it. If she had touched him then, he might have leapt to the ceiling, or crumbled into dust. She was awed by the way an artwork might connect and differentiate its viewers. By the painting's mysterious reflective quality. By what she saw as its capacity for enlargement.

Now, in the garden, she watched his eyes crease with a question. 'I'm not the first, am I, Miss Ogilvie?'

Catherine laughed. 'I have been tutored in painting before, Mr Rutherford, if that is what you mean.'

Tom smiled. 'And that was when?'

'I was fifteen.'

'And the fellow in question?'

'A gentleman artist of the Academy named Mr Barolo, who was instructed to introduce me to the skills required for basic representation.'

Catherine recalled how she had been made to sit each afternoon before large porcelain vases of heavy-headed peonies, clusters of irises, nasturtiums and lilac, and urged to draw and redraw, to paint and repaint, until her depictions were deemed lifelike enough to satisfy. Once the flowers were accomplished well enough, they moved to other still-life arrangements: fruits on a platter, a perfume bottle on a dressing table, an unoccupied cushion in the bay window. But she questioned it all: why was the cushion never occupied, why was the scent not applied to a wrist or at the collar of a dress, why was there no one to slice and eat the ripe fruit with the juice running between their fingers?

Romantic nonsense, Mr Barolo had said. And he'd gone on: her paintings lacked realism; she did not render objects with a natural effect; she did not show the world as it truly was.

'As if there were one correct way to see the world, one correct way to express it only. He had no feeling at all, no life in him.'

She glanced at Tom, who was listening with such concentration. He had hidden his hands behind his back; those sinewy, sun-touched arms that she had noticed on the hill, covered up now and trapped in his new suit. She willed him to break his composure. 'He made painting a chore. My eye was wrong. I took myself too seriously when I ought to be grateful for any learning at all. And I ought to be languid, my brush a graceful accessory. In short, I ought to paint like a lady.' She conjured a look of scornful humour and was charmed when it drew from Tom his almost shy, boyish laugh.

Those days had passed in a stultifying tumble as she faced off against her easel in the conservatory. The light was best there for painting, Mr Barolo said. Beyond the windows the sky rushed and puffed and bloomed, the gardener inched past on his knees, picking weeds from freshly turned soil, while Catherine felt she was wilting. She knew she could see the world clearly. She knew the lessons were designed to bestow on her a sanctioned level of skill and to discourage self-expression.

She knew she was being reined in.

In time she begged her father to take the lessons from her, pleading that she could not paint well enough to satisfy her tutor, and Mr Barolo did not equivocate. Then in secret she took herself off with her aunt – who never discouraged and would pose according to Catherine's direction. Beside the trickling fountain in the garden with a bonnet curved at her face and the wind in her skirts. Or at the pianoforte playing their favourite Schubert while Catherine attempted to show the motion of her hands and body within a static form. By this point Catherine realised it was much more difficult than it looked: drawing, painting, setting life on canvas, creating depth on a flat surface, showing movement in fixed strokes, finding the colour of the sunlight, getting the shadows right. It made her love the works she visited in London's galleries even more, and fed her ambition to somehow find her own path forward as a painter.

When she spotted Tom's watercolour of the sailboat moving upon the Thames, painted with such detail and expressiveness, she saw more than just a sketchbook with a single page revealed; she saw an opening, an unmarked door ajar and admitting light, a creative conversation to be explored. She knew she had been right when Tom was rendered speechless before the Turner, just as she had been the first time.

That they were alike in that feeling gave her hope, and some relief: to have found a common mind, a heart that could be as moved as hers, a temperament as open and, she suspected, riven with longing. She craved his otherness, too, to know the touch of salt and journey, the physical and energetic, every dawn and dusk, all that he had been before her. To understand what had made him.

Tom followed the flick of Catherine's wrists, the sway and fold of her as she lifted the blanket into the air and settled it onto the grass. Her face pinched in concentration. Satisfied, she knelt down and smoothed the blanket out.

'Aunt?' she called, lifting the lid on the picnic basket.

'You go on.' Cecilia raised her book as evidence.

Tom wiped the last of the pigment from his hands and left the oils to start their long, slow process of drying.

Catherine gestured for him to join her and offered him a sandwich. He finished it in little more than a single swallow and followed it with a second before realising what this betrayed. His palate had grown accustomed to the terminal dullness of weevil-infested sea biscuit, salted meat, the watered-down toxicity of grog. His hands he fancied to be two great paws beneath his bristling beard, too rustic for the straight lines of soft bread and finely sliced cucumber. But this feeling ebbed. The cool lemon tea Catherine poured for him slid down his throat like a summer breeze.

'I'll have to make the mizzenmast better.' He rested back, his arms bent like two firm braces, and stretched his legs along the blanket. The indulgence of such reflection was another curiosity he fought to make familiar. He strove to assimilate it all.

Within days, work would start on the *Majestic*. A solid new mizzenmast would be hoisted and secured. He could see it all, gaining in momentum: in a couple more weeks after that, the clipper would be released from the dry dock; they'd load and ready her hull, settle into the well-loved grooves of each plank and rail, and he would depart London – chief mate, returned to the sea as he had always intended. It shocked him, there on the blanket, lying flat to the earth, to find a seam of discomfort in the vision, a rupture already too deep to ignore.

'The mizzenmast?'

'The mast at stern, behind the fore and mainmasts.'

There she was, sitting next to him with the same determinedly straight back he'd observed at Richmond on the hill. Would she ever slump, soften her posture, make curves like a sailor bending into the wind? Yet she was animated when she spoke, and he could not help but absorb every gesture she made, heedless of the risk.

'I have no idea how a mizzen ought to be, but I should think for our first time painting together it is rendered well enough. It is only a first layer, after all.'

Our first time painting together. What a funny way she had of looking at things. She had made suggestions, of course, and he had made those suggestions come to life on the canvas, so perhaps she was right.

When she offered him another sandwich, he divided the small triangle into three deliberate bites.

'Your family has an interest in other parts of the world? Perhaps you have seen some of it yourself?' He was thinking of the lacquer and porcelain, the dragon motif, the myriad paintings in the hall that spoke in contrasting hues of people far from here. 'The East, for instance?'

'I would have adventures, but my father has rarely crossed the Thames these last five years and my brother follows his ways. If Papa were caught in the rain he would think himself lost at sea. He likes a quiet, hermetic life in his age and keeps close with his art dealer. I suppose a sailor might say he collects life rather than lives it.'

Catherine brushed at her skirt. She was lost to him momentarily.

'You, however, are likely to have many tales you might amuse me with?'

'Aye, they'll be different at least.'

Tom closed his eyes against the sunlight, opening to new sensation. Warmth flooded his chest and face like a river running over an unresisting plain.

'Did I make the lesson dull enough?' He spoke to the sky from his private darkness, wondering if she would understand.

'In that respect you have failed miserably.'

Lass, he wanted to call her. All this formality. They had so little time. Opening his eyes, he dared look up at her. Obscured beneath a broad straw brim, she was considering him from the shadow. Her face seemed still and intent. He wondered what it was she contemplated, and how she might arrange the pieces of him into a whole: not those simple mechanics – limbs, a torso, a pair of blue-grey eyes – but all this conflicting impulse and instinct in him. His intellect and emotion. All his depths and shallows. Could she identify a place for him in her world? Would he accept it?

He felt an exchange of questions between them as she studied him from beneath that hat. Then she became all light, twisting to glance over her shoulder. Cecilia, who had closed her book a fraction too loudly, was within sight on a bench by the scarlet-budded rose but remained for the moment out of earshot of their quiet conversation.

'She has no choice and I do love her so but it is a burden to have to be watched all the time.'

Tom had spent his entire life watching. He'd watched the clouds, the arc of a sail, the sway of a sailor pitched by the sea. He'd watched the stars, the moon and the sun all fall level with the horizon through a sextant. He had been watching her, and watching himself. He had barely considered Cecilia's presence, but he thought he caught Catherine's meaning.

Before he could unravel a reply, she pressed a hand onto the blanket at his shoulder, dropping her head closer.

'Shall we make it a regular arrangement – every second day?'

Still on his elbows, Tom smiled up into the trees, so aware of her next to him he didn't trust himself this time to turn his face. He could feel the weight of her as if she had rested her head against his neck. 'The day after tomorrow, then.'

9

The next afternoon together, she spread the blanket in the same spot. 'Show me through your eyes,' she said. 'Start at the beginning, your first time on a ship. Do not leave anything out.'

'That is not difficult. A man never forgets his first hours, his first days and months aboard. If he weren't small enough already, he is sure to feel it then, dwarfed by majesty and scale.'

'It sounds a little like falling in love.'

Tom drew back. What did she know of such things? What did he? But once she had said it, he knew it was true.

Wrecked by his father's death, he had been put together again by the same force that had caused it. Its tumults and calms understood his own. The sea had become his family, his solace and his every success. It provided the colours and shifting forms of his inspiration.

Had Catherine perceived some of this too? What else might she have intuited, waking and blinking in the quick of him?

Already he could see her hand in that first ship he had begun to paint for her, brought further to life on this second visit by a new layer of detail and now left to dry, evidence of an exploration in progress.

Perhaps he could trust her with this deeper kind of sharing.

'It's a long story,' he said. 'It would take many days to tell it.'

'Weeks even. As many as we have.'

'Well then. *Aurora.*'

'Goddess of the dawn,' Catherine answered. 'Heralder of new beginnings.'

From there it was easy. He could see that first ship of his childhood and described it for her with lucid vision: square-rigged with a brawny hull, it had listed out in the Forth. Masts like three bare trees, wintering, awaiting leaves.

It was as if he stood there again on the dock.

'Thomas Rutherford!'

At the call his mother's hands slipped from his face. Tom could not look at her, but threw his bag ahead into the longboat as the other boys had done.

Momentarily he bridged land and sea. Below him the dock's blackened foundations were lost to the opacity of uneasy water.

He'd left his bed nineteen miles away in Bo'ness when everything was smothered by night. Now the port of Leith brightened into a defined and active shape. The sun smiled from a turquoise sheet but the sea would be cold and relentlessly deep, and the westerly was building.

The longboat was lined with pairs of tousled heads and rolled-up shirtsleeves. A single wet space remained on the plank. He sat, with backside quickly saturated and cold knees almost touching the back of the boy in front of him.

He could sense his ma standing there, a hand on her stomach, watching as he took his place.

A smell of fish and brine layered metallic on the air. He tried not to find it unpleasant.

The first sounds of the sea as they set out from the dock: wind whistling at his ears; the slow, building breath of the other sailors; and the splashing of water cut through and transformed into wake.

Fixing on the broad back of the boy in front of him, Tom studied the rhythmic roll of shoulder blades with each pull on an oar.

'Put your weight into those oars, lads. Heave. Heave!' And Tom responded to the mate's call, heaving harder.

He turned his head to glance along their path. *Aurora*. Whose rise and fall he would soon take for his own breath. Becoming broader, taller with every surge. He leaned on the oar and drew back against the resisting tide. Leaned forward. Drew back again.

He imagined the figures still standing at the dock, waving their arms against the sky, his ma gesturing her hand in the slow and reduced scale of movement that sadness bestows. Tom wanted to raise his own hand in reply, but he couldn't stop rowing. When at last he looked up towards the receding dock, his eyes stung and he had lost her to the sun.

Even before the sails were unfurled and sheeted and the busy world on water revealed itself, when the future was still hidden below decks, Tom knew he would be all backbone. All eyes.

They spent that first night at anchor, readying the ship for its approach to open water at breaking light. The first calls sounded as the sun split the sky the following morning, setting it all in motion: 'All hands! Lay aloft and loose all sails!'

And the captain's commands kept coming. Around him the crew became a concerted force of activity labouring towards a single end. Arms, legs, mouths, hands working in unison; eyes skyward at the masts. Lines coiling, uncoiling, being made fast.

There was no time for anxiety, no going back. Tom would learn what to do through observation. He grasped a line when ordered:

a massive twist of rope that led to the fore topsail. It was coarse, heavy and surprisingly broad, and the burn in his hands and shoulders was almost immediate as he leaned his weight back and pulled, hand over hand like the men in front of him, hauling up the sail.

On the next command he let go the line, and the strong men began to strain at the windlass. Their arms thickening with muscle, they groaned, keeping on, bringing the anchor up from the deep.

Tom felt it keenly now, overwhelmed by the size and all the moving parts of a full-rigged merchant ship, one hundred and fifty feet from stem to stern, and the significance of the gesture Sweet had made in giving him a berth. He knew he could keep his stomach steady in choppy waters. He had a respectful fear of the sea and its power. The youngest boys were only half his age. Even so, Tom was hardly prepared.

The older boys had skin that was thicker-looking, ready for the elements. Tom saw the way they joked in an intimate fashion, like brothers. They knew each other's names, which foot to place where as they climbed the ratlines, how to properly reef and sheet the sails when ordered, and were strong enough to do so.

The captain's unmistakable voice had boomed from the quarter-deck in greeting the morning before and Tom had mustered with the rest of the crew to hear Sweet's words against the boisterous wind. Though Tom was attentive and patient, the captain's eye did not find his. Sweet had looked at him across the fishermen's graves with unsettling familiarity, but on deck Tom was as insignificant to him as any other boy.

Burly, solid, flanked by Mr Nelson, his chief mate, the captain stood with arms at his side and pipe in mouth, an unmoving conductor with a look of steadfast readiness affixed to his bearded face.

He set out for the crew how life aboard the *Aurora* would go. They were to work hard, learn their duties and perform them as ordered.

On the Sabbath there would be prayers; they'd be allowed some time of their own. It was up to the crew to keep life aboard peaceful. If they stepped out of line, became lazy or violent or thought too much of themselves, they would create their own hell on water.

'Know that I will have no worry enforcing order, men,' Captain Sweet swept a stern look across their gathered heads. 'And you will have no worry obeying, unless you wish to meet with rough discipline.'

Tom was assigned to the larboard watch, under the command of Mr Nelson. Their watch would alternate in shifts with the starboard watch, under the second mate, to tend to the daily work required for keeping the ship afloat, dry and on its set course. Each watch would climb the masts, take in the sails and attend the decks. They'd reef and knot and caulk and stitch and tar and haul and heave and scrub. It was their responsibility to do the tasks that would ensure the *Aurora* was kept a safe and clean vessel at all times.

At the call for 'All hands', the watches would be set to work together – and the captain made clear they would answer that call, no matter how tired, sodden, cold, hungry or queasy they were.

From Leith the *Aurora* would head to London. From there through the Bay of Biscay to Cape Town in southern Africa, around the Cape of Good Hope, and further to Port Jackson within distant southern seas. As Sweet outlined their route, Tom committed each place to memory, though he could not yet imagine their shapes. He'd been little further than the mouth of the Forth, fishing with his da.

Sweet had signed Tom on for two years with the promise of more work and many more ports if he proved himself. Tom was glad at the prospect of having food in his stomach each night. He was glad he didn't have to stand watch with the lanky boy who had hunched in front of him while the captain spoke and picked at his face until it was raw. He imagined he might find his father, out here at sea, not lost at all.

It was October and despite the morning's sunshine a chill had reared itself, cutting an ache deep in Tom's bones, stinging his cheeks. Each blast of wind came at him full of fine-tipped needles, piercing him with a taunt: *you're not a man, boy; you're not a man yet.*

10

She had let him talk to the sky and now he grew aware of her, tensed and poised next to him. In Catherine's face, Tom saw she had followed where he stepped and was waiting for what came next.

He had never told his story like this before. No one had ever asked. Even Seamus, who knew Tom best, had grown to understand him through a patchwork of rough-cut histories shared over many long journeys.

'There was no warm-bosomed nanny aboard to gather you and the other young boys under her wing?'

'No, there was no such thing.' He laughed. 'Though I suspect there was a well-disguised girl among us once or twice. They were quick and alert aloft, but seemed to disappear into the boards themselves below; so quiet, never making trouble. Kept their shirt on while washing, grew no hair on their cheek and sailed no longer than a single voyage.'

'Were they running from some situation, do you suppose, or seeking someplace new?'

'One looks much like the other, depending on where you're standing.'

'True,' she agreed. 'Imagine their terror of being found out, of having no safety behind them or ahead.'

'What do you know of the sea? Have you ever seen it?'

'Once,' Catherine said. 'Cecilia took my brother and I to the seaside. I was perhaps seven or eight years old, Alfred around four or five. We dug down, shaping a moat for our terrifically regal castle, and the sand was cool and wet. Water flooded over our fingers, filling in where we scooped our hands. We paddled in up to our thighs and cupped water in our hands to splash each other in glee, jumping in the little waves that broke near the shore. I remember sitting in the shallows as the sea foamed over my legs and circled my waist, tugging my body at its will, and feeling like I was at the edge of the world. How large and breathless life was in that moment.

'It did not last. We were soon back in the carriage, dry in stiff skirts and useless ribbons, returning to the walls of this garden. I watched the sky through the back window as the horses drove us on, and the clouds with their misty heads seemed to hang there, peering in, carrying me home.'

Tom imagined Catherine sitting there up to her waist in sand and water, sensing herself unbound and limitless. If they could go to the sea now, he thought, she would run and plunge headfirst beneath the largest curling wave. Offer herself to terror and thrill, no matter if she could not swim. He could sense the desire in her. Knew he would do the same.

Touch by touch, shadow by shadow, under a sallow afternoon sun she continued to seek the impressions of those early days at sea that Tom had long held inside.

The force of saltwater over the bow as they picked up speed, the aching chill that set in, the bellowing of the westerly wind. It was shocking at first, he told her, but within hours he'd grow used to it.

Leith, Edinburgh, Bo'ness and eventually all the coast would recede to a pinprick in their wake. The sea opened to them, he recalled, as if it could wipe their memories clean.

'But a ship is a conundrum,' he said. 'A contradiction of enclosure and sheer wildness, darkness and absolute light.'

Below decks the air was thick and sour. The ceiling sat with little room above his head, and the mast that ran through it caused a feeling of being caught in a limbo state. Their quarters in the *Aurora*'s forecastle were not spacious; they were dark, airless and perpetually rolling.

Tom's head had spun; he tried to gather things into a single form. There was a last glimpse of his ma lingering at the dock, straining her eyes towards the ship. The broad trunk of the mainmast puncturing the sky, Tom newly arrived at its base, filled with both awe and dread. And now this darkest belly that would house him and all these other strange boys and men.

'You, sailor, what's your name?'

A low and grinding voice. Tom turned to find a thick-torsoed seaman, saggy-jowled, and a Highlander by the sound. MacIntyre they called him. He was staring down at a boy of around Tom's age who was already hunched, his body folded and propped against the foremast as the vessel tilted, rose and resettled.

'Green, sir.'

Laughter. Tom smiled and waited.

'Green? That's unfortunate. And I'm no "sir". I take orders just like you. It won't get any better than this, so best set your stomach as soon as you can.'

'Damned sissy.' This came from another voice, somewhere in the darkness behind Tom. Muffled laughter followed.

Away from where Green struggled with his heaving stomach, away from the jeering, Tom stored his bag with the other men's sea chests and the hammocks that would be set up each night. What little he owned was rolled in a length of tartan inside his bag. Tokens of an earlier life. He catalogued them in his mind: a Rutherford clan badge. A locket from his ma, long ago broken off from its chain, and another drawing of his da he'd done the night before embarking, folded up small enough to fit inside for a makeshift memento. He'd watched his ma take the kilt from what had been his father's drawer, run her hand across it, shake it out and wrap in it these items Tom had selected. Some charcoal and parchment, too. A parting gift. His fingers felt for the initials inked into the corner of the bag: *JR*. Two letters that would do him little good if the bag were lost. But he'd resisted his ma's suggestion that he obscure them with his own.

Navigation, speed, currents and winds: as chief mate, all of these were within Tom's grasp. But for years, such wonders belonged to more experienced men. As a boy, his place each morning was on the foredeck with a holystone in hand, scouring the teak with the bible-sized sandstone block.

His fingertips burned in the wet and cold. His trousers were constantly soaked; his kneecaps sharpened with an ache. Here he was, performing a sailor's religious rite. *A clean deck is a safe deck.* The captain had expressed it in a way that admitted no question; it was a statement of simple faith.

Tom had knelt on wooden boards with a bible in hand before, but that had been in church with his ma and da, his head bowed in the wake of the minister's incantation. They'd looked to God for His blessing, giving thanks for what they had, however little it had been. But Tom wasn't going to thank God for his bloodied hands and aching back. No, it was nothing to do with God. And as for his da – the thought of him gone and never held again emptied him inside.

He kept his face down, his hands moving. Concentrating on his task. His skin prickled with awareness. Calls and counter-calls. Order all around; the men did as they were commanded.

Tom sat back on his heels, wiped the back of his neck and gazed up the length of the mainmast; along its outstretched arms, sailors clung. From where he knelt, it looked as if they were climbing into the sky. The mast could pitch from side to side and still they held fast, grasping the yards or flattening themselves against the rigging.

With the secure hug of land left behind and the horizon opening wide before them, Tom's breath caught in his throat. The sky fell around him; the North Sea stretched and curved. Out here there was nothing, and there was everything. The sunlit water dazzled and cajoled, drawing him out to seek the furthest limit of his vision.

He learned to listen for the bells. Ringing out from the quarterdeck at the half-hour, every half-hour, their careful ritual kept the ship afloat. Eight bells marked twelve, four and eight o'clock. He'd look to the sky. Check the light. It became second nature. Before long he grew accustomed to this new way of breaking down time. The watches alternated in four-hour shifts from the first night watch at eight p.m. until noon. But during the day watch it was all hands on deck. The ship felt busy then, like a schoolroom of boys hard at work, or a family, even.

There were dozens of knots to learn, and ways to secure the complicated rigging. All the sails to identify, the masts, the many stays, shrouds and braces. Within days Tom could loose and furl the royals and skysails. He proved adept with stitching, and assisted with the repair of a studding sail, earning the sailmaker's praise. He exhausted himself to complete his duties fully and to Sweet's satisfaction, but only ever saw the great bearded face from afar. All the captain's orders were conveyed through Mr Nelson, who somehow stood between them.

Time seemed to slide. He slept when allowed, not wasting a second to sleeplessness. Routine rendered the days indistinguishable. There was only the wind to concern them, which was mostly fierce, and a feeling of being small in the palm of the sea, which was their only horizon. Tom wondered if the captain ever felt as he did, like they were a speck in the lens of a giant looking glass.

'I had that feeling from Turner, too, in his snowstorm. From edge to edge, it is a whirl of light and dark. No sense of him at the centre.'

Tom shifted at Catherine's words, rolling onto his side and supporting his head in his hand. She was above him, sitting with her weight leaned upon an outstretched arm. The skin at her wrist was within his reach. The indigo vein that disappeared beneath the sleeve of her dress.

'Was he a seaman, do you know?' he asked, languid, looking up at her.

'No, but he wanted the experience to be true, to understand the feeling of it, and so he had himself lashed to the mast during the worst of the storm, when they all thought the steamship would be lost.'

'He did what?' Tom sat up, abrupt with the idea of it.

'For hours he was tied and washed by the waves, and all so he could observe it. Is it not astonishing?'

He was stoked with resentment. 'It is naive. And arrogant.' He had to stop himself from swearing. 'The sea is not for sport.'

Her face pulled in confusion. 'But he wanted to experience what you have: to feel the storm in his blood when he painted. To understand it. I thought you admired him?'

'As a painter, I do.'

'And his passion, his commitment? I wish I could do as he did.'

'Believe me, you do not. We are never tied. There is no safety. We work aloft hour after hour, day after day, whatever the skies are doing. We fall. Men die. Boys die. Their bodies break or drown.'

He saw he had shocked her, which he regretted, but there was more he needed to say.

'My father,' he began. Heady with it. His blood rushed.

She pulled her teeth over her lower lip. 'Yes?'

Tom told her of the wreck and its human debris. The fishermen washed ashore, their bodies bent and blue. His father lost and not recovered. How Sweet had turned up, speaking of James Rutherford's bravery, his loyalty, and the duty it entailed.

'The sea was never a choice. It was a necessity.' For his father. For Sweet. For Tom.

Catherine frowned. After a pause, she said, 'I suppose I am sheltered. What kind of man was he, your father?'

Tom exhaled with a memory. 'His voice crackled, like he had the wind lodged in his throat and could not remove it.' Catherine's mellow laugh released him. He thought, We are still on the same side.

'He taught me to swim,' he continued. 'But not by example. He pushed me over the side of the rowboat one afternoon and forced the learning upon me.'

Tom was perhaps six at the time – younger than Catherine had been when she visited the seaside. Though they were not far from shore, Tom was well out of his depth, coughing and spitting, slapping his hands at the frigid surface. His da threw instructions but offered neither line nor arm until his son proved he could not only stay afloat but propel himself against the tide.

Sweet's story had confirmed to Tom that his da had been no coward. And as he described the memory to Catherine, he shared his suspicion of what lay behind such a lesson: that his da wanted to teach Tom what he could not do himself. How truly lost he must have been when the fishing boat foundered against the treacherous rocks.

His father had been a muscular man but Tom recalled the strain in his face as he hauled Tom back into the boat that day. The next morning, his da rose from bed but did not fully unfold. Tom's ma rubbed warming ointment at the base of his back as he rested, bent at the waist, forearms against the table. Tom thought of the many other mornings like that, and the way his da had rarely lifted Tom onto his shoulders like the other fathers did their young boys, though he was neither cruel nor cold in word or temperament.

And he pictured his da holding on to Captain Sweet with every ounce of his strength, saving his friend from the sea. Straining every part of his body. Ruining himself, perhaps, in the act.

11

By his third visit, Tom had grown familiar with the westerly route across London from the docks and arrived ahead of time. He glanced through the front gate that stood sentry with its row of spears but continued walking as if he had never intended to stop.

Ogilvie House sat greedy on a block of its own, its pale limestone bulk opposing rows of narrow terrace houses that were perfectly bricked, cleanly painted. The trees he had sat beneath with Catherine rose behind the stone wall at his shoulder as he traced along one boundary and then the next. No one would ever know what took place behind that towering barricade. The whole world was made an outsider.

Approaching the entrance a second time, he assessed the light through the trees, confirmed with his pocket watch and decided to go in. It was almost the designated hour.

She was not ready.

A young housemaid led Tom through to a room off the rear of the hall. She gestured towards a dark leather armchair, requested he wait and closed the door behind her.

The room was north-facing and lay in shadow but his entry had awoken the darkness: two brass cages almost half Tom's height and raised on stands were now set aflutter. The atmosphere grew shrill with disharmony.

Tom moved to the bay window overlooking the deep green lawn, its edges curtailed by ornamental garden. A fixed scene, unmoving, firm beneath the sky. From there began the path down to where the roses grew and the bench from which Cecilia had overseen their lessons two days prior.

He scanned what he could see of the sky, out of habit watching for the sun, and surveyed the pattern of the clouds for an approaching storm. The cries from the cages at his back persisted, and he reached for the velvet drapery in the window. It soothed him, the running of fabric between fingers and thumb. The material was heavy and smooth, and blocked all the light where it fell.

Finally he turned back to the room, adjusting his sight to the dim interior as if he'd stepped below deck.

Two pent-up creatures shifted from one leg to the other on their perches at the far end of the room. They puffed out their breasts, ruffled their feathers and sought him with their large curved beaks through the bars. He had seen birds like this before, in Brazil; some kind of brilliant macaw, large and fierce, their plumage a wave of red, blue, green and yellow as they circled in noisy groups high in the canopy. Creatures that belonged under no roof but the sky. They'd been caught and caged there too, he remembered, lined up along wharves and quays, but Tom could never have expected to trace the result of that trade to this genteel London room.

The longer Tom stood in their sight, the more fevered the birds became, flapping their wings at their sides, unable to stretch their span. He wondered if they would be able to fly if released, despite this desperation to find air.

He retreated to the armchair, hoping the cacophony would quieten if he sat still. Catherine could not be far away. He imagined how she would swing the door open any minute and relieve him. And so when the handle finally turned and the latch gave way, his expression was unguarded and he was caught out.

It was not her.

The gentleman who entered was taller than Tom, likely a few years younger, dark and moustachioed, with deep, angular sideburns and immaculately high cheekbones. He, too, had been drawn up short. But there was no question of who was the intruder. The man's immediate air of insulted authority conveyed that Tom had been left to wait for Catherine in his private sitting room.

On his feet again, Tom strove for a neutral expression and offered a small bow.

The man had released the door handle but remained silent, his erect stance reminding Tom of the marble sculptures that decorated the entrance hall on neat pedestals. His jacquard waistcoat shone with all the alien richness of silk, patterned with a plum-coloured paisley that looked like tiny tear drops. Only the colour of his eyes, which Tom felt calculating him, was familiar. His relationship to Catherine unmistakable.

Tom was in his new suit, but he saw himself suddenly through the man's mirror, as if he had come sweaty and stained straight off the mast; his thick-skinned fingers and that little bow, so obviously acquiescent. The man reached for the bell but changed his mind as quickly, his chin raised towards Tom in a gesture that resembled Catherine's own manner of prompting. The question forceful but unspoken.

'Rutherford. Mr Thomas Rutherford. Chief mate,' Tom uttered. It wasn't so much an introduction as an explanation, a justification.

The man pursed his lips just enough for Tom to wonder if it were a smile. Closing the door, the stranger moved to where the birds still shrieked in their cages. Waving two long fingers he made a hypnotic shushing noise.

Tom observed the response: quick and obedient.

'That would be lieutenant, would it not, in Her Majesty's Service?'

A deliberate assumption, set like a trap.

The birds were all languor and calm, turning to nuzzle themselves beneath raised wings.

Now that the room was quiet, the pressure of the man's attention unnerved Tom further. He was familiar with brute force, base aggression, clear and overt power. He'd been tested before and had learned to forbear. But this was something else. The man was composed of a tightly wound energy that seemed poised for release; it was disdain, Tom thought.

'Merchant navy. Sir.'

'I see, Mr Rutherford. And the purpose of your visit?'

'I am engaged as a painting tutor to Miss Catherine Ogilvie.'

'Ah, so that is what you think.'

It was not simply what Tom thought; it was what he knew to be true. It troubled him that the man had turned his query into a statement, as if he knew something Tom did not. Still, Tom kept his eyes steady.

'I think you are my sister's little secret.'

Tom's indignation flared but he knew better than to react. The man's words implied a clever sort of threat, one that was made with the intention to provoke and the certainty it could not be countered. In his fascination Tom wondered if he were a fool after all to think Catherine sincere, if he were a piece in a game for which the rules were oblique.

And then, as if summoned by his thoughts, the door was thrown wide and Catherine rushed within the frame, a hand at her hair as if she'd just finished pinning it. A triangle of sunlight following her in across the floor.

'My dear Mr Rutherford! Our new girl, Mary, has been rather foolish to leave you in here—'

'Good afternoon, sister.'

In the sudden alteration of Catherine's expression, Tom saw what he had imagined in his own just minutes earlier. A face interrupted in its bright feeling and forced to reconfigure.

At the end of the room, her brother had picked up a glass jar, lifted the lid and was sprinkling its contents between the brass bars. The birds pecked and crunched at the scattered seed.

Tom roused a smile for Catherine, but his jaw was tight. He stood silent, but released his fists, realising he had been gripping them at his sides.

'Alfred, we were not expecting you until this evening.' Catherine gave a firm, slow nod in her brother's direction. 'It seems you have discovered my tutor, Mr Thomas Rutherford. Papa may have informed you already of my lessons.'

Alfred listened with a blank dissemblance of politeness, and continued to sprinkle seed. Tom remained on guard, physically poised for reprisal.

Instead, Alfred broke a proper smile, exposing his perfect teeth, and looked mildly towards Tom as he conceded. 'Yes, I have been informed of your little lessons. But really, sister, why should we talk of it. Such an arrangement is, after all, insignificant.'

'I agree,' Catherine replied. 'It is of no consequence to you.'

The encounter had the effect, however, of souring Catherine's creative mood. Alone with Tom again – Cecilia in their wake – she admitted so, and requested he join her for a walk around the garden instead.

Though Alfred was dear to her, his rigid conventionality was vexing, ever tiresome. Almost three years her junior, he behaved with the certainty of a superior status acquired merely from being born the male sibling. He had told her before: she must not burst into rooms; it was not her place to enter when men were talking.

'He was apoplectic the day he saw us on the hill,' she confided. 'Two unmarried women approaching a stranger with whom we had no introduction!'

'I was only startled,' Tom laughed. 'And charmed.'

'Charmed?' She smiled at his recollection. 'You were entirely abstracted, off in your creative world – swimming in the river with the sun on your face, raising a hand to the willow branches, down on your knees studying the colour in each blade of grass. Or so I fancied. We stood above you as you painted and you were not aware. How else were we to gain your attention and retrieve the glove?'

'Was the glove so important?'

She laughed. 'I was envious, you know. How many times I have longed to be able to walk and sit and draw entirely on my own on that hill without propriety getting in the way, without being waved back to the house.'

Tom glanced over his shoulder. 'Cecilia is not so terrible a chaperone. It cannot be pleasurable for her all the time either.'

'Alfred thinks she is too lenient, of course.' She paused. 'He would not chastise me in your presence – he is too proud for that, though you entered his world in so improper a manner.'

'I'm very glad you burst in,' Tom said, his voice quiet.

What was unspoken, hovering between them: Catherine had addressed Tom with a tone of familiarity in her brother's presence. So casually. As if he were hers. As if in entering the room she had offered him her uninhibited embrace.

She knew it was dangerous to betray this feeling in her. Desire could be turned back upon a woman as a weapon; love could be withheld, volition denied, choice negated. Catherine had seen it happen around her.

Still, she would push against all that sought to contain her.

She needed to exert a force sometimes. To create some small commotion. Otherwise she felt so invisible, a vague draft wafting at the ears of upright men in dining rooms and on dance floors.

When she confessed as much to him, Tom called those men fools.

It made her ache that he should say so, that his care seemed uncorrupted by design or status or power.

It wasn't that she went unnoticed in society. But she was unseen; her thoughts lay unprovoked, and she knew she was not meant to offer them freely.

Tom was less gripped by society's fist than other men she had met. In him there was a fluidity and ease. The tragedies of the Greeks that she had devoured last summer had not held her interest like his stories of the sea. His life on the water had been one of hardship; his sensitivity with the brush so at odds with his upbringing that it made her curious. And more: she suspected she could open her own dreams and thoughts to him and he would not rebel.

But the unpredictability of his itinerant occupation seeded anxiety. She understood he was bound in other ways. To the whim of the winds, the lure of trade, the structures and hierarchy of the mariner and his rank. And to something deeper, she knew. Of more serious threat was his own dedication to those great forces – the tremulous ocean and its sister sky. The very dedication that made him who he was. Their time together could be cut short at any moment by a captain's command, and when it was, Catherine did not want Tom to leave unaffected, with the same unattached ease as he had arrived.

Tom understood rank, order and regulations, but the arrogance of class and its human fabric so far seemed like folly. Nevertheless, he perceived its power. It was there to make him aware of his own humility. He'd stepped willingly into a world of opaque and unmarked rules and codes, which he judged, whenever he bumped up against one, to be as strong as the intricate structure of stays that held up a ship's masts.

Catherine's brother had been almost rigid with contempt. What might it mean for Catherine, and for himself, should the man's self-restraint slip?

As always Cecilia had greeted them warmly, but soon enough slowed her steps to fall behind. Tom now suspected this to be deliberate: a gift of liberty to Catherine, or Cecilia's own small act of resistance.

As they walked he said to Catherine, 'Tell me about your father. His papers.' It was clear there was a deep bond shared between the man and his daughter. Tom envied them both for it.

'He is writing a family history. I have only read fragments. He works at it night and day.'

'And your mother?'

'She is the reason for his words, I am sure.' Catherine glanced away.

'She is no longer with you?'

'Not for a long time now.'

'I'm sorry for it.'

'It is not Alfred's fault he is so tense and overprotective.' Her voice rose. 'I sometimes think he imagines himself to be the cause. She died with his twin brother still inside her.'

Tom winced, but it was Catherine's pain he felt.

'I, too, have lost loved ones. My da, as you know. And my ma too, in an accident a few months after, while I was away.' Siblings also, he thought, before they were born.

'So you understand.'

He didn't know what to expect when he met her eyes. If she was referring to the workings of Alfred's mind then Tom certainly did not understand. As for her grief, he knew what its cuts and grazes were like, and that they would never entirely heal.

Her fingers made the barest touch at his elbow. So fleeting he could not have proved it. So resonant it lingered.

Was it only manners that held her back from a greater expression? He wanted her to be bold. For him to be ready for it.

'We can be thankful they are at peace, I suppose,' she continued.

Had his parents found rest? He wasn't sure that were true. 'The sea I suppose to be my da's grave. My ma lies in Bo'ness, but I've never yet been back.'

Her face was swept with pity. 'I find it comforting to have a headstone to lay my hand upon.'

She directed them off the path, their rhythmic steps falling silent. Blades of freshly cut grass cross-hatched the toes of their boots. For Tom it was an impermanent layer upon indelibly salt-stained leather.

'Memory—' Catherine began, as if he had triggered a thought.

He waited, anticipating her capacity for truth.

'It is disingenuous, have you noticed?'

'You mean it is a lie?'

'Some moments from my childhood I recall with a full-bodied clarity. I taste what I once tasted, feel what I once felt. Sometimes it is as if I exist in two places, here in the present as an adult and back then in the past as a child, all in the same moment.'

Tom roughed a hand through the lavender that edged the lawn, unsure of what to say. He saw her for the first time awkward too, less self-assured.

'I have no reason to believe you should understand when I talk in such a way,' she continued.

He nodded. 'And yet you do.'

She smiled, her eyes darting to the distance. 'I recall the stipple of a marcasite brooch.' Her fingers spread to illustrate. 'It was in the shape of a bow. I remember it clearly, like the ribbon on a birthday parcel. I remember the touch of my mother's palm on my forehead when I could not sleep. I loved that feeling. She would smooth her hand gently, like this, and I never wanted her to stop. I had a nurse, of course. Perhaps I conflate the two? I was so young when my mother died, not yet three. So I wonder, which memories are true, and which are a stitched-up fabric, all those sensations muddled and conjoined? Perhaps I make no sense.'

'You make sense to me. It's important not to forget. And your father — he writes down his memories?'

'He grasps to hold a continually more distant past. It is a fool's game, surely.'

'It's not without merit. Nor sympathy.' Tom halted as they arrived back on the path and allowed her to indicate the way. She chose a shaded trail to their left, small and narrow, ill-marked, off the main garden walkway.

'I think where we come from is a part of where we're going,' Tom continued, suddenly sensing they were alone.

'Do you not believe we can change? That we might break free of what came before?'

'Aye, we can try. Identify a future and work towards it.' And then he felt embarrassed. 'But I am no sage, no wise man; I just know what I feel to be true.'

'Have you changed so very much?'

'More than you could know.'

'Since you were a boy?'

'Aye, but when I think of myself through the years I still feel like the same wee bairn who cried in his cradle all damp winter long with the fire the only protection from frozen ground. I still feel that in my heart. I expect I always will.'

Tom said this last deliberately, a kind of warning.

'Surely you cannot remember that long ago?'

'Likely it's a picture I paint. Like you, I cannot say if my recollections are real or enlarged. Perhaps it doesn't matter.'

Her smile reassured him.

'Your brother—' But they had reached the end of the path and were entering the wide expanse of lawn that would lead them back up to the house. Before them its limestone blocks appeared stacked in unassailable density, its windows a line of reflective shields.

Catherine stopped and stared up at the house. 'Other men mock my painting,' she said quietly. 'I have found no path to follow. I have been ridiculed and disregarded by my brother, so much that it forces a bleak contemplation upon me, and I wonder if I have not the talent at all.'

'Do not believe it.'

'I cannot believe it.' She smiled. 'If I believe it, I cannot continue. It would be an easier existence if I were content with the conventional path. I am told, like all women, that I must marry and bear children, support my husband and continue to live a good and accomplished life. I would like a family. But I wish also to paint and explore. Until now, I have had no notion of how I might achieve both.'

There was a vein of something richer running through such intimate words. Longing. Ambition. Desire. Hope. As she faced him, her head atilt and her eyes steady, he recognised shared feeling.

All that had lain in him unspoken for years rose to the surface. All that originated on the banks of the Forth, in the flour-cloth canvases his mother had cut for him, and the way she taught him that imagination was a person's true horizon. Everything that had flickered in him since he was a boy now found more oxygen at Catherine's side. He imagined he could fuse past and future together on one canvas.

He knew what opportunity looked like, and he would not be intimidated by her brother.

'Well then.' He offered his arm, sensed her gather the shape of him as her hand settled on his sleeve. 'Miss Ogilvie, are you ready to paint?'

12

Tom insisted Catherine take her place at the easel. 'That seaside you spoke of. Paint it for me.'

She picked up colour on her brush and moved it fluidly across the naked canvas, as if inhabited by the memory. Again she mixed a luminous palette, and onto the golden colour of a shore she scattered yellows and pinks in a suggestion of variegated grains of sand, as if the sun were glancing off it. He watched in fascination as she used looser strokes to agitate sea foam and flecked her clouds with violet in a way he never would have thought to do. The entire scene was suffused with light. He could sense in it the heat of the day. The anticipation of the gaze. Her brushstrokes, moving in all directions, gave it texture. She worked fast, with her canvas always wet, not waiting for a layer of paint to dry.

The sea of Catherine's youth was gentle and idyllic, with all the beauty that he knew and none of the violence. She painted a child's legs and toes, kicking up from beneath the water, as she remembered it from all those years ago. Energy was palpable in the movement of each foot splashing and lifting, as if communing with the force she felt in the water, the light, the concaving wave-drawn sand.

'What makes you make that mark, that stroke, that line?' he broke in eagerly, peering at the elements of her creation. 'Why?'

Catherine knew it before any tutoring with Mr Barolo, before the constraints of feminine accomplishments were imposed. There was a stream, running at her feet.

'One day you realise you are standing in it. Something inspires. The shift of fabric past a doorway. The light cast through the window and onto a cushion. The way a body moves to scoop up water in a hand and drink it. From there impulse leads to action; a pencil is plucked out of a drawer, drawn across paper. The result is pleasing, or not; the action is repeated, becomes sifted through emotion and intellect and imagination. Eventually it becomes greater in meaning, more personal: a part of yourself. Eventually you pick up the brush to hear the sound of your own voice.'

At an early age, she told Tom, she could please with her drawings, at first illustrating small cards on the occasion of birthdays and Christmas. Kneeling on the red and gold oriental rug before the hearth, she curled an arm secretively around the paper and bowed her body forward, eager to make manifest in miniature bright moments that pierced the quotidian. A worm lazily curled on the wet earth, or glossy pink and yellow peaches gifted in a box, and the yardage of ribbon brought by the dressmaker on spools that she had freed to run riverine and kaleidoscopic across the room. At other times she would leave drawings around the house for her family to discover – on a mantelpiece, next to a plate at breakfast – anticipating in particular the gift of her father's joyful surprise, the enveloping of her against his warm beard. His hand on her head.

Whenever her father had received a call from Mr Saxton, an aspiring dealer of art, she'd find colourful pictures slipped under her pillow, of an elephant-headed deity from India or a snow-stilled canal in Holland. She pored over extravagantly dressed French women walking arm-in-arm along a lamp-lit street in Paris. She slept with these images at her head and sublimated them into dreams rich with the touch and smells and colours of far-off places.

Tom wished he had known this girl, imagining Catherine smaller but with the same rushing smile and intense curiosity. All the world bright and gifted to her.

Some small part of her childhood story had grazed him, leaving a tiny hidden wound, but he could not identify the cause.

He could hear the tinkle of the gardener's trowel against pebbles in the soil. Catherine's breath. She was waiting for a response. Rose petals. Cucumber. Lavender. The smells of their days in the garden were becoming familiar.

'Why?' She had turned his question upon him, smiling. 'What makes you?'

She handed him his brushes, set out a fresh canvas and asked for his story to go with it. For him to take her back to the holystone and aching knees. The water over the bowsprit. To paint it for her.

'Leave me a piece of your world when you go.'

It grazed him further to hear her mention his departure. The world as he understood it had changed since she came into it, since he had been welcomed into hers.

He touched a finger to a small jagged white mark above his left eye. All that had made him: the sea's ravaging power and promise.

A memory flared. He was thirteen again.

'There was a wild night,' he recalled, 'perhaps a month after departing Leith.'

He mixed the colours of that green-black night on his palette, and it helped him find the words to share it with her. How he'd woken with a start when it was still dark: six bells, and a rapid thumping on the hatch.

All hands! Up now!

The floor dipped away as he rolled out of his hammock. The lamps swung on their chains. Up on deck the lean was horrendous, a merciless threat to gravity. What was once horizontal became near vertical, then shifted again. He was hit by the force of a storm's clenched fist. The howl of it. The smell of salt and anger.

Wet through and heaving, the starboard watchmen were huge with effort, urgent at the lines as the sea swept over the *Aurora*'s bow in a maddened foam.

Tom could barely hear his orders above the wind and the pulling of sails. Everything sounded like chaos. Nelson roared and Tom sighted the top gallant sail hard-pressed on the mainmast. MacIntyre was already hauling at the buntline, others at the clewlines, lifting the sail up towards its yard.

The deck was a mess of ropes and men.

There was no time to ponder his footing as Tom grasped the mainmast's net-like rigging, nor the lean of the mainyard arm that almost dipped itself into the water. His task was to secure the sail with Green before the gale could split it.

The ship careened. Tom climbed into darkness, assaulted by wind and wave. Pressed hard against the rigging one minute, hanging out above the sea the next. Each reach of an arm and press of a leg was an exertion. The night was like slate. There were no stars. One slip was all it would take to untether a boy from this world. He kept his head down, feeling his way in terror. He hoped death would be quick.

When he made the top gallant yard, Green was close behind, and together they began to gather in the sail and secure its heavy centre. It had been folded up towards them by MacIntyre and the men on the lines below, but still it pulled in the wind. Each sudden wrench sounded like thunder; a vicious slap in the air. Tom held on, leaning over the yard, using all his strength to gather in the sail, pressing it against his stomach to keep it fast. Then he lashed it to the yard with a gasket tie, winding the length of rope around and around, battling to fasten the knot with numb fingers. Next to him, Green did the same.

They would split up to secure the sail at each arm. Green was slighter than Tom and his feet almost slipped as he moved to starboard. Tom saw the rain strike at the boy. Silver in the lamplight.

Tom inched to larboard, grasping the next section of sail, pulling it in, wrapping it tightly. Moving on. Each time the mast struck out over the water he was hurtled towards the churning sea. His heart crashed in his chest. When the final knot was made, his knees almost gave way and he could hardly breathe.

At last he urged his legs back towards the mast to climb down. Green was returning too, his head pressed to one side against the wind. As he grew closer, the boy's face seemed fixed, as if carved of wood, and the knots he'd made appeared far from secure.

Tom yelled out to the boy but Green's feet were already searching for the rigging. He replied not with words but with the awfulness of his petrified face.

The icy rain lashed at them, a whip dealing ruthless punishment. The ship leaned deeply again. Tom cursed and moved past the mast onto the starboard arm, where the sail wrenched violently, threatening to throw all its ties. As he pressed himself along, he had less and less traction. He lost his footing and gasped to regain it.

One by one, he strove to remake each of Green's worthless knots. The sail strained under him. If it came loose it could carry him with it. He grew colder and wetter, his hands insensitive, his head pounding atrociously with the wind.

With relief he reached the last tie, and as he did it gave way entirely. Part of the sail whipped up above the yard, slamming him in the side of the head. He reeled, slipping sideways. Clutched at the rigging. His face was numb. The blow had hurt but how much he couldn't tell. He could have lost half his face and not known it. He was dizzy, his focus drifting like an unsecured buoy, and for the first time since setting sail he felt queasy.

Beginnings and endings were lost. He saw the fishing boat in the storm. The blue-bashed limbs in unnatural postures on the debris-filled shore.

Only by chance did he manage to grab the sailcloth as it blew back at him, and with a deep burst of strength he secured it. He felt unreal, a character in a dream that he observed from above, outside of himself. His body propelled by instinct.

Back on deck, he gasped for breath, hands on knees. Green was vomiting on all fours. Nelson loped over against heavy side spray and pressed a hand against Tom's shoulder, buttressing his own weight. Tom waited for praise, to hear the mate's relief. He turned his ear to catch the words. 'You're a bloody fool for risking yourself, Rutherford. And I thought you were a clever sort of boy.'

Every bone in Tom, every muscle ached. His eyes could not find focus.

'You're bleeding.'

Tom felt for his cheek, his temple, and could not tell if it were true.

'Get yourself cleaned up and kipped before the next watch.'

Tom watched the mate heading astern to the captain. They hadn't seen the terror in Green's eyes. He wiped a wet sleeve across his dripping brow and laughed at the uselessness of it. He'd never been so saturated and cold.

With his blanket pulled up to his chin and the cut at his temple throbbing, Tom thought of how these extremes would soon become commonplace. He had climbed, lonely in the sky, and survived. Already the body of the ship had narrowed with familiarity. He was a lowly boy, a ship's hand, a labourer, restricted from the quarter-deck and the cabins at stern where the mates slept and the captain planned, ruminated and surveyed the sky through his looking glass. His world was but a tiny and brutal orbit in a universe of undulating wooden planks.

Then: sleep came. Sudden, full-bodied, hard-earned. Unlike any he'd known in his life.

In time, Tom explained as he painted, fear lost its power; there was only so much effort a person could give to terror.

As he had learned to swim in the Forth, proving himself to his father, Tom scaled the masts, hoping to prove himself to Captain Sweet.

'And so you learned to forget your own bravery,' Catherine perceived.

'Is it bravery if it is ordinary?'

'I imagine more so when you commit to an action with the knowledge of risk,' she said.

Brave or not, each day the crew climbed and hauled. Near the equator, the air grew still and warm, and two months out from Leith the sun burned Tom's face as he sailed into his first southern summer.

Tiredness slackened into exhaustion. The men became restless and tested each other with fists.

To keep his thoughts from drifting, Tom practised his knots, making them fast and secure. Bowline, clove hitch, an eye splice, a double diamond. Casting a length of rope through and over itself. He didn't know why his father had died. Hitching, pointing, nippering. He didn't know why it was this path he'd been set upon and not another. But when he pulled two ends of rope, a knot tightened; when he eased it with his fingers, the ends fell free again. Above him the immense height of the mainmast waved like the needle of a compass against the sky. It never settled, swaying always in response to wind and wave, but it was strong. The trustworthy product of their own hands: carpenter, sailmaker, sailor.

The shifting light was something else. Tom marked the effects of sun and wind on water: jewel-like, white-bright, windward to lee. The way the waves rose, tipped and fell. The quality of light through the seasons, cerulean and rust, the lengthening and shortening of the days. All of it he stored in his mind: a perfect mental picture.

When he took his parchment up on deck each Sabbath, the colours rushed in like a storm breaking over the sides, though all he had to sketch with was charcoal.

'I saw that young boy once,' Catherine said. 'Standing before Turner's tumultuous snowstorm. I am certain of it. His face was awash with a dreadful kind of magnificence. All those memories just at the surface.'

Pierced by this, Tom let out a breath. 'When I look back the past is bright. It's made of particular moments that eclipse the whole. Like the way your mother's brooch shines in your memory, I suppose.'

'I think these memories must define us, tell us who we are.'

She was right, he thought. But there was no way to anticipate those moments. And so much back then was unexpected.

He had often felt alone; his grief lodged inside him. Nature felt so large. He searched for some connection through it.

Now he added the last of the white pigment to show the foaming at the hull and put down his brush, suddenly spent.

'Even the storm has beauty,' she said, inspecting what he had created.

Her face seemed to shift with anticipation as he stretched himself out on the grass. Those soft blades under his hand. A fluttering in the oak above. A clear sky to rest beneath.

'Forget the blanket,' he said, and held out his hand. He did this without thought, and before he could retract or qualify, felt her fingers clasp his freely.

Was it Tom she wanted to understand, or the sea? Was there a difference?

'Tell me something more.'

He lay back and thought for a bit.

'The bird.'

'The bird?'

'Does it sound foolish? I will never forget it.'

'Then it is not foolish. Or if it is foolish, we will laugh, and that will be worth the story too.'

He smiled at her, then gazed across the garden, up at the blue lid above them.

'We were approaching the coast of southern Africa. For several days the sky had been cloudless, the nights clear with the unfamiliar arrangements of southern constellations. Where we anticipated violent winds, favourable breezes blew us on instead. Fortuitous, you might think, but it kindled superstition among several of the men. Everything became foreboding, some dark portent.'

Table Bay had spread itself in a curve, a flat-topped bulk of mountain pushing up beyond the shore. 'Like the top's been sawn off,' the carpenter said. Working behind him with a pot of tar, sealing the rigging, Tom had trailed his sight along the line of that new land. A wave of fog unfurled, not from the sea like the haar over the Forth but from the interior, rising over the top of the mountain against a backdrop of striking gentian blue.

'Is it always like that?' he asked the carpenter.

'Often it is. Strange to see for the first time, I warrant you.'

Tom had never seen anything like it.

MacIntyre had told them of ships wrecked by winds that pushed hard upon the shore. 'The toughest hull smashed like she was made of glass.' He'd seen a leviathan, a humpback rising out of the water off that very coast, as tall as the sky sail.

Tom had spent hours in hope, watching for the great plume of a whale as it rose from the seas, picturing the leap and twist of an enormous body, and anticipating the noisy crash as it rebroke the surface.

He was searching the waters again when there was a sudden hit against the foreyard arm.

A winged body dropped to the deck at his feet.

Bending down, Tom saw blood seeping from the eye, open wide but unseeing. He had admired these birds as the *Aurora* first drew close to the coast, how confidently they harnessed the wind beneath outstretched wings. It was a mesmerising motion that held them aloft; to the human eye it appeared a kind of stillness.

One of the older boys balanced on the ratlines just above.

'Cormorant,' Tom confirmed, looking up.

'What in hell?'

Tom searched for what could have caught the light and directed it fatally at the bird, but there was no apparent cause. It was freakish, he thought, for it to be lying on deck, yellow-eyed with its once-graceful white breast and slender neck twisted too far around. One wing lay wrenched from its body, like the broken spoke on his ma's umbrella that would never again close properly.

One minute it had been a seemingly weightless creature skimming the sky; the next a dead weight dropping through the air.

He could not draw away.

Descending from the ratlines, the older boy directed a long, jeering laugh towards him. A knee angled itself with sharp and deliberate force into his ribs.

Tom crouched motionless over the bird. He saw how on one side of the impact had been life and on the other, death. Nothing separated the two. He felt for the innocence of the bird, which flew itself to its own end, never knowing what was coming, nor that it was so close.

It took him a long while to gather up the still-warm body and release it over the side. The large eye offered him a silent, glassy reflection.

Curled up in his hammock that night Tom slept fitfully, dreaming of bright stars against a blackened sky that became the shining eyes of the bird as it struck the mast, its wing bent to the side. He thought again of the bodies on the beach. He longed for his father, his mother. For the hum of their voices from the hearth and the comforting flicker of orange flames shadowing the cottage walls. And, at last, he allowed himself to cry in the darkness of the hold, falling asleep again without once making a sound.

13

Tom was proud of all he had achieved, how he had grown from humble origins, but his pride was veined with soft surprise. That Catherine took such interest in his life; that the poverty of his upbringing met her privileged nursery-raised childhood without resistance. She appeared drawn to the differences between them, not troubled by them as her brother was.

Alfred had seemed to imply he was a fancy.

Tom did not believe that. He and Catherine spoke with trust, sharing private thoughts and sensitivities they might otherwise guard. Sometimes he contemplated the ploy of his tutelage for all its implied possibilities: the tugging of stronger currents than a shared passion for their work.

As Tom had pored over her seaside painting, he felt a rush within him as if it were he who kicked and churned up the shallows, his own body alive with her quick artistry. When he presented the sketch he would work from for the *Aurora* in storm and mixed his palette of colours, she moved in close at his side and smiled her agreement that the lemon tint he'd use for the beam of the ship's lanterns, made with less white and more colour than he usually would, seemed just right.

'Does it ever make you feel powerful – the speed, the wind, the wild waves?'

'It can feel like freedom,' he replied after a pause. 'And humility in the face of power.'

Stirred by her questions, he saw his past igniting as he painted. He allowed it to flare and fade before them. The present was beckoning to the future in what was spoken, in what was merely intimated.

That afternoon he wanted nothing more than to have her take his face in her hands and cradle him for all the lost years of tenderness. The temperature had dropped but they continued to paint, with brushes and words, and blankets at their shoulders, until the light began to wane and Cecilia cast a conspiratorial shadow at their periphery.

Finally, on their way back to the house, her aunt made an excuse to slip ahead, and Tom reached for Catherine on impulse, again finding her hand. As he drew her nearer she took the chance to inspect the scar at his temple; she mapped it lightly with her fingers, and he willed her closer, found her eyes, intuited all that was subterranean.

Then light flooded across them from an opening door, and he lost her to the house once more.

He would salve himself that night, after Alfred and the captive birds and Catherine and the touch of her; all the murky feeling stirred up like sediment. There were two sides to him, and he felt loyal to both.

The tavern near the docks was comfortingly stale with the tang of foreign tobacco, bodies of brine and weeks-old sweat, the cadence of different tongues. Men of the Indian Ocean, the West Indies, the stretch of Europe. Those who worked the docks; those who'd just arrived upriver or were soon to depart. Each rounded himself to shovel his meal, and dogs lay at the feet of their various masters, heads on one side with their own mouths open wetly.

Leaning back in his chair after a plate of beef and gravy, Tom stretched and lit his pipe from the fire. His da had done the same at night, only using a scrap of kindling as a taper, his stockinged feet against the hearth steaming and smelling of the sea as he smoked. His mother would join him at the fireside with a pile of darning, her knuckles big and red in the fire gleam. She'd crack her skin on the laundry during the day, rubbing sheets and shirts by the fistful along the wooden washboard into a bucket of cold, cold water. There was always a line of washing hanging to the right of the cottage, and a line of fish hanging to the left, pegged like stiff flags to dry in the tepid sun.

A heavy round of laughter from the neighbouring table brought Tom back. Turning his head, he eyed four heavy-set men, surprisingly well turned out with shiny buttons but greasy skin. He caught their northern accents – English, from near the border – and saw the publican's wife recoil as she cleared their plates, shifting her hips to avoid a searching hand. Tom didn't need to imagine her indignation as she withdrew. Grown scarlet at her cheek, she let her voice grow sharp for all to hear, and he was suddenly embarrassed for her, for the men's crudeness, for his own role as witness.

Tom reached down and ruffled the satiny ears of a terrier mutt that had lifted its head at the sound. It trained its moist eyes on him and blinked when Tom pulled away again, dipping its head and resettling a broad nose against its paws.

'You never know when it's all going to explode.'

Tom looked up. It was Pickering, the able seaman who would replace him as second mate. Setting down a bottle of whisky, he pulled up a chair, making a sign at Tom with his hands. Phht, they said.

Tom raised his brow in wary question.

'This,' Pickering elaborated, jerking his head to indicate the general surrounds.

He was not wrong. Amid the camaraderie of convenient friends made over a bottle, there was an edginess and friction to the talk; too many bodies in one space wanting different things, or worse, wanting the same thing. Rivalry. Simple hatred of another's skin or faith. And sometimes situations did explode, scuffles and brawls, out of nothing.

Tom pushed his plate to one side and his glass forward for a pour. He toasted. 'Slàinte mhath.'

The old scar on Pickering's lip smoothed out as he gulped his whisky. Fistfight, he had bragged to Tom; took his opponent down like he was nothing. To the men in the forecastle he recounted tying a young Bengali lascar to the mast on a previous ship. Binding the sailor's wrists above his head and filling his pockets with lead. Dousing him with seawater for no other reason than sport. The tale was told as a boast or a threat, depending on who was in earshot.

Tom was glad when Captain Martin arrived at their table.

'How do you find the repairs, sir?' he asked.

'The man's a craftsman when I need efficiency. I've a mind to the Indian Ocean and do not want us to miss our window.'

Tom agreed, knowing he had learned to desire two things at once. It was two and a half weeks since they had disembarked at the London Docks. Nine afternoons Tom had spent with Catherine. Three of those at the house.

He protected his secret. Eager to take up his new position and command the larboard watch for the first time. But chafing at the idea of his departure.

Martin complained that the shipwright tending to the *Majestic* was frustratingly vague. It could be another week before the clipper was released from the dry dock; it could be another ten days. Tom made a different kind of calculation in his head.

'I'll lose half my crew at this rate,' Martin growled. 'They'll abscond, or be lost to the booze.'

'Steady on, sir.' Pickering lowered his whisky.

'You can rely on us, sir,' Tom said, tapping the rim of his glass.

'What is it you do with your afternoons, anyway?' Slipping topics, Pickering eyed Tom keenly.

'Oh, a bit of walking, a bit of painting.'

On the days he wasn't with Catherine he was learning about the London light, its frequent milkiness that drew a sheath over the eyes.

'We wondered if there was a woman involved, Mr Rutherford.'

'Got to be it, Captain.' Pickering smirked.

Tom looked down again at the terrier, which cocked its head, as if alert and complicit.

Turning back, he asked, 'Any other news worth mentioning?'

'Aye,' Martin acknowledged. 'Word in from Ireland. They're still dropping like flies. Hundreds of thousands of them.'

Tom shook his head. 'Poor bastards. Plenty heading out to America. Seamus Regan's young sister and his brother among them – he had word before he left for Oxford. Parents too weak to make the crossing. It's a damned shame.'

'Let's hope the Protestants and Papists can put their fists aside for the passage. As for Captain Franklin, still no word from the Arctic expedition.'

'Hmm, but they, unlike the Irish, are well supplied.' Pickering grinned.

'That's the truth,' Tom conceded. But the prospect was fearful. Two years had passed without message or sighting. It was said Franklin and his men had three years of tinned supplies stored within the hulls of *Terror* and *Erebus* to sustain their search for the Northwest Passage, but no one wanted to think what would happen should they find themselves stuck in the ice.

Martin and Pickering kept on with news from the docks and the pouring of whisky until Tom's head grew weary.

'I expect you sharp tomorrow, Mr Rutherford. I want us at the dry dock early for an inspection.'

'Aye, sir.'

Tom slipped into his jacket and left them to it. Pickering offered a vague wave; he would not be beaten when it came to drinking long and late.

The alleyways behind the docks all looked the same at night. Tom turned into one opaque, rough-cobbled passage after another, ducking under damp laundry slung across his way. He passed by men and women slumped in doorways, drowsing at his feet. Children curled into their mother's skirts. Rural labourers, he thought, driven to the city for work. For a moment he lost the direction of the river. The air was stagnant and dense. He wanted his bed.

Then: a sudden reek of wastewater. Barely missing Tom's boots in the obscure dark. A stink he could taste. He traced its path.

A face, girlish, yet more old than young. A hand that wiped at a skirt, another holding a bucket.

'Got some coin, mister? Show you what you're lookin' for.'

Her open look, her beckoning finger.

'No, miss.'

His head bowed, his hand pressing down on his hat.

'No,' he repeated.

He was tired, but not from physical labour. His mind felt like a dark and overcrowded hold with the hatch prised open to the light.

The evening was large and cloudless but he couldn't sense its expanse.

Out on the water he watched stars become moon become sun become clouds become stars. Capturing their halcyon bodies through the sextant glass to mark the ship's position, and in doing so marking his own. Understanding for a second what it meant to belong in a very small spot beneath an endless patterning of constellations. He longed for that sky, its ever-changing arrangement that needed watching. The air so bright and fresh. Depths of dark mystery beneath the hull.

Finally he emerged into a broader street and recognised it, teeming with bodies, lit by gas lamps erect in rows. He dropped his shoulders, took in the air and headed for his room. The night drooped at his back in a featureless haze of coal smoke. There'd be dew on the cobblestones in the morning again, but by noon no trace of moisture.

14

Undressed and unexpectedly heated, Tom lay on the bed sheet that night with his head still storming.

Whenever he painted with Catherine, he tingled with coexistence. To tell her about the sea, to tell her about himself, he was compelled to describe not what happened yesterday but what had happened to him as a child. The root of it all.

Recounting his first ever steps upon a foreign shore, he had seen Table Bay again, and he saw the captain. The pair intertwined.

Captain Sweet had been a watchful eye during the learning and labouring, the storm and the bird. The numerous daily brutalities of Tom's life. It was Sweet who had stood in their cottage and carved an image of Tom's father that Tom could hold close. Who withheld fatherly care until Tom gulped out of hunger. Who had, finally, reached out, enquired, and turned an eye to Tom's potential.

That young boy had learned to steel his tender self but remained wide-hearted. Had grown accustomed to the sway of oceans but of land knew only the touch of Scottish mud and rock.

Table Bay magnified before the bow in a scintillating flare of white heat. Closer, the shore with its jetties took on the appearance of veins and limbs, the wide curving of a coastal arm, the hump of mountainous shoulders.

The air was rust-tinged. Industrial. Cut with the freshness of rain-soaked foliage.

His skin was sweaty. A burning kind of ache dug into every muscle as he hoisted and shunted barrels and chests out of the *Aurora*'s hold. Single malt whisky. Always whisky. Iron. Pounds of folded cotton. The pain of a finger caught where it shouldn't be, or a foot. When the last barrel had been unloaded, they'd spilled themselves over the ship's side like ballast.

Catherine had asked: *Who was that boy who placed his feet on land after months at sea?*

A boy not quite fourteen. With a stomach that was never sated, even when Cook deigned to offer seconds.

The port reconfigured dangerously with moving cargo and steaming horses straining at their loads. The sticky air thundered with languages Tom could not follow.

Tom let the men and older boys slip ahead, confident he would not be noticed. They threw their jackets over their shoulders, tugged at their belted waists. At that age, much of their lewd talk was still lost on him.

Alone after so long, he felt a sudden sensation of shedding weight. The sun roared like a furnace and the stealthy fog, curling from inland, had disappeared without a trace. Even then he swayed out of habit, and saw his shadow shimmy on the water, broader and with a wider stance than when he had left his ma at Leith more than two months earlier.

So much had happened since then.

He had charcoal and parchment in his bag, but he didn't know where to start. And so he sat and studied the way the bay, ash-coloured and churned by traffic, slapped itself against the prow of each ship. He barely had an outline of a hull drawn when the voice called out.

'I doubt that'll be a very interesting picture, lad.'

Sweet had never once addressed him personally. Tom supposed the captain would continue on to the custom house to finalise his transactions, and so he dropped his hand and waited, legs dangling, looking out to sea.

The captain diverted along the boards. Tom felt the reverberation of footsteps, closer, until the man was at his back.

'It's just waves, lad, and haven't we seen plenty of those. Big waves, small waves, inbetweeners. After a while they all look like one big never-ending bastard of a wave,' Sweet said.

Tom nodded, turning to look up at him. Sweet appeared notably refreshed with a clean jacket and his hair slicked back.

'You've seen plenty of them already yourself. Clutching to the yards in storms like your da used to do.'

'Aye, sir.'

'Are you superstitious, Tom?'

'Perhaps, sir.' Tom tried to follow.

'Do you believe in God?'

'Don't know exactly, sir.'

Sweet's eyebrows rose into two bushy hillocks. 'Well, then, do you believe in the sea?'

'Aye, sir.' Tom had seen the result of its wrath, unleashed without cause. He would do nothing to provoke it.

'So you should, son. So should we all.'

The captain contemplated skywards, rubbing his clean-shaven neck. The skin there was creased and pricked with tiny pink dots.

'How do you find it all, Tom? Your first leg completed.'

'The food's not bad, sir. I improve at my duties.' What was expected of such open-ended questioning?

'And beyond the gruel and the scrubbing? What make you of this world at sea?'

The contradiction had become clear to Tom: theirs was a life lived in constrained quarters in the middle of a vast expanse.

'Well, sir.' Tom wondered how he might express it. 'It's both big and small all at once. I've learned every board of the decks. Every sail, every knot, every brace and shroud. But the sea is enormous, it spreads for miles, stretching beyond sight, and sometimes it's like sailing into—' He saw his ma's face by firelight, her feet at the hearth. Tom wondered if she still read each night, perhaps now to her unborn child, who might soon be a brother or sister to him. He pressed his lips together and inspected the wet timber of the wharf.

'Into what, lad?'

'Infinity.' Squinting, as if to obscure the word. He meant it as a kind of heaven and hell in one. He shrugged it off. 'That's what my ma would say.'

'Aye, it's a wee bit poetic, Tom. I wouldn't let the other hands catch you out with that kind of language.'

'She liked me to read, sir.'

'Clearly. And who was it taught you to draw?'

Tom looked down at his parchment, searching for an answer to a question he had not considered before. He felt something deep and powerful when he gazed at the sky in its variety of shapes and textures, at the colour of the sea, in which he identified not just one green, one blue, one grey but a multitude of hues. No one had taught him that.

He shrugged again. 'Just happens, sir.'

There were parts of his earlier life Tom had not told Catherine, not wanting to shock her and turn her away. Events he believed too harsh to retell: that Green had been whipped three times before them all for his failure to secure the sail. That Tom had been bullied after his private conversation with Sweet, beaten out of envy by the older boys until his ribs were marbled purple-black and he could barely inhale for the pain. A bucket of ice water had been dumped on him from up high. A blade pressed to his soft throat by a pock-faced Liverpudlian lad, and his weight levered precipitously over the side. Only upon the incident with the blade had Sweet, who had observed it all, stepped in. Bullying was one thing; it would make a boy tougher. But a captain couldn't lead a ship with a crew set to murder each other.

That night Tom would dream of the walled garden: roses that were the colours of bloodied skin, the backs of playing cards, the whites of eyes grown bloodshot from the wind.

Catherine had described the impulse in her as a river. It was a way of seeing, and her father had nurtured this sight by bringing impressions of the world to her, which she stashed beneath her pillow. Just as Lord Ogilvie decorated his study walls with paintings of other places, other people, other myths and great narratives. Just as he filled the entrance hall of the house and its echoing corridors with objects of foreign beauty.

Ah, there it was: that graze again and its unseen wound. He felt around for its sting a little more as he lay there on the narrow bed. Just to be certain. Eventually finding what it was that had caused it.

Was Tom himself an exotic and curious object to be admired and studied?

Was Catherine collecting him?

It was a deep cut, he discovered, but there was no blame for it.

Why did it matter if she wanted to put him and his stories under her pillow like tokens and continue to dream after he'd gone?

So what if he thrilled her, brought her joy in the short time they had?

He was a willing participant, bathing in the sweetness of her condescension like an opium haze.

Soon he would have to come to.

Soon he would need to depart.

15

Each day now was a shifting bead: both an adding up and a counting down. Tom wondered if Catherine marked an indefinite end point as he did.

Every second afternoon she was waiting to greet him before any servant could summon her.

She chanced to lead him alone into a small east-facing room off the hall that had been her mother's morning room. She loved the intimacy of this particular parlour, she said – she found it cocooning. Tom saw it was decorated with embroidered fabrics in floral designs and oatmeal-coloured curtains that filtered rather than blocked out the light, so unlike the dark leather and velvet of Alfred's private abode.

In this room he was avid for Catherine's visible imprint, signs of a life lived separate to him. There was the burnished piano, oily with wood polish, where he imagined her singing with Cecilia at the keys, their eyes on the sheet music that was held in place with brass wings. Here an indented cushion against which she allowed her back to curve after all; her preferred spot in the bay window where she spent the mornings with her legs drawn up. A book abandoned on the sill lay open in evidence of repose and leisure, cast off mid-thought. Elizabeth Barrett, he read from the spine. 'Now Browning,' Catherine said at his shoulder. 'Following her marriage.'

Collecting a lilac shawl from the piano stool, she guided him to a painting hung above a dark-wood mantelpiece of a woman with amber hair who observed them with an interrogative gaze.

'Your mother?' He needed no confirmation. The asymmetry of her eyebrows was the same as Catherine's; one was a smooth and even curve, the other triangulated into a peak.

'I have been passing some time here with her lately. She helps me in times of uncertainty.' Catherine pulled the shawl close at her shoulders.

'Are you in need of guidance?'

'I have many questions, and the answers my mother gives are unfailingly brilliant.'

'I suppose you please yourself with their import.'

The easy tumble of her laughter emboldened him.

'But you are close with your aunt?'

'I tell her everything.'

'Everything?' Tom wondered what topics she confided, and whether he was one of them.

'She gives excellent counsel.'

'She observes enough of your life to do so. And what of her? She has never married?'

'She is defiance.'

He searched her brilliant eyes. 'You'll have to elaborate.'

'At my age she loved a gentleman, and that favour was returned. Sadly, before they could be married, he died in an accident – he fell from his horse and broke his neck. She was courted afterwards by many suitors, but she did not love them, so she declined all their offers. My grandfather was furious and threatened to cast her off, but she would not be persuaded to marry another, not for wealth nor title nor security. Eventually no more offers were made, and when Mama – her younger sister – married Papa, my aunt arrived with her to live at Ogilvie House.'

He nodded. 'Your father's kindly.'

'My father likes novelties.'

'I see. And Alfred?' He barely dared raise the man who'd made his opposition to Tom so insultingly clear. Would Alfred Ogilvie reveal the same tolerance as the rest of his family?

'Well, my dear brother will have to marry eventually, to carry the family name.'

'Certainly,' he agreed, although it wasn't what he had meant.

'So you see, we are somewhat of an eccentric family. Are you sure you wish to be connected with the Ogilvies, Mr Rutherford?'

Surely she was teasing. He had arrived as her tutor, and not even a proper one. They had moved outside easy definition. He listened for softness, a catch in her voice.

Eccentric was one thing, but Ogilvie House and its world were far from Bo'ness, not merely geographically. Certainly his own mother was never dressed in such finery and painted in oils. And while she had wanted her son educated, not bound for the sea, she had lost that battle with God easily enough.

He didn't know where to look, so he shifted between the two faces: mother and daughter. 'It's a beautiful portrait.'

'It makes it easier for me to imagine her face reanimated.'

Tom understood that impulse, and how impossible it was to achieve. How some memories were fleeting and objects were required to take their place.

'Was she—' He didn't know how to express it. Was she of equal social level was what he wanted to ask, but it seemed so coarse to say so, and even more so to feel it necessary. 'Her family. They were from the same circles as your father's?'

'Naturally.'

Then Catherine bent in towards him, low-voiced, confidential. 'Not everybody can be a rebel, Mr Rutherford.'

He cleared his throat and waited. Dipped his chin lower, feeling her eyes fall on his neck. She was right there at his side. She hovered, as if to say *however*, and he heard her exhale. Then the door opened upon them and she started, stepping away from him. He felt suddenly exposed.

'Beg your pardon, miss. The master requests I inform you: everything is prepared and your aunt awaits you in the hall.'

Catherine was still, her sentence hanging. Tom waited, asking for her eyes. But she dropped her head, resigned to the interruption.

'I was introducing Mr Rutherford to the former lady of the house.' Her voice, slightly raised, was not for him.

Alfred was there as they left the parlour. Tom watched the man triumph with a curt nod from across the hall, the abrupt closing of his private door.

For a minute Catherine seemed to deliberate in her brother's wake, one hand clenched at her waist, and Tom wondered if she might follow.

Against this, Cecilia's cheerful greeting rang out from the foot of the stairs.

Tom recomposed himself.

Catherine did the same. 'Dear Aunt, are you ready?'

'I am. It is set to be a charming afternoon for reading outdoors. And for surreptitiously observing the talents of this young man across the grass.'

'You do mean his painting, of course?' Catherine took Cecilia's arm and led the party off. She was daring again, light-hearted. Cecilia blushed, and he fancied he must have too.

'You must join us for whist one evening, Mr Rutherford,' Cecilia said. 'It may surprise you that my nephew plays an excellent hand.'

'Almost as excellent as his sister,' Catherine added.

But Tom had long suspected Catherine of orchestrating a careful schedule, despite the levity.

Her father was warm, if distracted, whenever they happened to meet. Checking in on his progress with the Ogilvie history, Tom would be told: 'Yes, another chapter laid down, and so onto the next. There is no start and no end to history, my boy.'

Tom thought of this phrase in the days following as he shared porridge with Pickering and Martin at the boarding house, as they walked to the docks and checked in on the *Majestic*, when the pair queried his absences but were not interested in the reason, when he woke at four in the morning to soundless bells, when he painted next to Catherine and told her of his father's bravery in saving Sweet and how his mother liked to read poetry too, and how, further back, there was more that he didn't know even to speak of.

He pulsed with the idea that after this, this moment, this very second, there was much more to come that he couldn't know of either.

When he thought of Alfred, he began to think of him as a harmless spot in his vision that came as the result of staring into a candle's flame for too long. A moment in a longer history that would soon pass.

Neither Tom nor Catherine saw Alfred go to his mother's portrait after the house had fallen quiet. He released his fists and gave them the appearance of gentlemanly composure, though there was no one to witness. Whenever he looked at his mother he saw Catherine. He never saw himself. It was in his sister that his mother's vitality lived, not in him.

As children they had been close. Catherine loved him and had been loyal, but she was separate, always away in an inner world he could not follow her to, playing made-up games with candlesticks and figurines in the parlour, drawing with her pencils, and making forts in the wide hollow at the foot of the great oak tree. She would squirrel herself in there with her drawings and flowers and stones and stolen marrons glacés, and wield a stick at anyone who tried to draw her out to more sensibly girlish games.

From a young age Alfred had done everything with propriety and obedience, proving himself worthy of his survival, but he felt no ease. He found himself to be an outsider, the child at parties who stood apart from the other boys and girls as they laughed at the predictable spring of a jack-in-the-box. He would be a much older man before he would understand that at least some of this distance he felt from others was within himself, and that his assumption of rejection pushed people away more than was necessary. That convention might only be a veneer, not a master. But at twenty, solitude was his safest friend. Alienated from kinship, his stiff bearing and controlled conversation hardened further in self-protection.

Thomas Rutherford embodied all that he resented. Everything he wanted to be. This low-born man who had drawn Catherine and Cecilia and his father in with his quiet charm, a seeming naivety. His competence in adapting, in assuming new postures as if he had always been familiar with them. That self-sufficient strength that gave him a dignity not even an heir apparent could buy.

16

Above them, against the skin of the sky, the oak tree's dark spines spread like veins.

'You will not see this view from any ship,' Catherine said, her head rocking back. Her shoulders sighed with a new-found looseness, as if her muscles had warmed and softened.

Tom had often thought of a ship's masts and yards as akin to great, sturdy trees, but their forms were uniform, thick and straight. Here beneath the gnarled old oak he found the contrasting lines of nature: lines that were not straight but comprised knots and arches, bends and diversions and oppositions. There was nothing known or predictable about it.

'In autumn the garden is a tapestry of ochre and carmine,' Catherine continued with a languid determination.

The branches reminded him of the drawings Seamus had shown him of the body's circulatory system, its tentacles spreading out, pumping blood so a heart might keep beating. He described it to her like that, just as he saw it.

Paired with the same reluctance, the same wilful determination, they did not discuss what was upon them. He would be gone before they could kick through those red and gold leaves together.

Another day slid by, and another. The fact of Tom's departure was inevitable; the manner of his leaving was not.

Only the pace of each visit became urgent. They began to meet daily. Filled with ideas and confident Tom would not dismiss them, Catherine began work on a series of seasides, painting one new canvas and then another from alternative points of view: she studied herself from the clouds, and from the approaching waves. With each fresh palette she seemed to intuit the future. Anything useful she had gleaned from Mr Barolo about colour or perspective, she passed on. Where once Tom had known only simple impulse, he gained language for it and improved his technique, becoming aware of how he sketched out his own compositions, chose his colours, mixed the pigment to a particular consistency, selected a broad or thin, soft or coarse brush, and applied first one layer and then another to the canvas in his slower, more painstaking way.

Eager to experiment with Catherine's superior supplies, he swapped chrome yellow for the brighter, long-lasting cadmium, and took up her suggestions for exploring other vibrant colour pigments. Detail meant everything, and for this brief time in the sun-softened garden, released from the demands of the bells, he had long hours to devote to achieving it: the balance of mist and weight in sea spray or the perfect striations of semi-translucent shadow. An egg-yellow sun.

In the past his art had been limited to sketchbooks and parchment or small, unstretched canvases that could be easily rolled. For years before he was a mate, his shared quarters in the forecastle had allowed only for essentials: charcoal, waterpaints and paper. There had been no storage other than his bag in the beginning, no easy way to keep works clean or away from corrosive saltwater, no place to leave a large oil piece to dry. No time to paint one. His improved circumstances and more liberal quarters as chief mate might allow for what she had further opened inside him: this longing to describe his experience of the world through colour.

The more he worked, the more he understood he was her apprentice.

'This particular scene I would like to see framed and hung.' She spread her arms before the easel as if to measure the painting's effect.

It was a packet ship upon the North Atlantic, lit with a high summer sheen. Studding sails bloomed on the fore and mainmasts. A white-painted waist showed false gunports shaded in. Sun-shot waters drove at its dark hull, and a variegated ultramarine stretched before the bowsprit. He'd traced lines of burnt umber to show Catherine the set-up of the long stays stretching from each mast.

He had never had a painting of his set into a frame. He had never considered such a static endpoint for what he experienced as an enlivening process, something living, that was a part of him.

For Catherine, the celebration of a painting in public was a natural conclusion to artistry. Tom's process had only ever been just that: a process, ongoing and privately pursued. All of his ambition until now he had given to the sea.

'Perhaps you might travel someday as a passenger aboard a clipper ship – for they are fastest of all – and dine with me, the captain. The ship would be my own. We would seek North America, Siam, the Arctic, prevailing over icefloe and typhoon, hail and humidity.'

'I should like to believe it possible.'

'Aye, and then you'd know for yourself if what I paint is accurate, and whether art is as enthralling as life out on the water can be.'

As if she took his words as a challenge, Catherine surprised him in that final week by leading them across the creaking floors of London arts societies, into the long private halls of imposing stone houses even grander than her own, ushered by a servant or family member, dust particles swirling like a snowstorm. She guided him, a student avid to learn, a man intoxicated with unexpected possibility. Mesmerised him with visual riches in which together they studied the many different approaches to light and movement, techniques of composition and perspective.

Was it her pitch at persuasion before Tom turned his back on the city and the whip-drop of sailcloth convinced him of his rightful direction?

She showed him what she understood and loved: an artistic world of refined hands and hushed spaces where magnificent paintings were hung to be admired. This was how she learned of the world and its people, how each artist's visual story transported her away from Ogilvie House to other realities, other imaginations.

She showed him pigment and brilliant gilding laid down on wooden panels hundreds of years earlier, from which halos like golden orbs shone around pale faces. Paintings by Italian artists less ancient but unknown to him, in which a chiaroscuro technique created drama and depth out of shadow and light, or where the fat, peachy limbs of winged cherubs filled a sky that had been foregrounded in the top third of the painting, further challenging his idea of perspective. In his own work the sky always formed the background – he fitted it behind the ship, no matter how dramatic its tone and shapes – but the heavenly suspended angels that almost leapt out of the canvas before him made him reconsider the assumption of this approach.

In all this history he could not find anything similar to what she created in her own paintings. Nor could he find the genesis of Turner's snowstorm.

He thought back to that wildness.

'I want to show reality. I paint exactly what I see,' he said, thinking out loud.

'Surely all painters paint what they see?'

He'd never known another painter before her, had only lately come to see the creations of their brushes. He'd never articulated his own process or vision. Thomas Rutherford: painter. A new possibility took shape.

'Then we each see things so differently. You. Me. In Turner's seascapes, nothing is drawn clearly; the sky is as dominant as the water, close to the viewer; the ships are lost in a kind of illuminated mist but for the recognisable spines of their masts. Yet it's understood to be as it is. A ship in storm.'

'Precisely. I feel it too. In this lies the wonder of art.'

He felt revealed and demonstrative at once. His hand showed her not just what he saw, but the way in which he saw it. He was learning to express what he had felt since he was a boy on the *Aurora*, the way the changing light and its illumination of the sea – by night, in storm, in snow, in searing sun – moved him, and imbued him with a sense of expansion and space. His work showed who he was as a sailor; his attitude of awe, his dedication, his ambition, his mastery of a complicated kind of machine. And more. These weeks with Catherine had disrobed him. He stood before her a simple man exposed by simple desire for another human being. Through the creation of colours and lines he had allowed her to prise open his chest and touch what was beating inside.

When word came from the shipwright, it came too soon.

Captain Martin's instruction was immediate. He thumped at Tom's door, his curly head emphatic with the announcement. 'Good news, Mr Rutherford! Our time has come. We load in two days and set sail the morning after. I'll allow no further delay.' He left Tom with a rap upon the doorframe that presumed his enthusiasm was shared.

Tom emerged sleepy and dishevelled, rubbing at a tightness in his ribs. Hard upon the thought of departure came the relief of inevitability, an urgency for solitude and the sea. How much easier it would be to have such heady foolishness behind him.

Earlier he had thought to invite Catherine to the docks where the *Majestic* was resting dry with the repairs almost complete. Out of the water, the size and lines of the clipper would be even more imposing and impressive, the characteristically sleek and sharp bow so evidently designed for speed, capable of far swifter journeys than the *Aurora* had ever achieved. He would show her what his world was made of: wood and iron; canvas of a tougher kind and so much larger, waiting to be dropped, ready to capture the wind's full power. But he had been fearful that to do so might break some kind of illusion. That it was all too easily shattered. And so he had not.

That last afternoon came to them with a suddenness they could not have prepared for, four weeks after Tom's arrival in London. Canvases were abandoned and left to dry, their colours boxed up. The mood grew soft and plaintive. Cecilia led the way through the garden, ushering the servants ahead. It was a gift, a few minutes free of scrutiny, and Tom leaned in as Catherine turned towards him. He was kept at bay by her skirts and the wide brim of straw and ribbon that he wanted to dip his head beneath so he might kiss her.

'It seems unreal that I must go.' His hands at her wrists. That small territory of skin between glove and the lace edge of her sleeve. That indigo vein pushing blood under his thumb.

'Will you write? Am I able to write to you? Is that possible?'

He shrank from the hope of it. 'The seas will stretch between us. You will forget me soon enough. It is best that you do.'

If she had said the same, he would not have believed her.

'There is more we might share with one another.'

Off-balance, he retreated. 'Our lessons, do you mean?'

'Oh, our lessons. Yes.' She looked away, speaking as if to the trees and sky. 'Watercolours are lovely, but grand ships need oil and canvas. Promise me you'll continue when you are gone.'

'When I am gone.' He nodded. 'Will you paint how you want to paint? Say damn to the world, to the scrutiny of naysayers?'

But this made her sharp. 'Men can say such a thing as easily as eating breakfast.' She broke from his grasp. 'A woman relies on acquiescent fathers. Or a rarer creature: a husband who is supportive of his wife's ambition. Indeed, of his wife possessing any ambition at all.'

She did not ease him with her usual laughter.

'Quite simply, I do not wish for you to leave. It is not what I would choose.' Then she recoiled. 'But I know I talk too freely.'

He could see the tension in her neck. Her eyes darted with the effect of her confession.

His throat was dry, his mouth clicked as he swallowed. 'What path could there be for us? One we would be permitted to follow?' He had always assumed there could not be, but now he found his questions were genuine, and glanced up for a sign of movement at the windows of the house.

'I told you my father likes novelties.' The faintness of a smile, then growing, beckoning. 'There is no path. It is for us to make one.'

'My life is on the sea. That cannot be enough for you.'

'Many will say I am a fool to care for love. I do not ask for your sacrifice. But already you have shown a new kind of life is possible. I know you are a man who follows his heart, who shapes himself from his circumstances but is not bound by them. That may or may not be a risk, for both of us.'

Her words had him reeling.

'It is a risk I would take.' She spoke in earnest. 'Think on it? The rest is your decision.'

17

He decided his leaving would be like Seamus snapping a man's shoulder back into place: if he did it fast enough, the pain would soon be over.

On the morning of his departure, he sent a brief note.

I am changed by you, and will never forget this time we have spent together. The best path, for you, for both of us, is to let this tie between us sever.

Seamus was at the captain's table, returned from Oxford with news of the latest surgical advances and sufficient supplies to replenish the ship's medicine chest. Tom gave in gratefully to his friend's enthusiastic embrace and felt himself reassembling.

'Mr Rutherford, chief mate,' Seamus announced with pride.

Within hours they were on the water, and Tom felt the full effect of his shapeshifting. One form was lost, another regained. On the familiar decks of the *Majestic*, the crew was organised within unambiguous, demarcated boundaries. Almost sixty men and he knew them all as intimately as brothers; knew already those smooth-cheeked boys who showed up wide-eyed on deck with holystones as he himself had once done. Backs bent. Knees soaked and no doubt aching. Their hearts open and fearful.

Tom's slip into routine was immediate, full of muscle memory. In action he found relief, once more self-assured, intimately certain of the mechanics and rules of his surrounds. And that old, intoxicating feeling resumed its pull as they cast off their moorings: a deep anticipation of expanse. An unfolding. A knowing.

Within hours Tom was commanding his watch with the ease of a more experienced mate, yielding to wind and sky and the fresh beckoning of salt spray. Thrilling in the hard-won achievement of his new position. On the quarterdeck under a high sun with the weight of the sextant in his hand, he felt easy. Sighting the horizon, he saw the security of knowing one's place.

The *Majestic* handled like new. The rudder and mizzenmast had been replaced, the sternpost well repaired, the hull smoked for leaks and sealed up watertight for the journey. Familiar smells hit with a reviving slap, like smelling salts bringing Tom back from a haze. Tar and vinegar and recently dried varnish. The special pungency of already-stale bodies and soon-to-be rancid food. Somehow he had missed it all.

The sun slipped down in concert with the sound of the bells, and after supper Munro, the cook, beckoned from the galley as he often did. Tom and Seamus lit their pipes from the galley fire and smoked on deck to the sound of his whistling as he rinsed the last of the pots before joining them. Munro told stories of his youth along the Hooghly and in Calcutta's marketplaces. He would know where to source the ripest tomatoes when they anchored, and fresh fruit, knobbly roots of ginger as big as a hand, smooth brown onions. He would make their mouths water with recipes learned from his Bengali mother.

While Pickering grew loud in the forecastle and showed off his latest tattoo – a pair of dice, each rolling six on his right shoulder blade – Tom felt himself stamped with a different kind of image: a summer spent on land, worn invisibly on his chest. That imprint – the secret imprint of Catherine – kept him apart and separate, even from Seamus. If the men were to look closely, they would find only the nautical star inked by the old Highlander MacIntyre on Tom's first return north from the southern seas almost fourteen years before. The star on his left breast, which signified he would always find his way home.

Whenever the bells rang out, he felt time alter. The days in Richmond and London had passed with peculiar elongation and stealth, each second heightened and enduring. Out here he found himself transported away with time sped up. It was another life he had lived: Catherine Ogilvie and her artistic world. She was right: he'd shown how readily he might adapt to land.

He would sail through the next five months as though they were minutes. A confident man, now with a larger sense of things, further grown through his experiences.

Still, he was haunted. Could it be that he opened her world as much as she opened his? Was she thinking of him, this minute, and had her feelings altered? She had mined him for impressions of a life away from London, and he wondered how she might use them. In those last few days he thought she painted with greater deliberateness than she had on the hill, funnelling all her will and frustration into brushstrokes that were long and light, almost feathery.

He had reasoned it through numerous times: he had achieved rank. He had some money set aside. The word in shipping circles – for there were few secrets along the docks or on the decks – was that he was a skilful mariner, and tipped to get his master's ticket before long. Captain Thomas Rutherford. It sounded just fine to him. But it would not be good enough in Catherine's world. He had an education that was hard-won and patchy. He had created a veneer. He could get by. But Tom hadn't wealth of the kind Catherine was accustomed to and took for granted, and the difference in their backgrounds was far greater than it had been between his parents, the merchant seaman turned fisherman and the schoolmaster's daughter. He saw now how his mother had laboured under the poverty brought to her by marrying for love.

The audacity of their brief attachment was made clear from his spot on the quarterdeck. They had inhabited an unreal world with their paints and tiny sandwiches, protected from the truth by the tall walls of a sheltered garden.

The shapes of the East greeted Tom as he leaned in to study the charts. Captain Martin gestured above grid lines and coastal undulations, stabbed an index finger at the currents, and characterised the winds. A compass came into play. A course was drawn.

Their ship was in better shape than ever but the enforced delay in London would push their arrival into the unpredictable heart of the monsoonal change. The *Majestic*'s hold full of copper, brandy and cotton would be emptied in Calcutta and restocked with sugar, silk and aromatic tea, the brilliant red of lac shell dye and golden turmeric that had been dried and ground into powder.

As their prow pressed on into the South Atlantic and sliced the waiting waters, Tom wanted Catherine to see him there on the deck with sextant in hand, delivering orders and making calculations. A sailor in charge of his environment, second in command. Respected, knowledgeable and capable of assuming leadership. He wanted her to see who he was beyond what he could daub on canvas.

Against the increasing spread of ocean, Catherine grew smaller; a woman of privilege trapped in a London life that, with all its unwritten demands, was in some respects little larger than the bounds of this clipper.

They rounded the Cape and he lay awake when he should have been recovering for the next watch. His mind was full and his pulse too often racing. He couldn't stand this gathering of contradictions.

Near the end of their second month, just north of the equator, a core of darkness appeared atop the Indian Ocean amid a fierce split of lightning. Several miles off from the *Majestic*, hovering on the horizon. Visibility was brief, found in the quick of white light as sky and sea illuminated into an undifferentiated landscape, but it was long enough for Tom to be certain. When an alarm followed from the crow's nest, backing up his sighting, Martin took the glass himself to follow the line.

'Nothing,' the captain announced after a minute. 'Not a darned thing. Are you sure, Mr Rutherford?'

Tom raised his eyes to the heavens. Waited for another strike. For the wind to get up. A smack of breaking thunder. The atmosphere remained eerily still and heavy, and the oppressive grey mist had lowered itself around them again. The sea, once more obscured, was unreadable.

He described what he had seen: the same hulking ship they had sighted the previous day, stealthy on the horizon off to starboard, and now closer than Martin would care for.

They'd slowed through the night in opaque conditions. A thick cover had slung itself over the ocean and obscured danger until it was almost upon them.

'What's your opinion, sir?'

'No identifiable markings, no colours, no attempt to signal distress. We have a threat on our tail, Mr Rutherford.'

Regardless of intent, it was clear both ships were stranded by conditions outside their control.

Tom gripped the brass railing. Runnels of condensation merged and diverged, pooling against his skin. His shirt was a sticky, restrictive second skin.

'We are a sitting target, sir. There's too much at stake.'

'I am well aware, Mr Rutherford. But we can do nought with the clouds at our feet and barely a flap in the sails.'

They could see no further than their own mizzenmast's lower yard and even it loomed like a ghostly shadow perpendicular to the deck. Their crew was out there, midship and in the forecastle, captive to the opacity, neutered in action.

Next to the captain Tom was tensing, his shoulders pulled high and his jaw clenched. He saw himself stiff and lacking volition, like the rusted tin soldier he had once dug up from the yard in Bo'ness as a boy.

'Tell the men to hold, but stay readied,' instructed Martin.

'Aye, sir.' Tom's response was delivered with the sharp beat of his palm striking the rail.

More than an hour went by, two sets of bells resounding across the quiet seas. The *Majestic* inched in its misty shroud, with no way to make pace away from the other ship, which remained unseen but ever present.

Piracy was a constant threat that had remained unrealised. Tom was visualising their laden hold, estimating its value piece by piece, when a sudden gusting wind broke his calculations. Oddly disorientated, he saw their ship as if in a painting, with a round-cheeked cherub large and corpulent-limbed above them in the foreground, blowing down for sport. He saw himself painting it like that for Catherine, describing their danger stroke by stroke.

A second scorching of light across the sky. Martin raised his telescope to starboard. Sighted. Passed it to Tom. A tumbling of the mist around them now, accompanied by ricocheting thunder, a rousing of the wind, another strike of lightning. The silvery sheen began to dissipate from the decks, lifting itself like a fraying hemline.

'It comes nearer, sir, I am certain,' Tom urged.

Too distant for hailing, too close for ease.

The revived wind was gaining force, and its sudden shift in direction filled Tom with a vibrant sense of unassailability. He had known Martin to push the clipper to well above eighteen knots before, but the capability of their foe was unknown. They couldn't rely on pace alone. Tom had a plan to use the changing conditions to their advantage.

The mist was lifting to reveal a different kind of grey, which grew darker and would soon encase them again.

'I have a suggestion, if you'll allow it, sir. You may not like it, but I believe it could save us.'

'I'm listening, Mr Rutherford.'

'We sail past them on the opposite course, sir, and as close to them as we safely can, minimising our exposure to their broadside fire.'

'What you're suggesting is a gamble, and a large one. You can't be sure.'

'They won't anticipate the manoeuvre. That is our advantage.'

Tom's plan had them cutting directly across the path of the vessel in order to lose them. If it came off, they could avoid potential theft and murder. If it didn't, they would all be lost, regardless.

Each man on board could now make out the looming shadow of the other vessel against the sky, but a storm was also hastening towards them. The atmosphere formed and re-formed, fast and powerful. The sea hammered the hull and the sails began to bow.

'Risk may be all we have at our disposal,' the captain uttered, and to Tom's surprise, he assented. On Martin's orders, the *Majestic* bore away from the alien ship and the men re-trimmed the sails on the opposite tack. They were counting on the *Majestic*'s ability to find speed, with the wind now filling the cloth. They were counting on the element of surprise.

The clipper picked up pace, heading furiously in the direction of its target. The danger lay not only in coming within firing range, but also in their estimation of the ship's position. Rain pulled the clouds down now to the sea, a backdrop to a battle scene.

Tom clenched his fist so hard his nails dug into his flesh. As another flash seared through the clouds, he made it out more clearly: the spectre of a deep-sea dhow, now directly upon their starboard side and closer than they had estimated. Martin saw it too and barked his commands. They sailed so close and dipped so low to starboard that the men on the mainyard arm might have reached out and touched the angular sails of the other ship. The cries of exclamation from on board their target were unmistakable; as they neared the vessel they saw men scrambling across decks and up masts, hauling at the lateen sails, and recognised the bulky bodies of guns along its side.

Tom saw the *Majestic*'s own helmsman cross himself, and the gaping jaws of the young boys aloft. He understood how reckless the manoeuvre had been, but they sped before the ship without a touch, and kept on, leaving the vessel far behind in the falling darkness.

The anticipated boom of cannons retaliated off to stern, too close for levity, too distant to nick the hull.

The rain beat down.

Tom was not the only man who found his limbs weak and his chest taut with the aftershock of exertion. Martin was full of relief. 'All sense warned against the tactic, Mr Rutherford, but the responsibility is mine alone. We pulled it off and I am glad for that. May Lady Luck stay on our side – with a little less adventure hereafter.'

*

Beneath the first chameleon colours of dusk when all but a skeleton watch was at rest, Tom's breath rushed from him, exhausted at stern. They'd left the vessel behind only to confront the ferocity of the storm, and used every scrap of energy to fend that off too.

Great sinewy lines ran above him to the mizzenmast. The tension pulling at them made a solid heft of what had begun as loose fibres. The deck around him was criss-crossed and laddered by shadows.

Momentarily light-headed, he'd removed his jacket and loosened his shirt at his throat. His chest was thudding; his blood seemed to rush too fast. He clasped the rail and gave a cough, then let himself drop to his haunches to recover his breath, becoming small like a creature on the sea floor. Obscured, protected, blending into his native landscape.

Curved like that over the deck he longed for the weight of holystone in his hand again, for the perfection of the motion, for the boundaries of a simple equation. Every sailor was glad when they graduated beyond the gruelling task, but not one could respect any less the next boy handed the stone.

He had been that boy once. He had rowed from the purple thistles and grey skies of Bo'ness; from his mother, from the shore that had denied his father's bones; he had scrubbed the deck until his fingers bled.

And he had not stopped there.

How much could a man transform and yet remain himself? It was hubris, surely, a kind of treachery, to want to grow so far from your roots.

But a sense of potential moved him.

Get up, he thought. A cowering man cannot command respect, cannot lead those who disavow frailty. He urged himself to stand. In his head he was on his feet, riding the sea as the ship rose and dipped and rose. But he knew it was not true.

In frustration he landed a fist, first one and then the other, against the ship's side, and discovered how easily his skin could give way.

Above him the sky loomed immense and flat, an intense ochre slashed with red. It, too, a bloodied skin. The sea swelled with flashes of viridian amid an unreadable silver shimmer. A rolling land.

'Come.' He sensed a hand on his shoulder and knew the quiet voice. 'You can't be seen like this.'

18

Back in Tom's cabin, Seamus made him sit while he surveyed the damage to his hands and peeled some crepe for bandaging. The doctor's eyes led an interrogation as he tended Tom's wounds, but he did not speak.

Tom too was silent, avoiding his friend's implicit querying, unwinding from what had come over him.

As his pulse calmed, he saw how much had changed since the Atlantic storm that had broken the rudder, that had forced them into the dry dock, that had set him adrift on land where his certainty had been split down the middle. Back then he'd been accepting of death. Now he was not so acquiescent. He had suggested a reckless tactic to Martin. Daring himself with it perhaps. That Martin found merit in the idea had shocked him. As they'd cut across the bow of the foreign vessel, Tom's chest had caved with fear and a kind of nostalgia. There was more at stake than the chance to get it down in paint. For the first time he anticipated genuine regret.

Afterwards, he'd watched Martin take from around his neck a silver locket containing clippings of his wife's hair and that of his four children. Was the risk Martin had taken of a different nature, Tom wondered. Having made a choice, having nurtured attachment else-where, did he have to prove he still had a young man's appetite? Did he face death with a greater boldness if it meant ensuring his return?

Tom had worked for what he wanted. Chief mate. Martin's trusted right-hand man. And there was more to achieve still. He did not desire to return to the holystone.

'Seamus,' he said eventually. 'I don't know what came over me.'

'Aye, you do. We've known each other a long time, and if I'm sure of one thing, it's that you know your own mind. You're still the steady, calm captain-in-waiting I call friend.'

Seamus finished winding the bandages and pinned them in place. Tom shook his head.

'What happened, Tom, while you were in London?'

What had happened? On the simplest level it was life. His life. Moving from one point to the other.

Seamus went on. 'It's clear something else has your attention.'

Tom had no thought of gaining clarity, only knew the knot of feeling needed unpicking.

'Some*one*. I told her to forget me.'

'Her?'

'Catherine Ogilvie.'

'Why? Many sailors have wives and families at home on land, if that's what you're considering.'

'Why? My life is here, beneath the mast. Hers is in the finest drawing rooms of London. She deserves more than a seaman who docks for a few days once a year. Besides, her father will quite rightly have in mind some titled aristocrat. It would be better if she forgot me. She is certain to forget me.'

'You are trying hard to convince yourself. Did you convince her, do you think?'

'I do not know.'

That day in the garden he had told her he would not write. He was not in the habit of letters, and with absence their connection would surely only diminish. He had thought to let her go would be a kindness to her. That to do so was unselfish. Now he was not so certain that was the truth. His future was in a different direction: he would be captain one day. It was what he had worked for all these years. How could he stray from the path that Sweet had set him upon? Who would he be if he chose a different life?

He didn't trust himself to find the balance as she did.

On impulse he had sent a second note, swift upon the first.

Allow me this voyage to consider. Five months. Perhaps six. In my heart I would say to you 'Yes'. But, though parting brings its own pain, I do not know if what we wish for can be.

'Love is a many-faced bedfellow, Tom.' Seamus had pulled out his pipe and began to puff at it, circling a match across the tobacco. 'It has its own timing and its own demands.'

Tom snorted. 'I'm not sure I can cope with your philosophising right now, Seamus.'

'Well, philosophising is all I've got.'

Seamus had proposed to a woman in Dublin almost seven years earlier. Certain she shared his feeling. She responded with enthusiasm but later refused his affection in favour of a wealthier candidate, also a doctor, with an established practice on land. Seamus could not let go. He doubted her choice. And it seemed it had not been for lack of care that her decision was made. Even after the marriage they met whenever he was in port, to talk over tea as old friends do, but it seemed to Tom that this alone would keep the man hooked to a line that could never be reeled in.

If Seamus fought harder, Tom had always believed, he could free himself from that hook. Now he found sympathy for his friend, and told him so.

Seamus agreed it was more than inexperience that made Tom's terrain risky.

After weeks at sea, Tom wondered if distance had yet played its part. If Catherine set up her canvas near the roses thinking only of what she'd create upon it. If he had been any more than a tactic in her challenge to society and what it assumed of her. If she would have followed through.

He shook his head. He would let the question of her slip away, a half-articulated fantasy.

The doctor sighed. 'No matter what, Tom, I'm sure you'll do the right thing.'

In truth Tom had made up his mind. His decision was clear. But he needed time to move towards it.

Seamus left him lying fully clothed on his bed, his hands like wounded paws crossed at his chest. Tom slept fitfully, rigid with tension, and rose less than four hours later with a cramp in his side.

As they drew nearer Calcutta, the conditions shifted once more against their swift passage.

Tom laughed as Seamus emerged on deck with a crimson face one morning. 'Martin warned of contrary and sudden changes.'

'He was not wrong.' The doctor wrestled with his already damp necktie. 'I had the worst sleep in my entire thirty years, Tom. There was not a scrap of air to breathe.'

'It's some heat, old man, without doubt.' Since confiding in his friend, Tom had gained some relief and fixed his focus once more upon the horizon.

They had been lucky given their delay; the southwest monsoon had moved them through the blustery open waters and deep skies of the Indian Ocean. But it flagged over the peak-shaped Bay of Bengal as they were filtered through the estuary into the narrower stretch of the Hooghly. By then, the wind was all but gone. The sky clotted above the river, violet and grey. They inched towards Calcutta with limp sails and a rising sense of impatience that fed on the crew's tired and overheated limbs.

From the deck Tom took in the low, wooded coastline along the bay, the contours of the riverbank, the scurry of bodies at work along the water's edge, but for once he did not reach for charcoal or watercolour. Painting had become a painful reminder.

The stagnancy hit each of the men in turn, challenging their nerves, and by the end of the day Tom would no longer prove immune. The sight of the shore edging so close was a threat of sorts, and he too felt enclosed, almost enshrouded after their wind-fuelled path across the ocean. The air on the river was thicker; the weight of the heat infiltrated Tom's lungs. Without the sea breeze he felt the sun burning at his skin, despite the season beckoning to winter, and their anticipated arrival stretched away from them.

And then the rain: a sudden heavy fall that slapped the decks, washed away the salt of weeks, assailed each man with vertical force. Still there was no wind. The rain glimmered around the clipper as if they had sailed into the heart of a waterfall and the unfettered cascade from the sky encased them in sound, separating them from the coast, from the port, from the entrance to the river, from the bay. The river seemed barely to flow, but its rain-thrashed surface became broken up by concentric ripples that grew and disappeared, grew and disappeared into each other.

For three days it rained. Everything reeked of damp. The shipboard world shrank in the harried waters, a further reminder that they lived at the mercy of the elements. The rains stopped and began again without warning, thundering in angry intervals. Variations in breeze raised and dropped the crew's hopes time and time over. And then, just as suddenly, there was quiet. The skies cleared and grew calm, the water flattened into a dark mirror, the coast pieced itself back into view. The decks steamed then, the brass fittings became hot to touch, and the sails slouched in graded shades of eggshell white as they dried. The heat struck at the men more aggressively, fuelled by the wet.

The decks became wordless, the men merely grunting as they whittled. Even Pickering lost his pent-up force, belching at the stays.

Seamus advised shade but there was none. Munro grumbled about his damp galley and was always bailing. 'Fire won't hold beneath the pots,' he called. 'Cold salt beef is all you will get.'

'Honestly, Munro, the meat will boil itself,' Tom sighed.

Pickering hoicked over the side but said nothing, just unsheathed his wide, snide grin under Tom's glare. At port, over whisky or ale, he'd grow cruel towards the cook, taunting what he called his murky Britishness. Any show of restraint now was not kindness; Munro held dominion over their victuals, over each man's belly and bowel. Soon, if they kept his favour, there would be more than biscuit and peas to look forward to. When Munro's strong wrists bailed again, Pickering was forced to jump out of his path.

For days they languished on the river, but as a full week was marked on its length, the canvas boomed with unpredicted monsoonal violence, and lightning cracked across a fast-moving sky. With a thrust they achieved the last few miles under sail.

Two and a half months after departing the London Docks, the *Majestic* joined a configuration of vessels clustered at anchor in the riverine waters before the Calcutta custom house. The bare masts of clippers and barques struck an outstretched pose against the glare of heat haze, a series of wooden crosses replicating far into the distance. British ensigns flying. Chinese. French. American. Steamers with stacks still belching. Lighters and rowboats buzzing at the ships' great waists.

The crew slid from their stations like mercury drops coming together to form a single mass. They rowed across to the wharf, laden with precious goods, the numerous chests and barrels giving a uniform shape to textiles, metals and liquor.

In his new role Tom would oversee the ship whenever the captain was ashore. But Martin, lingering in his quarters with cramping bowels, sipping the last of Munro's ginger tea on Seamus's instruction, had requested Tom stand in on his behalf.

Tom stared out across the high tide to the custom house jetty, the ghat, and all the commotion of trade, waiting for the longboat to return to their side.

Munro too was ready to disembark, fresh in a long, clean shirt. His right hand above the thumb wore a fretwork of burns, the newer scars pink and moist.

'Off to organise our provisions?' Tom asked idly.

'A half-bag of weevilly flour won't get us back to London, Mr Rutherford.'

Tom squinted into the glare but did not laugh. 'Aye, there'd be mutiny, and we can't have that.'

A solid pungency hit him: fish, urine, coal smoke. A different taste of staleness. The chaos of dusty crowds, overseen by the pale, dominating bulk of Fort William a mile distant. Its imperial imposition.

Munro slipped away and Tom, loosening his collar, stood for a moment, lifting his shirt from his neck. The heat flattened him against the hard earth, half wet, half dry at his feet.

At the custom house he submitted the captain's manifest and paid the duty on their cargo. Feeling both detached and strangely aware, he observed the movement of his own hand as it pocketed the remaining coins and pushed open the door back into the street. The wood was warm to touch.

Following the noise towards the market, he fell into the syncopated protests of livestock and chickens, the urgent repetitions of hawker calls. Now he knew he walked with Catherine's eyes, an outsider viewing Calcutta for the first time. Underfoot, the ground was pitted and slippery with discarded mango stones. The smell of shit sharp beneath the sweetness of jasmine and the golden heads of marigolds being bunched for sale. After weeks of the sea's greys and greens, there were new colours now – reds, pinks, oranges, yellows. The voluminous bargaining of local men and women fighting for a price; the punctuating blare of British expats and other seamen. The push of children against his legs that urged Tom to check for the coins inside his jacket.

Then, an awful beam of light that forced his eyes shut. He felt it directed upon him, a burnt orange haze. He stopped still in the crowd, jostled as he shielded his face, pressed to the edge of the human flow.

A voice grew distinct above the throaty hawker calls and the slide of women's bracelets. When Tom opened his eyes, the light had retreated to a series of reflective planes organised in display across a stall front. The voice embodied itself in a chiselled but mobile face, and the man looked at Tom, stroked a hair-free chin and conveyed a few more words before presenting his weapon: a tri-fold mirror. He continued to gesture at his non-existent beard. In the mirror's reflection, Tom guessed his meaning. When he held the glass before his face he saw his own bronze-red hair, and his beard, grown coarse and rampant: an impenetrable crop beneath salt-dried cheeks. In need of tending.

The mirror reminded him of the small triptych paintings Catherine had shown him that summer, inlaid with gold leaf and shaped in an arch. In the mirror's wings he could see each side of his face. He could see himself from different perspectives at once.

In the middle pane he met his front profile but imagined the other two faces looking on.

The seller motioned, growing impatient.

Tom nodded, feeling for the coins in his pocket, trying not to lift the scabbing on his knuckles. 'You're a masterful salesman, sir.'

Dhanyavaad. Thank you. It was all Tom had ever learned. Time and again he and the crew of the *Majestic* would sail into a bay, trade what was in their hold, and set sail again for further shores, oblivious to their role in politics and power, the lives that continued long after they had left. The man dipped his head without a word and turned away.

With his mirror wrapped in cloth, Tom wound his way out of the market. Alongside the full and flowing river, upstream from the port, a group of bathers dotted the shoreline. Up to their waists in the impenetrable waters. Women calling, young babies at their backs, skinny boys wading. The day was so hot. The waters had been stirred up from the rains, and the riverbank was slippery. He couldn't bring himself to wade, but bent down and scooped his hand through the water, cooling his neck.

Looking up, he found eyes upon him. Laughter. At his back, cows worked their fat lips, manoeuvring their heft in the dirt, idling without masters. Bells resonated at each throat.

Behind the bathers, a series of longboats slid by, covered over with pitched thatching. The shapes of fruits and vegetables became clearer as they moved closer to the bank. They were traders too, Tom thought. Or gathering fresh food to feed their families. He noticed the man who stood upright at stern on the nearest boat, how easily he worked the long rudder. He called with what seemed an intimate familiarity to the boys at the oars. A father, perhaps, overseeing his children.

When one of the boys turned to observe Tom, a lone sunny-haired figure at the water's edge, Tom shrank back, feeling he had intruded on their lives, feeling awkward and separate.

The *Majestic* would remain at port just long enough for the winter monsoon to settle in with its dry and favourable northeasterly winds. Munro cooked chicken and potatoes in a spiced sauce, which they all gulped down, and the aroma lingered in the galley for days.

At anchor on the river, Tom began to intuit the potency of a shared vision. In the mirror he was multiple, both solitary and connected.

With the *Majestic*'s hold replenished with tea and silk and the path set for London, Tom judged the cost of his decision. As the clipper hit buoyant winds heading out into the bay, slicing through the swell, he wondered if there was a way to express all the parts of himself, even when they seemed to exist in opposition.

He tasted the sea and let it revive him. Felt the exhilaration of wind on his face. Stared into the diamond glint of light cutting the waves. The sun, a vermilion orb hovering low over the water, gave him courage.

When the following Sabbath came and the bells rang out, he was certain.

He picked up his pipe, rolled up his shirtsleeves in the warmth of the noon sun, and wet the first of his desiccated colours, draping a brilliant ruby sky across the hopeful landscape of his sketchbook.

19

Mizzen. *Miz-zen.* Foremast. Mainmast. Mizzenmast.

Catherine studied the lines Tom had made in those very first days at the easel. What could be amiss with the mizzen? It was present, tall and straight, at the back of the ship behind the mainmast as, apparently, it ought to be. How he might have improved its rendering, she could not tell. But it did not matter: there was something more she wanted for the painting, something she could add that would bring new dimension to an otherwise standard maritime scene.

Drawing her legs up in the bay window, she looked over at her aunt, who had paused at the pianoforte. Catherine could just make out the top of Cecilia's dark head, silver-flecked, behind the sheet music.

'I shall make a series of you, Cecilia, in everyday moments just like this,' Catherine said. 'At the piano with your face obscured by the lattice of the music stand. With a glass in hand at dinner and a distorted face – made up of boredom or disdain – when you think no one is attentive to you.'

'Why should any of that make for an interesting subject?'

'It is interesting for what is unseen. I have a world inside me, and I know you do too.'

At Catherine's back, the garden had dissolved, formless with frost. Inside, the candles and lamps were lit early and the parlour was big with heat. There would be fruits marinating in the kitchen downstairs for Christmas, and geese being cajoled across the country before being silenced and efficiently basted.

The last weeks of summer had waned. Gradually the earth had grown deep with autumnal decay, which Catherine painted against a backdrop of distant drizzle. How far away the sky now travelled. She had a sense of it wrapping around the entire world. Where she walked in Hyde Park alongside the Serpentine the sky was formless and grey, while she knew somewhere else it was beating with radiant light. On the lakeside path she slowed, dropping back from her companions to study the shifting body as a boot hiked through golden leaves, the triangulations of interlinked arms, and the broadness of Cecilia's skirts that obscured the simpler sway of flesh. Alfred's measured stance: as straight as the hat that topped his head.

As the season rolled by, Catherine collected all this detail, gesture, suggestion and flow. Influenced by the way Tom had brought colour out of the sky and softly laid it on the water, his confidence in trusting his own eye, she knew how to bring it all together.

'Do you recall the painting made by the Italian paintress two hundred years ago here in the royal court?' she asked her aunt from the window as Cecilia searched for a new piece to play. 'I cannot keep it from my mind lately.'

'Gentileschi, I believe?'

'Artemisia, yes. *Self-Portrait as the Allegory of Painting*.' The baroque artist had depicted herself as muscular and forceful, a woman Catherine imagined as wholly creative, with strong painterly arms and a fleshy, contorted body that cared not for the prospect of being viewed, cared not for a demure pose or sweetly averted eyes. Her body, her mind, existed for itself. She wielded oil paint like a weapon and assumed a masculine power through her physicality. It went against all notion of femininity as Catherine had been taught, which was prescribed and had a specific value: languid, graceful, decorative, non-threatening.

'Her body was a creative instrument.'

Cecilia looked up. 'It was her mind, not her body, do you not think?'

Catherine smiled. Surely it was in the mix of male and female that a true artist could understand and live in the world. Not as the expectation of woman or man but as a person, with a range of qualities and attributes. Even in its force there was a sumptuousness to the body presented: the artist worked with bare arms, just as Tom liked to do, and her breast was soft above her bodice.

Catherine told Cecilia of what she had planned for Tom's painting.

Her aunt agreed, sounding a trill around the note of C. She had helped in its creation, so why not add a symbol of that. F sharp. And would it matter if Tom never saw it?

Catherine raised her face at this.

Would she paint and pursue what she wanted, regardless?

'If you do choose a husband, he will need to be one who allows you to have and achieve that desire. Thomas Rutherford may be that man, but the question with him must be, will he settle on land?'

Catherine had grown expectant lately upon each delivery of mail. She'd silently eye the tray that arrived over breakfast with its wax-sealed squares of paper and spindly ink addresses. Waiting for his careful handwriting to be on one of them. When for months she had received no sign, it was with a painful admiration that she understood him to be a man of his word.

He was adrift under that wide, unending sky. No address, no consistent location, no fixed date of return.

Every word of farewell had been contradicted by the way his body had bowed itself towards hers. The care in his touch. It was a test, she thought, this absence without even a letter that could otherwise keep them tied. He insisted she forget him but left enough doubt for her to hope. It inflamed her pride. And in his paintings he had imprinted his life upon hers more evocatively than he might have done in a phrase. It was, in a sense, as if he had never left.

Returning to the National Gallery, Catherine retraced their steps. As she suspected, her eyes were different now. The sea thrashed at the hull of a ship more fiercely for knowing the name of its sails and masts, and the nature of men upon it. In Turner's storm she perceived a fearsome foe, no longer abstract. A sea that might take a sailor's life in a single surge, and often did. With this realisation she understood the deep dread that could be felt as a shadow to love.

She pondered the change in herself. Found no regrets. Tom's birth made him an unconventional choice, but he was not an embodiment of rebellious protest as Alfred might have presumed. It was simpler than that, and more complex, bound up in flesh and emotion and pigment.

In Tom's absence, Catherine worked hard at the easel and, one afternoon, convinced her father to accompany her to a public lecture at the Royal Academy. But she could barely pay attention. An inexpressible envy simmered in her at the sight of the easels set up around the room where young men could come to learn and become great at the feet of the Old Masters. Where they could take life classes and learn about the human form. When afterwards Alfred asked her for a synopsis of the event and she in her fury could not articulate it, this only proved that she lacked a man's intellectual capacity, and that the visit had been wasted.

She walked in London's parks, and rode in the countryside until she was heated and breathless. She suffered through a tiresome performance of *Hamlet* at the Theatre Royal, and read through autumn into winter. There were novels from two Bell brothers, who she suspected must be women; their stories were full of strangely passionate drama, which made her chafe at the loss of her own heady summer. More and more, she lacked focus.

Any fool could calculate the time it might take to sail to the East and back again, and Tom had confirmed it: six months at the most. Would he arrive back into London only to sail out again? Or would he leave those high dock walls once more to seek her? Distracted with anticipation, wary of having opened herself to injury, she was prepared to lose what could not have been contemplated until the previous summer when her turpentine-soaked glove was delivered to the red-headed sailor on the hill.

What remained bright: the watercolour image of the Thames that he'd lost himself in that day, the particularity of the colours and the way they'd coalesced into something greater than what lay before him on the slope.

'I believe he understands the power of transformation,' Cecilia offered as she built a minor arpeggio.

Catherine lifted her head. 'Yes, Aunt. That is exactly what it is.'

There was something in his demeanour, too. An uncertain smile that searched, then reconfigured with confidence as a conversation progressed. One moment a landscape of innocence lay in an unguarded expression, the next a narrowing glance suggested a strong and constructed persona. This latter Catherine had come to understand as a kind of fort built through hardship, labour and grief, designed to protect a sensitivity of spirit.

She had known soon after their first meeting that they both wanted more than they had been given by birth.

It was a collision of simple, unquestioned aspirations that had led him to her. If he had not the skill to learn and become a mate; if he had not the impulse to colour his experiences upon parchment; if he had not the adventurousness to climb on a little steamboat inland to Richmond, away from the Channel, away from the North Sea – but to what degree they could shape a future together, she did not know.

She examined herself as she imagined Tom might, weighing things up out there on the endless seas: she was a person of privilege and opportunity, freer in some regards than he had ever been, but with less control over her own future. She knew that she was protected through her father's love and relinquishing distraction, that she had grown into the image of her mother and that it touched him. She took care not to over-exercise what she recognised as a small grant of power, but she should not wait too long to make her request. Were Alfred the head of their family, she would surely lose the choice.

Leaving Cecilia at the piano, she took the stairs to her room and studied the canvas Tom had painted in the garden, the ship with its square sails taut in the wind, the prow lifting above cresting waves: would a sailor consider this rough passage or smooth? One condition was relative to the other, but she had no reference from which to judge. She drew close to inspect the figures in the longboat, which he had added in the foreground upon her prompting.

At twenty she had imagined running off to Paris and offering herself up as an artist's model to fund her own learning. It was a wild and scandalous idea with no serious basis. To do so would have killed her father, and she could not cope with the label of courtesan; she was neither as selfish nor as brave as that.

At almost twenty-three, she now considered the idea of living alone. That in marriage she would necessarily swap one journey with a trousered fellow at the head for another. But she would not wish to be under her brother's wing, an eventuality the line of entitlement would ensure.

Tom did not spurn her opinions or behaviour or desires.

She had long ago decided that whichever boat she took, it would be one of her own choosing. Like her aunt, then, she would have love or nothing else.

She stood before the canvas with one hand pressed to a hip, a paint-slicked brush held in the other. There it was.

The sailor at the back of the longboat now wore an emerald pin in his hat.

When Catherine visited her father late that night, she found him softened and folded over his desk, his eyeglasses tilting across his nose, their lenses glinting in the light of a lamp. In sleep his face appeared to slip to one side, like an avalanche of years tumbling to the desk. He seemed so much aged tonight, so vulnerable; shadowed and crevassed.

He snuffled as she bent over him, and she was grateful to hear his breathing.

'Papa, you must go to bed. You must take care of yourself.'

Catherine slipped the papers from the loose clutch of his fingers and touched him gently on the shoulder.

Behind him on the wall: Turner's fishermen, illuminated by the moon, eternally navigating the rocks. As her father slowly made for bed, she remained beneath the painting, supporting her weight with a hand against his desk, and found she could not look away.

PART TWO

London, 1848–1852

20

As the *Majestic* was hauled upriver, Tom found snow had made a quiet and suppressed monotony out of the industrious city. The London Docks were a filthy sludge. The streets outside their walls huddled in a single shivering breath.

It was another world to the west, with doorways freed of snow and each curtained window incandescent with lamplight. So crisp he almost flinched.

He ought to have sent a note ahead of his arrival, he realised too late. Unannounced in the hall at Ogilvie House, almost six months since his departure, he waited with his head low and his hands clasped at his back, contemplating all that was wrong with this approach.

Her steps were silent on that deep blue carpeting down the stairs, but he was alert to the faintest shift in the air, snapping his head towards her descent. Catherine, dressed in heavy midnight velvet, her pearl earrings suspended like small moons. No longer abstract; no longer the object of his sea-sprawled imaginings.

Bulked by the fabric's weight, she seemed both more striking and more serious than he remembered.

'Leave us,' she directed the servants. A gentler command than those he had given and responded to for months, but no less firm. From steps away her eyes took in the detail of him, but she did not indicate a room where Tom might make his case in private. He would have to do so here, he decided, among the umber shadows of ageing portraits; the inky dragon with its vicious heat; the deer, missing its heart and all its blood, at his feet.

'You proved true to your word.' Her calm, inscrutable expression held him like the still centre of a storm. 'You did not write.'

'It did not help my state.'

'Help?'

He noticed the confession of a single hand, moving to grasp the end of the banister.

His head spun, months of agitation and reprisals forgotten in a second of keen anticipation. He released his hands from his back. Let them waver openly at his sides.

'Now that I am here I fear you cannot have taken me seriously. That I return to find you engaged to some noble lord. Or with no desire for a husband at all.'

'It is true, I have pondered the possibilities many times.'

She stepped in, closer, so close to him now that he could smell the rose garden again. He recognised the teasing tone. A smile was forming.

'Noble lords, as you put it, know nothing of the world. They care too much for rules and status and have no feeling for art. Their confidence is tainted by arrogance.'

'I do not disagree with you.' His laugh was more an exhalation, in which doubt transfigured into something more hopeful.

Her smile broke fully then, as it had the first time on the hill.

'But I have nothing to offer you, Catherine.' The truth pained him but he would speak it plainly.

'I do not see it that way.'

He felt the light touch of her fingers against his.

'I have comfort and security, with or without a husband; my father would not see me suffer. So your birth and station – regardless of the interest I take in them – are of little importance.'

'Privilege is not something to be careless of,' Tom countered, pressing her still. He was split and arguing against himself, not wanting to win. 'Your father would be taking a leap. And what of Alfred?' It was best to identify what he was facing, as a dueller must mark his paces and turn.

'Alfred is more concerned about his own reputation. I suppose it is something you care about when it is all you have.'

'Having nothing to lose can make a man dangerous, in my experience.'

'He is full of bluster,' she said. 'He cannot stand in our way.'

Tom clasped her hand, circling a thumb around its fleshy heel. Her skin was warm and smooth. 'You imagine we can join all our differences?'

'Come,' she simply said. 'Ask your question.'

She took her hand back only to brush it against his neck below his ear, tracing higher over the clipped beard at his cheek, and he felt her watching as he turned into her palm with his mouth open.

'You know my answer, but I do not control our fate.'

Fuelled only by adrenaline after the busy docking, Tom allowed Catherine to lead him upstairs – already a pair, already conspirators – and left him to navigate alone the hushed gallery leading to the dark-panelled study with its many paintings. She promised him smooth passage. Her father was familiar with her wishes and would understand.

At the door Tom readied himself and paused. How firmly ought a man knock at the door of one he would have as a father?

Borne by Catherine's encouragement, he gave a distinct rap, once, twice, with the back of his hand.

Lord Ogilvie pushed back his chair as Tom entered. 'Why, this is a surprise, Mr Rutherford. You are returned.'

Fresh from the East, swell still at his feet and tar lining his nails, Tom was unprepared. He scanned the wall. The fishermen were there, just as he'd left them, and all the other painted faces captured in an unending moment.

Quickly he put his case, and suffered the lengthy pause as Lord Ogilvie rubbed at his knuckles and moved towards the hearth.

'I pitied my daughter when she first told me of her choice.' The man's fingers had become swollen and bent since summer. He splayed them like ineffectual claws before the flames. 'I was not convinced, however, that we would come to this moment.' The matter of certain shortfall between Tom's means and the necessity of Catherine's comfort was not small. It would call for a generous allowance from the family estate.

'I'm not what you would desire for Catherine, my lord.' Tom spoke as if consoling them both.

'Mr Rutherford, make no mistake: I am free to exercise volition in my affairs.'

'Of course, my lord.'

'I married for love and mourned my wife's passing. Why then should I set different rules for my daughter?'

In the uncertainty of a reply, Tom drew his eye around the room, singling out the detail. Condensation rivering the window pane. Twists of gold braid around a saffron-coloured cushion. A bloom of ink on the man's thickened index finger.

'How do you see yourself as a man on land, Mr Rutherford?'

'I have adapted to many changes in circumstance, my lord, and this shall be no different.'

'Note, I do not encourage the union,' Lord Ogilvie clarified, shifting to the sideboard and pausing, one hand upon a crystal decanter. 'But neither would I deny my daughter.'

Tom accepted a thimble of port, dissembling an unaffected posture while his breath stuck beneath his ribs.

'My condition is this: Catherine's place is here, with this family. It shall remain so, and you shall live together under this roof.'

It seemed a straightforward, even pragmatic, concession. 'We have your consent, my lord?' He wished it had not sounded like disbelief. He had not thought it could be so simple.

'It seems you do. But you must own it, Mr Rutherford. You cannot afford to betray surprise when you step out into the world.'

When Lord Ogilvie raised his glass, Tom did the same, beaming now and incautious as they sealed the arrangement.

Outside the door, Catherine was waiting.

Tom's self-restraint unravelled. 'You were listening? You heard it all?' He pulled her in by the waist.

The heat of her mouth that first time made him feel both earthy and unreal. He was all sensation. 'Yes?' It was everything he could utter in the slight space between them.

'Yes,' she laughed, ablaze with it. She bound up the expanse of the world's waters and brought them to him in that single emphatic syllable. *Yes*.

Tom traced the memory of summer in the cushioned bay window and the piano's latticed music stand as they waited that afternoon. The fire hissed at his back, generous with vermilion heat, and the spine of a leatherbound book facedown on a side table was made soft with it. Even his bones felt molten, no longer ice-brittle.

He offered Catherine modest gifts. Small quantities of spices secured in twisted paper wrappings, straight from the market in

Calcutta. Bottles full of coloured pigment they could mix together into paint. A reel of silver thread with a pair of embroidery needles to use with it. The tri-fold mirror that he had used to trim his beard. Holding it up, she moved the mirror's arms to show the myriad reflections of her own inquisitive gaze. He was secured by her expressiveness and that rising curiosity he had missed.

He did not tell her of the indecision he had suffered even as he purchased these gifts, nor of the pain in his cut knuckles, self-inflicted, before they healed. It did not matter. None of it mattered now.

Accepting her outstretched hands, he was certain his smile reflected her own. He was the nervous one; she calmed him. He noticed how the wood panelling at her back framed her, as if she herself were an artwork set into the wall. The house claimed her as such. Even then he knew it to be true, but he moved to her side and joined her watch of the door.

When eventually Alfred arrived in the parlour, Tom released Catherine's hands but remained attentive at her side. Alfred stood his ground in opposition, near to the fire, waiting for them to begin.

'Mr Rutherford has asked for my hand in marriage, and Papa has given his blessing.' Catherine's low voice was filled with a gravity that made Tom feel prized.

'I'm devoted to your sister.' It was a relief to hear his own words steady and assured. 'We ask only for your best wishes.'

But it did not matter. Alfred was direct in his response, brutally honest in the way assumed by men of high birth in the presence of those inferior. He ignored Tom, turning instead to his sister.

'Do you honestly plan to live life as a common sailor's wife, Catherine? Miserable, deprived, destitute, cast out by your peers?'

'You exaggerate the case, Alfred, for you know I will be none of those things. Tom is set to be a ship's master and, I believe, a great artist.'

'An artist. A merchant mariner. And you, a sea captain's wife!'

'Besides, you know I care not for what others think of my marriage.'

'I do not believe you.'

'That is because your name is all you have. Who do *you* love, Alfred? Who loves *you*?'

Tom would not wish Alfred the satisfaction of seeing his anger riled, but he stepped closer to Catherine. Her hand on his arm showed him she was not intimidated, but her look confessed she'd gone too far and knew it.

Her brother swallowed.

'You are so simple, sister. So naive. You ought to be more prudent.'

'I am not yours to command.'

'Father is old, and overly indulgent.'

'But he is our father nonetheless, and the head of this family. You are not.'

Tom felt separate as brother and sister faced off across the room. Each dark-haired, strong-willed. He saw for the first time that they were not so dissimilar. At their feet, a brittle collapse: cinders flaring and dying out on the hearth. Tom determined to hold fast. In silence there was less risk.

'You could have an easy life but you deliberately go against expectation, Catherine. Do not allow desire to be your ruler.'

'Why say that when you are free to choose everything as a woman cannot?'

'Free? What does freedom have to do with it? As heir I must be above reproach. But it is of no consequence.' He reached a hand behind his neck, as if supporting, physically, his composure. 'When we were children we were close, you and I. Do you remember? I thought we were alike back then.'

'Your memory fails, Alfred, or else you distort it. There was always affection – there will always be affection – but we were never alike.'

Alfred started visibly, but his face was stone. Tom felt the man sizing him up now, as if he were shifting units of weight from one side of a scale to the other.

'His circumstances will burden us all,' Alfred said, still weighing.

'I do not require anything for myself,' Tom countered mildly.

'You will be alone, Catherine. A widow to the sea.'

'I will be happy that I am loved.' Moving from Tom, she touched a hand to her brother's shoulder.

'Love?' It sounded like pity.

'I hope the same for you someday.'

Alfred pulled away, turning to the mantelpiece where the small brass clock moved its metronomic hands in persistent time. He straightened its position on the shelf. When he spoke his voice was tempered.

'You will remain in this house?'

'It is Papa's wish.'

'Then let us hope for your sake that your choice will prove me wrong.'

Perhaps Catherine was right; Alfred appeared powerless in the face of her father's acquiescence. But Tom suspected she overlooked something dormant, believing him harmless. Tom had seen cobras in the heat and dust in Calcutta, curled and stilled but capable of rearing up and striking, and he'd gone out of his way to avoid an encounter. Poison like that would fell a man more effectively than a violent punch to the head.

'I can assure you it will, sir.' Tom's voice broke in. 'Our future lies together, whatever it entails.'

Even in restraint his words felt provocative, compelled by a kind of shame. Tired of being mediated by Catherine's brother, he'd spoken with an intentional burr. It turned two pale faces in his direction, with very different expressions.

21

In that first week, the peculiar inner workings of his new world began to be revealed. Catherine gave him lessons in table etiquette and taught him how he'd be expected to greet people of title and rank. Positions and titles, Tom noted, that bore no relation to a person's achievements, skills or labour. He absorbed each coded requirement as if he were learning a new pathway home, making the necessary leaps to arrive, eventually, at a warm hearth.

At his Wapping lodging he sorted through his belongings. His father's tartan, which he thought to wear at the wedding. His tin bowl and spoon. A cloth-bound book with a broken spine, now faded to the colour of watermelon. Just these few small tokens, a stack of sketchbooks and some oils done on board.

Though Catherine's father had offered him residence at a respectable place nearer the house, Tom had refused. His reluctance was not simply a matter of pride. There was a necessary transition in effect, a letting go of one family that came with the embracing of another.

He wanted to knot these worlds together somehow, and so, on Catherine's invitation, Seamus met him after his midday meal and together they made their way west in a soupy drizzle.

The smell of damp wool rose through the hall as they shed their coats. The large wall of eyes – the mirrors, the portraits, the bodyless sculpted heads, the stag – revived in Tom both anticipation and anxiety. Seamus's gaze was incredulous, even as Catherine and Cecilia welcomed him into the parlour.

With the rain set in and drilling at the windows, they were secured in a private vessel against the elements. Soon Seamus was describing the amputation of an arm and the effect of frostbite on the lower limbs, the perils of opioid addiction and the ways to ease an unsteady stomach. He was frank but modest with the details as his audience leaned in. Embellished by the walnut seat back with its carved whorls, Seamus held his plate beneath his chin to catch crumbs of sweet lemon cake, and Tom grew easy.

As they talked on through the afternoon, Catherine took up her sketchbook and pencil. Her hand scratched across the pages and Tom, trying to decipher what it was that moved her, followed each line and crosshatch from afar. Cecilia donned a pair of steel-framed eyeglasses for her needlepoint, and eventually Catherine leaned across to her aunt, holding out her sketchbook conspiratorially. They studied a page together and lifted their eyes to Tom, shaking with suppressed laughter.

'Mrs Beecher would be lucky to have such a fine poodle.' Cecilia was almost giggling. Tom had never heard her so full of delight. Seamus, piqued, looked first at Catherine and Cecilia, then at Tom, then again at Catherine, who had withdrawn the sketchbook to her lap.

Motioning with index and middle fingers together, Tom determined to break open the joke. 'Come on,' he said. 'Show us all.'

Catherine gave no fight. 'You have not yet met Mrs Beecher,' she explained, preparing to reveal the sketch. 'She lives nearby with several adorable poodles that she meticulously grooms like show ponies. I thought this one was a fair likeness.'

Tom recognised his own face on the body of the pup, his wavy ginger fringe coiffed and his woolly chest sucked into a tartan vest.

'He's not wearing any trousers.' His indignation was only partially feigned.

'Why, how absurd, Tom. When did you ever see a poodle wearing trousers?'

Seamus roared, requesting the sketchbook for a closer look, and Cecilia's laughter rang with affection.

'Best that my climbing days are over, in that case,' Tom conceded, and it only increased their mirth.

With the light waning, Seamus made his farewells. The doctor would sail out with Martin and the crew on the morning tide, leaving Tom behind. Suddenly churned, Tom stood by in the hall as his friend shrugged into his heavy coat.

'You did not lie about the eccentric streak.' Seamus smiled, wrapping a scarf at his neck. 'I like Catherine a great deal.'

'My God, Seamus. I never saw this coming.' He had been running over the path to this moment, as if he could recheck some fantastical course drawn over a map. He thought he must appear stunned by his calculations. 'I'm sorry to see you go.'

Seamus grasped Tom by his shoulders. 'I am happy for you. For you both. And I will miss you.'

'I'm sure it won't be long until you're bandaging my foolish wounds again.'

'We shall see,' the doctor replied. 'Well, then. Goodbye for now, my friend.' And he gave his hat a decisive pat, leaving Tom alone in the hall.

Even with the engagement firmed, Tom and Catherine were observed and scrutinised. When Alfred and Lord Ogilvie excused themselves after supper, it was up to Cecilia to sit with the pair, but that night she swooned rather convincingly and blamed the airlessness on the fire.

Finding themselves in private, they did not know what to do with their bodies. Tom's mouth was dry and his pulse drummed. A kiss was easy to command, but a kiss was just a start.

Catherine stretched herself lengthways along the sofa opposite the fire. She was bootless, arms dangling. At the hearth Tom funnelled his breath, patient as the flames built higher.

'We have people to do that, you know.'

He eased himself back into a squat, as he used to when tending his ma's iron cooking pot full of thin kale soup or heating water for their bath. Only when satisfied his work had held did he replace the fire screen and shuffle across the floor to her.

'Oh, I can build a fire, tie a bowline blindfolded, gut a fish with a quick blade to the side.' Resting with his back against the edge of the sofa, he stretched his legs long towards the heat. His head was near her waist. Her fingers were in his hair.

'I am certain of it,' she said. 'But you have known a privation that I have not.'

'It is good that you have not. Hardship is not something to admire. Or pity.'

'I could never pity you. Do you resent wealth? Do you resent the way it has sheltered me?'

'It is circumstantial. We should try to live beyond it.'

'It is hoarded, by certain men. Wealth is power.'

'Then it is a power neither of us have. We are to be provided for by your father.' To say so out loud made him uncomfortable. His ma had taken in washing to help when food was scarce, and she had battled with his da to allow it. 'There are women who are forced into work to feed their children in the absence of husbands or fathers.'

'And there are women with less need but a desire to work. To train in a craft. I do not envy necessity, but I do envy independence.'

'On that we agree.'

The touch of her fingers drawing down his nape made him drowsy with arousal.

Was this it, he thought. Was he there yet?

'What you've opened in me . . .' he began, and then smiled at the fire. 'Well, I think my ma would be pleased for us.'

'Your father less so?'

'Aye, perhaps. I wonder at it.'

'I hope Seamus will make the wedding,' she murmured. 'He is your brother, in a way.'

'His calendar is the will of the winds. As for his intention, there is no doubt.'

Tom shifted, slipping the book with the broken spine from his jacket pocket.

Catherine roused herself at his shoulder. '*The Poetical Works of S. T. Coleridge: Vol. II.* How precious. It is so worn and well read. Is it one of your mother's?'

'No, I have little to remember her by. You might say it belonged to a father of sorts.' Even now he could hear the gravel in Captain Sweet's voice: *Read it well, lad. They call it poetry, but it's a damned fine yarn.*

It had been similar back then as a boy: this feeling of disorientation, the need to find his footing in a new world.

Now it was Catherine who ran her hands over Coleridge's stanzas, cupping the book where the cover pulled away from its stitching, and began to read the poem Tom had indicated.

'*The Rime of the Ancient Mariner: In Seven Parts.*'

Tom let his eyelids drop. Transported across so many oceans to another, younger version of himself that had first heard that rime, big with loss and even bigger with determination.

'I will have the carriage take you back tonight.' Even these prosaic words lilted like verse.

Catherine smoothed Tom's shoulder where his muscles twitched with tiredness. Only then did he realise she had finished reading.

'Stay for a while longer,' she whispered. 'Tell me more of the captain. Tell me more of you.'

22

'A whole world might spin, rearrange itself, with a single unknowing step,' Tom said.

A step onto a steamboat up the Thames. A step into a great hall, into its garden. Tom had entered Captain Sweet's cabin for the first time after four months at sea and his youthful world shifted once more. A journey far greater was set in motion. The view from stern led him out across the *Aurora*'s wake as if he were caught in its flow. It drew him for miles, across traversed waters, luring him with a sense of awe and achievement and ambition, for more of this: more seas, longer journeys, endless horizon.

He wanted to watch without curfew. He wanted to run for his charcoal and paper, to record this impulse. This yearning towards the ocean. But Sweet set him to work, explaining how things would be.

'It won't be an easy task.' The captain stood behind his chair and leaned over its back, a broad set of knuckles gripping each wooden arm.

'You'll continue to learn above deck. You'll work the night and morning watches just the same, sleep below with the hands at the bells, eat your biscuit and beef without complaint, and work as hard as any of the other boys. If you blunder, fall foul of command, neglect your duties, you'll be punished without favour. But during the day you are to perform the steward's duties, assist me as I ask, and learn the necessities of the cabin, as I allow it.'

'Aye, sir.' Tom took it all in as the captain spoke: the glossy painted crossbeams running above Sweet's head; the painting in dark and dour oils, shadowed with candle soot, of the King in admirals dress; and the long table where he envisioned Sweet sitting with Mr Nelson in tactical conversation. The captain's sleeping quarters had a real bed with soft-looking blankets and a plump pillow.

It riled the crew for days that Tom had managed to swap holystone, bucket and swab for tea trays and lantern lighting. But Tom had shown courage and withstood his share of punishment, and no one had liked Jimmy Sutton, the ingratiating sod who'd whined beyond the captain's door, wore an angelic look on the quarterdeck, and was finally caught with a pocketful of tobacco and two pints of grog stolen from the pantry, of which he was in charge. Sweet had let him go in Hobart Town, along with the pock-faced Liverpudlian who'd held a knife to Tom's throat.

'It is unorthodox,' Sweet admitted. Stewards who were doubly skilled as able seamen could be ordered before the mast in times of emergency or loss of man. But he'd no such precedent for promoting a sailor hired as a green hand to double in a vacant cabin role halfway through a voyage.

'But it solves a practical problem. You'll need to walk between two worlds, Tom. You'll need to keep your footing.'

'I won't let you down, sir.'

'No, Tom, I don't believe you will.'

He was excited for the change, though it brought little reprieve in his labouring. Already they'd skirted treacherous rock pinnacles less than ten feet wide, difficult to see from a distance, and cruised offshore along enormous land masses with their sails distended and the hull breaking through silvered waters. Tom had crossed the equator and saw how the seasons flipped in the opposing hemisphere – like time winding back on itself. He'd seen dolphins and one of MacIntyre's leviathans, a southern right with her calf, flicking a massively broad tail fin above the surface, her great arched back rising just off their port bow and then submerging, not to be seen again.

He'd turned fourteen and not realised it.

From Leith to Cape Town to Van Diemen's Land to Sydney, their hold was always full: linen, iron, coal and salt; timber, wool, whisky and tobacco. Sometimes saddlery and, once, a piano. They'd achieve one port and empty the ship's insides just to refill it again, following the flow of trade.

Tom embraced the strenuousness of work, and the accomplishment that came with it. He learned that sadness could be vanquished by physical pain, which demanded all his concentration; by mortal fear, which pushed all other emotions aside; and by the embracing of small details that became the sum of banality and routine.

Those perfect scarlet dusks and ice-blue mirrored mornings were the reward. He collected each hue and shade in his mind.

His voice had started its awkward transition and his legs ached at night; he wasn't sure if it was from the labour or because he'd begun to grow at pace.

Often he thought of writing to his ma, but each time he contemplated the words he faltered, fearing he would not be able to hold them back once he began. He imagined it, could sense it: a dam of feeling that, once split, would run like rapids. He wondered if she would recognise him, and not just physically. If she had delivered the new bairn, a baby brother or sister. Whether they were healthy. How they were keeping fed. If they had even survived.

His mother's features grew vague now, and his da's more so, but he hadn't forgotten the path the *Aurora* must take to make its way back home. The tremendous westerlies in the southern latitudes would soon press them towards the shattered rocks and potent treachery of the Horn, the site of his da's bravery and physical wreckage.

Sweet was imposing from behind: broad-shouldered, legs thick and long like masts themselves. Still, at noon he cast the slimmest of shadows. He conferred with Nelson in low tones and looked out across the tips and troughs whipped up by the wind. Training his sextant on the horizon, he calculated angles and lowered the instrument, verifying his coordinates against Nelson's own to mark their position-line on the charts.

At eight bells, all hands at work under the midday blue, Tom sought the captain astern under the high sun. Tom's fingers were bone-chilled, rough with calluses from scouring the decks and scaling the rigging. His jacket had become too short in the sleeves. He wrapped his arms across his chest.

'What's it like through the glass, sir?'

'Never you mind,' Mr Nelson replied for the captain.

Tom asked again as Sweet lowered the sextant. And was promptly cuffed around the ear by the mate.

Once more he asked the captain, a few days later when they were alone.

'Hold it like this, lad,' Sweet instructed.

Tom raised the brass sextant to his eye and aimed its telescope to where the sea flattened itself against the sky.

'Now, sight the sun.' The captain showed him how to move the instrument's angle until the sun fell to the horizon through the lens. When Tom achieved it, Sweet noted the time and the position of the heavenly body to measure their nautical position.

For the first time Tom had moved the stars at will. He had sighted the farthest horizon. The vision he gained was not a simple matter of calculating a position-line. It was his own future he saw within the glass, contained within the barrel of an instrument providing near-certain trajectory.

From the moment he had been pressed with a knife at his throat, he'd resolved to harness the captain's mathematical world. He would understand ocean curve and the art of celestial navigation. He began to fill in the silhouette of a future that did not involve scrubbing timber with sandstone. He'd never allowed himself to look forward in this way before, to feel his only limit was the capacity of his imagination. When he looked through the telescope, his breath quickened.

'I gave you a yard but it seems you want the whole mast.' Sweet's voice was like a low wind at his side, and Tom felt a quick pat at his shoulder.

He wanted to say: Didn't you once, too, sir? But he couldn't take his eye from the lens, sighting the sun once more.

Slowly the pieces began to fit together. Small parts made a whole. He felt he had become mutable, capable of changing forms like the sea, no longer a boy, not yet fully grown, neither a green hand nor a seasoned sailor, no longer ignorant, not yet learned, both bound and unbound by sea and ship.

When he returned the sextant to its wooden case in the captain's cabin, he understood that he wasn't afraid of what he saw out there through the telescope; he was afraid of what he saw within himself.

Tom's embrace of Catherine was a grateful anchoring. Her speaking of Coleridge's verses entwined the boy within the man. She reached out to them both.

There was no notion of lingering evenings such as this, he said, taking the book back from her and smelling the sea in its pages. They'd had less than the stretch of a bell for it each time.

That brief reprieve after he'd cleared away the captain's and the mate's empty dishes; before he must return to the forecastle for the night watch. Back to the swearing and farting and constant catarrhal hacking of the other boys; the closeness of them all, brothers on top of each other, strong and able and toughened by the sea's demands. He didn't mind it so much. *Aurora* and her inhabitants had closed around him in the nurturing form that familiarity takes. The cabin, though, was oddly quiet. Spacious. How different it was for there to be just the two of them, Tom and the captain, with the breathtaking path of ocean visible through the stern windows. The space was more than physical, he understood as he opened the book to the *Rime* to read aloud; it allowed for thoughts and feelings and sensations banished by physical labour.

The fair breeze blew, the white foam flew,
The furrow followed free;
We were the first that ever burst
Into that silent sea.

It was true: Tom felt as if he were the first that ever burst into the silent sea, into the vocal and boisterous sea, into the sea in all its chameleon states. He wondered if the other boys felt this way. He wondered if this Coleridge had ever been like him.

All in a hot and copper sky,
The bloody Sun, at noon,
Right up above the mast did stand,
No bigger than the Moon.

Sweet nodded, and Tom's confidence grew with every line.

The dark symbol of the albatross shadowed the room. He couldn't imagine the killing of such a regal and auspicious bird. But what of those creatures that killed themselves, however accidentally, in your presence?

Silence fell as Tom lowered the pages. The ghost of the mariner lingered, the bird limp at his neck. Tom followed the wake foaming astern in the lantern's newly lit flare. His mind was a loose line in the wind.

'Captain Sweet, sir, you once asked me if I was superstitious.'

Sweet pressed thumb and finger to his eyelids as if awaking, and shifted in his seat. 'You're a sailor, are you not?'

'What if a bird flies to its own death? Have you ever seen such a thing?'

Sweet stretched for the dark-glass bottle at the end of the table. 'A captain sees everything.' He uncorked, poured a swig of rust-coloured liquid and downed it in one loose gesture. Leaned back then, still holding the cork. 'What do you believe in, Thomas Rutherford?'

There it was again. The captain had a way of asking Tom large questions that felt like a shove in the gut, that somehow left him reeling.

But now Tom knew the answer.

'I believe a man could fall from the mast at any time, and when he does, he should have no regrets, sir.'

Sweet nodded once more. After a moment he gestured to Tom to light his pipe for him and settled back to smoke with his legs outstretched and crossed at the ankles, feet on the table. Tom echoed the pose. Sweet did not demur.

Over the following days, the captain told Tom stories of himself as a young sailor, and of his good friend for many a voyage,

James Rutherford, who consistently beat him at cards – usually poker, usually played against orders – and of the pair of them being punished for their gambling and drinking with double shifts of night watch during the worst of the stormy weather. They'd been eighteen, nineteen years old. Wild with independence and invincibility.

As the life of his father took shape, Tom heard again the narrative of Captain Sweet's debt to a man who had saved his life. He was back in Bo'ness, pulling in the fishing line, looking to the sky and hearing his da tell him, *It's all in the wind, son. When it changes, be sure you're ready.*

He'd tried to submerge his questions, but they remained full of breath, close to the surface. Had his da resented Sweet for his injury? How far would his ambition have taken him? What would he think of Tom now?

Perhaps the captain was wondering the same thing. 'The illusion grows stronger, Tom. Sometimes I look at you and mistake you for someone I used to know.'

'We're almost at the Horn, sir.'

'I never forget it.'

When they neared the Cape, the wind struck the boat with bald ferocity, but they harnessed it in their sails, navigating the ice floes both east and west without incident.

'*Cabo de Hornos.* It sounds much less terrifying in Spanish, doesn't it, Tom?'

Captain Sweet's stubborn determination kept them at the lines and yards unceasingly. Tom could barely see out there in the swell and spray, but it didn't stop him imagining. His da's body may have been lost without glory off the Scottish coast, but his spectre lived on full of courage here at the Cape, the most hellish point on all the seas.

As they rounded the Horn, Tom's hands began to cramp and his face was lost to numbness but he had never felt so proud. He hoped his da would feel the same.

That first voyage from Leith and back was over too fast. More than seven months they'd spent cresting oppositional waters, alert for each sighting of land, until before them once more: Britain. Beckoning, as yet veiled by distance. Behind them: the surging wake. The trail of their journey drawing long and wide before fading.

The Sabbath reading and prayers at an end, the men played cards, stitched their clothing, sat back to smoke their pipes into the breeze. Tom closed his eyes against the warmth of late summer as it flickered in a mottled haze above the sails.

Sweet was relaxed on the quarterdeck. 'Why don't you make my likeness, lad, so you can draw a real picture.'

He offered in a way that was distinctively an order.

The captain straightened his jacket and struck a pensive pose, with his eyes lidded against the glare.

Tom obliged with a sketch, clumsy and distorted, of Captain Sweet in his best attire with his back to the sea and his hands clasping the rail.

Even then he knew it was the sea itself that came to life in that flat charcoal image, voluminous and raging at the captain's back, taking up the majority of the background, with the man a small, overshadowed figure in the fore. And although Tom had got the perspective wrong, he was pleased with the attempt. He would have liked to have held onto it, but the captain took the parchment and stowed it safely in his cabin. Tom imagined Sweet's wife unrolling it as Sweet looked on, waiting for a response. The figure of the captain would be smudged and greyed, but the sea behind him would be bolder than ever.

*

Tom and Catherine could have slept all night before the red embers of a softening fire, pliant and tender, but when a figure entered to tend the room and see that the fire was out, they awoke. Tom made his somnambulant way back to Wapping, giving no objection to being driven in the carriage.

23

The arrangements moved at pace. By mid-April Tom and Catherine would sit at the head of a long table laid with identical spheres of translucent china and crystal goblets, toasting their wedding vows. There were menus and flowers and linen and footmen to be organised before then. Bolts of silk and samples of handstitched lace to inspect. Table settings to be considered. Would they use the Crown Derby or the Wedgwood? Tom picked up a fish knife for consideration, turning it in his hand to admire the engraving on its fat silver blade, and could only say: 'It's all very beautiful.'

Such embellishments meant nothing to him. He knew love was as strong unadorned. He could hardly wait until they could close the door on the world and face each other in the quiet of their private room for the first time.

They were thrilled to be at the easel in each other's company once again. Tom began work on the thatched longboat on the Hooghly with its family of men and the colours of vegetables in the hull, tall ships distant on the river with masts in various degrees of sail. Catherine took pains over the icy gleam of a wintry Serpentine and the colourful promenade around its banks. Her style had developed since last they were together. Tom saw an integration of detail in the inked outline of a ribbon and the fine length of a trouser leg, and such motion in it all that he perceived further ways to enliven his own technique.

Although she refused to spend too long away from the important work of her art, Catherine took delight in orchestrating the formalities of the marriage ceremony, not in service of convenient union or female obligation or wealth-making designed by the patriarch but as a celebration of genuine affection.

Alfred's simmering at their announcement had cooled into a benign resignation. Tom was grateful for the veneer of harmony, but just as uncertain of his motives.

'I see you are as useless as I in all of this, Thomas,' Alfred intoned from the hearth one afternoon as Catherine and Cecilia conferred in the box window over fabrics and their preference to keep the guest list small. 'All this fuss.'

'Fuss?' Tom replied, holding his gaze. Immediately he resented the implication of comradeship, the pairing of them against Catherine, the supposed frivolousness of the women. And the slight against him at its heart: *Fuss. Over what? This insignificant union?* He decided to see Alfred's behaviour instead as a test to determine how securely Tom might plant his feet.

Tom would not allow himself to be tripped.

Nevertheless, it was true he had little role in the unfolding preparations. And so when Captain Richard Sweet sent word from the London Docks eight weeks before the wedding, requesting Tom sail with him north to Leith, it settled things with an unexpected but serendipitous reunion.

'He heard you were here in London? I am glad he remembers you. But am I to lose you so soon?' She frowned, half-serious.

'You know you are losing me to nothing and no one, and you never shall. But you don't need me for—' He gestured to the seating plan in her hands, cringing as he heard Alfred's echo. 'I'd like to see him after all these years, share my good news.'

'Go,' she kissed him. 'You should go, of course. But do not leave me waiting on the day, or I will haunt you.'

Almost ten years had passed since Sweet had reluctantly yielded his young apprentice to the service of other masters. The captain was greyed and expanded at the waist, but little altered in manner.

'Like old times,' Sweet called as Tom approached the mooring.

'Except I am your second now, sir.'

'You have the same look on your face, lad, like you are concentrating to keep your balance.' He threw his arms around Tom then, as a father would his son.

Up close his eyes were rheumy, his beard sparse and bristly. Tom felt his own youth, his brilliant future. He felt strong and alive.

He cleared his throat and gazed up to the vessel at their side. 'She's all yours, sir?'

'Aye, *Swift*'s a rakish wee Scotch clipper-schooner, perfect for coastal jaunts. She'll make an easy fourteen knots with the wind.'

Years had passed since Tom had made his way down the Thames to the wide river mouth only to set sail to the north. The Atlantic stung as he fell into a rhythm with Sweet, and he was proud to be able to show the captain all he had learned.

Tom would let excitement fill in the years. Sweet would be on his side. Sweet would understand.

The captain had given Tom a chance for a future, to become not just a sailor on a fishing boat but a ticketed master mariner like himself. A chance at the life he believed James Rutherford should have had. A life James would have wanted for Tom.

'If only I could have stayed under your command, sir.'

'If you had, you wouldn't be where you are today. You should thank me for letting you go.'

Within two days the icy wind had driven them 416 nautical miles north of London, up the coast and into the pallid grey of a Scottish winter's morning. In the deep harbour at Leith they dropped anchor and prepared to discharge their hold full of leather and sugar. From his spot at the gangplank, Tom breathed in the familiar air and sensed Sweet staring down at him. He pulled his shoulders back. He'd been lucky in a way, he thought, looking up at the quarterdeck and touching his hat in silent reply, but Sweet had made him work for it, too. He'd let the bullying go on, allowing it to toughen Tom, until that blade had been pressed at Tom's young neck.

Now he was a grown man, almost married. South in London, Catherine beckoned while he dropped anchor here in his past.

Tom was perhaps three hours from Bo'ness by road. As the hold began to empty, he felt it all unbidden: the weight of the casket at his shoulder and the sink of loam with each awkward step. The ache that had settled in his jaw that night, and the persistence of the tide as he waited for his father's cheek to graze the shore. His stomach churned. He could smell the damp of their simple cottage, eased open the bedcovers stiff with the cold, watched the salty bodies of silver-scaled fish empty from his father's bag, saw their mouths wide and eyes blank as his ma taught him to split their sides and prepare them for supper. He shook it all off, physically shrugging his shoulders, as his men hoisted and heaved at wooden crates and barrels and the customs inspectors arrived, inspected and departed.

'Careful,' Tom warned to none in particular, forcing himself back to the moment.

'Aye, Mr Rutherford, sir,' came the exhausted replies.

He looked out to shore. Rubbed at a cuff of his jacket. They'd had simple meals, nourishing and satisfying. They'd had no wine, no silver utensils.

He thought and felt and told himself he could not be spared to make the trip to the village. The quicker they restocked the hold, the quicker he would return to Catherine.

Still he imagined the bones of the men at Bo'ness, rotted into the earth; their spirits trapped, dry and restless, longing for salt-spray oblivion. Praying to remain with the sea. Part of him was grateful his da had been spared such a fate. As for his ma: he paused and swallowed. She'd been found pinned beneath the upturned cart in a storm, the harnessed horse full of distress and rearing, and the bairn had followed her into darkness before they had known the light. A letter sent by the pastor reached Tom six months too late. The words lost their form on the page as he read, the heavy mist of the Atlantic a sympathetic substitution for the tears he could not allow to fall. The letter grew so wet it fell apart in his hands.

He had been fourteen years old. The *Aurora* had driven through the wild ocean; the momentum did not cease. The sails stretched and wailed above him and his heart barely held together with each press in his chest.

He would not go. There was nothing in Bo'ness for him now. His home was elsewhere, scattered around the world, in the cabins of tall ships, and in the arms of his soon-to-be wife, in the southern city stretching along a great river.

By afternoon Tom had updated his logbooks and Sweet returned from the custom house.

'I need an hour, no longer, sir. Just to freshen with a walk.'

Sweet nodded. 'Tomorrow evening I will rest with my family. I find a wonderful sense of peace restores me when I return home. I was of a mind you might experience it too, lad. Go further if you like. Take the night. Drink it away if that is what you prefer, or use it to see what there is worth remembering here.'

Then Tom understood. 'It was no coincidence, was it, sir? You had heard the news of my marriage and that I had left Martin's service. Were you curious as to why? Do you wish to convince me otherwise? Did you lay off your mate deliberately for this reunion? I'm trying to understand your calculations.'

'Call it the will of a higher power bringing our paths together.'

'I never would, if you remember well,' Tom replied lightly.

Sweet laughed. 'Call it chance then, fate, whatever you wish. But do not waste it.'

The sky hovered in lapis-grey, but Tom felt like walking. Moving simply for pleasure, without intention. It was a start, he thought, as he drew his collar high against his neck. The docks were more sheltered than the ship, which sat exposed at anchor in the bay, but they captured and transmitted a deep, resonating cold as if the earth had never seen the sun.

He circumnavigated the east and west docks and passed the port offices, the tavern already rowdy with naval custom, with no thought of entering. Instead he stopped to observe the flurry of the curing yards, where newly delivered barrels of herring and cod waited to be weighed, shiny and silver and still smelling of the sea. He walked past coopers, salters and packers, men off the herring boats, whalers from the north. Scraping and scaling and gutting. Women in woollen shawls, hands bound in strips of flour-sack cloth, wielding sleek blades, aprons dark and bloodied with guts, slicing and cleaning, salting and storing the fish in barrels.

His footsteps scattered groups of gulls pecking at the detritus of a haul along the boards; they squawked and flapped their wings at his ankles, lifting off and circling just long enough for him to pass before settling back to scavenge the sluice.

Taking out his flask, Tom warmed himself with a swig. A weak line of late afternoon sun overcame the turbid sky. The light spilled across his boots. He had arrived at a small assembly of market stalls, away from the action of the docks, where he found a mismatched line of assorted offerings and services. His knife did not require sharpening. He was in no need of tallow candles nor soap. But there, in the midst of the prosaic offerings, a colour caught his eye. He knew it straightaway though he had never before seen a specimen, only conjured it in his imagination. The gold stone of the inland Cairngorm mountains. He recalled the poem of Byron's that his mother had liked to recite, in which the craggy, towering Lochnagar of the Cairngorms had loomed.

White hair curling at the sides of his cap, the gem seller was hunched in concentration, polishing the stone in a soft cloth. He held it up to capture more light. Tom took the stone when offered and did the same, and the two of them stared with eyes raised, captivated by the smoky amber glimmer.

'Odd shape this one. Distinctive. A rare beauty.'

Tom nodded, still absorbing what was in the stone.

'You know its name, sailor?'

Tom nodded again.

'It would make a fine wee brooch.'

Tom reached into his pocket and paid what was asked, with no thought even of bargaining.

He knew then. There was still time. He found a driver and jumped aboard before he could change his mind.

It was a modest wooden cross that marked the grave of Marion Rutherford and her unborn child, laid to rest in the same wintry grounds as the fishermen.

Dusk cut a violet scar low across the rows of the dead, deepening as evening set in.

Tom crouched and immediately regretted his haste. The ground was frosted and unyielding, without colour or petal of any kind to offer her.

'Ma,' he began. 'I'm sorry it's been so long.'

His throat stung, and not just with the cold. His breath was almost a wheeze.

'Ma. I received a letter. Months too late.'

Just the flare of his own exhalation in the air, the crunch of frost as he shifted his weight.

'You were given so little, and what you had, you passed on to me.' A hand out for balance on the hard earth; he was heavy with guilt.

'Do you remember you would read to me at night? Anything you could find. Byron. Shakespeare. Burns. The shipping news. An atlas of the world.'

Her cheek was sometimes warm, sometimes cold when he pressed his own against it, holding her near. The smell of soap and onion in her hair as she bent into him. *Sleep well, my darling.* Pulling the covers up to his chin with a kiss to his brow. *There are worlds that lie beyond us.*

He was overwhelmed with an ache, not unlike rage, not unlike love. How close grief could bring those feelings.

'Ma, I wish I could know you now, and that you could meet Catherine. I wish you'd had comfort, opportunity. Ma, I love you still.'

He left the churchyard and marked a spot on the shore for perhaps an hour, listening to the swelling tide and its retreat, crunching stones and broken shells under his muddy boots as he walked up and down. It was black out there, just as it had been the first time. His father's death would always be unseen. There was no place Tom could rest his hand and know the truth.

Afterwards, he lay in a room at the tavern in Bo'ness without taking a meal and stared and stared at the indifferent ceiling. He was returned home but not home, both peaceful and stirred. Out of habit he felt alone, embracing the quiet of it, but then he realised that was not true, and he was grateful and glad.

*

By the third morning at port, they had loaded the hold with whisky and iron and were ready to throw off the bowlines. Side by side they stood, the captain and his chief mate, as the island-studded coastline receded. Scotland returned to memory, as intact as Tom had left it years ago.

'That damned road was always so rutted. If the horse was spooked by lightning, bolted perhaps, the cart would have easily tipped. If only she hadn't been out in such weather. If only she had been born with comfort.'

'If she had, you would not exist as you are.'

Tom smiled. 'She would have liked this.' He took the stone from his pocket. 'A gift, for my wife.'

'Impressive indeed.'

'Thank you, sir.' And Tom meant it in manifold ways. As a boy to his mentor. As a man to a wise friend. Grateful for every guidance, every opportunity.

Sweet tapped at his pipe. 'I'm slowing down, Tom. These bones are creaking and it won't be long before even the coastal trade will be too much for me.'

'No, there is plenty of life in you, sir. I've seen it.'

'I take some hope from that.'

Tom didn't bother to mull the question. 'Would you come, sir? Would you stand by my side at the ceremony?'

'I cannot. I will be further north by then.'

'You think I'm making a mistake.'

'No, lad, you've always had your eyes to the horizon.'

Before the prow: England. The clipper hit ten knots and they fell into silence.

24

'What colour is your hair, Tom?'

'Some say red, some say blond.'

'What do you say?'

'To the ship's surgeon? Reddish-blond.'

'And what do they record?'

'Red.'

Catherine drew her hand through the curls that swept his forehead and framed his freshly clipped beard.

Intoxicated still with champagne, they lay there long into the night, languorous, sated, confident in what they shared.

'And what do you say to yourself?' Her face close to his. 'Is it fantastic?'

'Shamefully so.'

'Tell me.'

'Strawberries.'

'Oh, yes. I love strawberries.'

'Or Siena. The light on the stone.'

'A colour?'

'Italy.'

'How much you have seen.'

'Siena is a hilly, medieval warren, with a church perched at height, overseeing it all.' He paused with the memory.

'Like God, in architectural form,' she supposed.

He was outside of himself again, watching them lying entwined, he a poor boy dreaming up descriptions he never would have uttered before now, wrapped in embroidered white linen and resting on silk pillowslips. Her breath hot against his neck. He could no longer distinguish a difference between the two of them. She was a part of him, as he was of her, and together they were simply the fullest and brightest expressions of themselves.

All he had, he offered to her again. A description of his travels gifted in small parcels of colour and light. The slide of boats along the river through Calcutta. The sounds and smells; the sense of the earth under his feet. Confessing he had imagined her there with him, that it was illuminated for him even now because of her.

Catherine placed her palm against Tom's, raising them together. A steeple. A mountaintop. With her fingertips she followed the creases and calluses of his skin. With her cheek against his chest she discovered his heat.

She had pressed at the limits and demanded life grow larger still. He had come to her with new horizons, but between them there was no yearning for power, no need for rescuing nor desire to rescue.

Placing his hand on her breast, she showed him how he could explore her body. In the absence of experience she allowed sensation to be her guide, confident he would be open to its expression: her breath full and open-mouthed, her body charged and sensitised, lengthening, moving towards him.

Laying themselves open they were undisguised, fearing no judgement. It was both a long, slow draw of emancipation, and a mutual, willing entrapment.

They kissed without pause as they moved together, he cradling her head and she raking her fingers through his hair and catching it in her fist. His hand on her hip, pressing at her thigh, now encircling her at the waist. Wanting to be gentle. Needing to be forthright. And he could feel the same assurance in her: the way she grasped his arms, pressed her hands flat-palmed against his back to bring him towards her, arching in a single fluid movement. The way she shifted, elongated and swayed like a sail above him, her long loose hair falling across his chest and face.

Tom was startled by the intensity of their intimacy, by her certainty, by the clarity with which she articulated her desire and how he might fulfil it. But with each gesture he felt himself take in the experience, assimilate it and become changed. Sensing with minuscule degrees what those changes meant, what it felt like to emerge from her embrace yet another version of himself.

He had no sense of how long they had lain there afterwards. Wordless, with just the confession of their exhalation. The cooling of body heat. He was captured by the weight of a single finger tracing the points of the star inked on his chest.

Eventually Catherine shifted, stretched out an arm. Finding what she searched for, she held it over their bodies. In the wings of a small tri-fold mirror she framed them both.

'Fire flames on a cold night,' Catherine countered.

'A collision of copper,' he met her, not pausing to consider.

'A riot of russet.'

'Burnt sunset.'

'Flames of the phoenix.'

And they laughed at such a fantastic triumph.

25

'Here?'

'Not here.' She looked around.

'Here then.' He pulled her in against the foot of a broad oak.

'Yes.'

They pressed two bodies into one beneath the shelter of her parasol. There was nothing in that brief embrace but skin and heat and permanence.

'Don't worry. There's no one around.'

'You have no idea how easy it would be to cause a scandal, Tom.'

They had been married five days.

'But we have so much to catch up on.'

'Yes, because you were away in the East for all those months, and kept me baited like a little fish.'

It was an intimate honeymoon in Richmond Catherine chose, symbolising their first meeting. She knew Tom to be more at ease outdoors and wanted the relaxed Tom, the Tom who would stretch himself out next to her and roll in close as the clouds hung above them like nests of spun sugar.

She revealed a token she had kept from their first meeting almost a year before in the same spot where they now sat. Her lace glove, laundered, but tainted still with solvent.

'I suppose it was superstitious of me to hold onto it, but the glove was a link to you, and then it became a bond, and then eventually a promise.'

They sat on a blanket of mid-blue Rutherford tartan, identical to the new kilt worn by Tom for their wedding. He had intended to wear his father's, carried with him on his first voyage from Leith and kept all those years, but when it was shaken out from his bag into the London light they discovered the fabric had lost itself to mould.

Instead she had pinned the new kilt with his Rutherford clan badge. *Nec Sorte, Nec Fato.*

'Neither by chance, nor fate,' Catherine had translated that first night as they undressed.

She looked out at the light breaking through woolly clouds, pale yellow threads dropping to the muddy Thames.

At their feet: a river hurrying with vessels.

It was true. Everything was in their hands. They would draw a new future.

Released from chaperones, freed of servants, Catherine and Tom sat shoulder to shoulder with sketchbooks propped on their knees. Sharing a tray of watercolours. Free to dilute and spread paint in their individual ways.

'Thomas Rutherford, I think you need more azure in that sky.' There was no hesitation as she draped a line of blue across the corner of his picture.

Tom made no objection, only gave his boyish grin and incorporated the marks she made.

When their paintings were put aside to dry, she poured them each some ale and they rested back.

'Isn't Ogilvie a Scottish name?' Tom asked after a while.

'Now that is something never to be mentioned in good company.' His eyes were full of mirth. 'Ah, the shame.'

'It was a long way back. Everyone has forgotten it now.'

'Aye, but it seems to me that you've returned to your roots, lass.'

'Perhaps you are right.' She leaned into him, searching for the pocket watch at his waist, but he moved his hand to cover hers.

'Let's not go back just yet.'

'We will not be popular if we are late.'

'I'm not popular to begin with.' He laughed. 'I've no trouble with routine, but why should you, a married woman, be at your brother's bidding? Let alone myself, on our honeymoon.'

'It is only for tonight and then we will have our privacy restored.' She paused. 'Give it time. Family is important, Tom.'

His hand pressed her own more firmly against his body.

She made to pull from his grasp but was enjoying the stubbornness of it, the feel of his rough skin against hers. 'As are you, my husband.'

He moved to kiss her. 'Look, it's caught the light.'

Looking down, she saw it was true. A smoky ochre quartz, taken from the solemn and lonely Highland plateau that sliced its way flat-topped across Scotland. Dug up, she imagined, from a snow-bound isolation. Cut, polished and transformed into a brooch, a gift to her on the day of their vows, which she'd admired through a tri-fold mirror. It hung from its pin at her breast like a light-filled little purse.

'Cairngorm,' Catherine searched for the Gaelic 'r' in the roof of her mouth.

'Cai-rr-n-go-rr-m.' Tom sounded it out again.

'Perhaps a few minutes more.'

'Good. Let's see who can paint the sky the fastest.'

26

At the periphery of his sight: a stream of faces, an observant watch. All eyes were drawn to them, tracing their path around the gallery rooms.

'Goethe wrote that yellow is light that has been affected by shadow,' Catherine was saying.

Tom knew the fellow's name, perhaps from a spine of one of his mother's books.

He was aware of the weight of her hand looped above the crease of his elbow, and the slight curve beneath the fabric at her waist. He knew the change was as yet imperceptible; they were nurturing a secret that would reveal itself in its own time.

The Exhibition had opened that May, but following their time in Richmond there came a bout of discomforting nausea that had made Catherine cautious about outings. It was July before they made their own excited viewing. They were almost three months married.

'Whereas blue is darkness acted upon by light,' she continued.

He thought about it. 'So one tempers the other, creating something new?'

'I think you can apply this to people, too,' she said.

Tom knew her decision to be the subject of scrutiny. They were magnetic north as they moved from painting to painting. The hushed words behind them were overt enough to be intuited, subtle enough to remain indirect in their accusation.

'I believe they are fascinated by you, Tom.'

He knew this was not true. They were peering in hope of finding tar and grime at the cuff of his wool suit, or the dirt from his humble home lining the arcs of his nails. If they looked hard enough, he thought, they were bound to find what they were searching for.

Catherine was not so naive; her words rang with irony. They had been indulged and were protected, so far, by her father's good standing.

When Tom allowed himself to be dressed each morning and relieved again of his clothes at night, the eyes he looked into appeared no different from his own. The fabric his manservant wore was of a lesser quality, but there was flesh beneath, a beating heart, no doubt similar loves and fears. He felt the lie of his attire fall away, yet still he chafed. He would not distress Catherine with this feeling. In time it would gall him less, he supposed. He transcribed the question into one of hierarchy: their servants were no different to a crew.

Tom negotiated his new position as he did an unsteady deck. He kept his balance under any circumstance. He donned his apparel and wore it with aplomb, hiding any uncertainty, as Lord Ogilvie had instructed him to do. Despite his openness with Catherine, he was used to solitariness, and certain inner thoughts and feelings remained a private world he could protect.

At supper he was a boy learning the ropes of a new ship. Studying Catherine's lead. Silently observing. Which utensil, which glass, which gesture, which order, which language.

His sensitivities to others and to art mostly served him well. Where he kept them hidden on deck or aloft the mast, here things were reversed. He wore his inside on the outside, like showing a new suit jacket's gleaming lining to the world.

Tom and Catherine stood together beneath Holman Hunt's depiction of Madeline and Porphyro from Keats' poem *The Eve of St. Agnes*, observing the bloodhounds that appeared as intoxicated as Hunt's revellers. At the right, the two lovers slipped by the fallen guards, making their escape.

Tom had looked forward to the newest creations from Turner, but the painter showed nothing at this Exhibition – for the first time in years, Catherine sighed, equally disappointed – and the circling conversations in the gallery mentioned the artist's worsening health.

'What else do you notice, Tom?'

'That most people here are more interested in being seen at the Eightieth Exhibition of the Royal Academy than in viewing the art?'

'Yes, there is that, I suppose. But look. There are so few paintings by women on the walls. And most of those that have made it have been skied.'

'Skied?'

'Hung at the top, so close to the ceiling they cannot be properly viewed.'

'Anyone can enter, you say?'

'Which is not to say everyone is selected. Would you believe the Academy was more progressive in 1768 when it included two women as founding members? Now they do not even permit us to train in the Academy schools. We are more often subjects than artists, though it's likely more than one feminine hand is hiding behind the initials that are signed, and that some of these names are pseudonyms. I am certain there are many women who could show here with just a little encouragement and education. Who might be included not as an exception, but because they are worthy.'

He ran through the names he had read on the plaques. She was right, though in truth it had not occurred to him that it would be otherwise.

'Sometimes it is like speaking with a hand over your mouth. Knowing you are incomprehensible, and that no one is interested in listening anyway.'

He touched her at the waist.

Her eyes shone with it.

'What happened?' he murmured.

'My submission was returned without comment. Along with a rent in the canvas.'

'One day, Catherine, it will be different.'

'My paintings will never be accepted, even if I have the talent you suppose I do.'

'You're challenging in a way that is not easy.'

'I am a woman who is challenging. That is the thing. We both know it. But you, Tom, your eye accords with the general view.'

'The view of the Academy?'

'The view of men who say what is art and what is not. You show the mariner's world in loyal detail. Through you it has a moral value: a life at sea as a worthy pursuit, heroic and yet humble. I can see your work hanging on a great wall of the National Gallery.'

'That's some dream. Can you see me being accepted as a member of the Academy?'

'Turner is the son of a barber.'

'And prodigiously talented. And half my age when he was admitted,' he laughed. 'All those years of training.'

'I will not give up on it.'

He shook his head. 'I lack a technical education, just like you. I cannot think that being judged by Academicians will bring us closer to our dreams. I'm not of their realm, and though you are born to it, they keep you from it. Why do you want it? There will be another way, no doubt, in time.'

'You are deserving, Tom.'

'As are you. And you know very well being deserving has nothing to do with it.'

She was astride him that night, her skin warm, her thighs capturing him at his hips. Salt between her breasts when he tasted her there.

Catherine interrogated every limb, every ridge and contour of muscle; that intoxicating line of hair that led down from his waist. Drawn by touch.

Laying her length along him. Her face against his: intentional, provocative, determined.

They could kiss like this for hours.

When she pulled herself upright, he raised himself to his elbows, caught still beneath her weight. No wish for escape.

'What do you see?' she asked, pushing her dark hair from her face.

It was her hands he watched, forming into flat lines, first below then at each side of her face.

'You have an artist's fingers, in defiance of these soft, soft limbs that move them.' Here he flapped her arm above the elbow to prove its yielding nature. 'I see curving breasts, a growing belly, and I imagine what we have created inside it. I see a mouth I would kiss again. And more besides.' He stretched towards her.

She dropped her hands from where they had been framing her face. 'Tom. I wish for you to draw me.'

'Oh, that's what that was about?' He fell back again, enjoying the teasing.

'Well?'

'No, Catherine.' Tom laughed. 'I can't do that.'

'I wish for you to paint my portrait.'

'You're impossible to capture.'

'You have the skill, so why deny me?'

'You make it too hard. Your expression flits, faster than any gathering storm, or a changing sky, or the spray over a bowsprit.'

Brushing her hair from a shoulder, he began to kiss the soft skin of her arm.

'I am a simple maritime painter. Besides, I don't want to paint your portrait.'

'Why would you say that?' She pushed him back.

'Contain you? In a single pose or expression? You're more than one moment, one gesture. I prefer the living, breathing you, the version I have to watch and try to understand.'

'I thought we did understand each other. I feel that we do.'

He agreed with this; he felt it too. But he thought time and observation would deepen that understanding, as it did the more a sailor observed and gathered evidence about the seas.

'There's much to learn about you still. Perhaps there's no limit. Perhaps I don't want there to be. No, I won't paint you.'

Her hands dropped to his chest, fanning across his ribs.

'But I can love you,' he whispered.

'Then show me,' she said, beckoning.

'Yes.'

27

They walked along the twenty-acre stretch of the western dock, past the stern brick warehouses guarding priceless merchant bounty: coffee, port wine, wool and rum. Past the huge tobacco warehouses, which had the most capacious storage of all. Tom brought her here as he couldn't before, no longer afraid of breaking an illusion.

Catherine continued to surprise him. It was not the smells of fish guts, waste, coal and tar that overwhelmed her. She was drawn by the shouts of command and response from on board the variety of barques, brigs, clippers, schooners and steamers at their moorings. The disciplined scrubbing of decks; the flight of sluice off the teak and into the water; the continual heavy syncopation of boots progressing up and down wooden gangplanks. Gulls, shrill and circling over their heads; and the strength on display, the muscularity and unaffected force that hoisted casks out of holds and shunted barrels right at her side. The size of everything.

It was October, and she'd wrapped herself in moss-coloured velvet and knitted wool against the turning season. Though she had gifted him soft leather gloves to match her own, Tom did not find a need to wear them. His body was used to the elements and he did not mind the colder days.

Each morning he'd wake and rise with the sun, leaving her curled on her side under the covers. He'd slip into his dressing room and press himself as straight as a board, pushing his body off the floor, lowering back down until his arms ached, his muscles shook and his breath came large from his lungs. He wanted to stay active, to feel the sensation of blood rushing, of being at the ready. And when she leaned against the doorframe, following his motion, her hair loose over her nightgown as the light cut through, he longed for the weight of her on top of him. The way she would place a bare foot in the middle of his back and push him face down to the floor. Turn him over with a nudge of her toes at his ribs, wordless, and unwind her body along his length so that they lay breast to breast, her feet falling between his own. Kissing his eyelids, pulling his arms around her.

Now Catherine was six months pregnant and unable to lower herself with the same ease. Her stomach had become suddenly firm and rounded, and Tom would press his cheek against it whenever he could, hoping for a sign of the child.

Her feet tired easily, but she urged herself out, keen to absorb all she could before her confinement.

'I understand more deeply now how difficult it must be.' She craned her neck to study a ship's yards as she considered this. 'The work you must accomplish so high in the air, the activity on the ropes – all while the ship is moving.'

'Lines, we call them, rather than ropes. Those are the forestays, those the shrouds, those the backstays – they support the mast. And these ladder-like nets are the ratlines. On those we climb.'

'The masts are so much taller and wider up close. It all looks very complicated.'

'Aye, it is. Yet intuitive in a short time.'

'I suppose that is why you feel so vital up there – because you are so close to death.'

Her perceptiveness, as it always did, made her seem both remarkable and deeply familiar.

'You were just a child up there in the storms. So many of you, only children, at grave risk of falling.' She brought her gaze back down to him.

'You need not worry for our child,' he said, knowing that it was true, but that it was not what she had meant. He was proud of what he'd managed as a boy, and in these surrounds that pride made him defensive against compassion.

As usual these days the London Docks were at capacity. St Katharine's, though more recently built, was not sufficiently deep to dock larger vessels. Along the quay, several ships were loading. A milk cow bucked her head against the rope that led her from memories of grassy pasture to below decks within a strange floating enclosure.

Tom would come back early one morning, he decided, to paint the docks with its resident vessels when the dawn was a clamour of apricot against darkened stone and wood. Though his recall was well tuned, it would be easier to work with the water before him, so that his colours and brushstrokes responded freely to the alterations in tone and the texture of sky and water.

As he turned to say so to Catherine, he felt a slap at his back, not forceful, and was caught by an unexpected but familiar voice.

'I begin to understand why you made the choice to leave us, Mr Rutherford.'

Captain Martin returned Tom's smile with a generous shake of hands, his head a dark flourish of curls as he raised his hat for Catherine.

So the news was true. Although Tom had read in the shipping columns of the forthcoming arrival of the *Majestic*, he had not sought out the clipper. Martin had been blindsided by Tom's decision. It would be a temporary hiatus, Tom had explained to a baffled reaction, to take a honeymoon, to get to know each other well.

'You understand,' the captain had said, sharp with disappointment, 'that although I would wish to do so, I will not be able to hold your position.'

Seamus, too, had left Martin's service; he had stood with Tom at the wedding and afterwards signed on to a packet run between Liverpool and New York. His sister, Maeve, and her husband, Patrick, were expecting their first child in Brooklyn, and they'd asked Seamus to be godfather. Pickering and Munro were certain to remain among the clipper's number, however, and the decks would be full of mostly brotherly faces. Catherine would know Tom then, he thought, were she to see the ship and those on board, but he wondered, would he still know himself?

As they walked with the captain to where the clipper was moored, Tom pulled at the sleeves of his new jacket, noticing the sweet scent of the soap he had used that morning.

Martin had since commanded the *Majestic* with a new chief mate. He was competent, the captain informed an attentive Catherine, though not daring like her husband, which was perhaps not a terrible thing.

Tom felt a pulse in his stomach at the mention of their last journey to Calcutta, and of his replacement. The hard-won prize he seemed to have given away. It felt like a different life he had lived.

'You are docked for how long, sir?' Scanning the hull he knew so well, he was relieved not to meet with any familiar face staring down at him from the ratlines.

'A few days. Then on to the Black Sea, Odessa.'

And when Catherine enquired, Martin reeled off the manifest to her: pounds and pounds of wheat, linseed, wool and tallow, all to be stored in the *Majestic*'s spacious hull.

'Well now, I have more business to attend to yet.' When Martin clapped a hand on Tom's shoulder in farewell, looking him in the eye, Tom resented that it felt so final.

He saw his own silhouette disappearing along the dock with the captain, among the bodies of immigrants with cases at their feet and the skittering hooves of livestock. Plumes of pipe smoke puffed in contentment from the mouths of other sailors.

This was why, he reminded himself. He knew it when Catherine took his face and kissed him in the carriage on their way home, his hand gentle at her belly. When together they set up his new easel that afternoon, a wedding gift with sturdy wooden legs that folded and was so easy to transport. When they painted side by side on ample canvases – with the same weave as Turner's, she explained, and sourced from the painter's own colourman. When the redolence of linseed oil and turpentine, the careful studying and mixing of colour on his palette, and the sublime feeling of relinquishment and discovery took form from that first preparatory wash.

Tom would train his hand into naturalistic representation, just as he had trained his body aloft on the *Aurora*, patiently learning the nuances of his tools, the desire and force of his own expression, and the hastening current of a new and competing ambition.

The sea was his great source but it was Catherine who led him to what he'd sighted through the telescope as a boy: the possibility held in a shifting horizon. The potential for change.

28

Breakfasts were a collision of sorts – too many commanders in the same body of water, navigating different routes. The family was thrown together over their coddled eggs, their smoked herring, their bacon and buttered bread. The churning influence of newspapers, letters, politics at the table. Desire and expectation, even if it were simply about how a man might spend the day with his new wife.

Alfred's response was predictable. It was dangerous, not to mention unseemly, for a woman of Catherine's status and condition to be parading around the docks.

'You need not worry, Alfred. I will take care of my wife.' Tom offered an easy smile as his first cup of coffee was poured.

'That is hardly my point, Thomas.'

'Did you hear the news?' Cecilia turned to Catherine. 'Your cousin has had her portrait made by photograph. I am to visit next Wednesday for a viewing.'

Tom watched Catherine's face across the table, knowing where this would lead.

'A photograph? Tom refuses to paint my portrait though I have made myself small and begged him.'

'What is this about my daughter begging?'

'Good morning, Papa.' She kissed his cheek as he bent down to her. 'I have determined to have my portrait captured by the camera.'

'A very quick determination.' Tom grinned.

'I must say, you have a perverse interest in all things modern, Catherine,' Alfred said, sorting his correspondence.

'What is so perverse about finding interest in new discoveries and machines?'

'There are artists other than myself in London who could capably render you in oils,' Tom said.

'What, do not say you two are in agreement over this?'

'Photography is so flat,' Alfred muttered.

'It has no texture,' Tom agreed.

Catherine shook her head at them both. 'Will you also refuse to board a steam train, Alfred? Tom, you have travelled by steamboat, up and down the Thames. Do you deny the extraordinary progress being made around us?'

'Not at all,' Tom replied. 'River steamers have aided and eased the labour involved in hauling into the docks.'

'You nautical men will perhaps forget sail for steam one day,' Cecilia took it further.

'Yes, Tom, imagine the world then.'

They cut to the heart of him somehow. Tom was not averse to change, but paint and sail were the totality of who he was, of all that gave him meaning and purpose.

'Steam requires vast amounts of coal. It's costly and time-consuming to coal a ship for long voyages. Regardless, a clipper in full sail is simply capable of greater speed, and need not stop to re-coal time and again.'

'But that will surely change,' Catherine persisted.

'Perhaps, and I'll admit I'm intrigued by these advances. But shipbuilding is an ancient art, as you would know from reading your Greeks, Catherine, with techniques refined to create sleek and efficient wooden vessels. On just such vessels Britain has triumphed over France, explored and traded into the East and other lands, all on the bellow of wind. I have no love for conquest as an ambition, but overcoming the fickleness of the elements is part of a mariner's striving and achievement. Part of the artistry of sail.' He paused, surprised by his own ebullience.

'That is true. If you all had seen the size of the *Majestic*, which Tom has commanded as chief mate, and the intricacy of her sails.'

'Must we talk of the docks again?' Alfred hovered his teacup at his lips. 'It is improper, Catherine, to be out among sailors from God knows where.'

'Sailors such as her husband?' Tom was mild. 'Have you never wondered how that tea you're drinking makes it all the way from Canton and into your cup?' It was bemusing that a man could be so detached from the passage of the goods he consumed in his own home.

'The world is far greater than you or I know, Alfred.'

'That is nonsense, sister.'

'Papa?' Catherine looked to her father for guidance.

'You are both right,' Lord Ogilvie replied, spooning jam onto a corner of toast and opening his newspaper.

'The name Ogilvie will become laughable. Women who marry the wrong men. Women who don't marry at all.'

Tom drew back. Alfred's sharp tongue could still surprise him. The man's simple unwillingness to accept and move on. His awful disdain. It was with curiosity that Tom understood such outbursts to be the most revealing, most honest moments they shared: Alfred's pride ensured he would never speak so harshly of his sister and aunt in public. To let go these unguarded words in Tom's presence was, Tom believed, an unconscious acknowledgement of Tom's accession – even acceptance – into the intimate family circle.

Still, the offence was obvious to them all. Catherine had dropped her knife to her plate, but Tom realised she was not indignant for herself. Her wrists hovered at the table edge.

Alfred, it seemed, understood the same.

'Forgive me, Aunt. I misspoke.'

'Indeed you did. And you are forgiven.'

Cecilia did not stop there as Tom supposed. Suddenly firm, dropping the semblance of shadow that her chaperone status had imposed, more and more she revealed her true solidity, a surprising quality of persuasiveness.

'You believe women should have no agency, no choice. I understand this. You are a product of tradition, and you have my respect for that. But Catherine and Tom are more modern creatures.' Here she stopped herself. 'Though nevertheless bound by convention, both legal and familial.'

'Choice,' Alfred countered, 'is a luxury. For us all.'

Tom hiked his brow at Catherine. He could barely stomach the man's privilege.

'If you are so bound by rules, brother, perhaps you ought to improve your attendance at society engagements. Choose yourself some young woman of impeccable breeding whom you do not love and be done with it.' Catherine's back was imposingly straight. Tom wanted to reach for her fingers. They gripped the edge of the table in furious pink and white.

Lord Ogilvie cleared his throat as if to moderate with so slight a command.

Cecilia looked to Catherine. Shook her head.

Napkin discarded, Tom was poised, ready to push to his feet, but he found it difficult to estimate the seriousness of these sibling spats.

Perhaps they even enjoyed it. This punishing of each other, and the forgetting and forgiving that came soon after.

'Shall we begin our walk?' he suggested to Catherine. 'Cecilia, will you join us?'

'The problem,' Alfred cut in, 'is that such behaviour leaves little room or allowance for the rest of us.'

'And what exactly is it that you need allowance for, Alfred?' Tom's tone was detached but his impatience was rising.

Lord Ogilvie turned to him. 'Tom,' he cautioned.

But Tom had not been the only one to speak out of turn.

'On the contrary,' Catherine continued. 'It could very well give you the freedom to follow suit, to make a choice that fits you well also.'

Alfred was on his feet then, dropping his napkin to the table and gathering his letters. 'My sincerest apologies.' He even gave a small bow.

'Oh, sit down,' Catherine suddenly cried. 'Society cannot see you now.'

To Tom's surprise Alfred paused, then did what she said, replacing his napkin across his lap without a word. Catherine's conciliatory laughter broke the tension, and when Alfred made no further remark, Lord Ogilvie and Cecilia returned to their plates.

'Islay, single malt. I thought you at least might appreciate it.' Lord Ogilvie raised a cut crystal tumbler.

The whisky was heavily peated and far smoother than Tom was used to.

A pair of armchairs had been drawn up for them near the fire in his father-in-law's study. The wooden mantelpiece gave off a comforting smell of polish as it warmed. It took him back to Sweet's cabin – newly varnished, shiny and heady with fumes one winter as the sleet threatened at the window and the lantern swung to the rhythm of the ship's protesting.

'Do not mind Alfred, Tom.'

Catherine had said the same thing that afternoon. Though she had done her best to ignore the quarrel, Tom saw it had left her churned. Painting with Tom in the conservatory under a sodden sky, she stood by her anger, and even accused Alfred of overstepping. When Tom agreed, however, she recoiled from his criticism. Her look was sharp and alien, torn between loyalties. And so he subdued his resentment, not wanting Alfred to win through his anger, not admitting how this confused his own sense of place and purpose.

She had decided to paint and caught the shapes of the cerise-petalled cyclamen lining the flowerbed outside, rendering them as wings of colour overwhelmed by the grey mist.

Tom would not let tension set in between them. 'Mr Barolo would hate it,' he whispered at her ear. 'But I love it.'

'Well, it is just as well Mr Barolo is not my husband.'

In those tense moments at the table she wanted to take Tom away, she said, lead him to salt and return him to his natural state.

He touched her shoulder, then pressed a thumb into the looped plait of hair at her ear. 'I would like to see this loosened. Watch it spread on the water as we float.'

After supper she retired to rest her legs, and Tom released the weft of hair at her request, sweeping the stiff-bristled hairbrush over her scalp. His fingers in the valley behind her collarbone, holding her steady. She breathed deeply as her hair fell free.

'We are in this together, you and I,' he said, and when he had finished she was relaxed and chose to stay propped up in bed with a novel set on some hellish-sounding moors.

Alone with her father in the quiet living spaces of the house, Tom sensed the movement of uniformed women and men downstairs, busy preparing and cleaning and organising, like pieces of an efficient ever-moving machine. All that effort beneath his feet enabling this illusion of repose.

They sipped on the whisky, each silent within the autumn night so deeply drawn at the window. It seemed as if the garden and the westerly streets, the carriages, lanterns and coat-tails, the taverns, ragged alleyways and shit-caked cobbles further east downriver that abutted the chaotic docks had all been folded up indiscriminately, rendered into a dimensionless, uniform opacity.

'Alfred does not manage the same ease in relationships as you and Catherine.'

'Your son is unhappy?' Tom asked, and wanted to add: *Or does he simply despise women and the lower classes?*

'Catherine has been allowed to choose wildly, Tom. I will admit it. And you, likewise, are not bound to the same standards against which Alfred measures himself as heir to the Ogilvie estate.'

So he was resentful. Tom added it to the mix.

'You do best when you show forbearance. Indeed, my boy, it is something for which you display a talent. Though I sense in you the same stubborn wilfulness that is within my other beloved children.'

His father-in-law did not mark the sentiment, but Tom trusted the precision of his wording, and was warmed by it. He accepted a cigar when offered, clipped the end as Lord Ogilvie had done, and relaxed his head. The cushioning eased, warm under his neck. The smoke spiced with pepper and clove, the muted expression of their mouths puffing at the tobacco, and the slow waxing and waning of red embers at the end of each cigar coalesced into a hypnotic atmosphere.

'I am of good acquaintance with an art dealer, Mr Saxton, who may be interested in your ships, Tom. I understand he has an enterprising notion of holding private exhibitions at his own gallery, separate to the Academy's.'

'He is familiar with Catherine's work?'

'Oh, a gentleman is our Saxton. He has extended kindly encouragement and humoured her attempts, of course, but there is no future in it.' He chuckled. 'My dearest Catherine and her funny little paintings.'

'Her work can be difficult at first, I admit, but does Mr Saxton not consider the control and expression, the determination for invention?'

'Invention? That is the last thing we desire. You are in love, my boy, but do not be fooled. When Catherine is gone—'

Tom blanched, and Lord Ogilvie quickly patted his arm.

'As we will all be gone one day, Tom – her work will be good for the bonfire alone, and her spirit will be thankful. That she enjoys the occupation of painting is pleasing to me and fitting for her, but it is misguided to encourage it as serious ambition. Soon enough she will be a mother in addition to a wife, and that will bring a natural end to it.'

He indulged with one hand and pushed back with the other.

'You, however, with the right introductions, may meet with favour.'

Tom drew on his cigar, mulling a response. Catherine had mentored him, and his loyalty was steadfast.

'It is flattering. I'm encouraged,' he replied after a pause.

And he was. But surrendering his art to the gallery wall was a different proposition to surrendering himself to the canvas. The more he painted, the more he resolved he was not ready to expose himself to the scrutinising eyes of London's critics. If Alfred were a marker of attitudes, they would see through him in a minute.

In one sense, painting was a leveller. With brush in hand, he lost himself in the process. He was no longer Thomas Rutherford, a fisherman's boy from an impoverished pinprick of a West Lothian village; he was both more and less. He was nothing. But if he was nothing, then Turner was nothing. All the more learned, moral British gentlemen of the Academy were nothing in the same way. But once made, a painting became an object, vulnerable to hierarchies and scrutiny; what started as colour and lines became good or bad technique, appropriate or inappropriate subject matter. All the rules and divisions reappeared. And his birth was present in the wash beneath everything he painted.

In the conservatory, Catherine had expressed her turmoil through an indistinct grey background pierced with almost geometric delineations of pink cyclamen. As ever, he found her unafraid to reveal her unique inner view. What if – he reached for clarity – what if she were talented beyond ordinary vision? Beyond easy appreciation or neat categorisation. What if it were not her eye that was mistaken, but everyone else's?

Assuming her talent, then, what was the difference between them: Catherine and the rule-breaking Turner? Her brilliance, if that was what it was, went unacknowledged; and still she persevered, firm with a greater belief in her art than Tom had ever had in his own.

Tom had suffered Catherine to frame and hang a single painting of his. It was not his best expression, but it was the first he had created with her, a symbol of that first summer, and for reason of the green hatpin alone he agreed it should hang in their bedroom.

'I'm still a novice,' he spoke again.

'Ah, you are a perfectionist, my boy. I admire that.'

Tom shook his head. He thought of Turner's kind of white heat, of his sun suffusing light haze over water, of the flames in his depiction of the House of Lords ablaze – heat and embers both burning up the sky and lying flat as reflections in the stilled river. He was no such artist, but perhaps one day he might imbue his scenes with such luminous emotion. Only in art did it seem possible for such a thing to be expressed.

Was this what Catherine meant when she spoke of Goethe and his theory? Colours were emotion; emotions were colour.

'I was an apprentice for many years before I became second and then first mate on the *Majestic*. I imagine the process as an artist is no different. I'm enjoying the learning.'

And sitting there with her father, this educated, comfortable, blinkered man, he felt a deep internal building. An expectant wave, a notion waiting to be grasped.

29

Now that the time was close, he became fearful.

Christmas in their first year of marriage. Catherine slid one hand against the arch of her back, the other flat atop the piano. After one song Tom saw she was out of breath. The child sat high and pressed beneath her ribs, and she hadn't enough air for a second tune.

He lifted her feet as she settled back upon the sofa. Smoothing the skirts at her ankles and lingering there, his hands upon her legs, softly bracing.

'How else can I help?'

She, more impatient, keen to reclaim her body as her own and to finally see the face of their making, shook her head.

'You are doing all you can.'

She had loosened her stays further that morning; he had heard her complaints as she dressed. Her body was expanding, beyond any ability of fashionable control, unwilling to be confined and tamed by lacing. Now, seeing her ache after a single ditty, he felt certain she would do away with her corset completely, no matter what was insisted on in the morning. She might find some necessary ease and breath, if only for a few weeks.

'You would be more comfortable in bed.' Alfred spoke from the hearth. A log shifted and heat flared then fell away. He pulled at the bell hanging on its cord by the door. 'This fire is almost out. We cannot have you catching cold.'

'Alfred, you ought not fret. I am not as delicate as that.'

It was not that her body was delicate at all, she had marvelled privately to Tom. It contained an uncommon strength that she had never heard attributed to women who were with child. She might topple easily, suffer thickened ankles and a painful lower back, but there was a fire in her that was fierce. Something protective, she imagined.

'Tom, you must give me your voice in Catherine's stead.' Cecilia dropped her hands back to the keys, beginning a new carol. 'Do you know it?'

'You ask too much of the man. He was raised on a ship after all.'

'Alfred, please,' Catherine laughed.

'Well, is it not true?'

'Aye, you don't lie,' Tom replied. 'But we did have Christmas at sea, and we did all have voices to give to it.'

'Perhaps this one?' Cecilia played a few bars.

'Indeed, a perfect choice.' Lord Ogilvie settled himself, the amber of his port glass and the rich burgundy of his jacket glowing in the renewed firelight.

Tom approached the piano, arranging himself at its side as Catherine had done. He cleared his throat. Cecilia had chosen kindly, and he recognised the introduction to 'I Saw Three Ships'. It was a tune he had sung with the watchmen as the sea stretched away, icy and obsidian dark in the north, roseate and glinting in the south. It was never sung solo before a scrutinising audience.

Warmed by glasses of sweet port, he positioned his feet on the drawing-room carpet and gathered his breath. Cecilia gave him a nod, and Catherine's assuring gaze made it possible to begin.

At his left, the orange flicker of the fireplace and the elongated shadow of his brother-in-law. Before him, Catherine and his unborn child, her body a reposing line of sage-green silk and cream wool, triumphantly curved and cocooning their most treasured creation.

Hands behind his back, palms open and loose: a posture not unlike the stance he adopted on deck. His steadiness drawn from every widening wake and fetch of wave he had ever admired. His firmness, his watery spirit, revealed.

Fixed on the floral ceiling mouldings in the far corner, pitching at their dispassionate bloom, he threw his tenor to the waiting ears of his new family.

Safe within the shadows of their bedroom that night, Catherine slackened all her weight against Tom so he could share in it.

She was grateful for him, for his care. But she longed for her mother. She did not know exactly what it was that she was missing. Some all-knowing maternal comfort, some greater guidance. Tom was reassuring, as was Cecilia, but they had no more knowledge than she of what was to come next, and no way to comprehend or help her articulate what it was that had made her feel both fluid and igneous with strength. She was being transformed, inside as much as out. It was a process with its own volition, exceptional, beyond her control.

Tom smoothed a palm across her forehead, just as she asked him to. Just as she recalled her mother had done. Or was it her nanny? She would never know. But the action was consoling, and through it she knew she would be capable of offering the same calm assurance to her child.

When she gasped at a sudden, extraordinary pressure, Tom immediately placed his hand on her stomach, eager to feel where their child was moving inside her.

'Are you frightened, Catherine?'

She adjusted his hand to where she imagined a little foot or fist stretched out impatiently in her womb. How would it be to bring this tiny wonder into the world? Would there be pain, and would she survive it? So many women did not.

'A little,' she confessed.

'And after? When the bairn is born?'

'No. It is easy to love a child.' This she knew must be true.

'Of course,' Tom agreed. 'But you lost your own mother so young.'

'What do you mean?' she asked. He had griefs of his own. Was he afraid too?

'I'm not sure. Last night I had a dream: I had a line thrown out into the sea and was about to pull in a beautiful fish. I was elated. I could feel its weight on the line and saw the glint of scales beneath the surface. But when I made to reel it in, I found I was kneeling on a raft of splintered wood lashed with fraying rope and I was sinking with each tug. I looked around for help, and there was no ship, but I saw you were there, on land, atop a promontory, holding something in your arms. I could see you though you were so far away.'

She heard it in his voice: a crack of fear. A pre-empting of loss. 'I am right here, Tom. We will love this child. Sacrifice everything for them. Our own breath if we must. That is what parents do.'

She caught almost roughly at his beard and kissed him, inexplicably fired by a fresh and acute desire.

'We will know what to do when the time comes,' she said. 'I am certain of it.'

And when that time arrived, her cries were as raw as a man losing an arm.

She lay splayed, half uncovered. The insides of her thighs were stained with blood.

Her hands searched for him, for Cecilia at her other side. Her skin burned under his touch, wet with exertion.

Tom was helpless as Catherine pinched her eyes and strained with a deep and awful moan.

'Mr Rutherford! You cannot be here!' The midwife, working around him with cloth and water.

'Where is the doctor?' he hissed over Catherine's wracked body.

'We do not have time to wait.' Cecilia's eyes revealed the truth.

Another cry from Catherine speared him, gutted him like a fish. She let go his hand now, pushing him away. Reached for him again. Gripped him with uncommon strength.

The midwife's hands were on Catherine's stomach.

'Mr Rutherford! Sir!'

'Leave us, Tom,' Cecilia urged.

A prolonged, agonised cry, and another, wrenched from darkest depths. Catherine let go his hand, pressing both fists into the bed as she summoned all her strength.

He was outside the room but unable to leave his wife's distress. His head against the door, a hand poised to snatch it open in a moment. He could hear it all; it did not end.

The midwife's urgent commands. 'Push now! You must push!'

Catherine's vocal, language-less replies.

He wanted to go to her.

From behind the door he heard the final wretched spasm.

Then a gentler elongated moan.

He saw the baby first. A tiny swaddled, bloodied being cradled in two hands by the midwife as she left the bedroom and whisked straight past Tom and along the hall. He had heard no cry.

He wanted to follow the child. He wanted to go to Catherine. He was barred at first from both. The grandfather clock at the end of the hallway circled its arms past one a.m., moving nearer to two.

At last Cecilia opened the door to the bedroom, where Catherine lay dried and clean on fresh sheets, left limp after her effort. Her eyes were closed, violet-lidded.

'You cannot leave me.' He half begged her, half demanded. 'You cannot leave our bairn.'

But with a touch of a thumb to her lips, Tom felt her breath. And then he heard it: a spluttering cry from along the hall that grew more forceful as the baby was brought in to them.

'A glorious baby boy,' Nanny announced, hovering the child above Catherine as she opened her eyes.

Tom was weak with relief. Catherine sighed and slowly raised her arms, her face strangely pearlescent as the baby's cries hushed against her breast. Bowing his head against hers, Tom touched the warm little body of his son for the first time.

By late morning Catherine was less ashen and her eyes had brightened. Tom had spent the night on the chaise at her feet, not wanting to leave her. He woke when the maid came in to rejuvenate the fire, still in his clothes, his neck stiff from restlessness. He would not allow the curtains to be drawn just yet upon the cold clutch of January. Catherine needed to rest, and he craved for himself a still moment in which the outside world did not exist. This was a new kind of exhaustion, a depletion that weighed time behind his eyes.

January 15, 1849.

He was a father now.

Lying there, trying to understand it: this intense feeling of love and responsibility. Closer to his own da, somehow, through the experience.

Exhaustion had fogged him. But his body, when roused, was ready. As vigilant as always.

'Tom?'

At his touch she blinked with slow and heavy lids. He dropped his face into her hair and breathed in with a kiss, once, twice, then left her to settle back to sleep.

Steam curled around him like little fingers, reaching from the water into the cooler air. He had asked for privacy. He'd bathe unattended this morning. Dress himself, alone.

Tom had held the child, their son, and felt inexplicable grief amidst the joy, for the soft little creature who smelled milky sweet and in whose tiny face he saw reflected both his own future and his own past.

That first uncertain noise had thrilled and frightened him in equal measure.

He would return to the boy, with his own skin warm, clean and bath-wrinkled to match the baby's own creased body. Looking forward to studying the child's face, to identifying all the parts of himself and all the parts of Catherine that had ended up in their boy.

At the nursery door, he stopped short.

Nanny, cradling a small shape, one hand resting on the baby's stomach, as Alfred reached out from the blue-black shadows in the shuttered room.

'The boy looks like his mother,' Alfred said, not looking up.

Tom fought to restrain his possessiveness. He resolved to give Alfred a minute, and that would be all.

'James,' he offered. 'We have named him James. After my da.'

Still Alfred did not raise his eyes from the child.

'James Ogilvie,' he pronounced over his nephew.

'Rutherford,' Tom corrected. 'James Ogilvie Rutherford.'

30

James would not hold still. One month old, he waved an energetic fist, worked free of his swaddle, then stretched his face in a sudden cry. Catherine and Tom were used to laughing at each of his intimate noises and peering at his expressions. But now they suppressed their mirth into forced faces as the headless photographer, obscured beneath a tent-like hood, captured them from across the drawing room with an acutely slow closing of the shutter.

Tom had been right, Catherine declared afterwards as she loosened her body and made an intentional flop into an armchair. She had felt so rigid, afraid to twitch an eyelid. But how incredible the chemistry of it, to see themselves revealed on photographic paper. To have this precious pictorial token to place upon the mantelpiece.

James was a ghostlike blur in Catherine's arms. Catherine, seated with her back stiff and her head angled towards the lens, had her arms overflowing with a writhing little body that became frozen in its movement. Tom, awkwardly arranged at her back, had been instructed to pose with his right hand on her left shoulder in a way that made him feel separate to them, and as if his wife too were an infant.

*

How the birth of a child could change things. The house was glazed with ethereal harmony. Tom marvelled at the small being they had brought into the world. Catherine could not resist touching the curling lips, the soft cheeks, the tiniest of wee fingers.

Whenever Nanny entered with the child, each of the family was eager to take the baby in their arms, to soothe him when he cried, and contort their faces to elicit what they might then proudly interpret as a smile.

Alfred was placid in those early weeks, dealing four hands for whist around the card table each night and declaring the suit of the trump upturned in the middle. Tom played on Catherine's team as she energetically challenged her brother and aunt to better her clever trick-taking.

Though Alfred prodded with each play, it seemed he leaned towards fraternity. 'Ace of diamonds, Thomas? You are, I believe, out of trumps.'

The world continued outside their domestic sphere. The *Observer* reported the continuing rush for gold in California, of pure mineral abundant in rocky crevices, and dust idly panned from rivers as travellers were stopped for tea. The *Morning Chronicle* tallied the lives taken by cholera across Britain, and in the *London Illustrated News* there was a sketch of the *Icarus*, lost to rocks off the Barbary Coast with barely a survivor.

'You knew of this ship?' Lord Ogilvie enquired, dropping the newspaper to his lap.

Tom did not, but the Mediterranean's southward current along the North African coast was known to exert a strong pull, requiring a master make numerous adjustments to maintain their route. A vessel would certainly be drawn into danger if too direct a course were attempted between Gibraltar and Malta. Tom watched Catherine's distracted frown as he outlined the likely causes for the foundering.

In truth he had woken for days with his mouth dry, becoming drier, and then finally tasting of salt. He sucked at his gums, drawing saliva into his mouth. He took to the bedroom floor and moved forcefully through his push-ups. Catherine was up and already with the child, and he missed the touch of her toes at his ribs.

They had help with James, but she was devoted, leaning over the crib as the baby's limbs writhed and jerked, waiting for that smile. It was something that won them all, the breaking wonder that lit up James's face, like an endorsement of their goodness, their beauty, their worthiness as human beings.

Tom pressed on with his oils in those early months but distraction was high, energy low, and Catherine had less time to join him for their work. Playing cards at night with a languid Alfred and a half-finished painting upstairs in the small studio they'd been given made Tom query if he'd lost his old centre. His hands craved the rough pull of a line, the theft of his breath in a gale.

When the opportunity arose, Tom conveyed it to Catherine with careful, practical reassurance. Sweet had asked for him on the coastal route. The work would not take him far from his family. He would not be absent for long. Tom would sail for a week, and spend the remainder of the month at home with Catherine and his son.

She was sanguine at first. 'Since James arrived, we have slowed with our painting. I know you share my happiness, but you are more idle than you are used to, and I would not deny your creative inspiration.' It was a change she had, in fact, anticipated. She did not begrudge him.

An outline of Tom's plans received blithe assent from her father, while Alfred, for once, was silent.

Tom understood the undemanding contract was a favour from Sweet: a compromise to keep him on the water; a way to keep him close to his family.

Brushing her dark hair that night before bed, Catherine paused mid-stroke. Her eyes pierced him from their lamp-lit reflection in the dressing-table mirror.

'Those rocks took your father, Tom.'

'Sweet knows the North Sea mile by mile,' he assured her. 'There is nothing to fear.'

But when she did not look away, he moved to embrace her, his voice low with determination. 'They won't take me.'

Sometimes Tom dreamed his body was weightless, suspended like a flag from the mast; that he flew loose-limbed above a hallucinatory flare of water.

Still, when *Swift* set sail to Scotland six months after James was born, those first moments of separation cut him like a blade.

As they ploughed the roiling North Sea into a feversome northeasterly, the bucketing rain sent ice fingers down his neck, soaking him through. He was enlivened by the keen, boisterous clamour of the elements as he returned to the sea, which was his first home, and by all that was raw and newly excited in him: the warmth he'd found in his family, which fuelled him equally at his core.

Time and again they would watch for the rounded hill near Dunbar and beyond it the North Berwick Law, steering north-west from St Abb's Head to pass the craggy width of Bass Rock, steep and chalked grey-white with the dung of roosting gannets, signalling the entrance to the Firth of Forth. They'd navigate each rocky mass up the Forth, which Tom counted off like digits on his own hand: Craigleith, Lamb and South Dog; Fidra and Ibris; and Inchkeith in the middle of the Forth with its crumbled fort and lighthouse. Each time they anchored safely at Leith he showed a defiant and satisfied fist to a God he was not sure he believed in.

The first year of James's life went quickly this way, so set was their rhythm.

Arriving home from Leith, eager to see his family, Tom would discover Catherine and her brother had taken the child out to Hyde Park, or he'd find James on Alfred's lap in the parlour, a picture book being read sweetly to him. Tom told himself not to fret with this new orientation. The blazing joy in his son's expression echoed his own when he lifted James into his arms and the boy clutched at him tightly.

Each night before bed he visited the nursery alone. With his head low over the crib, he would watch the small, almost translucent features whisper faintly with each breath. The sleepy spasm of a finger that had escaped from the swaddle. Unsure whether he was attempting to memorise the face of his son, or to imprint James with the image of his own.

After a time he learned to miss them less. He understood that being apart did not make them separate. He felt it hardest in the first moments of departure, and again on his return when the sea let go of him and he opened himself again to life on land. When he became atom and impulse, alive with pleasure just to see Catherine and James.

Somehow Catherine understood what he could not articulate. To be split between two worlds entailed one life continued elsewhere, without him.

She came to him one morning with the photograph of the three of them together: silvered, stiff and bled of colour.

'You need this more than we do.' She pressed it into his hands.

From then he set the portrait upon his cabin wall for each voyage north, adjusting the frame to vertical whenever it slipped, and fell to sleep watched over by their faces. He'd take it down again each time before disembarking, carrying them with him to and from the sea.

31

Of almost 1500 paintings hung upon the panelled salon walls of the Royal Academy that season, 1850, it was Millais' depiction of Mary, Joseph and Jesus set amid wood shavings in a humble carpenter's workshop that drew indignant criticism. While Dickens spat vitriol in his reviews, the *Morning Chronicle* declared Millais the most obtrusive sinner against all laws of taste and art. But Ruskin was enthused, and Catherine too went against the grain, enjoying the way Mary was depicted as a real woman, kneeling on a dirt floor and seeking a kiss from her son.

'Wealth does not speak to divinity,' she said, as she inspected the painting with Tom.

'It does not.' He was thinking of his ma.

The human side to poverty was no more than simple reality to Tom. It gratified him to see the lives of ordinary people – people like him, people like those he had loved – presented before ladies and gentlemen who had never known less than affluence. For Catherine to see it, too. But how easily scandalised they were by such a blasphemous representation of the divine. He thought back to the idealised fleshy-armed cherubs of the Renaissance masters, idyllic with their smooth, peachy faces, which Catherine had shown him on their earliest outings. Here, Joseph's lean limbs were those of a workman, with blue-veined arms practised at wielding the plane, the mallet, the saw.

'What a rebellion against the staid umber scenes beloved by the Academy,' Catherine said.

Tom heard a breath drawn behind them, a tittering. It was likely in response to the painting, but he checked his hands for filth out of habit.

'How brightly lit it is,' Catherine continued, regardless.

Millais had achieved such brilliance across the scene, in the illuminated fabric of the figures' humble clothing, the golden warmth of the wooden workbench and shavings-strewn floor. Tom absorbed the simple but potent contrasts of vermilion, sapphire and white, and added it all to his understanding. Wondering how he might take this light to his seas.

For several sailings he worked patiently with wood and cotton fabric. The rigging, hull and fittings were the perfect replica of a topsail schooner. He had given the model ship a scarlet waist and bright white sails, and the name *Lady Leith*. From London to Leith and back again, he had not lifted the lid on his watercolours for all the work on this gift for his son.

Returned to the house with salt-thickened hair, Tom looked forward to setting the model ship on the water. But James would not be persuaded. Almost two, he pulled at his father's hand and twisted his face. He would not be led to the garden. He would not go to the pond. He would not sail the ship with his da. Energised by his command with Sweet, Tom met with the fierce immobility of a child who would not respond to authority, directive or reason. Tears out of nowhere. The cries. When Catherine came running, dismissing

Nanny and bending to soothe her son, brushing his damp hair from his face and wiping his cheeks, Tom threw his hands open in a baffled questioning. Her face wore an apology as she gathered James into her arms and led Tom to the nursery.

There stood the root of the disturbance, resting in the corner with a long blond mane, wide eyes painted by a clumsy hand, and a child-sized leather saddle complete with miniature reins. When James was placed on the horse and Catherine began the gentle rocking, there came at once laughter and spontaneous cries.

'It was Alfred's idea. He is obsessed with it.'

Tom stood there with the *Lady Leith* in hand.

'Poh-nee! Poh-nee,' James slurred in excitement.

'I'm sorry. You were not here. I did not know.' She motioned her head at Tom's ship. 'It is wonderful.'

That his brother-in-law should trump him like that, with a gaudy and no doubt expensive rocking horse, carelessly, as if they were playing a hand of whist.

Though he caressed the head of his laughing boy, he felt pushed out and belittled, childishly hurt by what had occurred. Catherine had not known – it was to be a surprise for her to share in – but Alfred had seen the cuts of wood weeks earlier and enquired about their purpose.

For the rest of the month in London, Tom busied himself with colour, forging his frustration into a new ship on canvas. Borrowing from Turner's fishermen, he layered the sky with graphite clouds above a pitched sea, a barque navigating away from a rocky coastal strip in search of safety. Small figures worked upon the rigging. The topsails strained above the mountainous North Sea, lost in a haze of spray. He illuminated the ship with a golden light from above, a parting in the darkness.

He had grown familiar with a conflicted state that accompanied his efforts: there was the elation of having realised a vision, the grief of letting it go, the regret at what he could have done better, and the determination to start all over again.

When Catherine discovered the painting, completed and drying in their studio, she crouched beside him within her volume of skirts, a firm hand cupping his shoulder. It was easy for them to be together in silence, but as the seconds went by and her study of his brushwork continued, Tom found himself holding his breath. This one he had thought expressive. Admirable, even.

At last, she pronounced, 'These paintings ought to be hung for London to see, not hidden away in this house.'

Tom laughed at that. 'Ought they be?' He adored her certainty, but London might also roll on just as well without them.

He asked her: Would he ever feel he'd learned enough, developed enough, expressed himself in the perfect way? Was there an end point, where completion meant an ideal had been attained? Or was it a case of letting go when the sense of imperfection felt less threatening?

A part of himself answered: *You are a sailor, first. Always and forever of the sea. That is where your true ambition lies.*

'There is one way to find out,' she said. 'We ought to show your work to Mr Saxton.'

Tom fell quiet. He had avoided the topic since her father had burdened him with the art dealer's opinion on Catherine's style.

As usual, she was ahead of him. 'I know he requires persuasion about my own pieces, but I feel confident he will fix on your work immediately.'

He nudged her hand with his chin. 'What of you? I am not agreeing I am ready, but what of your own ambition?'

'There is something I have been considering. If I were to introduce him to your work myself, then he must become convinced of my good eye. And if he trusts in that, perhaps in time he may be led to consider, and to appreciate, my own work.'

'That is a clever plan.'

She smiled at his leap. 'It is a path, at least. He is not a fool, and I am not naive.'

He heard the retreat in her voice.

Joined by wide skies and affective light, their styles were rich with contrast but not incompatible. Would Saxton intuit the conversation between them in the pigment? Could it cause a difference in his opinion?

'It is skill we need,' he replied. 'Not deception. We work until we have our most perfect imperfections ready to show.'

And, as she pushed off triumphantly from his shoulder to her feet, he added: 'We should guard our desires. Say nothing for now, not even to your father.'

32

Catherine took Tom's words and turned them to her own efforts. More and more she was entranced by the human form. With the greater freedom granted to her as a married woman, she arranged to visit the home of a Miss Eliza Fox, who had been permitted by her father, after much persuasion, to study at Sass's Academy, and who now invited other women artists to attend her private drawing classes, in which they were free to work from an undraped model. Catherine studied the intimacies of musculature and flesh, the contours of ribs and cheekbones, and how each different body curved and fell and moved in its particular way. Alfred and her father would never have approved – but Alfred and her father did not need to know. Cecilia and Tom had Catherine's confidence, but this was something for her alone.

Back from the coast, Tom painted with renewed enthusiasm and the cool touch of the North Sea on his brush. And as they resumed their routines, working together in the garden or the studio, she began to talk more of her dreams: that they might travel together when James was older – to Paris, to Rome, to Venice, to Athens. Visit the ruins and classical statues and tour all the great galleries full of paintings and sculptures. They might themselves paint in those new places, among other artists. She wished for Tom to take her inland to Siena, where she might see for herself that specific light he spoke of, to look out upon it reflecting off the terracotta rooftops.

On the first day of May, 1851, Tom and Catherine gazed at a magnificent glass ceiling arching high above them. It spread out in four directions like a cross, and through its pink-hued panes light was intensified into heat.

The Crystal Palace, it was called, and within its vast enclosure were promised the innovations and wonders of the world – selected, shipped, curated and displayed beneath Joseph Paxton's colossal construction of iron and glass. The effect was to be a glorious showcase of Britain's industrial leadership.

Tom was struck by the ambition and elegance of a structure that had been built from a material he thought of as delicate, easily broken. Elms stood tall within it, reaching to the roof. Balconies dense with spectators lined the palace's wings: a sea of coat-tails and shawls, skirts in mauve and tangerine. It seemed half of London had flooded into Hyde Park for the opening. A gallery wall constructed of stained glass beamed colour across them all.

James had lately found impetus for lifting unsteady feet and finding speed. 'Hold tight to Mama's hand,' Tom instructed him, and Catherine clasped the toddler near.

At noon Tom lifted James to his shoulders and they skimmed a wave of top hats to catch sight of Queen Victoria and Prince Albert standing before dignitaries, declaring the Great Exhibition of the Works of Industry of All Nations open to the public.

Catherine eagerly led them on their tour. Half of the glass palace was devoted to Britain and Empire, the rest to foreign exhibits. There was pumice stone to inspect, kauri gum and rope made of flax from

New Zealand. A grain reaper from Cyprus. Textiles from France. Surgical instruments, printing machines and looms.

Tom loved Catherine's curiosity, her fascination with other peoples, the various riches of the nations, the invention of machines. That she wondered how different life might look beyond London and Richmond, beyond Britain. How much their lives might change with craft and engineering. What would the world look like for their son?

At a congregation of taxidermied kittens, balanced on their hind legs, James shied away, hiding his face behind Tom's knees. Though Catherine coaxed the toddler, James could not be induced to look at them, and Tom simply murmured, a hand on his son's soft head, 'Leave him be.' Such re-creation of life in death struck him as morbid.

'Let's move on.' He twisted to lift James to his shoulders again and urged Catherine away from the staring eyes and rigid bodies.

'This from a man who has speared, scaled and gutted a fish, and seen a grown man's limb crushed to nothing,' she teased, taking his arm.

But that was not it.

A quick glance was enough to be chilled by the fact there was nothing beating beneath the skin.

At the Indian court he was quiet as they examined an elaborate ivory throne and footstool, a regal howdah for riding an elephant, and a large and priceless diamond that was now the possession of the Queen – surrendered by the child maharajah of Lahore through conquest.

He lifted James to view several miniatures of twin-masted wooden sailboats, thinking of his own gift, which had since been taken out successfully on the pond and lived on the mantelpiece in the nursery.

'Papa. Sip.'

That James pointed to the sailboats and looked at Tom, making the connection, warmed Tom with pride and gratitude. It was the particular power of a child to bestow such a keen sense of validation.

As they moved past a flurry of plaid trousers, gloved hands and expressions of astonishment, he ruminated on all that was presented. The way it had been set out for them on newly laid floorboards, backed by fine drapery, roped off and captured in gleaming glass cabinets and bell jars. The enormity of the display inside Paxton's palace was a wonder, he could not deny it, for those passionate about technology and industry, for those who would never see foreign shores. It conveyed, as intended, the reach and power of empire. But it did not reveal what he had experienced from the swampy Bay of Bengal or riverside on the Hooghly. It spoke nothing of the labouring push of water carriers and barefoot rickshaw wallahs through the market, the pain of breathing through dried-out nostrils, the meagre servings of daal and chapati eaten right there in the street. Calcutta as he knew it was not so tamed or made pretty as this; it writhed under the Company thumb. Here, at the Great Exhibition in London's Hyde Park, none of the mechanisms of empire were shown for what they were.

Thoughts such as these he kept to himself, standing amid the sanitised awe.

33

May 5, 1851

Mr Rutherford—

The urgent nature of my request requires brevity. My chief mate is injured and I require an immediate replacement. I prefer to sail with a man I trust to do the job.

We sail for Valparaíso from the London Docks within the fortnight.

I appeal to our shared history and await your soonest reply.
Captain A. W. Martin

That his breath rose long and deep as he read the note gave him his answer. Tom felt lighter in weight and his body thrummed. In a single moment Martin's request reoxygenated that craving for open seas, broader skies, the clarity of command. It gusted in him with sudden force.

For more than two years Tom had confined himself to the coastal route, swaying each month between sea and land, with just enough saltwater to quell any cravings. He'd weighed out his desire to stay close to Catherine and James against his need for the quarterdeck and, for a time, he'd succeeded.

Lately Sweet's talk was of retirement, and what would Tom do then?

Those clear dark eyes of Martin's had appraised him many months ago on the docks and made him consider, if only for a moment: had he reached too far? Had he lost his way?

Life had grown both larger and smaller since his marriage. His position in London, within the Ogilvie ranks, was murky-edged, ill-defined, but his ambitions as a sailor remained untouched: to become a ticketed master mariner, to command his own crew. The child that his da had thrown from the boat and into the water was still eagerly paddling.

'South America?' Catherine thrust Martin's missive back at him with indignant surprise.

'There's profit to be made in trade.'

'Profit?'

'It's not the reason.'

'You have been stirred again. I blame Crystal Palace.'

'I am as I always was. You know it.'

Each time he left, would it become more difficult, for Catherine, for himself? He trusted his ability to shift back into his sea-borne self for a longer voyage, as he always had in the past, and that occupation and exhaustion would alleviate the mourning.

'How long?'

'With favourable conditions eight months, perhaps nine. Then I am back here in London with you and I promise I will settle again.'

For a man who had spent half his life at sea, it was a mere moment. He might once have gambled away six months over a nip of rum.

Time had altered since his son was born. Now Tom understood the preciousness of a single day. But if the thought of being separated from his wife and son brought pain, it was tempered too. No matter the physical distance, he was secured by Catherine and their shared dreams. And the returning, the reunion, would be the sweetest.

'I cannot let Martin down.' He raked at his beard.

'Cannot? You will not. And so James and I shall sail with you.' Catherine was firm. 'I shall experience the world as you do, beyond stories and paintings.'

'James is too young, and besides, my men would be rendered useless through distraction with you on board.' Tom laughed at the thought. 'We'd be sunk before we left the Channel.'

'Oh? Only your men would suffer distraction?'

He bent into her indignation. In his palms her fingertips lay quiet and cool but her determined face hit him hard.

His words had twisted around on himself and his desire. How often he had imagined Catherine on board with him, wanting her to see him as a man in command of his surrounds, wanting her to know that side of him. Now, looking around at their comfortable life – the fullness of her immaculate skirts, the way they swept with her expansive stride; the softness of James's wee body and his impetuous limbs – he could not see a way to bring it all together.

'It's a demanding life. One I wouldn't desire for you.'

'For a woman, you mean?'

'Aye, for a woman.' He sighed. 'And for any man born to the land. I've seen men die on deck, wasted from sickness, claustrophobic; unused to the rations, the constant motion, the exhaustion of labouring. I've seen bones broken, flesh pulped and men fall from the mast.'

'You have survived it. More than that, it seems to thrill you.'

'I have sea in my veins, like my father. And I grew up with a stomach accustomed to privation. I need now and then to return to something of that.'

Catherine's voice was brittle. 'Do we provide you with too much comfort, Mr Rutherford?'

He flinched, quickly shaking his head. How smooth her hands were; how softened his own had become. His calluses had not simply signalled the abuse of his skin through hard physical labour, they were part of a sailor's armour, a protective shield built over time.

'You would not like to be separated from your family. Your father would not let you go.' He recognised the conflict in her eyes.

'Is it not enough to sail your ships across canvas, Tom? You are a marvellous artist and soon we might show that to all of London.'

'Nothing is changed. Those ambitions remain.'

He saw her break a little with a reluctant smile, but she dropped her head towards her shoulder as if to hide it.

'I saw you on the hill that day and the ground began to make sense for the first time, Catherine. But, in truth, I cannot live without the sea.'

She took hold of each of his wrists then – keeping him near, pushing him back, he was not certain. 'And for all my dreams I cannot live upon it,' she said. 'We understand that now.'

Lord Ogilvie waved away Tom's announcement with a fistful of papers. 'Go, my boy. Bring me a souvenir of some kind, won't you?'

But Alfred was stony.

'What kind of a man are you? That you should disrupt this family so with your base mercantile missions.'

Tom faltered. Alfred had surprised him with a beckoning nod the following morning, and he could not refuse to enter his private room and engage.

His first thought was of the colourful birds, but he found both cages empty. Alfred appeared in no mood for an explanation and left Tom to guess their fate. Since his first and only accidental visit, this room had remained visceral in Tom's memory with its captive creatures and threat of reprisal.

Lulled by the familial truce that had followed James's birth, he had not supposed his impending departure could be so aggrieving to Alfred, yet here he was, furious that Tom was abandoning his sister and nephew. He was a disgrace for invading this noble family; he was shameful for leaving it. He was a fool for thinking Catherine could love him. He was a brute for casting her off. Did he, Thomas Rutherford, have any notion of how fortunate he was?

Tom listened until he could do so no longer. Confident that a calm response was the most effective defence, he marshalled himself, striving for a mellow tone, and still the words came barbed. 'What would you have me do? Would you care to sail with me and experience the true meaning of life and death?'

Alfred was measured too, in a way that felt unyielding. 'I would have it that my father had never agreed to make you his son. But as surely I cannot rewrite the past, I simply wish you to depart at the soonest and bring this business to an end.'

Tom slipped back into bed next to Catherine that last morning, fully clothed and ready for the sea. With her warm and drowsy against him, he promised her every hue and shimmer, each placid reflection and muscular storm. The simple banality of clear azure. She'd have it all in paint and story.

Her voice came raspy but firm. 'I will speak with Mr Saxton, Tom.'

He supposed it was a fair trade. 'Ask the question. But no more until I am returned.'

And she pulled at his jacket, his waistcoat, releasing their buttons, kissing him in a way that made him feel deep-rooted, dug into the earth, unshakable in a way he'd not understood before.

In the nursery Tom lingered with James while Catherine dressed, joining his son at play and reciting snatches of rhymes that lifted from the deep of his own childhood. Wondering to what extent the child's features would change in the time he would be away. Lamenting he could not take his family with him, that to indulge one part of himself required forsaking another.

With his son enclosed in his arms, he whispered his hope to return by the boy's third birthday, three weeks after Christmas, and a promise of all the presents he could wish for.

'This is where your da will be.' He placed a small watercolour on the mantelpiece, next to the *Lady Leith*. It had taken him much of the night to complete the likeness of the clipper that would take him around the Horn to the west coast of the Americas; the vibrant wash, each loving line, gleaming with anticipation.

Her white glove stood out like a beacon in the crowd. She was not frantic like others around her, did not bow her head or turn to another for comfort as the ship pulled away from the dock. She stood quite still, with a smile held in place, her hand raised in the air with its open palm cupped, as if it were close enough to be resting against his face. He closed his eyes as he stood on the deck beside Martin, and he could feel her touch on his skin.

34

Linseed oil. Peppermint. New leather. And his own particular earthy scent, she recalled, as if he had been born in the long summer grass and not known it. Tom would return and his skin would taste of these things, mixed with salt and sweat. Each morning Catherine woke with the visceral memory of him on her tongue.

At dawn she felt the fire of day build and she greeted it with bare feet padding across the floorboards, dressed in one of Tom's shirts, the cuff of it smelling of laundry soap, that faint lemon whiff, which she inhaled as she slipped down the hall to their studio. The quiet broke now, dust motes responding to the creaking door; already a fine layer of particles occupied the shelf where his paintbox should be.

She did not brush her hair. She did not pretty her face. With the long mirror at her side, and the small tri-fold mirror in one hand to give her the angles, she set straight to work with watercolours in a new red leatherbound sketchbook. Alone, with her reflection and the first flush of light creeping through the window, she sought to capture incremental change. To know herself in some new way. To make herself visible, perhaps. Interrogating what lay beneath scalp and eyelid and rounded jaw. Just her face washed onto paper, broken into parts. A shoulder too, perhaps, and occasionally the length of an arm. Each self-portrait was a variation of shade and tone and tint: flesh was not flesh-coloured in that moment. It was lemon. It was pink. It was blue. Whatever the light showed; whatever the skin revealed.

For a long time after her son was born she had felt her body a strange sort of covering to be carried around in. She'd concentrate on her book or sheet of music before realising her shoulders or neck had stiffened, that her ankles had been so tightly crossed that a leg had lost feeling. Wooden and heavy, as if it didn't belong to her.

She had come so close to losing her son. She had felt her body crack open and almost give in to the pain that grew warm and flooding and stole every thought. There had been only her alone against this enormous force, and just as she feared she would surrender, it loosed its grip and left her fighting again, determined once more for breath.

Twice since James's birth there had been bloody clots that passed between her legs, her womb in a spasm, refusing to hold anything further.

Now she built a new relationship with the woman she had become. Even before Tom, her body had been aroused without understanding what it was that it desired. She pressed a pillow up high between her legs as a girl of sixteen, under the cover of hugging it for sweet companionship, but writhing in the darkness where it drew against her, and her nightgown became moist and her nipples hard where the silk slipped across them. When it brought her to an unexpected spasm she gasped, and the feeling spread and did not abate for minutes. There was shame at first, and fear of insanity and disease, which Nanny had implied through obscure language to be the certain outcome of self-pleasure, and so she hid this magnificent experience away, over time fending off notions of sin, finding herself feeling quite well, not ill at all, and instead savouring her unmentionable secret.

A woman now, with new knowledge of touch to draw on, she found a way to keep Tom close, and her body was again attuned and refined, her own touch assured and precise. It was an entirely unsanctioned accomplishment, and she laughed in triumph at how self-sufficient a woman's body really was, how pleasure might be made, despite all she had been told about women suffering a wife's duty to her husband. Despite the great taboo.

The sea could have her husband for a time, but it would not win. It was more than merely physical, this bond. She felt herself stretched out to Tom in an impossible way, leaning when he leaned, like a compass drawing one arm across a map of the oceans, the other holding fast at the centre. A favourite poem of Donne's came to mind: 'A Valediction: Forbidding Mourning'. She understood what the verses suggested, and in this way her ache was eased.

The test Tom had first set for her had long become established: he would not write. They were together even when they were not. He would bring her the seas on his return, and in his absence she would imprint her life with James and Cecilia onto her canvases, so he too would not miss out, so he too could share and witness the bloom of their child, and share in both lives, both aspects of himself.

The sketchbook, however, was private, a visual journal in which she made handwritten notes after she had painted her image each morning: loose threads of thought that caught the air and moved before her eyes. A study. An indulgence.

In the garden, painting was a different task, with oils and canvas and serious attempt. And although she had borrowed from Tom, as he in turn borrowed from her, it was suggestion, not detail, that moved her. Layers of colour and instinctive shape that she'd trace and fuse into an attempt at pellucid meaning. The movement of light across a scene, the movement of a figure through that light, the way time passed through them, and the heart that beat beneath with a thousand hidden joys and griefs.

Each day with the chirrups and laughter of her son, and the flick of pages as Cecilia read, and the peck and scurry of nesting robins above in the big oak tree, it grew clearer. Tom would go to the sea and return with inspiration: paintings sketched, paintings half-finished, paintings yet to be started; ideas for colour and vastness and deep, deep feeling. Everything he did was inspired by the sea. It was the living force of his creativity. She wanted that for herself because she had been barred from it. But she had begun to learn, within the daily bounds of the house and its high-walled garden, that she didn't need to run away to Paris, or stand on the deck of a clipper, or travel to every part of the world. Everything she needed was inside her.

Her world was endlessly wonderful and changing, like the wind or the waves. The growth of her little boy, his trundling legs; the way he showed to her the slowing of her own father, his gentle hands stiffening at the joints. The softening in Cecilia's face, small shifts in her own, and the differing swing of each of their bodies in nature. The light glancing off bark and thorn and rock. The minor and domestic and feminine and quotidian just waiting to be transformed. Or simply to be revealed for the marvel they always were.

35

No sooner had Tom's trunk been secured than he rapped on the carriage roof and urged the driver make haste. Bracing with one hand, jolted over cobbled stone, he was tense with anticipation.

January 15, 1852. His son's third birthday, and in his tin trunk he'd secured small trinkets wrapped in muslin – a carved wooden whale, a portable compass, a miniature ship in a bottle.

He was filled with the thought of lying with Catherine that night, their bodies recalling the shape of each other, eight months of absence expressed in careful but forthright desire. And after, with the fire crackling and the covers pulled up, he would tell her of his travels, accumulated in detail for this moment. She would urge him on, examine him with intuitive questioning, appraise each scene. He would tell her of the American navigator Eleanor Creasy and her captain husband, Josiah, whom he had met at port in Valparaíso. He'd describe how Eleanor had learned the mathematics of winds and ocean current, and together she and Josiah had made blistering speed from New York to San Francisco Bay. A record eighty-nine days. Catherine was no daughter of a mariner, but it made Tom wonder. Perhaps there were new ways to balance things. They would talk about their future. It would take them much of the night to transmute his recollections into mutual living memory, and to confirm them afterwards with limbs unfurling and lips firmly pressing until they each fell away with a cry. They would not mind a night of sleeplessness. They would not mind a week of it.

The closer he got to the house, the more urgent he grew.

He'd find James growing fast now, holding tight to his mother's hand. Childhood happened so quickly. First it was the mobility of a toddler, now crawling, now climbing. Next incoherent sounds became syllables. Changes in the face, the emergence of a characterful boy from within soft, undelineated babyishness. He felt an overwhelming kind of love for his son; it gripped him with fright, left him feeling full and alive. The child had flashes of Catherine in him, and he loved him all the more for it.

Out on the tremendous Pacific he'd made quick sketches. Water-colours of the mast reaching up to low-hanging clouds, of distant scudding surf, and the slamming gale in which the two oceans beat against each other. Small oils on board that catalogued swell and sky and sail. All these he'd translate into larger works on canvas once he was settled back home, when he would have time to puzzle more deeply on ways to imbue a flat and static plane with the sensation of motion. The South American coast had provided him with all the light and shade he needed to fuel his art again; the decks had been his studio; his cabin a gallery. He felt greater ease at the prospect of showing his work to Mr Saxton, and wondered if the dealer would prove as interested as Catherine had hoped.

Many of his crew would return to a home – some loving, some unaffected – but few were to sleep such as Tom would, beneath silk and plump down, chandeliers and stuccoed ceilings, his bed turned down and warmed in advance by one in the family employ. He did not talk of it. Wealth was an accessory to Catherine and his son. It was not intrinsic, nor of import beyond the assumption of comfort, which he received gratefully.

Under Martin's hand the *Majestic* had won the tempestuous Horn from the east, and then hugged the long Chilean coast to their anchorage. The hold was emptied of textiles, iron castings and steel; re-loaded with copper ore. So far to the west, Tom's thoughts led him further, to the distant waters of California and San Francisco Bay, and to a fresh resolve to apply for his master's ticket on his return.

At the London Docks, he lingered on deck while the ship became still at anchor, waiting for them to appear. He trailed his telescope up and down the quay, imagining her late and emerging breathless with loving apology. The crowd was full of colour and commotion, and then it thinned. The passengers had disembarked, their dark travelling trunks with embossed initials hoisted onto the backs of carriages. The crew was unloading, the hull emptying beneath Tom's feet. His trunk was packed, he'd washed his face, his mouth was fresh with peppermint and cinnamon candy. He traced every detail of the quay again, searching for the flare of her white gloves, or the golden heart of the cairngorm signalling to him in the sun. Not a shadow of her to be found.

Moisture gathered in the creases of his fingers. In the hall of the house, he allowed his bag to drop to the floor beside his trunk, the deliberate weight of it causing a startling slap. Everything else sounded hollow.

Attuned to a change, but not understanding its nature, he found his voice and cast it into the void.

'Catherine?'

First there had been the laurel wreath at the door. Now he saw the windows were shuttered, and the mirrors in the entrance hall had been draped. The statuettes, even the portraits, were covered over.

There were lilies in vases that wafted their awful perfume over the sweetness of beeswax candles in slow burn.

Now the eerie whisper of black-clad servants, one bending to take his bag.

Sickening with each new sign, he grasped at the wrist of another, who wilted, shaking her lowered head.

'Where is my wife?' His question a command, as if he were on deck.

'I will find the master, sir.'

'No.' He recoiled almost as she had done and when she dared to raise her eyes, he caught it all.

Across the marble, onto the carpet. He raced up the stairs, two in each stride.

'Catherine!'

Through the empty corridors, his calls like blows to an unresponsive body.

'Catherine! James!'

When finally: the opening of a door. He thought he'd found relief. His breath pressed harshly as a face emerged and she came in close. He could smell his own sweat.

Cecilia's skin was as white as zinc. Her eyes glossy, lids lost to red. Her hand, reaching for him.

He shrank back, knowing that a single touch would change everything. His heart was thudding in his ears but now he could not seem to breathe.

'Catherine?'

Cecilia made no sound, just allowed her face to collapse. Tom's mind was scrambling, running from itself. He noticed a chip at the bottom of the polished door. Perhaps James had run into it with one of his toys, or the housemaid had caused it with a broom. In the corner near the skirting boards, wallpaper dared to curl. Cecilia's feet were hidden beneath her plain black dress. He felt her hand on his arm now. As heavy as lead.

'No, Cecilia, no, no—' His head was moving, his words slurred with horror. And as she spoke it bent him low with a guttural howl, like his back had been broken.

It had erupted so suddenly, a fire that had taken hold of a dry forest floor and scorched the earth in minutes. Catherine knew her attempts to cool her father back to consciousness were both frantic and feeble, but she could not stop, would not stop trying. Tom had often described to her a feeling of detachment that he experienced when he was painting, and now here she was, hovering above a scene with herself in it: a desperate daughter curled over her father's bed, trying to thwart what was beyond her control. Alfred would not stop pacing. Her father's breath was a shiver, his body quavering and drenched. For three days he struggled, lying in the wet of his own heat before a strange and sudden exhalation made him still, his crooked hands releasing at his chest. Only when Cecilia placed a hand on her shoulder and the doctor drew his fingers over the dead man's eyelids did Catherine stop wringing at the cloth she had applied over and over to her father's burning forehead. Only then did she slow into the swirl of a new reality and accept that something had changed. Something had been taken. Everything now would be different.

She needed Tom by her side, for his strength to prop her up as the grief made her crumble. She would have him cradle her beneath the bedcovers, and they would not emerge until they were old and grey themselves, petrified like stone together and no longer afraid of death.

All her joy at Tom's imminent return was cut with desperation. She was stricken by what she had lost: her dear weakened father. She longed for what was absent: the warm-bodied solidity of her husband. Thomas Rutherford, the sailor–artist, whose canvases she had shown the week before to the art dealer Mr Saxton, who was impressed with the detail and use of light in his watercolours and oils and would consider, he promised, an exhibition of the promising young painter's works, if only Tom would meet with him upon his return.

She thought of this as she lay aflame with fever herself less than two days later. She revisited the sketchbook propped on Tom's knees, the winding of the Thames, the weight of the cairngorm as he pinned it to her dress. She held out her hand but it remained empty. She asked for the stone but it was not brought.

As Tom sailed up the Channel towards Gravesend, Catherine felt the distance between them grow suddenly greater. It was not he who was far away, it was she. The tie that stretched grew thin, barely a thread. She was in her body and out of it. No longer firm at the centre. She fought Cecilia as her aunt mopped her skin, pushed Alfred away as he moaned and stroked her shoulder, writhed as every bone, every muscle ached within her, as she burnt at her core and could not keep still.

Tom. Where was Tom? Why was he not here yet? But there was his face, younger, paler, unlined, with darker hair. It was the face of Tom, in her son, and he rested his head at her hand and cried.

She was not alone at the end, Cecilia consoled, holding Tom to her. She called for you, and we took her hand in your place. She tried to hold on, but now she can no longer suffer.

Her body, washed and dressed and anointed, had been lowered that morning into the ground, next to her father. The infection, Cecilia pleaded. The risk of further illness. 'We could not wait.' The more her words slipped over him, the more confused Tom grew, and he shook his head and pushed away from her in a silent daze.

When James woke to his father's cold touch, the boy's cry was a mewling. He clutched at Tom's neck with a ferocious grip. Seeing his own grief expressed so unadorned, so unmitigated in his child almost cracked Tom in two. Too young to understand, James intuited his mother's absence. With his own throat in spasm, Tom let the child weep, smoothing a palm across his forehead as Catherine would have done. He imagined his hand was hers. He imagined her watching him. He imagined him watching her. It all seemed the same thing. Reciting, when James had calmed a little, the words from a favourite picture book as he had heard her do. Eventually the boy drifted off, his dark eyelashes wet with tears. Tom lay beside him as he slept, his heart in a void, split from time. Warming himself with the softness of the boy's breath. At once it was necessary to memorise the curl of a fist under a chin, the way an arm clutched to a stuffed bear. He had been barely able to whisper the story, and its happy ending had stung like mockery.

In their own bedroom Tom ran his hands over the quilt, tightly tucked and smoothed to each corner of the bed. Now alone, he rested his head on the covers, drew up his knees, and could smell the soap she used in her hair. It crushed him to see Catherine's side of the bed empty. When he slipped his hand under her pillow, he found one of his shirts folded underneath. He lay there on his side, bunching his shirt at his chest, staring at that pillow, eyes fiercely wide, until the cold descended over him and he fancied he was dead too. He thought perhaps if he did not move it could be true.

Then, a housemaid: murmured apologies, the swift crackle of a fire and the drawing of curtains. The final relief of darkness.

It could have been hours he lay there. It might have been days. In the surreal draw of time he shuddered at the awful sound of his own sobbing. He'd never heard anything so frighteningly animal. He'd not known he had it in him.

One thought only would restore motion to his body in the morning. He must rise, carry on. He had a son to love and care for.

36

He had been summoned to the study at two p.m. They would not discuss matters over breakfast, as some brothers-in-law might do. Instead, he felt he was attending an inquest, or a meeting with a notary determined to scrutinise his debt. It was likely the point, he realised, as he pushed open the door. It was designed to put him off-balance, to show power now that the soft buffer of Catherine and her father had been removed.

Alfred sat beneath the painted fishermen at what had once been his father's desk. Tom recalled the thimble of port and the warm handshake after making his nerve-wracking request four years earlier. Now Lord Ogilvie's son was in his place: two pale hands spread on the dark wooden surface; his mourning suit pressed into sharp seams.

'It is sad to be in this room without him,' Tom expressed.

'Grief cuts us all.' With his fingers at his neck, Alfred seemed far away.

'We couldn't have talked over breakfast?'

'What we have to settle has nothing to do with my aunt.'

'Settle?'

Alfred nodded, opened a drawer with a slow hand. Only when he handed Tom the document did his expression flicker.

Tom was no legal man. He fought the desire to skip words, instead slowing to comprehend what the document imparted.

'Catherine's wish, which your father agreed to upon our marriage, was for the annuity to continue in such a circumstance, so that I might provide for our son.' Tom held back his anger as best he could, determined to firmly articulate what he believed had been decided.

'There is no such arrangement.'

'The marriage settlement . . .'

'A clever piece of legal work, granted, in which detail, rather than intention, is paramount. I do not expect you to understand the intricacies of Equity law and the private protections in place to safeguard this family. However, any annuities agreed to by my father are derived from the estate. In the absence of my father, there is but one person responsible for that estate. Without that person's consent, the allowance cannot be granted.'

'You mean you will not grant it, Alfred.'

'Thomas, you cannot sincerely believe that I would allow you, a common man, a northern man and a sailor, to be a beneficiary of this family's noble legacy. Catherine may have been extended leniency by our pliable father, but I will not offer the same.'

'I care nothing for the wealth myself. You know this, Alfred. But what of your nephew? I can provide adequately for my son, but I cannot school and care for James in the manner to which he is accustomed, in the manner Catherine intended for him, on a seaman's earnings.'

'Of course you cannot.' Alfred's face sloped with affected regret.

Tom smacked the paper down on the desk.

'I will care for the child, I assure you of that,' Alfred continued. 'He will have everything he requires. But you will not see a penny.'

'You will be the beneficent arm that extends for his education, his housing, his clothing, his every comfort and privilege? While I plug the holes with nurture and sweetness, as if I am a wet nurse?' Blood pulsed at Tom's temples.

'I will honour him as a bearer of the Ogilvie name.'

'Then I will take him, Alfred. To hell with your noble legacy. What do I care about that? He is my son. I will provide a life for him, give him opportunity. You can remain here. Alone.'

Alfred's eye betrayed a twitch. For a moment Tom thought he had gained ground. But it did not last.

'Indeed? What kind of opportunity would that be for James? One that involves gruel for food and grinding dangerous labour at sea? Will you take him with you as your cabin steward perhaps, or leave him behind with some stranger in place of the love of his mother?'

Alfred's aim was instinctive and sure. Tom could not think.

'The choice is quite clear, Thomas. Provide for your son as your dead wife would have wished, or do not. Take him with you halfway across the world on a precarious wooden vessel, subsisting on paltry nourishment, stealing from him a great family legacy and depriving him of opportunity and learnedness . . . or do not. It is of course up to you.'

Twenty-four hours, Alfred offered, for Tom to consider. One day, one night. Forty-eight bells.

At times, Tom thought, they had managed accord. An uneasy brother-hood. Now Alfred reared with a venom Tom had once suspected, while Tom was weakened with grief, unsure of himself and his future, knowing he would never belong in this world alone without Catherine.

He thought back to James's birth, how it almost cost Catherine her life, how precious the child was, and the presumption Alfred had made at cradling him in the nursery as if he were James's father.

And then he realised: James might in time become the Ogilvie heir. Alfred had waited patiently to cultivate him as such, to take him and mould him in his own image. Perhaps it had always been his desire: for Tom and Catherine's son to be his own.

'Can you dissuade him?' he pleaded with Cecilia that afternoon, breaking her slow arpeggios with the news.

Her response was piercingly simple. 'Think it through, Tom.'

He saw Catherine in her aunt's damp eyes and their puffy lids, in the empty bay window cushions, in the portrait of her amber-haired mother.

'Don't tell me you agree with Alfred?'

'I agree with you – there is no easy option. You have to understand, Tom, I have no position from which to urge him, no wealth of my own.'

'Nothing from your family?'

'My sister's husband was kind enough to take in her intentionally unwed sister. My own father did not feel the same charity.'

Tom cursed them all, for her, for himself.

'Tom, please.' Cecilia's head lowered again over the keys.

'There must be a solution.'

He stood and waited, but it seemed neither could find an answer worth uttering.

Tom went to James again at bedtime. The child had indeed grown over the last months. His face still resembled Catherine's but now Tom saw his own father in the curling of James's mouth. Strange how haunted we are, he thought. The dead live on in all of us, unbidden.

He eased the blanket up to James's chin, and rested his own face close. Touching a flushed cheek with his lips, he kissed him goodnight. Thankful for the innocence of a child when all was a nightmare around him. Wanting to protect that innocence at any cost.

Perhaps it was possible to set James up with Cecilia in a modest home, funding them with his earnings. But he would have to spend every day offshore to bring in enough to do so. So James would be without mother and father and comfort. And what kind of life could it be for Cecilia, even if she were persuaded to agree?

He could take James to sea, teach him the ways of a seaman, assist him to rise and achieve rank as Tom himself had done. But it was a hard life, and it ought to be of one's own choosing. James was still too young, still used to soft cradling. It would be years before decisions could be made about his future. Tom could take him to the colonies, perhaps, where fresh starts were readily available. But what kind of existence could he guarantee? And who would be there for him when his father was at sea? Any option seemed to confirm Alfred's view that a life with Tom would ensure not just the loss of privilege but deprivation.

Perhaps it was only his pride that would be hurt with the proffered arrangement, he concluded.

He left James reluctantly, wishing he could sleep the night beside his small form.

Closing the door, he leaned back against it and stared into the half-darkness. His breath fled from him suddenly and he gave a sharp cough. Then the hammering in his chest started. At sea he'd thought such sensations were to do with the roiling seas, the wind, the intense exertion. Here on land, it shocked him. He was forced to draw slow, deliberate breaths.

When the breathlessness subsided, he stepped sightless through the hallway, recalling the way from memory: where to make a step up, where to round a corner. Falling into his own bed, pulling the covers over his exhausted body.

*

In the end, Alfred's strongest weapon was one that pitted Tom against himself. It wasn't physical. It wasn't made of iron or stone. It was much more simple, and far more cunning. It was as if Alfred held up a mirror to Tom and forced him to judge what he saw.

Tom returned to the study in the morning, conscious of his heartbeat, his legs that felt like they were asleep though he had not closed his eyes all night.

'I agree to the arrangement,' he said eventually. 'On the condition that we continue to live as we are in this house. That Cecilia may provide some substitute for Catherine's mothering. That James knows nothing of our agreement and his childhood is interrupted by no further grief.'

He'd thought about it in the dark, lying flat on his back, his eyes flitting across the unseen ceiling as he comprehended the contingencies, as if deciphering a complex navigational calculation. What did it matter that Alfred controlled the fortune? What would Catherine want him to do?

He had lain with one hand on his chest, too aware of his breathing.

'Thomas, you are really in no position to bargain. I must insist you sign a contract so we have our arrangement in writing.'

'A contract?' Tom sighed. 'Draw it up.'

'In anticipation of your acquiescence, I have done just so.' Alfred rose from his desk this time, produced a fresh document from his drawer and held it out.

Tom reached for the paper and read it slowly. There it was in binding ink. He could not believe Alfred's audacity.

'What the devil is this?'

'Keep in mind, Thomas, you are talking to the man who has the fate of your son in his hands.'

'Guardian!'

'It is the only way for the child to be supported. He must have the family name.'

Tom's breath caught. He could see it so clearly. He was of the sea. His son was of the land. Without Catherine, he had no way to bridge the two.

'What, shall we pretend to him that I am dead, too?' Bile in his throat. Tom spoke with sarcasm but saw the effect. Alfred's face lit with sudden clarity.

'There is no need for deceit, Thomas. The truth will suffice: his father is gone to sea, and I am in his place.'

Tom lost all speech. In his head he could argue right and wrong for hours, but his gut was churning.

Alfred pushed further. 'An enduring absence would be best. For the boy's stability.'

It was horrifying to recognise the feeling he'd first known as a thirteen-year-old boy. The raw storming of grief. Tom began finally to bow, depleted blow by blow. He was in a swirl, a gale, off his feet, out of his body.

He tried to reason it out. Sacrifice, she had said. That was what parents did. That was what was required. His son would have all that Tom had not as a boy. All that he would not be able to provide as a father.

His own father had been lost at sea. Tom knew what that looked like.

Alfred offered the pen and sat back at his desk. As Tom's hand wavered above the document, his brother-in-law waited.

PART THREE

Melbourne and Port Chalmers, 1853–1871

37

At the end of the pier Tom dropped his bag and stood, legs wide. Once more the strange shock of land. How solid it was. How ungiving. The earth shimmered in the heat and he looked forward to the falling of the sun. It was mid-April, late afternoon, yet it seared his face from one side, a flaming ball in the west.

Melbourne. The light here stole colour from everything it fell on. The sand, the stone and the wooden pier, bleached by its brightness.

They'd anchored just after dawn off Sandridge in the broad stretch of Hobsons Bay. Once the cargo was discharged, there was nothing more for Tom to do but relinquish command and leave the arms of the clipper. From the quarterdeck he watched his crew disembark onto barges then disappear along the sandy shore, feeling the loss. A deliberately constructed shield wall broke down, piece by piece. For weeks he had passed the nights in their company, unwilling to be left alone with his swirling insides. The mates had taken turns to play him at cribbage while ruminating on the changeability of the Southern Ocean, and Tom had tested himself by charcoaling each man's likeness. His subjects had been pleased by whatever aspect of them he had captured, as static as it could only be, and afterwards he had offered the portraits to them, so all he had to show since leaving London was a handful of seascape watercolours: a sunset hovering over iron-dark waters off the Californian coast; the Indian Ocean emblazoned with ethereal blue-white light; and a study of narrow Port Phillip Heads with its dangerous eddies through which they had passed with the aid of a pilot.

Tom's throat was parched. His legs heavy. He shook them out, one limb at a time. He was to meet Seamus in this broiling southern town, where the dust rose up and made everything rust-coloured and gritty, where there was an alternately pleasant and piercing smell of tea-tree and horse shit.

Turning his back on the bustling port and its comforting humanity, he made his way south around the bay, seeking shade when he could beneath the mottled spines of red gum trees. He walked beneath the screech of yellow-fringed cockatoos gathering their full white bodies in clusters high in treetops, the brilliant slip of lorikeets, the grey-green sway of weeping leaves. On he went in a long stretch of unvariegated blue, through the ochre kicked up by horses, until he arrived beneath the freshly whitewashed ceiling of his room in a boarding house on Alma Road, St Kilda. He lay down on his bed, separated from the sounds of the sea, and there he was: still the same man, holding the same burning ashes in his hands.

That first night his dreams returned. He was swimming in the tidal motion of her breath. Her strong legs pushed against his thighs. He reached for the slope of a shoulder.

Catherine.

He was breathing beneath the sea. She was floating above him at the surface, sunlight surrounding her. She had become opaque, a shadow. He kicked through the water, found her, ran his hand along her back, the muscle of her. Touch had become his only language.

He couldn't see her face. His chest was merely bones, ribs unsheathed of flesh; he was letting in water.

He woke tangled in sweat-soaked sheets, ragged-breathed. He was always exhausted in these early hours. Raising himself to pull back the curtains he rested on the edge of the bed before washing, feet flat on the floorboards and parallel. He allowed the sun to warm his body through, drying the wet at his navel and the base of his neck, and absorbed the strange complexion of the sky as the morning grew brighter. It was a tepid and timid first light that flourished to a confident vibrancy. He couldn't have mixed such boldness in his palette.

He'd pass many more mornings this way before the pain began to ease. He'd dream of Catherine and wake alone, always in awe of the sunlight and the heat, belittled and moved by the expansiveness that promised relief but never delivered.

News flowed fast through the port, and Tom waited that first month to hear what was being said. But the talk off the ships at Sandridge and Williamstown was only ever of tides and profit-taking, abscondment and prospecting, injuries and record-breaking navigation. Seamus had departed Liverpool at the start of April but it would be winter before he passed the Heads into Port Phillip Bay. Until then, Tom's other life could remain in shadow.

Gold had hit Victoria with a kind of fever. Lured by promises of wealth to be picked, sieved and panned from the region's soils and rivers, sailors were deserting in droves to head inland to the goldfields, and thousands more diggers arrived ashore each week to follow: English, Irish, Chinese, Italians, Americans, determined to stake their claim on a land already turned upside down. Many relied on native guides to lead them safely over country they did not know or understand.

Melbourne town was a billowing entity that grew and dispersed like a dust storm, three miles inland from Sandridge. Firmly aspirational and engorged by golden wealth, it cut a neat grid formation on the Yarra's northern shore, but its streets were awash with effluence.

The prospectors, thieves and hopefuls who had flooded in were living in the chaos of a canvas city pitched along the southern riverbank. Surprised by a knife one night, Tom found crime was rife, petty theft and pickpocketing adroitly done. Hold-ups of gold transports were a common affair. Murder far from unheard of.

The force of settlement was startling to any eye that had seen this place in earlier years. Where cockleshells once piled on hills and beaches around the bay, harvested from the reef offshore, the land had been disturbed by spade and bluestone slab, taken for cemeteries and quarantine stations or overlaid by groove-cutting drays. At the edge of the town along the ancient river, its flow newly polluted, ten more acres had been claimed that year for a cricket ground to be built near where the Yarra tribe still camped. Among the wattle and river red gum trees, bark huts were the shelter of these native men and women, now unwelcome in the town, and camp fires burnt bright on the land. Further out still, acres of plentiful grasslands had been grabbed for sheep and cattle as if they'd lain dormant for the purpose. A blackfellow who thought otherwise would be reminded of their place by the pull of a righteous trigger.

Tom himself had unloaded cases of brandy and barrels of gunpowder to this shore over the years. Watched livestock in the hundreds escape the dark of a hold. Sometimes he imagined the sea flowing like arteries towards a giant, bloody heart.

He kept to himself down by the bay at St Kilda, three and a half miles south of the town. Many times he woke at night to the sound of screaming, and by dawn it was the unfamiliar cacophony of foreign birdlife that brought him back from Catherine and into the light.

Rising, he'd wash with a pitcher of icy water at the basin and dress not in his captain's jacket but in a cream-coloured shirt and vest beneath a coat the colour of roasted chestnuts. It reminded him of Christmas at the house. The marrons glacés Catherine had always been fond of. It reminded him of another life. He wound a necktie at his throat, and his hair flamed above it. He'd taken a blade to his beard and the effect was boyish.

From his lodging, it was a mile or so down to the foreshore. Setting up his easel on the small wooden jetty, inevitably he would be obliged into conversation with this crewman or that captain, about which ship had just docked after a searing run east through the forties, or the outrageous number of hands taking off to the diggings, or how well the newest American clippers were handling around the storm-thrashed Horn. They asked Tom when he would next head out, none thinking to remain longer than it took to unload and refill their hold. When he said he did not know, that perhaps he'd take a break from the decks, they laughed at his words. Such jest, they said.

Sometimes Tom wished he were more like these mariners with their sea-grime roughness, brusque manner, and the way they saw everything in black and white, as if the world itself were the simplicity of a ship's tall dark masts slung with big white sails.

When he uncorked the bottle, the smell of turpentine came potent with memory: Catherine, on the hill, daubing her bold and energetic brushstrokes with a defiantly straight back. What would she make of this? Beyond the bustle of barges and cargo, he estimated at least one hundred ships resting at anchor across the bay's wide curve, their sour wafts of sluice and tar carrying on the breeze. He studied these masted residents in the haze of dawn, under the bright sting of noon, and as the lurid touch of dusk spread across the sky. The mixing of colour, the neatness of detail, the concentration on line and form kept him focused now. A bare canvas was full of potential, and the hesitation he felt before laying down the first wash was only ever fleeting. For a moment he could forget the life that fell in his wake, forget what was here at his feet. He could rein his ambitions once more to what he understood: the sea and its inhabitants.

38

From Sandridge they walked to St Kilda and on to the hotel at the junction, Tom burying his head in his collar against the sharp June wind, contemplating the necessary words.

Seamus was ready with his response. 'Why on God's earth did you not bloody well tell me?'

Tom might have anticipated his anger. For months Tom had roamed the seas with a canker rotting his insides, as Seamus now described it, and his friend had not known a damned thing about it.

'I was at your wedding, Tom.' And then, after they'd claimed a quiet corner in the tavern, 'Have you learned nothing of friendship over all these years?'

Tom only nodded, concentrating on a series of wet rings left by his whisky glass on the table. He rubbed at his aching jaw. When Seamus leaned in and secured his wrist, it was the first reminder in a long while of what care could be like. Trapped in his friend's reassuring grip, he felt utterly and irreparably exhausted.

In truth he had told no one. He'd signed with the first captain who would have him and readied to depart London on a word. Not one of the crew was known to him, and he was glad to have it that way.

259

He could not afford to fall apart. All he could think of was the crystal vase that had been knocked to the floor at their wedding as he and Catherine danced in celebration; it had a greater density than that of breaking glass, and the shards were infinitely smaller, and never to be put back together again.

The scent of Catherine had barely left their room before the pillow slips were removed and replaced, her books dusted and stacked by someone else's hand, her hairbrush cleaned and aligned with its matching mirror as a shrine to a long-lost face. Within days Tom found her easel and canvases carried away and her brushes and pens tidied in a drawer. He spun, clutching for small tokens. The tri-fold mirror, and a sketchbook with a red leather cover that was new to him. He guessed the cairngorm to be at her breast in the earth and wished he could have pinned it there himself. Her canvases, however, along with his own, he willingly let go; he would regret it later, but at the time the innocence of those lost selves, shared in hope and once believed to be permanent, felt curdled and unbearable.

It was not one decision that had forced his departure but a series of responses to Alfred's deftly erected hurdles. At first Tom moved speechless through rooms in a house that was no longer his, seeking a still-warm imprint of his wife. He had held on to his son in disorientation. As had Alfred.

With each action and reaction Tom sought to protect James. Each attempt had led inevitably to their separation. Never had he felt so reduced and small. Worn by an ache he had not felt since he was a boy watching the shore for the return of his father.

Within a month he was gone from the house. Gone from London.

He had kissed James while the boy was still drowsy under the bedcovers. Of course he would be cared for. His uncle would see to it; Alfred's love for the boy was not in doubt. Tom had left for the sea many times before; why should this be any different?

It would not be forever, he reasoned, turning to his son for a final time at the nursery door. He would find some way to unlock them from this. For now, at least, the boy was safe.

Before Catherine, the decks had been Tom's home. He'd once thought he'd require no other. So he turned to them again, signing up as first mate on a ship bound for San Francisco where, on arrival after a hundred and fifty days, he found a bay clogged three ships deep and slung with fog. The ghostly groan of vessels at anchor, abandoned in the hope of gold; the hammering of construction a constant ricochet across the water. He returned to Liverpool, uncaring of destination, doing everything by rote: scanning the skies, commanding his watch through storm and heat and violent winds, and sleeping a deep negating sleep in between.

On British soil again, he applied for his master-mariner's ticket and was successful. When he grasped the accomplishment of a long-held ambition, it felt flat and bitter. Each night at port he passed with sketching and whisky, waking with a headache to castigate himself for. But he did not dream, and for that he was thankful.

He was a shadow at the local port office, and avoided news of London. Should the loping gait of a sailor suggest a familiar face, he'd turn and walk the other way, hiking up the collar of his jacket and studying the footfall of his weathered leather boots: on guard against the curly-haired darkness of Martin crossing his path, the brusque scratch of Munro's call, the sympathetic glance of Seamus. Fearful of any softening.

A year was spent this way. His will began to flag. His jaw throbbed, his neck clicked with tension. He tried writing to James, to Cecilia, but he didn't know what to say, and he had no address to give for their reply. When might he see his son next? He did not know. And James was so young. He would not understand.

London had grown distant. Tom had lost his place there even before he set off. One day he would return, he told himself. He had made a promise to his son. But not yet.

Fortitude, a hunkering down into an innate privacy, served Tom now. A technique well known, forged as a child. His first job as captain: commanding a clipper, newly built, from Liverpool to the distant south; the ship itself was to be delivered along with its cargo. He signed his name with a quick scrawl, before inertia threatened.

And so, Melbourne: a town settled in the uppermost curve of a sheltered bay at 37 degrees south. The southern hemisphere, the British colonies, the child at the ankles of the Motherland. A place where he might continue to forget and be forgotten.

The scars on Tom's hands remained evidence of Catherine, of a life unexpectedly rerouted. The scars of her absence, however, were invisible. No one could see that kind of bleeding. Not even Seamus could patch him up from this cut, or assure him he would be healed.

In one way only could he hold on to her: the new paintings he created, now drying in his room on Alma Road. Their number would grow as he dedicated himself to the manifold steamers, schooners, clippers and barques punctuating Hobsons Bay. To view his work was to discover the full array of hull and sail, and he would show them to Seamus, he said, looking at his friend over his whisky glass. But they did not tell the whole story.

Tom considered what it was that made a person crave power, made a man think he could take what he wanted from another. Ambition alone was not the cause. Was it simple hatred or greed? Was it weakness? Was it fear?

As Tom laid out his history for Seamus, the softness of his inner cheek gave way to the metallic tang of blood. With his glass a prisoner in his fist, he breathed in each of Seamus's questions as they were given air, wishing they could be unasked, or made less sincere, less caring.

'My son was supported but I was not. You understand, Seamus. I could not suffer in that house with Catherine's ghost and my son fed by another man's hand. In any case, I had to leave to earn a living. Should I have brought him with me? Should I have stayed? I thought with time I'd have a plan. But it seems I do not.'

'A plan? You did what you had to do, Tom. Any man would have done the same.'

It was a relief to unburden himself, to describe to Seamus his life within the Ogilvie fold; to tell of the opportunity he'd taken to voyage with Martin to South America, and the regret that he had done so against Catherine's wishes. The stoic wave of her white lace glove that final time; his naive optimism. She would never know how desperate he had been to see them both waiting for him at the dock on his return. Instead: the coldness of the bedcovers, smoothed over as if she had never lain beneath them.

Seamus's reassurance could not wholly assuage his guilt, and the fault was Tom's own: no matter that his hand had been forced, Tom alone had made the decision after Catherine was gone. He'd picked up the pen and signed his son away as Alfred watched and grew satisfied.

Seamus sighed. 'I'm sorry I cannot stay longer.' He had less than a fortnight before departing again for Liverpool and on to New York.

Tom responded lightly. 'Nevertheless, I'm glad you're here.'

39

Catherine's hand was at Tom's shoulder, then reaching out and worrying the hard scales of a tree's dark bark, finding where it was broken, touching the stickiness with her finger. She pressed it against her thumb. When she held it to his face, he breathed the tang of resin. Her skirts shuffled against his leg.

'Does it matter to you that our upbringings are so different?'

She smiled. 'I am more interested in our future.'

'I never was one to accept limitations.'

'So let us not accept them.'

'People say I'm beneath you. That your father's a fool. That you—'

'They do not see our private selves. And no other detail matters.'

She had been wrong, he understood upon waking, and so had he. The details had mattered in the end. He lay there in the still of dawn, breathing the phantasmal scent of sap and thinking, Who had that man been? Who had he become?

Dropping his bare feet to the floorboards, he sat on the edge of his bed as the light came in. With Seamus here he could no longer run.

He reached for Catherine's sketchbook and placed it on his knees. Both hands flat and gentle on the red leather cover. Assessing its solidity. For all these months he had kept it hidden away, frightened somehow of lifting that cover to the past. He had imagined every sketch, of course: there would be dusk behind the old oak, its leaves in late summer the colour of limes. Or its branches drawn like veins, viewed against the midday sky from the grass. Cecilia under a parasol by the roses, with James holding her hand. The mobile face of his son, upturned with a smile, his small fingers, reaching. Tom brought the leather to his nose. It was not these images that would injure him anew, but all that he would not see: she who had bent herself so seriously over the sketchbook, behind the brush. Forever now invisible.

Only he was wrong. When he opened to the first page he saw he was utterly wrong, and unarmoured against the surprise. His hands shook, fumbling to turn through each self-portrait, quickening, revealing more and more: Catherine, Catherine, Catherine. All of them, every one of them, pictures of her. He was a stranger admitted to a private world, and what lived there, bold on each of the leaves, pulled from him an involuntary moan. He lifted his face, pinning his eyes open against a gathering sting. Breathing out. If his tears should fall to the page, they would run down her face too, washing it away.

She met him now, her eyes so close to his, each image of her beneath his hand presenting itself anew and reinterpreted. An image of one he still loved, caught willingly in the passing of time.

He drew a finger along each differently shaped eyebrow, the arch and curve of them, her mouth small and pursed, the sweep of her narrow neck. Collarbones. Cool like sand. He'd turn a page and begin again. Never had he known her like this. She had peered beneath the skin to articulate what rushed and wrestled there. All her intimate moods in strange hues and unconventional brushstrokes. What was it that ran through her in that moment, what did she hope for as she painted? Was it summer still as she worked, was it autumn, was she warm sitting there in his shirt, had she smelled him on the cotton, was she wearing his slippers too, had she gone to James already and kissed him?

Where was her husband, where was he, where was he?

The answer was not a mystery.

'Where the sailor ends the artist begins.'

Just how long the man had been standing at his back Tom could not say. By afternoon he was detailing the drape and fold of sailcloth taken in along the yard of a Boston-built clipper, running a thinned sheen of Naples yellow over the palest areas of the main topsail where the light flared. The voice brought him back to his body, and he grew conscious of his feet on the wooden boards, the resuming hum of the jetty.

'Forgive the intrusion. I do not mean to interrupt.'

But the man had done just that. Tom kept his eyes forward and his hand raised to the canvas a little longer, resentful, regretting the loss – the taking away – of his painterly state.

Catherine once described it as being pulled from a magnificent dream. There was no boundary between himself and the canvas when he painted. It became his only world, and he moved within it at speed, a feeling like pushing a ship to eighteen, nineteen knots, racing unhindered across the surface of the world. Such pace and sublime forgetting were never permanent, but each dash gave him hope and purpose.

As his momentum flagged and the man's presence hung behind him, awaiting a response, all that was material and tangible folded in on him again.

Tom lowered his brush and turned to a dark-haired gentleman carrying a sketchbook of his own. He was perhaps similar in age to Tom, wrapped in an overcoat the colour of slate.

'The tone is impressive, and the verisimilitude outstanding.'

'You're very kind, sir,' Tom said, newly conscious of the southerly.

'Goldstein. Ambrose Goldstein.'

'Thomas Rutherford. Captain.' He made a show of his pigment-speckled palms.

'Of course,' Goldstein said, withdrawing his hand, still cheerful. 'I shall come to the point. In August there is to be an inaugural exhibit of the newly formed Fine Arts' Society – formed by myself, that is, and a small group of other landscape and maritime artists who find ourselves washed up on these shores from various parts of the globe.'

Tom rested his brush now, and wiped his hands with a muslin cloth.

'We do not know each other, of course.' The man cleared his throat. 'But I have noted you working down here on occasion, and have been captured by the persuasive quality of your ships. I wondered if you may be interested in joining us?'

'I'm flattered, Mr Goldstein.'

'Your work would be an admirable addition.'

'Thank you, but no.'

'Of course, Melbourne hasn't yet the grand galleries of London that you would be used to.'

'Forgive me. That's not the reason.' And then it occurred to him. 'London?'

'Yes, at least, that is what I heard. Your accent may mark you as a Scot but I understand you are connected to a family of some name back in England.'

'You heard?'

Goldstein adjusted his necktie. 'I like to gather a little on all the artists who turn up in Melbourne town. Especially those talented enough to join us at the society. I hadn't any background on you and didn't recognise your name. Judging by your subject matter I thought you to be a man of the sea, and so I asked around. I apologise I did not approach you sooner.'

'You were, what, spying behind my shoulder as I worked?'

'Observing.' The man laughed. 'Observing, Captain Rutherford. From a respectful distance, of course.'

Tom pressed his lips against each other, realising his thirst.

'You exhibited in London, I presume?'

'I did not.'

'Well, I must say I am surprised. Your work is quite fine. Why not join us? Let us show them what we colonists can do.'

'Only my wife sees my work.' Tom heard the tense and his face twitched with the effect. 'My paintings are not for show.'

'Well.' Goldstein lingered for a second or two, glancing from the canvas to Tom and then back, as if in confusion. 'Well, Captain Rutherford. Should you change your mind.' He wrote in the back of his sketchbook, made a fold along the page and tore along it, offering it to Tom. 'There is still time.'

Tom listened for his retreat down the jetty, then turned and watched the fellow step quickly across the hard, wet sand towards the foreshore track.

Standing back from his easel, Tom wondered if there'd be rain again tonight. He enjoyed the freshness in the mornings after a pour, all traces of yesterday smoothed away. He sighed and swizzled the first of his brushes in turpentine, wiping it clean with the cloth. Goldstein had disappeared. The bay was loud with the crack of gums being chopped and cleared. Bricks and bundles of firewood were being heaved out of a dinghy along the beach.

Tom had thought himself obscure beyond the comfort of the jetty, the calming regularity of the tide and the undemanding sailors whose attention was on the taverns, payday, their next departure. Seamus had been his only companion, and soon that too would be at an end.

Now it seemed Tom had drawn attention through the very method he used to keep himself contained.

He knew what Catherine would wish for him to do. But he had been painting for one purpose only. While Goldstein might see expertly documented maritime scenes – ships and harbours and coastlines rendered in earnest detail – only Tom, only Catherine, could know the alternative history, buried in the pigment of his paint and the lifting and resettling of his brush.

'They call this winter, but it's not as we know it.'

Tom looked up and was ready with a smile. 'Indeed, doctor.'

'Are you ready?'

Tom surveyed his canvas a final time.

'Who was that fellow you were speaking to as I was walking down?'

'He was speaking to me. He's some painter himself, apparently.' Tom finished packing his paints and folded the legs of his easel. His still-wet canvas he placed into a handmade frame that covered the surface without making contact and allowed him to carry it.

'Good. You should seek company, Tom.'

'What I seek right now is a wee cup of whisky and a plate of lamb roast, Seamus, if you'd care to prescribe that for me, too?'

The road up to the tavern at the junction was a rosy flurry of boots and skirts and hooves as the sun dropped and the air grew cooler. The smithy was still hammering in a molten glow, but the apothecary closed up as they passed: the tinkle of a brass bell, a wooden sign flipping over in the window. Seamus gave a wave.

'You got what you needed today?' Tom asked.

'I'm prepared for anything. Physic, that is.'

The sky was like the skin of a peach. Tom wished he could pull out his canvas again right there in the street and add a fresh sweep of colour to capture the bloom. Night would soon fall. It would be too dark to paint after supper and then, with his hands stilled, Tom's mind would wander.

At the junction, bullock teams thick with muscle pushed by with cargo-laden drays. A craggy stockman lumbered through on horseback, shooting commands over one shoulder and forming a piercing whistle with two pink fingers in his mouth. Tom smelled the leather and oils and spirits and sweat-soaked wool as he and Seamus dashed in front of his path. A pair of lean native youths rode erect behind, and at the call they urged the stockman's mud-caked beasts over a land so changed, trampled by hooves.

In the tavern a fire was roaring, and wafts of roast meat and gravy and ale fuelled Tom's hunger. The bar heaved with the newest clutch of diggers to arrive off the goldfields. Made obvious by their gaunt profiles, unkempt beards and clay-encrusted trousers; the possum skin rugs bought from native traders among their scant belongings. They stood with their bundles at their feet and drank a pint in a single gulp. Tom fancied he could judge by their eyes who had won in the efforts for a shining nugget. Who would return jubilant to their abandoned wives and children. Who would not.

He sat with Seamus and raised his glass. 'I'm sorry to lose you to the Atlantic again.'

'I might have stayed if my contract allowed it.' Seamus's smile was rueful. As he sliced into a plate of lamb, he prodded. 'Back to the man's question, Tom. Why don't you consider it?'

'Aye, Seamus.'

'Well, that sounds like a no.'

Pursing his lips, Tom topped up his friend's glass in reply.

'Well?'

'Well. I barely know the man. What if he's some charlatan?'

'Then your paintings don't sell and maybe I get to keep that one I like of the schooner with its sails slack at sunset? It would brighten my drab cabin enormously.'

'I hadn't thought about them selling.'

'There's a lot that might be fixed with coin.'

Tom considered this for a moment, rubbing at the muscles that had tightened again in his neck. 'It's too late. And it could never be enough.'

'Enough for what?' Seamus asked. 'Tom?'

'To take back my boy, Seamus. I am no longer his father.'

40

Tom could not sleep. Whenever he closed his eyes, he'd bolt awake again, ready to leap to the quarterdeck. He missed the distraction of the men, the shifting of the ocean. He missed many more things, which hurt too much to think of. By candlelight or dawn, he pored over the images Catherine had made of herself, searching each face for its differences. Bathed in red light, bathed in gold, bathed in a strangely harmonious blue. He picked a gaze and absorbed its mood, focusing on those eyes, that smile. Tasking himself with knowing her in every way.

> *It rains through me today and I am dusky blue, peach and*
> *sap, watery, muted, longing for reunion.*

Only when he'd grown familiar with each nuance of mouth and brow, had marked lovingly the little dip in her cheek that accompanied the merest sort of grin, only then did he shift his attention to what she had written on the pages facing each image. First he was simply happy to see the looping flow of her hand, and could intuit the rapidity or languidness of her thoughts through the neatness or distintegration of her copperplate. He skipped to a page somewhere in the middle, not wanting to read from the beginning to an inevitable end. He'd subvert the path of history this way, circumvent her fate, keep her alive in an ever-changing narrative. Her writing – journal entries of some sort – did not appear to connect in any case. Sometimes she'd inked a solitary line. Sometimes several sentences, a paragraph, an entire page. No matter their number, the nature of her words were like alcohol on a wound; they stung, but perhaps that would help with the healing.

These things are greater than us: the pull of the artist, the stream that runs through our bones and blood. And the sea for you, I suppose, is the same, the currents are competing: one tide comes in and the other goes out, and then they swap, and they tussle, and you are drawn in turn to one and then the other. I know, as you surely do, that the tide will always go back out to sea. And I trust, as I hope you trust, that it will then always return you to shore.

In this face, a morning of thoughts, clouds across the window. You have gifted me your life in images, when I know you to be quiet and protective, and now I do the same – not here, not in these indulgent jottings – but with oils on canvas in our walled garden, so you might share in all you have missed on your return. Oh, do not expect me to tell wild and adventurous stories. Alfred says lady painters lack in noble feeling, that my art is, necessarily, all too 'domestic'. Where is the soaring of the soul, he asks, the moral discipline, the rigour and understanding? As a woman I am accustomed to hearing of my deficiencies. But are war and history and religion the only moving subjects? They are someone else's subjects. What surrounds me has its own meaning: is this not luminous too? I am certain you will understand.

I picked some roses the day you left, and now they are dying in the vase and Mary has scooped the fallen petals up with a tut. So often I walk into a room to tell you something and you are not there. It takes time to adjust. What long and tugging shadows love casts.

That morning, as dawn crept in, the candle stub still burning at his bedside, Tom woke from his eventual slumber with Catherine's pages lying open on his chest.

It was not quite seven a.m. when he sought the dining room. His landlady, Mrs Mitchell, was on her knees, sweeping soot from around the hearth: the night had brought the rain, and high winds.

'One thing I'll say for you sailors: you're punctual,' she greeted him, cross-hatching kindling over the fire grate.

'Aye,' he replied. 'And we never complain about the food.'

She huffed at that. 'You like your porridge salted?'

Tom nodded. There was something peaceful in that second of stillness and light before the kindling blazed into flame. 'Thank you.'

'You'll have to wait though.' She warmed her hands before pushing off from her knees. The skin on her knuckles, inflamed and scaly, seemed to cause her pain as she did so.

First she brought him coffee, which Tom sipped gratefully. His heart still banged with every line of Catherine's he'd read.

There were immigrants newly arrived in the dining room this morning with unwashed hair and jaundiced babies in arm – born on the ship, he surmised. The whirr of a toddler, tipping near Tom's table, bottom onto boards. He wanted to reach out, set the child upright, but her mother was there, quickly to the wee one's side.

'There, there.' She soothed the child of tears.

What kind of lives might they have left behind, he wondered. What ambitions did they nurse; what frailties, what regrets?

At the ring of a bell, heavy feet trampling down the stairs. He heard the closing of the front door. For a moment he was in Richmond again, lying awake in his strange bed and listening.

'Tom?'

Seamus was shaking out his jacket, draping it over the back of his chair. He had listened as Tom opened up over the days and, like any good physician, gave a measured diagnosis. Grief had a way of conjuring extremes in temper, he said, and he wondered if, with the salve of time, an equitable solution might still be found. Alfred, after all, had been mourning too. 'You bundle yourself into a self-made enclosure too readily,' he had summarised for Tom the previous evening.

It was true. But Tom knew no other way.

Seamus had a talent for giving his opinion freely without pushing too far. His words grew like seeds – they took hold, reaching their roots down deep.

'You ought to consider Goldstein's offer, Tom.' There it was as he reached for the coffee pot. That careful dose of insistence in his voice.

'Aye, Seamus. Good morning to you, too.' Tom exhaled with a laugh.

What he ought to do, Tom thought, was return to the sea. Return to what he understood and where his command was clear and respected.

What would his father think of him now: a sailor idling and drawing pretty oil colours across canvas? James Rutherford would never have contemplated such frivolity when there were mouths to be fed.

Only Tom didn't have any mouths to feed, except his own.

'Catherine believed in you, Tom. Goldstein is clearly impressed. You ought to make something of it. It's not your way to be so shy of ambition.'

Goldstein's offer was an opportunity. It was also the shadow of a lost dream – Catherine's dream. He had tethered himself to it. This was not London, and he was not the same man. Absence was one thing; they had weathered that before. She was gone, in all finality, and no matter what he did, she could only grow more distant.

He swirled the dregs in the bottom of his cup, knowing he would have to slip free of an invisible knot.

Whose eyes had her words been meant for? Were they for her alone? Would she have shown him those deepest inner thoughts?

'Tom?'

The only certainty was that he would always be a sailor. Without the sea, his painting had no fuel, no subject.

'Listen to this.' Seamus was reading from the *Argus*: 'July 8, 1853. Matthew Perry and his "Black Ships" have dropped anchor in the bay at Edo and demanded to trade.'

Tom looked up. The docks were already aflame with the news. He'd heard it straight from the mouths of sailors. Nevertheless, here it was, confirmed in smudged columns and an assertive typeset headline. The great unknown empire. Commodore Perry had broken Japan from two hundred years of seclusion, forcibly revealing its secrets.

'What do you know of this American, Perry?'

'Little, I'll admit.'

He'd not bothered to enquire. It was the sea Tom cared for; the journey, not the port. All land appeared the same from a distance: a low-lying shadow that took time to clarify itself from cloud. Drawing closer, there was a moment of suspension, a space of imaginative proposition. It was never clear whether it was the land that was solid or the sea. The sustaining microcosm of a ship could keep a sailor riveted year after year to the sea's reliable roll and liberty, but whenever a dark form on the horizon slowly deepened, variegated and gained dimension, all certainties became sea-felt contingencies, pinned to the vacillations of water and the shadow of land.

Every voyage was threaded with risk. A sailor accepted it whenever the anchor was weighed. Even so, Tom hadn't understood its reach before Catherine. That to be swept into the swell of another, to be known and embraced, meant that when they were gone there was a pit of loneliness, a sense of being adrift, and no longer by your own volition. He'd been changed by her, and by his own ambition, and he saw there was no returning to what had been before.

'You know what Catherine would want you to do, Tom.'

'Aye, Seamus.' He gave in, acknowledging the truth of it. And when Mrs Mitchell arrived with the porridge, he ate with wholehearted hunger and smiled at his friend and drew his own privacy out, asking about Maeve and the new bairn, urgent to show how grateful he was before Seamus picked up his jacket and bag and made his final farewell.

When the time came, Tom embraced his friend sincerely. Having allowed his solitude to be breached, it would be hard to settle again.

'Safe travels, doctor.'

'Aye, and to you.'

'Oh, I'm not going anywhere,' Tom laughed.

'We're all going somewhere, Tom, even if we don't yet recognise the destination.'

41

'Thy firmness makes my circle just, and makes me end where I begun.' It seems Donne knew something of our state, dearest Tom.

It was a week later that Tom dashed off his note to Ambrose Goldstein, writing in haste before he could change his mind. He had been punishing himself perhaps, for all his missteps, but he was not suited to stasis.

He dreamed again, in vivid colour. Waking, he thought of the photograph of himself and Catherine and the blurred bundle in her arms that was the infant James. Had she ever spoken to Mr Saxton in his absence, he wondered, and what might the art dealer have replied? What had happened to her paintings, to the new oil canvases she described in her sketchbook? To those of his own he had left behind?

Catherine was whispering a story in his ear, fuelling a fantasy. Would she recognise the man beside her and want him still? Each painting he had created to forget his pain, and each had instead become a tribute to her memory.

He marked his signature: *T. Rutherford*. With an almost paternal care, he spelled out the titles for engraving:

Moonlight on the Hooghly
Storm over the Bay, Rio de Janeiro
Dawn, London Docks

At the beginning of August, the dark-haired painter guided Tom around the space provided by the Mechanics' Institution on Collins Street for the exhibition.

'Goldie, if you please, Captain Rutherford. Though of course the name is ironic.' He gestured to where Tom's works were now displayed. 'We've set you in a prominent spot.'

Tom clenched at what he had done. Soon his imagination would be bared, his private self framed in local wood and hung on a wall. So very many eyes, so many opinions and judgements roving his exposed creations as if across his skin. Would they intuit who he was beyond the surface of the image?

'They've hung very well indeed,' Goldie assured him.

Tom had only ever attended galleries with Catherine at his side, guiding the way. He had only ever been an observer. It had been her hope that he might show his paintings to a London audience, and he'd worked hard to learn his new craft and justify her belief.

He hoped he had enough in him for a single bluff.

By late afternoon the doors opened for the inaugural exhibition of the Victoria Fine Arts' Society, and the atmosphere was fast aswirl. Each wall a study in aspiration and nostalgia. Scenes of Adelaide, where the streets looked too clean; Sydney Harbour, and an idyllic Dights Falls on the Yarra Yarra. There a sleeping nymph, an Italian peasant girl, the interior of a church in Holland. Windsor Castle. Walls made up of juxtaposition, where Europe and the mythology of ancient Greece appeared as strange and distant as the Victorian bush; all of it made unexpectedly foreign by the artist's eye. Goldie's watercolours of the river and bay were affecting, and several women had sculpted flowers out of wax, declaring weeks of painstaking effort. It was the intricacy Tom appreciated. The dedication to a single labour.

Some names were known, but most were obscure – to Tom, at least – and he grew less uneasy. There had been no particular hierarchy to defer to and he did not feel a fraud. The wide and dusty streets of Melbourne were not what Catherine had in mind for his paintings, but he imagined her proud beside him regardless.

He waited, and listened for the quiet conversations as people stood, studied and moved on before his ships.

   . . . the veracity of the rendering . . .

   . . . affecting and unusual tonality of sky and coast . . .

It seemed like honest praise. To his surprise, when later he ran his eyes down the ledger, they would also sell. Paid for with new wealth, untitled and ignoble, dug from this ancient earth in the form of sparkling dust and gleaming nuggets.

When the time came, it would unsettle him to relinquish those ships he had painted for his wife, to witness them held in gloved hands, brought down from the wall, covered in cloth and lifted into the carriages of strangers.

But he had let go of what he had loved before. What he had loved more fiercely.

On that first night, after the doors had shut to the public, Goldie offered a toast.

'To Captain Thomas Rutherford: the artist is a sailor. The sailor is an artist.' Tom's last-minute submission had been a boon for the success of the exhibition, he applauded.

*

It was a small victory, but enough to rouse him. Tom set out his brushes and pigments with fresh determination. Was it too late to put things right?

He re-created all eight ships in miniature oils before they were taken from the walls at the close of the exhibition. Labouring to match the colours and quality of feeling, to recapture the same light and shadow, and the detail of the riggings at such small scale.

Later he parcelled them up, each perfect miniature wrapped in tissue paper, boxed for protection and secured with string, and he addressed the package to London.

Tom could not write to the boy; he did not know where to begin. Instead he signed his pictures of the sea: *T. Rutherford, your father.*

42

Did you see the moon last night where you are? Was it the
same? As full as a gold coin, barely different to the sun,
only more tender. To think of all the times we have observed
the same constellations, each from a different spot on earth.
That we were joined and had no notion of it until we met.
And when we are separate again, still we are not. Have
you noticed how still a night sky is? While Venus burns
bright the moon seems to hang at the neck of midnight, barely
breathing. It is a talent to be able to render such atmosphere
in pigment. Instead I prefer to capture the flame of day, the
pulse of it, the way shadow only makes it appear brighter.

Catherine's many faces were alive for Tom, who opened the
sketchbook each morning in greeting and began to be soothed. She
had seen him and understood, and to know in return the depth of
her heart, her energy and fullness, eased the fact of his loss.

Revived by the exhibition, he sought greater occupation, and felt
a small surge of optimism. That first winter and spring surprised him
with colour. The brightening of wattle flowers into little balls of gold;

the eucalypts that bloomed crimson and lemon and blush. The scent of tea-tree hanging in a fragrant veil after a sudden downpour.

By summer he was ready to return to the water, allowing the *Lady Bird* to draw him in: a sweet little three-masted iron steamer, easy to run, free of pretension. Half of the reputable crewmen around Melbourne had skulked off to dig near Ballarat, but he would need barely twenty bodies. He did not mind that they might be untested, nor where they came from, so long as they proved hardworking and willing beneath his command.

Launceston was a modest 277 nautical miles south across Bass Strait, achievable in two days, but rough passage was guaranteed. Time and again fierce winds would keep the crew labouring for the entire crossing. The waters they must navigate were pressed between the might of the Atlantic to the west and the vast Pacific to the east. And every departure from Melbourne, every arrival, required they navigate Port Phillip Heads, an exactingly slender passage beset with complex eddies, enough to wreck a competent steamer on the rocks.

Stavers at least knew the coast.

'You can grip well enough, if required?' Tom nodded at the American's hands. He had watched him flex his knuckles as if his missing index fingers were still there.

'Still strong enough, sir.'

'Goldfields?'

'No, I had enough of that in California. God-damned best way to wreck a man. No, sir. Hong Kong Bay.'

Short on options for a chief mate, Tom did not push for details.

With each successive dash across the strait, Tom grew fonder of the steamer. When Catherine and Cecilia had proposed the future of steam around the breakfast table all those years ago, and the idea that Tom might one day embrace it, he'd been adamant. But Catherine had understood he'd not shy from progress if the opportunity arose. Steamers had their place. Their reliability over short runs was undeniable, and he found he needed something he could put his faith in.

There was a neatness to his circumference now, and the regularity of the Launceston route meant it was a matter of days before he was back at his easel.

On still mornings the light flared prettily over the water as they arrived at Low Head and waited for the pilot to board. Tom was forever moved by the coastline, by the shimmering light, while sometimes he looked beyond it to a darker fate. Imagining himself in a line of convicts, shuffling with putrid feet down a government gangplank, wary of the possibility of survival. Without Sweet, he could so easily have fallen: a stolen loaf of bread justified by an urgent stomach and the punishment a free ticket to Van Diemen's Land. He had been fortunate. Now transportation was at an end, and he'd sail many a convict to freedom on the mainland with pardons in their pockets.

For the people who had lived there long before any British foot clomped down, there was no reprieve. There had been talk of resistance and warring on the island when the *Aurora* had docked there twenty years before. He'd been warned not to stray from port, told of the organised Black Line of British rifles that had mobilised to rid the island of its 'hostile natives' once and for all, and had damned near succeeded. He'd seen that the land had never been empty.

All such shadow existed beyond the light. Beyond the painter's chosen frame.

Near to the end of December, the early heat was already dense. Tom watched for the signal from the coast. When the oarsman arrived at their side on his own, they discovered the pilot had been delayed, and the silty Tamar up to Launceston lay clogged with vessels.

'Could be several hours,' the man called up to Tom before pushing back off the steamer's side with the blade of one oar.

Tom saw the sky catch at the man's back and redouble its hue in the rippling aqua.

It would be a hopeful scene he worked in watercolour, expansive and in search of salvaged beauty. The reclining sky resting with a soft salmon-pink wash over the coast. Even the lemon-green earth succumbed in the distance to magenta. He lost himself in the reflections that were cast out over the water. The lighthouse on the rocks met its double in the mirror-like surface, with buoys glinting in the foreground as they bobbed in the gentle swell. The sun threw an intense lemon burst across the surface. Cumulus clouds clustered above a shelf of stratus, and wisps of cirrus flecked across the background. Further back still, the empty sky opened up beyond his eye. He'd colour *Lady Bird* last, adding her into the scene with a signature cadmium red band marking her waterline.

'Where are all the people, Tom? Have you learned nothing still?' Catherine's sleeve brushed his own. Her finger assessed his scene. 'Where are you?' He longed to wrap an arm around her waist, burrow his face there. Ask her the same.

He would paint himself into the picture and marvel at how she had revealed herself so inventively in her sketchbook. He was merely a bowed head in the longboat. He wanted to draw her too, facing him as he pulled on the oars, but he knew it was impossible.

He rested his brush. Tested his newly regrown beard with the back of his hand and studied what he had done.

In time it would be Goldie who noted the altered tone in Tom's work as he translated his watercolours and sketches into oils. The artist would continue to visit Tom well into the new year, finding him wherever there was shade along the St Kilda foreshore, after the jetty had washed away in a storm. Tom's paintings had become less urgent, Goldie declared. More studied. More keen on restraint. The detail was there, as always, and stamped him as a mariner, but gone were the tumultuous seas, the assaulted skies. As if an inner evolution had quietly taken place.

Tom kept on, losing himself in paint, commanding his unlikely crew across the strait, and by winter 1854, *Lady Bird* slackened its speed into Hobsons Bay to find a whirl of vessels and a crowd gathered along the shore.

Stavers met him as he moved amidships to get a better view once the anchor had been dropped. 'What in hell, sir?'

There in the bay lay the famous clippers: *Lightning* to port and *Red Jacket* to starboard, their sails dropped to dry in the sun. The details were gleaned from excited mouths as they alighted at the Sandridge pier: *Red Jacket*'s run from Liverpool tallied sixty-seven days. Bully Forbes's *Lightning*, with less favourable winds, made seventy-seven. Wagers worth thousands of pounds were riding on their race for circumnavigation.

Tom planned to return at dawn, curious to meet the relentless Forbes, a Scot renowned for his temper as much as his blistering speeds. But it was more than this that energised him: he knew what his next painting would be.

Instead he woke in a sweat with the sun already risen. They came upon him from nowhere still, these flushes and internal excoriations, his sleeping mind articulating what he held back in the light. He dreamed of James as a newborn, bloodied and crying, and his chest felt tight.

Though a stillness appeared in his paintings now, it was a lie. He emerged from sleep with a question that rose from him in a gasp:

Had he made the right decision?

The sweat washed away, porridge stilling his sickened stomach, he arrived refortified at the harbour to find *Red Jacket* and *Lightning* joined by *James Baines*, and with this fortuitous timing immortalised all three record-breaking clippers on canvas.

Hobsons Bay was charged with gold and silver, its flat, ethereally lit water stretching beneath each hull. Each mast, each stretch of sail stood out against the brooding clouds, which crowded a distant sweep of light blue. In the foreground a shadow darkened the water; in the top left background, a single black harbinger of storm moved into an already cloud-scudded sky, threatening the luminous scene at the centre. In the quarterboat, five figures, white sleeves, two sets of slender oars slipping into the water. Again he drew himself, guiding the boat from stern.

Tom submerged the sensations of his night terrors deep beneath that water; no sense of distress disturbed the surface in his image. He used feeling to his advantage, instilling his art with tenderness and certainty. It was the best method he knew for transmuting his grief, for honouring Catherine and his boy. Such burnished stillness conveyed an emotional gravity that viewers would shake their heads at, caught by a visceral tug, and for many minutes they'd gaze at the scene, reluctant to pull away. Goldie suggested it was love they saw in the picture, and Tom, gratified, knew he had got it right. One of his finest paintings, *Red Jacket* would fetch one hundred and fifty-seven pounds in Goldie's exhibition the following year, and many of his other works would sell too.

Success would break Tom's bayside bolthole wide open. Goldie could not be quiet in his praise, and Thomas Rutherford became a name spoken with familiarity and respect not only among maritime men. His red hair an iconic beacon; his paintings beloved among the colonists. Again Tom re-created his artworks in miniature before they were removed from the gallery walls and transported to their new homes. He parcelled their replicas for London, unsure if those sent two years earlier had ever been received. Nevertheless, he signed each work with the same message as before: *T. Rutherford, your father*.

Success, in the end, unwound him.

As he waited in line at the post office on Bourke Street, the old feelings of regret and shame returned. This time he did not try to dampen them, but let them flare and burn.

43

The plan was simple: Tom would finish his contract on *Lady Bird*. Stavers, freshly ticketed, would replace him, and Tom would follow his paintings to London.

For the first time in his life he journeyed as a cabin passenger, conjuring James next to him as if they were already sailing away together from London, south again across the Line. Without the ship's command to occupy him, he gave space to optimism and grew hopeful, while anxiety and grief smouldered in his bones.

By February 1856 he was disembarking once more at Wapping, four years since he had departed.

Winter again. He knew the layout of the docks, how to navigate them, what to expect, but on this frigid afternoon he arrived as a stranger at what had once been his own door.

Ogilvie House was a haunting. Memories in stasis. The smells of lemon, carbolic soap and over-steeped tea leaves. Catherine on the staircase. The stretch of her, guiding him, ghostly desire in each footstep, everything that was now cold and lost. A feeling that almost brought him to the floor.

And then the warm touch of Cecilia, securing his hands in her own, made him flesh again.

'You bring it all back with you, dearest Tom.'

'Aye, I feel it too.' Hugging her to him, he felt her thinness. He dropped his face to her hair, the dark that had faded wholly to silver. Would Catherine have looked the same at her age? They would never know it.

Pulling away, he looked around, asking the question.

Alfred was not at home, Cecilia assured him. But neither was James.

She led him to the parlour, where they were brought tea with neat slices of lemon. Tom had forgotten how studied, how dainty everything was here. How empty the room felt without Catherine's energy to fill it.

He spilled his questions: how was the boy, now that he had turned seven? Was he happy? How terribly did he miss Catherine? Had the red in his chestnut hair finally ceded to brown? What was his height, how was his voice, what made him laugh?

What he could not ask: did he think of Tom? And if he did, in what way? Was it love that lingered when he thought of his father, or was it hate?

'I will discuss the matter with Alfred. Time must surely have mellowed him,' he confided.

'But Tom, what you speak of is a dream.' The melancholy in Cecilia's voice planted the first seed of precariousness.

'Catherine once described you as defiance,' he urged her.

'I have let you in, have I not? He would not allow it.'

'Where is my son?'

When she sighed, he simply repeated his question with greater insistence, shifting to the edge of his seat, hands flat on his knees. 'Cecilia?'

'Alfred would not permit this.' Nevertheless, she moved to the desk and wrote an address on a small card.

'Go then,' she said, placing the card in Tom's hand and covering it with her own. 'But go quickly. And do not say how you found out.'

More than a mile he dashed on foot across the wintry cobbles, with the closeness of tall brick houses pinning him at his side, their narrow chimneys belching above him.

The address led him to a tutor's residence, secured behind tall wrought iron fencing. He resolved to wait, observing the gate from across the street, for an hour, two, however long it might take for his son to be released. There was plenty of time for Tom to scrutinise his crumpled trousers and spattered boots. The fashionable of London skirted him as he tidied his unruly hair and fended off nausea with every passing minute. But his breath had dropped like a calm sea in the eye of a storm. He would stand here forever if he needed. *Test me if you like, Alfred, you bastard.* Forbearance was a talent, and he had imagined this moment. How he would greet the boy, explain, take his hand.

But when Tom saw his son for the first time in four years, he found himself transfixed. His hair was neither Tom's own red nor Catherine's brown, but a mix entirely particular to James. His features had further refined from their formless infant softness, hinting at the developing personality underneath, and a flash of Catherine's smile stole Tom's strength. Fascinated, he held back, watching the boy emerge from the house and run ahead of a manservant along the white-stoned path to the gate, slinging his leather satchel across his small body, determining on tiptoes to open the frosted latch himself. How proud Tom was in that moment; how proud he knew Catherine would be.

He did not see the carriage at first. His focus was fixed on his son. How long his legs had grown. When he heard James's voice, it scorched him with joy.

'Father!'

He raised his hand in reply, now off the curb, crossing the street towards his boy, ready with an embrace, an explanation. Ready to put his plan in motion.

Once more James picked up speed. His feet were on their way towards the carriage parked a short distance from the gate, calling again.

It was then Tom realised: it was not to him his son had called.

He could not tell if Alfred had been alerted to his arrival, if he had watched Tom wait all this time just steps away. Visible now through the open carriage door, Alfred did not raise his eyes to meet Tom's anger, nor move to salve his pain. He reached a hand to James. He kept his actions neat. Was it a deliberate denial? It did not matter: James was already inside, his face now a curious sphere at the window; the horses were whipped, and the carriage quickly gone.

Had James seen Tom? Had he known him?

The completion of Tom's loss hollowed him. He bent in anguish. A minute, two.

Even then, he imagined he could set things right.

Again through the streets. The northern climate stung; the wind increased its pressure. Gas lights bloomed but darkness fell like a cloak: everything seemed to oppose him. When he banged on the door at the house for a second time that day, determined to make his claim, he could barely feel his hands. He clenched them, held at the ready, his breath billowing heat.

A curtain wavered at a window, releasing a slit of light to the outside. No one answered. Were the servants too under instruction? He banged again, more urgently. Fuelled now. Ready to fight.

Cecilia had warned him earlier that he should not be there, and the understanding that Alfred now certainly knew and was blocking him made Tom heady with rage.

When Cecilia herself eased open the door, drawing a dark knitted shawl across her shoulders, her face calmed him a little.

'Tom, you're so cold.'

As she rubbed at his hands, it hit him again how much she reminded him of Catherine.

He waited, but she did not lead him inside.

'He knows I gave you the address. You did not manage to speak with the boy?'

'You must let me in. I need to reason with him. I won't leave until James is with me.' His tone, low but urgent, required all his control.

'The law is clear: you cannot take James without his consent, and he will not allow it.' Her voice wavering, she held a hand against his chest now.

'He is my son, Cecilia. I must see him.'

'It makes no difference. Alfred has sent for the authorities. He has the papers you signed at the ready.'

'Damn him.' Tom stepped back and looked up at the light glowing in what he knew to be his study. 'Alfred, come out!'

'Tom, please!'

'Alfred!'

He moved in towards her again and made to push at the door above Cecilia's shoulder.

'Tom! Tom, listen. This will not distress my nephew. It will only distress your son.'

Though he called out again, he was aggrieved to find his resolve giving way. He moved his head involuntarily, both agreeing and not.

Cecilia's hand still pressed at his chest. She did it to block his way. He knew it, and yet it was the single most intimate gesture anyone had offered him since Catherine died.

'Hang the police.' He was wretched.

'I beg you not to risk yourself. Who will they believe?'

'I'll get a lawyer of my own.'

She shook her head. 'Think of it, Tom. You saw James? Before returning here?'

'Briefly.' He pressed at his temples. 'He is grown, so much, and looks well.'

'He is. You need not be concerned for James's welfare. He is loved and cared for.'

He felt both relieved and betrayed to know it true.

'He looks like his mother.' He almost begged her.

'Yes, he does.'

Tom became quiet then, as soft as sandstone, worn away, and so she continued. 'He is cared for, and loved, and knows peace now. Hold on to that memory, Tom; take it with you when you go. Know that you have chosen the right path.'

Cecilia slid her arm around him, leading them away from the house. He turned again, watching for the door, for the small body that should run with its satchel over a shoulder towards him, but theirs was the only movement, and he allowed her to take him to safety.

Though Tom accepted he had not the power to change Alfred's mind, it would not stop him stalking the house each day for a month. It was as if its residents had halted all movements to convince him they did not exist, or that he himself were a ghost. And the law was watching. He could not risk it. A peeler walked the street routinely, shaking the gate to check it remained secure. Another he saw stationed near the front door. He was not a criminal. He had to restrain himself from striding up and saying so into the policeman's face. He was not even a father any more. Alfred had shown him that.

How quickly he fell into old habits again. Two more years measured out by the surety of the bells. Making port beneath a shroud of canvas, settling into his role as captain as though it would be his last, fixing his sight on the waters before him.

He swore he would never again rest upon land.

He joined the Canton trade, and in the following spring raced the Americans back to Liverpool with the early harvest of tea, swifting the fragrant leaves to market first so the merchants could trade it at the highest price. He wrote to Seamus care of the port office in Liverpool – short missives that lacked detail – and used his constant watch of the sea and the responsibility of command like an opiate to blur the pain. Craving the anaesthesia of forgetting, he was fair but aloof with his crew, and grateful that his surgeon, a teetotalling Welshman, was not the kind to broker private confidence with his captain.

But feeling, as it always did, crept back, a shadow on every watch. Aiming his sextant at the horizon, fixing on the harshness of a southern sun, he could see neither future nor ending. The nights became long, the view from stern an unreadable narrative.

They came to him then in the light of a lamp. Ghosts, in a way: his ma, his da, and then Sweet, and he understood there was legacy there, a debt that ought to be honoured. Perhaps there was a way through it all if he would give himself the chance to discover it.

When finally he allowed Catherine to come to him, she rested her spectral body on top of him where he lay and he imagined touching a thumb to the soft flesh of her elbow. His fingers in a gentle clasp held her close again, and it was over. She told him so herself.

That is enough, Tom.

Two months later he found he was not sad to pass through the Heads. Port Phillip Bay opened up with familiar light haze and his first steps ashore were a salve of eucalypt and warm sandy earth.

Returning to Alma Road, he lay down in his empty room, restored to him by Mrs Mitchell. He had sold or given away all his paintings except for a single one that he had carried on the long journey back from London. This he would never sell, never paint over. It hung now at the end of his bed and he woke only to lose himself in it each morning. Catherine's hand was there in the detail: the green hatpin she had painted for the sailor in the longboat. He had not thought to take the painting with him when he left after she died. He had not thought of taking much back then, except the boy, whom he could not.

This time Cecilia had found Tom at the docks before he embarked, confessing she had taken the painting from Tom and Catherine's former bedroom after the disturbance at the door, fearing it would otherwise be removed and lost. The small figure in the longboat would be missed, she had confided, touching him on the chest one last time, but it was right she should go with him.

His son would know that Tom loved him, though they must live apart. Cecilia would make sure of it.

The mizzenmast should be shorter. Tom knew it definitely as he lay on his bed, unmoving, until the room was again in darkness.

44

You cannot know how much I have resented you at times.
How I wished to be you. Would it shock you to know it?
Slowly, though, this falls away. I become more content with
what riches I have, and work as an alchemist must work,
turning a world bounded by garden pebbles into something
greater and golden. Still, though we are apart, you are here in
the light of this room, the paint on my brush, the flick of our
son's hair as it settles at his nape – it behaves the same way
as yours does. The touch of you I feel even in your absence.
Love, once found, does not retreat simply because our bodies
are apart. Nothing I do is without you. You move, I move
with you. We are strong enough to stretch across oceans; there
is plenty of us to cover all the world.

Grief distorted everything. It caused the past to seep, and could change a person's vision. The ideas it seeded in Tom grew with a peculiar and propulsive logic.

He had cut through the bluestone laneway on his return from the colourman's studio on the east end of Collins Street. A small pile of tiles had been abandoned against the brick wall midway down. On impulse he stopped and turned, dropping into a crouch. Square, cream, ceramic. They were each the size of his hand. Some broken, most only slightly chipped.

Whenever he'd lain back to soak in the bathtub at Ogilvie House, his eyes had roamed the illustrated tiles that covered the wall beyond his feet. Blue painted on white. He'd search among their number for those Catherine said she loved most as a child: the girl with her face to the sky, holding a basket of tulips. A Dutch windmill. A nimble hare. A swordsman on a rearing horse. There was a three-masted ship in full sail – a fluyt, Tom thought – and a figure of indeterminate sex – Catherine refused to believe it was a man – who wore pantaloons and had raised a telescope to their eye.

He could see that blue-and-white tiled wall again as he picked through and chose several of the discarded ceramic squares. Early the following morning, he sat himself at the table under his bedroom window with brush and indigo ink. He selected the first piece. It was small enough for him to make a tentative start. Its surface capable of taking a design. The result would be utterly private.

On this first attempt he gripped too hard, and a sharp edge on the underside of the tile surprised him almost as much as his enjoyment of the pain. The sight of his own deep-red blood rivering down his index finger reminded him that he was still alive, despite those nights when he woke in the coldest hour and felt his pulse dip and careen.

Catherine had shown him what was possible in her self-portraits, and now he sought to honour her request from long ago. For the first time, he attempted to re-create her face.

The new year came, 1859, and he practised both his arts: one public, framed and displayed with pride on respectable walls around

Melbourne; the other furtive, inked for no other eyes to see. In one he chased immortality. In the other, release.

'Charlie, sir,' the boy said.

Tom was again in the lane, selecting more tiles to take back to his room, when he was alerted by the boy's breathing. It came almost as shallow as his own. Twisting on his haunches, he discovered the sad mouths of two leather boots, barely holding together. Further up, two deep-set eyes in the face of a sandy-haired child, dirt-smudged, perhaps similar in age to James. When Tom stood and asked the boy's name, he wasn't sure which of them wore a greater expression of humility: Charlie, for skulking in a laneway where no cared-for child need be, or Tom, for having revealed an unfathomable, private fragility.

'What's it you got there, sir?'

Tom held a completed ink portrait of Catherine in one hand, brought with him from Alma Road. He'd had the peculiar notion of resting her there as a kind of exchange, allowing her to bear witness to his grief while he attempted both to bring her back to life and to let her go. A critic or dealer would be sure to look twice at Tom's oils were they to uncover such aberrant impulse. But this boy was hardly one of those.

He considered his response and decided on simplicity. 'It's my wife,' he replied, holding out the tile and knowing it was strangeness he offered.

Charlie accepted the face of Catherine with two grubby palms. Assiduous in his study of the inked portrait, he asked, 'Why's she on the tile, sir?'

'I'm not sure.' Tom could only be honest.

Perhaps grief is best dealt with in offcuts, he had thought when first he began the ritual. The tiles he'd found were pocked with irregularities, their glazed surfaces cracked and threaded with vein-like fissures that made it difficult to create an accurate likeness. And despite all his experience and skill, he still could not create her image on canvas: in life, her features had challenged him with their mutability, the quickness beneath them; in death, there was too much expanse into which the forgetting could take hold.

'I'd like to have a picture of my mother,' Charlie said, 'but I would want it in a giant frame on the wall so I could look at her when I couldn't sleep.'

Tom thought of Charlie waking from his dreams in the darkness, but instead he saw himself in a child's bed, opened his eyes in a child's body, and felt what it was to be a boy again.

'Perhaps I can ink you a picture.' Tom didn't know what he was offering.

'She has no face that I know of, least that I remember. Pa always said she was beautiful, though.'

'Where is your father?' For all Tom's warmth, he had to resist the urge to snatch Catherine back from the boy, to cradle her image before placing her face, drawn in Prussian-blue ink, onto a window ledge; to touch his fingers to his lips, say her name once, and walk away. He knew this wasn't right. But it was the most luxurious discomfort to feel he might let go of it all so easily.

'Don't know where he is.' Charlie tilted his head at Tom. 'Not for a long time, sir.'

As if intuiting Tom's intention, the boy ran a careful finger over Catherine's face. When finally he offered up the tile, his eyes were full of persuasive scrutiny, so that Tom, acquiescing to their implicit request, returned Catherine safely to his pocket.

'Don't have no home, sir,' Charlie whispered. 'I'm hungry, sir.'

*

At the nearest hotel, the publican eyed them but made no comment as his wife delivered a bowl of stew and a plate of bread and cheese to the table. Glad to avoid enquiry, Tom tried to pick it all apart. There was regret at being denied the execution of his private indulgence, and a sense he was being asked to return from the dead. Though he could not know what Charlie's presence meant, he was certain of what it would not lead to. The boy would be fed, given some coins, and that would be it.

'Wash your hands. You're not at sea,' Tom said.

Charlie reached for the cheese.

'Wash your hands!' Tom pointed across the dining room to the dark-stained door.

When Charlie returned, he kept his face low and slid like water onto the chair.

'And use a spoon for that stew.'

He worked the utensil so fast that Tom could barely follow. It was a silver arc, painted between the plate and Charlie's mouth.

Next the boy shredded bread between his teeth and swallowed loudly. Gulped down water. Filled his mouth again.

Tom knew the deep ache of a stomach exhausted into emptiness. As a child he had sometimes felt light-headed, waiting for his da to return with fish for their plates. He had known the urgent pangs caused by heavy labour when he was an apprentice at sea, and was thankful that James never would.

Tom swirled his ale as the image of his own son superimposed itself on the figure seated across from him at the table.

He was back in the nursery at Ogilvie House. James, kneeling on the floor with his dressing-gown tails flung behind him and a brightly illustrated book open on his lap. James raising his face as Tom kissed him goodnight. 'Papa?' Tom brushing the boy's hair from his eyes, nodding in affirmation.

Did Alfred now do the same? When Tom thought of his brother-in-law, it was as Turner might have rendered the man: a swirl of umber and white, pierced with blue-green. Those Ogilvie eyes. Tom would never set such a thing in paint himself, but in his mind, that was what he saw. A menacing imprecision.

He had misjudged how it would go, of course. Charlie, once fed, coins in his pocket, became soporific. He flinched when Tom guided him back to the laneway where he had found him. The autumn air had cooled and their breaths shimmered eerily against the bluestone.

'Where were you staying before? Can you not return there?'

Charlie's outstretched arms clutched at Tom's jacket. As the boy tipped with weariness, Tom saw the mottled bruising above his wrists. When he checked his doleful mouth and found the gums inflamed, he gave in with a sigh. He knew the symptoms. The boy would need lemon juice.

'One night,' he said, quick and firm. 'No more.'

Tom made up a bed of blankets on his floor at Alma Road, inserting his own pillow beneath the head of the already sleeping boy.

'Damn,' he whispered to no one as he lay there uncovered, his head flat to his mattress. 'Damn it all.'

He dreamed again. Unsure of how deep he was, or how much breath he had left. All around him, a murky sea. Nothing but a green-black room of water. His hands searched, directionless, rotating like oars in front of him.

Sweaty and overheated he woke with the early light. Tom had been a strong swimmer since he was a child, ever since his da had thrown him overboard into the Forth and compelled him to save himself. Moving against the prevailing tide had once been an enjoyable challenge, a kind of creative pleasure. Perhaps, he thought, it was this same contrary determination that had led him to stay in

London, marry above his rank and forge his ambition in places he was not meant to.

A soft whistling sound from the small figure on the floor.

Charlie.

The boy who threatened to depend on him.

The boy he wanted to be another boy.

The boy he wished he could toss overboard with all his unwanted memories.

The boy he longed to be again himself.

45

Tom touched a hand to the back of his neck. At the open sash window, sun-bleached curtains, swaying. A memory of Catherine's summery skirts. His skin was burning.

Mrs Mitchell had served a special request of fried eggs with golden yolks that left buttery grease stains on their plates. His face close to his meal, Charlie did not pause. Sweat hovered precipitously on his lip as he ate.

'You spoil the boy, Captain.' Mrs Mitchell wiped two irritated palms down the front of her eggshell-coloured apron.

Tom did not agree. He'd known deprivation and plenitude, and this was not the latter. After eight months of regular feeding, Charlie still coveted each meal like the first.

He glanced at the clock on the mantelpiece. Almost noon. The walk from Sandridge in the December sun would be punishing. Seamus had been informed of Tom's failure in London, but what exactly would he make of this?

Half an hour later the doctor's leather bag dropped to the floor in the doorway, a discarded jacket quickly following. Tom, impulsive with pleasure and embarrassment, pushed back his chair with a rising exclamation. Seamus had barely wiped his wrist over his brow in the wake of Tom's embrace before his eyes darted to the young boy crunching on egg-soaked crusts at the breakfast table. He looked back at Tom, full of incredulity.

'Tom? Why, I thought . . .'

'Aye, Seamus. Calm yourself a moment.'

'James?' The doctor came closer, head on one side, peering at the boy.

Tom shook his head, his eyes full of warning. His cheeks aflush.

'Charlie, this is Seamus. He's the best damned surgeon you'll find this side of the Line.'

Charlie swallowed, paused, looked up.

'What do you say?'

'Pleased to meet you, sir.'

'Tom?'

'Aye, Seamus. We'll need whisky, and lots of it, my friend.'

After waking on Tom's floor that first morning, ministered with a large dose of lemon juice and warm salted porridge, Charlie had been less inclined to leave.

'Where is your father, Charlie? Perhaps we can find him. Where was your last home? Do you remember?'

The second morning, Tom said, 'There is a place, Charlie, for boys like you. I can organise it. I'm sure it wouldn't be so bad.'

'Please, sir. I can work and earn my keep, I swear it.'

Something would have to be done. The boy couldn't continue to sleep in Tom's room. He couldn't be sent back to sleep in the streets. Tom didn't have the heart.

In the kitchen he found his sweat-browed landlady at work with a large ball of dough. It had not been easy to persuade her.

'The boy should be in the orphanage, Captain Rutherford.' She wiped her face with a sinewy forearm and resumed kneading.

'It's a temporary solution.'

'I won't be responsible for every ragtag child left to his own wits in those streets out there. You'd better not be thinking of bringing any more beneath my roof.'

But she needed help in the sinks and with the coal scuttle, axe and broom. And there was a small room, empty now that her own son had followed his father inland to seek what fortune could still be made from the dwindling gold.

'I've got diggers banging on the door every day for a bed, Captain Rutherford. They'd sleep under a table if I let them.' Her flour-caked hands perched on her hips.

Tom placed a handful of shillings on the table. 'Some extra for the boy's board.'

She narrowed her eyes and counted them out.

'Don't expect me to mother him,' she called after him.

That was the last thing Tom expected.

He explained it briskly to the boy. 'Mrs Mitchell needs some help around the lodging, Charlie. In return you'll have a warm room of your own and food in your stomach.'

Charlie's pinched face stretched into a grin. 'Thank you, sir, for looking after me.'

'It's only until you are well.' Tom would have to be clear. 'I can't be a father to you.'

Charlie considered this a moment. 'Why not? I have no other. You have no son.'

Tom paused before answering. What the boy said was true. 'It's not in me to do so.'

'I would be good.'

'That's not the problem,' Tom snapped.

The boy peered at him still.

'At the end of the month, Charlie, we must say goodbye.'

Charlie would sleep when Tom slept, eat when he ate. He helped Tom carry his painting supplies to the newly built pier each morning, and Tom taught him how to clean the bright pigment from his brushes. Together they studied the skies from the foreshore and watched the maritime world play out on the bay.

The end of the month passed.

By day it was easy. At night Charlie would beg as Tom sent him to his bed. 'Another day, sir. Please, let me have another day.'

Tom needed him to leave willingly. He couldn't abandon the boy.

He brought out his broken-spined book with Coleridge's poem and read it aloud at night. He couldn't work out if it was for Charlie he read, or for his own son, who would never hear the words, or for the boy who had been forced to leave his ma at Leith with his father already lost at sea.

'Do you know your letters, Charlie?'

'Some, sir.'

But the boy could not read. Tom sounded out vowels and consonants with a rounding and elongating of his mouth.

'Now you try.'

As Charlie grew, Tom let out the hem on his trousers. Kneeling at the boy's feet and biting the thread with his teeth.

'Did your wife teach you that?' Charlie asked.

'No.' Tom laughed. 'She could stitch but it was purely decorative. Mending was done downstairs, out of view, like magic.' He straightened the finished hem, sitting back on his heels. 'Any sailor can sew. I'll teach you, if you like.'

When Charlie caught his first fish from the pier and determined to reel it in without Tom's help, a feeling of pride took Tom by surprise.

Reluctantly he saw he'd underestimated. The bond had set on both sides.

He wondered if, despite everything, he was capable of loving still. It was a feeling, an action, that had been stored in him. Potent but barely used.

Even so, he'd shown himself unworthy of devotion. He didn't deserve a second chance.

'Are you sure you can't think of anyone, any family? Someone who might provide a permanent home?'

'My mother was a laundry maid, sir, I know that. And my father worked with coal, black on his hands and face, eyes like empty saucers when he arrived home. Hardly enough to eat. Less after she died. And then . . .'

Charlie wasn't sure of his own story after that.

The diggings, Tom thought. Gold did devilish things to desperate men. It wasn't at all the same as his situation, he reasoned. He had not left his son to fend for himself.

Later Charlie added, 'Born on the ship, sir, so I was told.'

But he was not of the sea. Tom could tell by the way the boy tracked the water at his feet, alert to its movement. He would shy away, stepping back whenever it broke with unanticipated force against the piling.

Charlie had spent months of his life crouching in doorways for shelter, sneaking through windows for bread. He did not know how old he was.

'Don't know what year it is neither, sir.'

'Well, it's 1859.' He looked at Charlie. He was small, but that was likely the impoverishment. 'Let's say you are ten.'

When standing at a distance, unafraid for his safety, Charlie expressed fascination in the repetition of waves as they skimmed along the beach. Tom agreed: it was a marvellous thing to watch, but this was just the bay. Past the Heads, you'd see a powerful furling that rose in both height and momentum before dropping, dispersing into white foam, drawing back out to sea. You could clear your mind staring at those waves, remake yourself, find your energy, he said. He didn't expect Charlie to understand.

'I always dreamed of a bathtub, but this is bigger even than that,' Charlie said. Against the line between sky and water, tall ships and steamers moved imperceptibly in the warm northerly, and the smell of the town blew over the pier and out to sea.

'True enough.' Tom laughed. 'Let's say this is just the beginning.'

Along the foreshore, distant figures were lugging and scaling and hammering as new bath houses were constructed. Tom shielded his eyes, then returned to the water. 'Would you like to get lost out there, Charlie?'

'Lost?' Charlie hesitated. 'I don't know about that, sir. I've been lost before and didn't fancy it much. Don't fancy drowning neither. But my pa did once tell me off for thinking too much about adventure and I never did much learning.'

'I was only a few years older than you when I set off for sea. My ma taught me to read and write, and I did the rest of my learning on board ships, between scrubbing the decks and polishing the captain's brass till it shone. But it's learning that gets us somewhere, Charlie.'

'You don't talk much like a sailor, sir. You sound more like some gentleman.'

'Some wouldn't agree with you. Some would say the circumstances of your birth can never be shaken. But it's true my own ma would struggle to recognise me at times.'

'Why's that?'

'Well, I suppose in part because I haven't seen her in years.' Tom smiled at him. 'She died not long after I left home.'

He'd often imagined what he did not see: his mother lying trapped under the wheel of the cart, her hip smashed and her head wrenched away towards the Forth. The horse pulling at the harness and thrashing its head. The lightning-scorched sky. Each time, he saw crimson blood, the indigo of his mother's dress, white tips on the grey of the firth, and the violet of thistles by the roadside. Strong colours, intense colours; colours that rendered indisputable reality from an imaginative landscape. Without this palette of certainty, there would be too many questions left unanswered.

The low-hanging sun cast two skinny shadows with elongated limbs as Tom and Charlie stood side by side on the St Kilda pier. One was almost twice the height of the other. Tom allowed his imaginings to go further: he was back on the quarterdeck; Charlie was his apprentice. Having given up the Atlantic, Seamus would soon be free to join them as surgeon. It wasn't so far-fetched.

Tom felt Charlie's eyes upon him.

A captain could use a trustworthy and quick cabin steward. He'd been given the chance himself once. And the boy needed to earn his way.

It didn't mean he had forgotten.

'Where is your wife, sir?' Charlie's voice was barely audible.

'It's just me, Charlie. It's just me.'

The water churned beneath them, thumping against the pilings.

'I wouldn't have to call you "Father".'

Tom focused on the damp algae-green wood rising out of the water. He felt queasy, but the sea wasn't the cause.

46

Though his work with the tiles had soothed him at first, the power of it waned. The ceramic squares were too small to depict Catherine with the nuance and depth she deserved, and too large for it not to matter.

Only Charlie knew of Tom's unusual habit. Only Charlie could look at him without pity, accepting whatever came his way, as early hardship had taught him to do. And so, not long after Seamus returned, Tom replaced the lid on his ink pot, set upon his windowsill the only tile bearing a decent likeness to Catherine, and discarded the rest.

In time he would learn to populate his oil paintings as Catherine had always desired him to: a blue-jacketed sailor on a sloping deck would extend his hand to a woman in white gloves, the clipper *Caribou* racing on, confident with the wind. The figures would be small against such a great background, so he would not have to concern himself with fixing Catherine's features in a single expression. But this would take time. Until then, he painted himself into the longboat, heading out to sea: a man of varying dress – sailor, artist – accompanied by small, unidentifiable figures at oar in the foreground.

*

The new decade arrived: 1860. When a two-year position as master of the *Pirate* was offered, Tom accepted, with Seamus signing on as ship's surgeon. Though his stomach was often unsettled, Charlie would prove a passable steward as they pressed back and forth across the turquoise Tasman Sea between Melbourne and Port Chalmers, New Zealand. Twelve, thirteen days at sea each time, carrying Her Majesty's mail south.

As the bells rang out after supper on those long, luminous nights and the watches switched seamlessly, Tom emerged on deck for air, greeting his passengers with a touch of his hat. Though the wind was fresh, their passage was the result of hardworking engineers, firemen and trimmers below, toiling with boiler and engine, responding to Tom's various commands with the desired speed. The persistent chug of the engine room had become a beat of confidence. Pipe in mouth, Tom relaxed at the rail, taking weight on his forearms: a demonstration of what years of sea living did for one's balance. His hands laced together high above the pearly wake cut by the steamer's deliberate hull. Sometimes he imagined Catherine beside him, sharing the garish drama of the sunset as they put it all at their backs. He smiled at her exhilaration, saw her lifting her face into the wind.

When the pain had subsided, memory turned out to be a magician. Catherine was always with him, her face and words in the sketchbook just part of the reminder, her love still warm at his shoulders. He thought of the poem by Donne she had treasured, written out more than once in her looping hand, and its lines: *Thy firmness makes my circle just, And makes me end where I begun.* He knew what she meant by this, and it brought him comfort.

In his youth Catherine had shown him what he would not have seen on his own: an image of himself in a tri-fold mirror, both multiple and connected. In his advancing age, she was still holding up a mirror, and helping him rebuild all the pieces.

Tom woke at anchor on the flat palm of Otago Harbour, sheltered from the Pacific by the long peninsula, a nodule on the rugged east coast of New Zealand's South Island. The bright, pelagic scent and potent sheen of daylight filled his lungs with easy breath.

The crew of the *Pirate* would be hard at work already, both above him and below, and each morning the reliable Charlie came knocking at his door with coffee pot in hand, reporting eagerly on the activities at port and above decks.

'Seamus is draining a boil, sir. The sky looks like someone lit a flare and tossed it into the clouds. The engineer says he's fixed that piston.'

'Aye, he reported so late last night.'

If he wasn't needed above, Tom reached for his sketchbook after that first sip of hot, metallic caffeine, wanting to capture the light over the hills and the water at its freshest. Larger sailing ships were anchored further out in the harbour, visited by lighters, and several smaller steamers lined up closer into shore and at the jetty. A whaleboat that had been transformed into a schooner with a painted bow made its way up from the Māori settlement at Ōtākou. Tom gave life to his observations in charcoal and watercolour as he had as a boy, thinking back to when he'd first sketched his old captain's padded figure against the blustering sea.

Whenever time allowed, Tom packed up his oils and a tin lunch box, enjoying the discovery of a sheltered spot under the brow of a ragged cliff near to port, surrounded by flax and the feather-like plumes of tall grass called toetoe. He tried to convey the feeling of this small but bustling place where summers threw a veil of pearlescent light and winters came opaque and harsh, just as they did in Scotland. For the first time, he tried to do so in words, too, beginning a practice of private notes and descriptions alongside his sketches, and occasionally becoming expansive.

Though Charlie still offered to carry his paints and easel to shore, and took time with Tom to observe the changing hue of the harbour – alternately churned into a despondent grey or flattened into a tranquil, glittering aquamarine – he would leave Tom alone and return to his steward's tasks, and an ever-more avid application to his studies. He'd lean so close to the flame with his books after supper that Tom, a hand at the boy's forehead, would have to warn him not to singe himself.

Tenacious, resilient, a quick learner, Charlie reminded Tom of himself as a young boy, but although he had taken to his reading with surprising aptitude, the boy's stomach for voyaging remained poor. Tom had hoped he would grow accustomed to the movement beneath him, but he knew it could not last for long, this kind of living. He would need to make a decision.

In the end, it was Seamus who fell ill. The doctor lay in bed for a fortnight, feverish and coughing, weakly issuing Tom and Charlie with instructions for tending him. A dose of this, a compress of that, an extra blanket, and then one less. A dousing in a storm off the west coast of the South Island had set a clammy treachery into his chest. Attentive at Seamus's bed, Charlie had a light touch, keeping him comfortable whenever Tom was required above.

At night, when his friend lay rising and falling between sleep and waking, Tom worked the idea over, thinking himself safe in Seamus's confusion. He placed the fragments together and began to see how they might fit into a new shape.

'Maybe we need something other than this, Seamus.' Tom swept his gaze around the doctor's cabin. It was far smaller than Tom's own, with a porthole view out to sea. The doctor had framed a photograph of himself with Maeve, Patrick and the bairns – and another man, who by looks had to be Seamus's brother. His medicines and instruments were secured in the ship's chest, but his medical books were stowed on a shelf above his desk, with an ink pot and a notebook to record indications, diagnoses, treatment, prognoses. Perhaps those pages would receive his private thoughts, too, some of which Tom fancied he knew already, the rest he knew he did not – and he enjoyed the idea that his friend might have this other life, something just for himself.

But was it enough?

He discovered he had said it out loud.

If Seamus's eyes registered disbelief, he had no voice to put to it.

Tom disbelieved the notion himself. But he'd dropped a kind of anchor now, and felt curiosity at what strange terrain it had caught on.

'Something to see us into our ageing,' he said. 'Something for the boy.'

When Seamus was up and walking, leaning on Charlie as he emerged into the fresh air, he nodded his agreement.

'I feel you have a plan, Tom. And apparently I am no longer a young man.'

'Inspector of Steamers, here at Port Chalmers. What do you think?'

'I think I'm listening to a different man. What have you done with my friend?'

'The position's free for the right fellow.'

'And you think that might be you? A post on land?'

315

Charlie was quiet, deciphering the words of one man and then the other, eyes roving, propping up Seamus in the swell.

'Were you not listening to the plan, Seamus?' Tom laughed, and as the sun shifted behind the mast Charlie and Seamus watched on as one side of his face became illuminated with a golden glow, as if a mask were dropping.

47

Magnetic Street. Perhaps his direction had been plotted to the south all along.

His signature drying on the contract, the money paid, Tom had surveyed the land one final time. A vein of regret pulsed through the optimism. He pushed it aside. What harm could it do to accept it now, to allow himself the pleasure of this small satisfaction?

They would soon live here, in a house on the hill overlooking the harbour, an odd shipwrecked family washed up at the southern reaches of the globe. In the past he'd propelled himself to new ports to escape a darkness. This time, it would be different. When next his helmsman navigated Taiaroa Head and steered them up the harbour towards Port Chalmers, when Tom traced the peninsula's now-familiar ridges of bush and fern scrub, it would be by choice, the embracing of a future.

Charlie was by now little different in age to Tom when he had first left Leith, though it was clear he would always be without sea legs. The poor boy had lost his stomach almost every time the steamer passed through the reliably rough Foveaux Strait to round the southern coast.

Now Tom broke the news: he would command the clipper *Lightning* for their final passage from Melbourne to Port Chalmers.

'Just one more voyage, Charlie, but under sail, so you'll know the true skill of a sailor.'

Their hold was full of rabble, almost a thousand diggers embarking with pans and picks still caked in silt, deserting the Victorian goldfields for the alluvial workings in Otago, where the yellow dust would either make them or ruin them entirely. Within days Tom was forced to confiscate booze and break up fistfights, confining the worst offenders below. Unafraid to lay down the law, he did not come off unscathed.

'You're lucky that fellow didn't break your nose, Tom.'

Seamus angled his face towards the light and felt along a cheekbone. 'You'll live. But you'll be less pretty for a time.'

'He was as stout and brawny as a tug, sir,' Charlie consoled, watching the way Seamus tested the bone for breaks. He handed Tom a muslin cloth wrung with cold water to apply to his skin, which would burn scarlet at first, deepen to a puce bruising, then give in to the hue of jaundice.

'Damned rogues.' Tom tasted blood and spat over the side. 'They're out of their minds. Forgotten how to control themselves.'

'I could hear the filthy protests from the hold on my way up.'

'The Bluff will be far enough, Seamus.'

'Oh?'

'They can find their own bloody way north from there.'

He wanted peace aboard, not to have to play gaoler. Days of stern enforcement followed, but when the time came to slip through the stormy strait, Tom stuck to his word, despositing the men at the frigid tip of the South Island before continuing up the coast.

It was a relief to trace those final miles with a calm and orderly hold. A day out from Taiaroa Head, the Pacific surged against the hull in an impenetrable inkiness, the ropes and wind singing beneath a burnished sky of constellations. The Southern Cross guided them without need of the glass.

Perhaps it was the quiet on board, the isolation, the lengthening distance, the feeling of no return. Tom had a sense that life was lived in half circles. Unable to see the whole: what truths, what stories lay beyond our perspective? All that we would not understand, until history, too late, provided the long vision.

Supper had been cleared hours ago. Charlie was at his books, despite his sickness, and soon for his bed. The bone-chill of evening seemed to be waiting above, shallow-breathed. Tom buttoned his jacket against it. Seamus, drawing on his pipe at Tom's side, allowed him to talk.

He had been naive, that much was certain. Yet it wasn't clear-cut. If there had been weakness in his choice, there had also been strength. It remained the greatest sacrifice he had ever been pressed to make.

'She found it hard to bring him into the world. I almost lost them both, and then we were so grateful to have him. We wanted James to have brothers and sisters but it wasn't to be. Catherine joked that perhaps we had used up all our chits with the heavens.'

'Do you believe God keeps a ledger?'

'Don't ask me, Seamus. If God exists, I don't understand Him, nor His designs.'

'I can offer no clarity, Tom. I am, after all, a man of science.'

'So here we are.'

Seamus blew on his hands. 'Gone are the days of flinging holy water over a body and praying for mercy. My faith is in education, in our modern developments. I believe in medicine, chemistry, biology. Whether or not there is an overriding plan, it does not matter to me. I do my best to heal the body even when the mystical fails us. When we cannot make sense of what befalls us.'

Tom nodded, mulling it all. After a while, he asked: 'Do you regret never marrying?'

'Speaking of what we cannot make sense of, you mean?' The doctor shifted his weight against the rail. 'I suppose there is some regret but I am happy enough. Like you, the sea has kept me company.'

'Circumstance was at play, as it always is.'

'How would you have managed back then, Tom? You would not have been satisfied with coastal trots between London and Leith your whole life.'

'I was for a time. And when I wasn't, everything changed.'

'Coincidence.'

'Perhaps I should have made a choice. Given up one or the other. I tried, once.'

'I remember. And I never want to see your hands like that again.'

Tom unfurled each fist and studied the tiny white lines that wove a faint lattice still. Even now he sought a way to find balance: land and sea, art and sail. He felt it closer now than ever. That an orphan boy recovered from a bluestone alley might have helped him on this path surprised him, warmly and sharply.

'Now it seems a contradiction, and too late, that I am ready to commit myself to land.'

'We all change, Tom. We must.'

'After Catherine's death I ran to the sea and let it take hold of me. It was a way to forget. And a way to remake myself, too, I suppose.'

'A deliberate drowning?'

Tom pressed a hand against his chest, stifling a sudden cough. 'Just the wind.' The doctor was not long over his own illness and had become alert for any sign in Tom.

Seamus nodded. 'And your ships on canvas? It must be hundreds you've painted by now, and gained reputation for them. Is it the same feeling?'

'I suppose they're what comes out of that feeling. Catherine talked about painting as a translation of some raw force in us.' He laughed. 'She understood so much.'

'She certainly seemed to.'

For a quiet moment they leaned at the rail, and then Seamus pushed himself upright off the brass, calling, 'Time for a glass of something, Captain.'

And Tom agreed, dropping an arm to Seamus's shoulder.

48

From Observation Point, high above Otago Harbour, Tom saw how it might unfold. Slips and yards could be built. A graving dock for repairs. The George Street jetty would need enlarging to accommodate the influx of steamers and sailing ships that passed Taiaroa Head each week to anchor in the deep lower harbour.

Port Chalmers too had gold as its constellation. The glint in alluvium was responsible for many a foundation stone as the village fattened into a town. Unlike the broad arc of Port Phillip, the harbour here was long and curving, knobbled with bays and points. Like a sea serpent, Tom thought. Or a bent leg, Port Chalmers at its knee. Stunningly rugged. Much of the peninsula was still thick and imposing with ferns, flax and mānuka, towering tōtara and rimu, but land was being cleared apace.

Wooden cottages already speckled the slopes around port, and buildings were emerging block by block, board by board, from the dust along George Street. A chemist shop, which doubled as the post office. Three hotels, offset by the hillside gaze of two churches – Protestant both – looking down on it all.

On the harbour below, ketches and whaleboats returned silvered and slick with cod, mullet and flounder, heading up to the jetty at Dunedin. Kāi Tahu fishers and their ancestors had caught hāpuku, barracouta and crayfish on these waters for centuries. They knew the seasons, what lived where, how to harvest it. Their knowledge had surely been a boon to all those who came after. They'd kept the whalers fed, and then the settlers from Britain, who now contended on the water for the fisheries trade in ever-growing numbers.

Tom had bought crays from Māori fishers who'd sailed up the peninsula from Ōtākou. The creatures were a deep healthy green, freshly taken from the sea, and were being sold for a bargain straight from the pots. It was strange the fishers hadn't taken their catch further up the harbour to sell at market in Dunedin, but Charlie's eyes had almost watered with anticipation, and that night Tom had boiled three huge specimens in salty water over the fire. They watched the crays transform from green to a magnificent red as they were cooked, and then they ate, speechless with pleasure as the juices rivered between their fingers and soaked into their shirt cuffs.

Since the signing of the Treaty more than twenty years earlier, large blocks of Kāi Tahu land had been purchased by the Crown for a modest few thousand pounds, and with promises to provide hospitals and schools and reserves of land so the natives might flourish.

Ship after ship of immigrants had followed, mostly Scots, to make a new life. Eight miles from port in the shallow upper harbour, the newcomers had set to building up the town of Dunedin in the image of something foreign, something northern: Edinburgh.

To Tom's surprise, it felt like a home he had almost forgotten. The Water of Leith meandered between grassy banks, and he recognised the burr of his own accent in the voices of many he met in town. They had journeyed here through an impulse he understood:

the desire for expansion, to be creators, to be something more than what they were born to.

It would take a year to prepare the section on Magnetic Street and complete the build with the help of several strong Māori labourers who understood the local wood. Charlie and Tom sheltered during that time under a wattle-and-daub cottage on the section's edge, lucky to have found a spare roof in the burgeoning town where many camped under canvas. The days here were differently divided, not by the bells, but by mealtimes, Charlie's school hours, and the work that Tom did to oversee the many steamers that flowed through the region.

Seamus made temporary accommodation at his rooms on Beach Street along the waterfront, near the makeshift custom house. When the surgical practice had been vacated, Tom had been happy to invest in a share of the premises. The kinds of malady Seamus would treat on land would be little different to those he'd seen at sea: injuries from the jetty and lighters; fevers, influenza, cholera, typhoid, venereal disease and other ailments brought off the ships or treated in quarantine.

'Constipation, as always.' He continued his salubrious list. 'Boils. Headaches. Hangovers.'

'Scurvy,' Tom suggested.

'Pregnancy.'

'Measles. Consumption?'

'Already ripped through the peninsula, Tom. Hit the Māori hard.'

In his new role, Tom's knowledge of clippers and steamers, of the world's waterways and docks, came together. Looking back on all his dogged determination, he discovered it had amounted to something unexpected, something tangible in the certificates he signed off that declared seaworthiness and capacity of berths for each steamer; in the reports and recommendations he made to the Harbour Board; in the way his advice was followed.

Quarrying would soon begin for the bluestone needed to build the graving dock and a retaining wall along the beach. The board would arrange for further works on the jetty to increase its capacity. Tom was called to survey the location for a new lighthouse at Dog Island, south in Foveaux Strait, and the treacherous Waipapa Rocks upon which many a ship had foundered. All of his expertise now had manifest results.

And, finally, there was the house. The double-fronted wooden structure with its wide sash windows and generous fireplaces drew plenty of curious eyes as it developed. On its eastern face, large bay windows looked out above the harbour. Far from being an aristocratic manor in the local bluestone, neither was it a humble single-room cottage. They would have a private bedroom each. There would be a dining room and a separate parlour. A verandah on which they would sit at night while watching for movements on the glinting water.

Keys in hand, he pushed open the gate for the first time. Seamus had come up from the clinic with his bag, and Charlie ran through and opened up all the empty rooms, still perfumed with varnish and paint and wallpaper glue. The toffee-coloured wooden floorboards would soon have carpets running along them. Solid-legged beds would be made up with pillows and soft coverings, which would slide off in the night only from restlessness or the heat. Tom's sextant, telescope and portable chronometer could be stored, along with his charts and nautical drawings, behind glass in a cabinet and secured with a little brass key.

It had come too late, Tom thought fleetingly as he followed Charlie through the house with steady steps and a blooming feeling of accomplishment. But there were other achievements to be proud of too. He was not alone. And he could provide for Charlie as if he were his own.

'Is it really all ours, sir?' Charlie's delight was infectious. He understood in a way Catherine or James would not have been able.

'Aye, it really all is.'

What little they owned was pulled from trunks to be folded in drawers, hung on walls, draped across beds.

Charlie chose several of Tom's maritime scenes to brighten the dining room and parlour. Others they would take to Annabel Murchison and her husband, who had gallery windows on George Street, where they were known to display the works of local artists and sell them for a worthy price. For his own room, Tom reserved the sailor with the green hatpin to hang at the foot of his bed.

They slept as if weightless that first night, and woke to greet the same view brightening at their windows as had darkened them the night before. Drawing the curtains, turning to the painting, Tom found the angle of the morning sunlight transformed its surface into an unreadable sheen, and so he shifted his view to the verandah that stretched along the side of the house towards the water, along to the southern rata they'd left standing at the boundary line, and caught the darting of a tui, its puffy white throat, its iridescent feathers of midnight green.

On the third night in the house, Tom rested back on the sofa, packing the bowl of his pipe with tobacco. Charlie riled the embers in the hearth and piled on another log before replacing the iron stoker in its stand. He had been curious to join Seamus, who had returned to the clinic after supper to tend a burn sustained from a boiler, but the night would run late, Tom thought, and there was schoolwork still to be done.

It was just the two of them alone.

As Tom struck the match, drawing on his pipe as he shook out the flame, he noticed Charlie inspecting the photograph Tom had placed that afternoon on the parlour mantel.

'It is your wife, sir? I have only seen her in ink.'

Tom stood and dropped the match into the fire. So much time and they had never before come to this point. The house brought them all together. At Charlie's shoulder now, he hovered. His eyes too were on the image; the boy, now fourteen, with hair already maturing his young cheek, awaited his reply. In that moment all he could do was cross the room to the window and raise the sash for a whiff of soothing harbour breeze, though the warmth Charlie had just built would escape and the chill off the harbour take its place.

It had been many years since Tom had last unwrapped the photograph from its cloth. He'd never again hung it in his cabin. Now it felt right for Catherine to be part of what he had created. Proud of their comfortable life, he knew she'd appreciate this at least: the way the fire enlivened every texture of the room with vermilion reflections, flickering there in the brass bases of twin fluted lamps, here across the sweep of polished rimu wood, along the back of the well-padded chairs, and within the amber liquid swirling in his whisky tumbler as he raised the glass to his lips.

'She helped you learn to paint, you said, in London, when you were younger,' Charlie prompted. 'But that's almost all I know.'

'Aye, she did. She was an artist too, and I owe my success to her. Catherine died of fever, before I sailed to Melbourne.' Tom chose his words with care from the windowsill. 'And I cherish her still.'

'Is that a baby, sir?' Charlie was peering closer at the blurred bundle in Catherine's arms. 'You did not say?'

Tom held his whisky up to the light before drinking again. He closed the window, sat again on the sofa. It seemed he had not thought it through.

'I lost him when I lost my wife.'

It was, after all, not a lie.

Charlie glanced at him, then replaced the photograph with the same reverence he had given the tile portrait in the laneway four years earlier. It seemed he accepted the obvious interpretation of Tom's words: children were frail. They died all the time.

'I'm sorry, sir.' Charlie studied him, breaking his thought.

And Tom smiled in wordless apology, wondering if he had been grimacing.

Later, when Charlie had left for bed and Seamus returned from the clinic, Tom and the doctor would sit with just the fire's persistent embers and the little wooden mantel clock tracking time towards midnight, and Tom would explain as best he could the roiling tension that came at him now like a wave.

How could he tell Charlie about his son, his real son, now? What could it do except unsettle their relationship, muddy it with betrayal and questions?

Charlie was more than a substitute. There'd been no response from James to his careful paintings, parcelled up lovingly in lieu of written letters, and Tom had mailed nothing further. It was possible Alfred had never let him see them. Alfred, whom James had been encouraged to call 'Father'. What did it matter now?

That first year in Port Chalmers, Tom had not looked back. He'd felt no uncertainty, no misgivings. He worked to create a secure home for himself and Charlie, free from the struggles they had both known. The irony of this path was clear. It was laid down in unconscious defiance of whatever it was – God, fate, rogue chance, the structures of class and wealth, the meanness of a sole man's wilful decision – as if to say, *See, I could have been a good father after all. I might have done this if circumstances had allowed.*

But perhaps, after all, it was only to himself he was trying to prove something.

All the paintings he had created, exhibited and sold over the last ten years had brought him the coin to build this roof, that hearth, those windows to the sea. Magnetic Street, so named because it ran between magnetic north and magnetic south. As if all the times he had sought to bring the sun to the horizon through the sextant, it was this he had been looking for.

It wasn't a destination, but an arrival.

49

In the boom that began with gold, the once humble village of Port Chalmers transformed at Tom's feet. Wealth from the goldfields and fisheries brought prosperity to the settler population, and Dunedin continued to swell with newcomers from northern seas.

Around Magnetic Street, the once denuded hillside flowered with planted gardens, while at the port, the graving dock began construction. No longer would ships be scuttled needlessly but could be repaired and given longer life.

With each passing year the house became known to Tom, almost human. Each room, strip of patterned wallpaper, brass door handle and knobbled carpet pile an extension of his body. He'd run his hands across the wood of the verandah railing, trying to learn the pathways and patterns in the grain. The history of this new place they'd arrived to. The solidity that had come to mean so much to him.

It seemed all the more fortunate to have found peace here when war had erupted in the North Island before the roof was on the house, and had raged a bloody path since. They read of it each morning in the *Otago Daily Times*: the defiance of the northern Māori chiefs, unwilling to sell more land; the strategic supply lines and attacks on this pā, on this village in response; a fierce resistance in Waikato and Taranaki; and the confiscation of lands from those the Crown called 'rebels'. In the south, the settlers called for separation: why, it was asked, should the peaceable south pay for the expense of all that bloodshed?

By 1868, Tom would travel by carriage to Dunedin on a Saturday afternoon to hang his latest works in a small but respected gallery on Princes Street. Opposite him sat Annabel Murchison, who had framed all twenty of the paintings herself; each choice of wood and moulding she had matched to Tom's ships and their seas; each corner aligned in an exacting example of craft. It had been her skill all along, Tom realised, all these years, even before her husband died.

He admired her work and told her so. She had a keenness for art and conversation that he appreciated, a maturity wrought by experience, and a way of carrying it all with lightness.

'You are not the only talented one, Mr Rutherford.' She smiled in return.

'Indeed, I am not.'

She was, he estimated, a little older than Tom, and had chosen to remain at Port Chalmers after her husband's death. It was the skies, she said, the evanescent radiance that held her there. And Tom agreed.

That afternoon, however, it was as if someone had blown out a candle in the sky. The sun disappeared, strangled with storm. It was not so strange an occurrence to be caught out when the weather suddenly turned, but it was only luck that just minutes earlier they had left the last of Tom's paintings safe inside to be hung on the gallery wall.

Together they dashed along Princes Street, hands securing dripping hats as the rain dropped violently. Annabel fought the darkening weight of her skirts; Tom reached out for her elbow. They passed where the Toitū stream used to flow before it was diverted underground, and where a Kāi Tahu landing site had once been a heaving market with baskets of fish and potatoes exchanged for coin. Through the rain, Māori fishers retreated to exposed boat hulls down on the waterfront. Perhaps they would upturn them for shelter. Tom knew the long return down the harbour to Ōtākou would be impossible in such conditions, but the native hostel, long unsanitary on the bank of the polluted stream, had been buried three years earlier under the rubble of reclamation works.

The wind cut everyone to the bone.

Hotels filled as settlers took cover.

Tom and Annabel found shelter in a carriage that would take them home.

The wild rain pressed itself like millions of gleaming eyes at the windows as the horses made a mud-slowed pace back to port, and Annabel laughed at the state of her sodden hems. Tom smiled at her light-hearted ease.

By the time they arrived, only a scattering of raindrops continued to slip in the sallow moonlight.

'That was quite the adventure, Mr Rutherford.'

'The pleasure was mine.'

Tom climbed the hill alone to Magnetic Street, his eyes falling to the earth as his breath rose. George Street was full of Scotsmen and women like him and Annabel, in the bank and the butcher's, the chemist and the printer's, who would make their way back to wide, warm hearths in newly built homes, so proud of their new beginnings.

Arrived at the house, Tom placed his hand on the gate, grateful for it.

The ancient peninsula rose before him in the dark and at its base the harbour curled, a question mark in a larger history still being written.

*

At the public viewing of Tom's latest paintings the following week, Charlie and Seamus added to the ecstatic applause. They were convincing in starched collars and tidy whiskers, no sign of salt about them, and Tom saw himself in their image.

He'd begun to slow and wish for simple comforts: a hearth at night, the quiet patter of rain on the slate roof, the sight of chimney smoke curling through the dusky morning skies and the warmth of a bed firm to the ground.

It wasn't just his own silvering beard or the threat of illness or Charlie's inability to live at sea that made Tom consider the roots he'd set down. This new life gave him companionship, something to strive for. More than that, he felt all the separate parts of himself finally merging into a coherent whole.

At his easel, he was still patiently searching, despite all Catherine had taught him, despite all he had since accomplished. Through Turner he had learned to use light and colour as emotional forces, drawing a viewer in through feeling, and with Catherine's influence even now he strove in the study of motion: how to make each wave, current, eddy, wake and ripple appear fluid and energised.

How to illustrate a state of persistent change.

A painting captured life as it was in a single moment, its subject necessarily fixed and inert. Motion must be implied, through light and shadow, through an illusory application of colour and an intuitive layering of brushstrokes. It wasn't so much magic as a kind of channelling. Turner's playing with perspective – the losing or merging of distinct foreground, midground and background into one – added to the intensity and movement in his work, but Tom's ambition had always been for realistic detail, to reveal the world in all its technical intricacy.

*

With affectionate curiosity Tom looked on as Charlie found his own form. In the early years it was mathematics and poetry and new school friends that occupied his conversation at night. Then it was his interest in working with Seamus at the clinic, and their visits to the chemist, where he became fascinated by the measuring of powders and liquids, the prophecy and hope inherent within each bottle, tube and tin.

The boy had not known his own age when Tom found him in the bluestone laneway that first strange day, and Tom had been reluctant to impose his own vision on one he saw as a kind of blank slate. In the end he realised it didn't take much to allow a child to flourish: food on the table helped, a warm bed, a feeling of safety and certainty. It was something he wished he'd understood earlier. The rest was the child's imagination and resilience, and Charlie had plenty of both, as well as the persistence to follow Tom's lead in one thing: to take opportunity whenever, wherever, it presented.

Charlie had grown into a young man, independent of mind, with confident sideburns and a moustache, and an authoritative knowledge of ailments and their treatment, gained under Seamus's guidance.

They celebrated his birthday on the date of Charlie's own choosing: April 15. Neither he nor Tom could identify the exact day of their meeting, but Tom knew it had been autumn, and he recalled an aching chill to the stone. And so they settled midway through the season. The symmetry appealed to Charlie's sense of precision and love of calculation.

Seamus took the whisky bottle in hand for a toast on the verandah, and the three of them shrugged on their heavy jackets and angled their hats low.

'Here's to us.' Tom's glass was up first, assuming the glow of lemony dusk that reflected off the house.

'Twenty-two. A very happy birthday to you, Charlie,' Seamus chimed in.

Three glasses touching, a faint trill upon the bass of the harbour.

There was an ample fire being built in the parlour by the housekeeper, and there would be cake waiting for them inside, but the harbour view continued to lure them, as if they stood upon the deck of their own unswaying vessel. Tom had an immunity to the frigid clime, a fortitude hewn from years of exposure. It made him feel alive, that southerly wind that laughed at any shield of cloth and headed straight for a person's bones.

'You have a glow, Charlie,' he observed after a while.

'Do I, sir? There was not much sun today, and I was at work in the surgery for most of it.'

'It's not sun that makes a fellow look that way.'

'Well.' Charlie flushed. 'Then you know the rest.'

He revealed the silver pin gifted to him that afternoon by Kiti Thomas, the chemist's daughter, who helped her father in the dispensary and understood the calculations and power of each precisely measured potion. A small fern, with filligreed fronds like those that grew on the hillside behind the port, which had been first a gift to her grandmother, a Kāi Tahu woman from the peninsula. It was her choice, she had said, closing his hand around it, to make a gift of something so dear. Though it was perhaps somewhat feminine, Charlie thought he'd wear it on his lapel.

'And do you have a special token for her, Charlie?' Seamus enquired later, stoking the fire after they'd warmed up over supper.

And the young man blushed. 'We'll see.'

Tom too had felt something lately. It was fleeting. Never acted upon. But with the youthful vigour of Charlie near, he could admit to himself he had enjoyed the awakening. It was surprising, the way a new face had slipped into his dreams. Anna, he would like to call her one day. Was he too old to start again?

The many echoes of Catherine at once drew him closer, and stayed his hand.

He had visited Annabel Murchison numerous times in the small shop where she had framed and hung Tom's paintings over the years. Paintings that had brought him attention, wealth and renown. It had come upon him gradually, as if he had been looking without vision.

She prised him open each time he brought her a canvas and she measured it for framing.

'Your ward?' She had once referred to Charlie, enquiring after him.

'My son,' he had corrected her, surprising himself at the ease of it.

Her smile told him she understood, and he thought of how it would be to have her sit with him of an evening, to share a wee dram with her and Seamus and Charlie. How it would be to share a kiss and mean it again.

How, even now, the horizon beckoned.

50

Monday, 6th of March, 1871
No. 83, Yokohama
Japan

Mr Rutherford—

Or may I call you Father? I hesitate to write that, but I know it to be true. I remember only flashes, incoherencies that I piece together to make a whole: the scratching of your red beard against my face, small pictures of sailing vessels that sat on my bedside table, and the feeling of being raised up and placed upon your shoulders.

I confine myself to this short missive, for I suspect there is no end to my wonderings should I allow them free rein.

You were a mariner and a painter. Great-Aunt Cecilia confirmed it in the days before her last breath, at this recent summer's end, while confessing the precise circumstances of your absence and all that has been kept from me since my mother died. Now I am also a painter of ships, recently arrived as an artist to document steamers in Yokohama, Japan.

Why so far across the world, into this strange environment? To get away, sir, to explore, to find the truth inside myself.

Father — that is, my uncle, as I am determined to call him now — greatly disapproves. Perhaps I risk my inheritance by accepting this post, but for now I put that aside as a consequence of a vital journey. It is a rebellion — I admit it. Still, I wish to understand myself as an independent man. From what I have lately learned, it appears I am too much like my mother. Too much like yourself.

My aunt said that you came for me once, wanting me in your own care. I was not aware. It may reassure you to know that I had a happy, though I suspect constrained, childhood, with excellent care and schooling, of course, and every opportunity I desired.

My uncle finally married when I was thirteen, though it did little to alleviate his solitary habits, and I have been given no siblings. He spends much of his time in recent years with a good friend of his on that gentleman's estate and appears content enough. I have comfort and great privilege. But it does not satisfy and I do not know why. Perhaps you can help me understand.

I have in my possession a series of wonderful unframed illustrations in oil, of ships under sail, of seas both settled and torrential, painted by you, I understand. 'T. Rutherford, your father.' I cherish these small parcels, kept from me for so many years and only in the last few months discovered.

Upon the certainty of Aunt Cecilia's death and the revelation that preceded it, my uncle grew full of remorse. Undesirous of further regret, he rescued these treasures for me, which had lain secreted in his study.

There was another thing, stowed with your paintings, which I daren't enclose for fear of its being lost: a marvellous cloudy, golden stone. When I showed it to her, Aunt Cecilia betrayed great surprise, for she had long believed it lost, and explained it was my mother's, and that you would know of it. The stone remains safe on my person until it can be returned to you, for I believe it was a gift from you to Mother upon your wedding, and so it is right that you should be reunited with it.

I enclose instead this image from my present home: in Japanese it is called 'ukiyo-e'; it is a print made of a woodblock method, very popular and the best examples of which are extremely skilful. The artist of this particular print is of the name Hokusai, who is now deceased. This is an especially agreeable example of his work, and I have been fortunate enough to acquire it. I enclose it within this letter as a sign of good faith. I am collecting prints from various artists as they fall out of favour due to the rise of modern image-making. Perhaps my current occupation too will fall victim in such a way. The world and its technologies are ever-changing, and so are fascinating to me.

I am posted here in Yokohama for one year, and then shall return to London. But my aunt informed me, before she passed from this life, of a modest note she received very lately from you, containing for the first time your address in New Zealand, and a plea for her to think of you, and a mention that you were thinking of me. You should know that she did think of you — and thought of you often, in fact, as she confided to me in those last sad moments — as I also have over the years. And yet now, more than ever, I wonder about you, and the life you have lived apart from me. Your painted gifts and recent communication indicate to me that I was not forgotten, and so give me hope.

Should you receive this letter and be inclined to travel, I request you find me at this address. If that is not possible, or not desired, perhaps you will allow me to journey south before I return to London in the following year. I should like to meet with you.

I await your reply, however brief it may be, as I have been warned to expect little more.

Yours affectionately,

James Ogilvie

51

Tom had set this in motion. He had shoved a handspoke into the windlass and turned it, dislodging the past and hauling it up from the deep-sea floor.

Sending a short but painstakingly phrased letter to Cecilia the previous year, had he not wished that a reply might come from his son? He had been too cowardly to ask for it.

Now, here it was: his dark desire. All its joy. Its difficulty. All the reckoning it would require.

When Charlie called to him down the hall, Tom could not immediately answer. He heard the young man's footsteps, the slap of his satchel onto the floorboards, the pause in which he would be hanging his coat by its collar on the wall hook nearest the door.

When Charlie called again, Tom's reply lacked air. 'In here.'

It was all he could muster. He heard the door handle turn and saw Charlie's boots first, just like he had that first time in the laneway. Well stitched now. Well polished and adult in size.

Tom had read the letter twice over, and was struck by its contents so intensely that he had pressed his back to the wall and sunk to the floor. With his knees bent up and his arms resting over them, his head was thrown back to better get some air. The strange accordion-like folds of the letter written from Japan hung from the tips of two fingers. Slipped to the floor from within those pages: a simple blue-and-white print in a foreign style, a wave building, threatening to break.

His breath had gusted from his chest. An involuntary cough. His head tightened, blanched of thought, and his pulse hammered.

When Charlie arrived, he insisted on helping Tom up onto the sofa and sending at once for Seamus.

'I am fine.' Tom batted his care away, his breathing calmer now.

'You don't bloody well seem fine to me.'

Tom smiled at the vehemence. They'd celebrated Charlie's birthday the night before, and Tom had felt high with promise and pleasure. Here was a young man, with all the passion of youth, finding his voice.

He refolded the letter and secured it in his pocket.

Seamus arrived in quick time, and pressed a cold stethoscope to his chest. 'Your pulse is a little fast, but it's regular. I'm not too concerned.'

To Charlie, he said, 'He's still strong.'

When Charlie left the room to organise an early supper, Seamus pressed Tom about the cause, and Tom handed him the letter.

'Aye, that is a shock,' Seamus agreed. 'I want you to rest anyway.'

Tom did not disagree. Overcome by a deep exhaustion, he dissolved into sleep from when the birds sang at dusk to when they woke him again at sunrise.

Seamus was softly snoring in the chair at his bedside when he hauled himself upright against the headboard. The letter was where he had left it, on the low table next to the bed. As his fingers fell upon its folded edges, he breathed at the touch. For a still moment he held it unopened while gazing at the painting on the wall. He could not make out the green hatpin in the peep of dawn, but he knew it was there. She was watching him. Watching over him, perhaps.

The click of Seamus's pocket watch snapping open.

'Christ, Tom. When did you wake?'

'Not long ago.'

'Thirteen hours, when I've barely known you to sleep through six. How do you feel?'

Tom rolled his head and smiled. 'Revived.'

'Good to hear.' Seamus stood and stretched, arching his back, and moved to lift the sash for air. 'What will you do?'

'Straight to the point.' Tom laughed. 'And we've not even had breakfast.'

'I'm sure you've a notion.' Seamus leaned on the windowsill.

'Aye. I will go to him, as soon as I can. Catherine would not wish for me to wait. We are not getting any younger, and I should like to know my son. We could make it in six weeks under sail, if the wind is our friend. I will not wait and miss this opportunity.'

'And Charlie? You've kept it from him for so long.'

'You know my reasons.'

'I do. And I've supported them. And yet you must tell him now. If you do not, you are a fool, and you make an even greater liar of me.'

Tom nodded.

'Do you not think you owe the boy the truth by now, anyway? What makes you any different to Alfred, if you do not? He has made his confession to James. So should you to Charlie. Who knows, perhaps they should like to be brothers one day.'

Tom had jeopardised their equilibrium. How should he explain?

His missive to Cecilia had been heartfelt. He was relieved to have sent it before she passed, and saddened to learn she was gone. He was overjoyed that he might so soon see his son again. But he feared to injure Charlie, and hated for them to be separated by a voyage. Yet he was resolute.

Charlie, it seemed, was ahead of him.

Sitting on the verandah with the glint of harbour at his feet, he was the first to speak. 'Are you here to tell me about the letter, sir?'

'What do you know?'

'I read it.'

His eyes lifted, dark and deep with feeling. Tom was sorry for being the cause of it.

'While you and Seamus were asleep. You cannot have expected otherwise. It was so unusual in its construction, and the state in which I found you – you slept for so long, I grew concerned. My punishment for invading your privacy is clear. It seems he is your son. Your true son. Lost no longer.'

The truth seemed so easy when he said it. Tom wondered if he did so to relieve him of the confession.

'He is.' Tom sank onto a chair next to him. Glad they had the water to focus on. 'We were separated when he was very young. Long before I met you. I'm sorry I did not tell you earlier, but I swear it does not change anything between us, Charlie.'

Charlie's brow furrowed. 'His words brought a great shock, I admit. But afterwards I was filled with grief and hope for you. Why would you think otherwise?'

'I never thought I would see him again.'

'And now we all hope that you do.'

'Are you not angry?'

'I don't know what I am. Hurt, angry. These are simple words. Loss is hard to bear; sometimes you have to lessen the load to carry on, I suppose. I see what Seamus always says about you is right: you're damned infuriatingly closed.'

Tom laughed.

'And what also aggravates is that I am yet again required to keep my stomach on the open seas.' His mouth twitched with a smile.

'I do not ask you to sail.'

'Of course I must sail, as Seamus must sail. You cannot make a voyage such as this alone. We're family, are we not?'

'We are. As is James. I gave him up, Charlie. It pains me to say the words, especially to you. It felt necessary at the time. Circumstances . . . My circumstances . . . Well, I found a line I could not cross.'

'He's a gentleman, sir?'

'He is. Raised with every privilege, but in the end none of that matters. I must go to him. His mother would wish it.'

Charlie was silent for a moment. 'I've been lucky that you needed a new son. I think my mother would've wished that for me.'

There was a strength in his levity that moved Tom.

'Why did you never tell me?'

'Many reasons.' Tom shook his head. 'At first I had no hope to ever see James again. Later I was ashamed. And then I became afraid you'd lose your faith in me. Time had moved on.'

'And now time has circled back,' Charlie said. 'If I am to make this journey, if I am to understand, you must tell me what I need to know.'

Tom closed his eyes. Saw the storm and a turpentine-soaked glove. Opened his eyes again to the silvered light, and smiled. 'Then I ought to begin.'

Tom knew of a ship. Of a captain grown rheumatic and tired who would happily take pay to remain at port while Tom took his place. The crew were known to Tom and proven seamen; he had their respect, and the chief mate was eager and more than competent.

Fifteen years earlier Tom had sailed from Melbourne to recover his son. Back then he'd been an uneasy passenger, full of optimism, only to become bowed and further estranged. Now he would sail towards James with purpose. Occupied with command, he would have less time to stoke his imaginings and let hope grow too great.

They advertised for cargo, and would embark for Yokohama in four weeks' time. They would take no passengers. They'd be back for spring. A fortnight's stay in port would be sufficient for Tom and James to start to know each other, and if it turned out there was no future for father and son, Tom would be home soon enough. But he dared hope he might show James the view from the verandah one day. Perhaps the following summer, when the pale toetoe and blood-red flax flowers would wave in the light against the harbour's cerulean edge.

In that final week, out of caution, Tom bid the solicitor draw up a will that would secure Charlie's future, and confided in the young man the exact arrangements. The house would be his, whatever the future brought.

He had sent a reply:

James, my dear boy, I am moved with urgency to see you again.

He confirmed he would sail at the soonest.

And although his commitment to do so was steadfast, to Seamus and Charlie Tom revealed his concern: that James had written while caught in grief and rebellion – as he had named it – and that by the time he received Tom's reply, a month and a half from then, he would have had time to cool, and might regret his correspondence.

Late autumn came sharp and clear on the hill. Soon after the mauve spill of dawn, they wrapped themselves in coats and hats and thick woollen scarves that sat high to their ears. Tom closed the gate to Magnetic Street and almost choked with uncertainty.

Charlie's hand on his shoulder. 'Seamus is still at the chemist's, sir.'

'Aye, he'll meet us at the wharf. You've said your own goodbyes?'

'A farewell for now, yes.'

As they stepped into the lighter that would carry them to the ship, waiting at anchor in the gelid harbour, Tom looked back, tracing a line to where his home stood hidden behind the port on a street running to magnetic north.

The lighterman waited as two sets of footsteps drew nearer along the wharf, syncopated in their rhythm. Seamus's certain and steady gait, slowed under the weight of his supplies. And another, lighter, faster: the post boy, flush-skinned, big-breathed, leather satchel clutched to his hip.

His hand waving rapidly as he called. 'Another letter for you, Captain Rutherford!'

52

Sunday, 2nd of April 1871
No. 83, Yokohama
Japan

Father—

I could not help myself. I write this brief note in support of my original epistle, even as you cannot yet have received the first, to beg you of its honesty and redouble my request to see you, which is in truth a plea.

It occurs to me that you may not respond. That you may by now have some other family. That I may be no more than a shadow. I have been told before I should not take up the pen after so much wine, but here it is, and I imagine you may take some convincing.

There is something further I wish for you to know, for it surprised me wonderfully to discover it. Quite a number of canvases I found stored in my uncle's study — most of which were unframed — and at first I assumed them to have been by your hand, except for their style, which is vastly different to your own, evidenced by your miniature ships. Would you believe, the signatures showed them to be the work of my mother.

My uncle dismissed them rather, claiming most were unfinished and unformed, but in my view they are complete, and rather extraordinary. The use of vivid colour and vigorous brushstroke is curious and inventive; in fact, so fresh as if they had been painted by the most modern among us today. The style reminds me of the work being done in France lately, and I feel these paintings might find some small open-minded audience, at least among those of us who will give time to the work of a lady painter. I should like to try and organise it on my return to London, and I would hope to do so with your good wishes. Aunt Cecilia described how you always supported and admired Mother when others could not appreciate her.

In any case, with these words I send you all love and affection.

Your son,

James

PART FOUR

The Pacific, 1871

53

11 June 1871
Pacific Ocean
N 4° 15' E 178° 53'

I lie here as the wood groans in time with my aching memories. It's a sympathetic element to surround an ageing body. Fifty-two. *I am fifty-two years old.*

I say it out loud, as if to make myself physical again.

My name is Thomas Rutherford.

I press my hand against the timber panel at my head, and wonder how many have done so before me. Whether they turned inwards to the cabin instead, unconcerned with the walls, compartments and divisions that surround us, that confine us. It has a deep colour, this wood, a fire in its heart that causes a crimson sheen in the light.

What befell us last evening no captain would wish for his crew. In a delusion brought on by heat and stagnancy, a man had thrown himself overboard. What cruel illness could impel a sailor to such dishonour, to such awful waste?

The sea is still. We are without wind. Our clipper is a true but now ageing example of its kind, lacking the auxiliary steam that might save us. The men are overcome. We are all awaiting an ending, a single discrete moment that holds hope in its centre.

How have we come to this?

Twenty-five days have passed since we left the bony arms of Otago Peninsula, but we languish in steamy air atop the flat lustre of the equatorial tropics. Barely had the ship crossed the Line before we found ourselves becalmed, squeezed now in the doldrums for seven days – longer than I have ever known possible in the Pacific. The water is clear and deep; a hand plunged beneath its surface can be viewed just the same. The silvery flash of fish in the depths is the sole movement we see. Our charts taunt us with the simplicity of their clear navigation lines; to cast an eye to the horizon is to conclude we are not moving at all. It is only precise calculations made from the sky and its roving inhabitants that reveal to us otherwise: we drift incrementally. I chart our position each day, waiting for the slightest breeze so we might fill our wilting sails.

On deck, the men pray for rain. For cooling rain to wet their cracked lips. Whenever it comes, it is heavy and hot, too soon lost to steam. They swear at the sky then, and at each other if that's not enough, but at least lethargy keeps them from their fists.

Fresh water runs lower. It is tainted with the taste of rust and I have had to ration the grog. We are victualled for sixty days at least but our biscuit is already more weevil than meal, our remaining beef giving way to mould. Yet it is not our bodies I worry for.

We find ourselves with an affliction on board that is the cause of the crewman's morbid impulse, and it is one neither I nor Seamus can arrest. All we can do is counsel the men's nerves, administer quinine to calm the fever, and hope they have enough fight in them to overcome it.

For my own part, other shadows rise from the calm and eerie quiet of these expressionless seas. Ghosts, returning after so many years, brought on by your words. I imagine what I will say to you, my son. I find I still don't know the shape of that story, and so I practise it while I can.

On our first night out from Port Chalmers, I fought to sight my course, there was so much feeling blurring the lines. Are you familiar with some of the paintings of JMW Turner? His later works, in which detail is eschewed for the inference of light and movement? It is as if I have tipped to his way of seeing after all.

Regardless, I keep on. I'll rise and take my command, awaiting the wind, and when it comes, as it must, I'll urge the crew towards your shore.

Charlie has been and left my morning coffee. The aroma draws me up as it cools.

Who is Charlie? I am searching for the words to tell you.

Feet on the boards, shaking this sticky shirt from my chest, I take out the first of your letters as a reminder of our purpose. The paper has lost all its crispness, creased from being opened many times. It has been carried in my jacket pocket through cool drizzle, against my chest in swelter, studied in rising light, dreamed of at night. The sea slips from its folds: it is flat in perspective and confined to paper, but raging nonetheless and breaking with great impetus. If only the cresting wave of this image were ours: *ukiyo-e*, you say it's called. A woodblock print. It's hard to believe such artistry could come to be considered ordinary.

I take this wave as a sign of your forgiveness, and it keeps me keen for our arrival. Despite the trial of our current state, our destination remains set: Yokohama. A port I had not thought to see but which now eclipses all others.

54

I will describe to you what I see.

Men with eyes fixed wide. Sweating day and night. Muttering words that to us signify nothing. They flail for the doctor's hand like it is an oar thrust out to save them.

Seamus has moved these fever-afflicted sailors into sick bay, but whether he can rescue them is not yet certain. He spends all day in the forecastle tending to them with Charlie's assistance. The pair confer with lowered heads between rows of damp men, assessing what can be done to give them comfort. Charlie follows Seamus's orders with as much dedication as I have seen any sailor follow their captain, and a confidence he will never have with the sail.

At night Seamus greets me in my cabin, as weary and overheated as the rest of us.

'No improvement, then?'

'We can but wait, Tom.'

Seamus is a skilled medical man and we have made many journeys together. He is also my closest friend. He offers me a swig from his own flask, and the whisky smacks at my throat as we recall once more the mate's anguished call of alarm last night before eight bells –

that is, close to midnight. By the time we had reached the deck and hung a lantern over the side, the water was again flat and unaffected. When it became clear that a sailor had willingly dropped himself over the side, it struck every man among us hard that we could do nothing to honour the loss.

We have recovered no body.

Desperate to rouse the wind, several of the crew afterwards took up their knives and stabbed at the mast, holding to a superstition, but the heavens did not respond. We scarcely list on the water.

'How is your own health?' Seamus asks me this question after his long day with the fevered souls. He is never off duty, it seems.

'I am not so concerned for my body as my idle mind.'

He mulls this. 'It is a worry I share for us all.'

I tell him I am eager to know who my son has grown to be. That I wonder, are you the man you would have become if I had succeeded that winter's day in London?

'If James is half as good as Charlie,' I say to Seamus, 'I shall be proud.'

'With Catherine's blood and your own I see no other likelihood,' he replies.

Perhaps I should not have kept the truth from Charlie for so long. But I could not bear to draw a string of connection between the two of you. I had failed already and wanted to start again, to do my best by him.

I believed I would never see you again.

When Charlie joins us, his back is an ill-fitting curve against the chair.

'What could bring a man to such an act of abandonment, sir?'

I can't find an answer. Though he has experienced much already, there are many more things for him to learn in this world. I look to Seamus. Receive no assistance.

'He was a competent and reliable seaman, Charlie. Right up until he wasn't.'

Is it possible our own nerves will give way before we make it? One morning I will wake and find my men the living dead of the ancient mariner's tale.

An albatross limp at my neck.

How have we come to this? It's the outcome of a simple but potent equation: my estrangement from you; your accordion letter.

I had received no word from Cecilia, no word from you. Not for fifteen years until an unusually thick message arrived with perfect copperplate handwriting on one side. When opened, its strange pages unfolded towards the floor, and changed everything in the minutes it took to read it.

Your second letter surprised me as much as the first, and so narrowly reached me before our departure. I can still hear the post boy's flat footsteps hitting the wharf. Recall the glistening of exertion upon his wispy upper lip, the resettling of a leather satchel against his hip as he met us, heavy of breath.

Until then I had wondered: had you changed your mind? Were you full of regret? Was I again too late? I cannot describe what happiness burst in me to read your plea.

Aboard the clipper I took command, ensured the watches understood their duties, eager to be moving. As the men strained at the windlass, bringing up the anchor, I still did not know what we were headed towards.

Setting out, we were buoyed at first by plentiful winds. They gusted like great bellows as we sailed past Taiaroa Head and north into the Pacific. It seemed such fortune, to be making easy speed. I felt charged with optimism. Ambitious, in fact; a searching and confident force that I often experienced as a younger man. But like many heady moments, it did not last. With no land in sight the wind flagged, losing its impetus in stuttering increments over three days, while the heat rose and we met with this: this perfect stillness.

I am urgent for reasons only Seamus and Charlie can know. In the morning I lean over the rail and stare into the deep, unmoving sea. It seems a man could topple into its calm without a splash; it's all so still, so silent.

For the first day, for the first two, I was confident I knew what it was to be becalmed, and had no fear of the evasive wind. I've borne storm, monsoon and drought many times over. This would be a frustration, a common disruption to our journey, nothing more. But the damp and steaming air soon infiltrated the ship with an oppressive stillness. The sails have remained lifeless, and we have borne this stifling heat for so many long days without hint of change, no rippling wake nor whirling eddy, no alteration in sky nor horizon, that all the crew are brought low.

Most have taken to sleeping above decks. The air is less stagnant and cooler than the foul quarters below and so I permit it.

Eight days now. Floating under a blazing light, fixed upon this reflective sea. My logbooks confirm it, but it's as if time is no longer passing and the sun and moon are illusions above the mast.

At noon I check our latitude, pressing an eye to the sextant and adjusting the angle until the sun meets the horizon. I hold out my hand and feel no resistance. No surprise when I make note of our coordinates and convey them to the helm. The deck is all bare backs and low voices.

'Why not give the word, Mr Rehu.'

'Aye, sir,' the chief mate replies at once. 'At ease, men. But be at the ready for command.'

Barely a sigh in response to his call. The men are exhausted by the pointless trimming and hauling they must do each time we sense a shift in conditions. We hasten at breezes so small we could catch them in our hands. In my anxiety I remain alert for some change, some shift, some lightness, any kind of movement.

The men bend, seek shade anywhere they can find it, light pipes with slow and precise gestures, as if measuring out time, making it count. A single bell is struck.

'All yours, Mr Rehu.'

'Aye, Captain.'

I seek refuge in my cabin. The wood is warm to touch and by afternoon the sun punishes through the stern windows. Charlie is waiting for me, back from the sick bay. Mopping a handkerchief along his forehead. I sit across from him at the table and pour us both some tepid whisky.

'So.'

'Yes.'

Even speech has gone. I turn my empty glass and it catches the light. He reaches for the bottle and for a moment the action surprises me. Still I see his face as it was when he was a boy, though over the years he has tended me as I have tended him.

When he is gone, I re-read your words.

55

Love and affection. Your son. Your second missive reassures me, James, although it may be influenced by the passion of a bottle, and therefore changeable on a whim. I am moved that you should declare yourself so. That you respond in a manner both unguarded and incautious instils me with hope for your genuine feeling, and I am pained for this delay to be at an end.

That you find beauty and merit in your mother's art brings me extraordinary joy. I would like to set eyes on those canvases myself one day. Some I may remember; some others may tell the story of my absences. I have a sketchbook of hers too, which I have upon me, ready to share. I anticipate the surprise that awaits you in its pages. You will know her face, perhaps even for the first time.

You say you are an artist – well, that makes three. I'm proud to learn of it, as your mother would have been. I hear Yokohama is a busy international port, and I look forward to seeing the vessels you paint. Do we have a similar eye?

You say you are seeking, and I understand. Perhaps when we meet you will allow me to confide some of what I have learned: that a voyage is less about new shores than what you discover within yourself. I thought I glimpsed it once through the telescope on the *Aurora* when I was a boy. It wasn't tangible like a coastline, a bay, a breakwater; it was an intimation that I had no bounds. Your mother brought out this feeling in me, further urging me towards fresh ambition.

Of course, there are limits. Imposed by those in power. By the elements. By oneself. Perhaps of all forces, it is one's own determination that is the most powerful, and the one thing we can hold on to.

If I've failed at things in my life, it was not because I did not try. I still question if what I did was wrong – if I betrayed you – and yet I made my choice to protect you, to give you the ability to become whatever you desired to be, without the struggles I'd had in my youth.

I wonder: have you ever before travelled so far south as New Zealand? I know nothing of your adult life beyond what you have penned me. No doubt you will be full of surprises. Your mother certainly was.

As an artist, you may understand. I'm forever attempting to capture the ethereal light that characterises our home, the low and invitingly luminous pastel suffusion that hangs across the sea and can turn with little warning to dramatic puncturings of indigo or vermilion, icy blue-white and thunderous charcoal. Skies that are spun and scattered at the will of the Antarctic. On the steamship *Pirate* years ago, we would chip ice from the winches and helm in winter, salt the slippery decks, and blister our fingertips by warming them too long on hot tin mugs of grog. In summer, we would scorch beneath the southern sun, our necks burning above our collars. But within the extremes of this climate, we were sheltered, living far away from the concerns of other places. Until then I had always been shifting my weight, never coming to rest.

After your mother died and you were lost to me, for some time I allowed the sea to be my forgetting. But Catherine brought me back to land. And it was Charlie who kept me there, just as you might have too if we'd had the opportunity to live and grow together.

I didn't understand it when I was younger. I was still searching for the ends of myself. But in New Zealand, I have found some repose, a gradual accord between what lies within and without.

Perhaps age is at work in this. My body creaks, slower than in my youth. There is silver in my beard now and on my head. I feel somewhere between young and old. More aware of my mortality. Of all I still want to become. Proud. Regretful. Keen to put things right. I thought I'd missed my chance with you; how glad I am to find myself wrong.

In Port Chalmers I work among the locals and the harbour men. I've given my voice at town concerts and meetings, and once caused consternation for coaling a vessel on the Sabbath. I imagine your mother would have laughed at that. I sail on occasion across the Tasman and back again, but I'm always relieved to return to my home. Not all I have done has endeared me, but I'm judged on my actions and achievements, and that is all I ask.

Some things have not changed since you were a boy: I am always at my easel. In both oils and watercolours I've painted the many vessels that enter past the Head, and our wonderful little port with its floating inhabitants.

It was more than I asked for, perhaps more than I deserved, to find favour among a small community weaving history into its growing fabric. Though I paint for my own satisfaction, I'm proud to say my paintings have been admired over the years, framed and hung on walls, discussed in newspapers and in quiet gallery rooms.

First I became a man with coin in my pocket. Then I became a man with a home to my name. The house I built on Magnetic Street is modest in Ogilvie terms, but for a boy from Bo'ness it is substantial.

Earlier I spent some years in St Kilda, Melbourne, shaping my grief into a new form, but the town was full of a darker detritus. Charlie, too, was haunted by its dusty laneways, the eternal question of his father. He was convinced the man was dead, as he knew his mother was. He mourned. But there was no evidence. I have always supposed the diggings to have claimed him. Many men did not return from injury, despair, the bottle, bankruptcy.

Aye, I took him in.

It does not mean I forgot you.

Now Charlie is a man himself, twenty-two years old and standing eye to eye with me. He is in fact the same age as you.

When I am gone, he will not miss a listing deck, nor even this still one. I have taught him to read our path from the stars, but it is Seamus who has something to offer his future.

I see them watching me, the doctor and his apprentice. The fever concerns them and I am charged with the care of so many souls. They wait for hesitation in me: an old cough I have, some occasional breathlessness. Yet there's life in this body still. I imagine how it will be to reach the dark shadow of coastline, to enter this last port as if it were my first.

I tell all of this to you as if you were here. In the swelter I allow the past to come over me, and the events and thoughts of these hazy days I confess to you, practising my story. An attempt at reconciliation. A man looking back to find a way forward. Your mother showed me how it might be attempted, and now I do my best to describe my thoughts in both watercolours and inked sentences for you, as she once did. I tell it as it happens, for all time is one in the doldrums.

I hope soon to tell this story in person, with it all behind me. I hope you'll understand me when I do. And if I cannot, if I do not get the chance, well, at least there will be some tangible record. My life laid bare in ink and colour for you to measure.

56

Last night we lost another. From the quarterdeck I saw him myself: with buckling knees, he approached the side and slipped to the water. He did not go quietly at all, rather hit the surface with a heavy slap, the sound breaking the silence.

'Man overboard!' I cried.

'Man overboard!' Charlie echoed.

And the call was repeated along the body of the clipper till all knew of the event.

In the black we hung our lanterns over the side.

'Anything, men? Anything at all?'

Nothing beneath the surface. No swinging of arms, legs, nor a face bobbing to the surface, nor a mouth gaping for air. No fight. It was two hours before the next cry came to me from the bow, and then a white shirt could be seen, billowing on the surface at starboard. A man lost to us days earlier, already risen in these warm waters. It pained the crew to be prevented from recovering the body. They were on the edge of disobedience, but Seamus warned of the fever spreading this way, and I reminded them in sad detail of the likely degradation to the flesh, so there was nothing to be done. Soon scavengers will swoop and pick the skin from him. In a week the bones will sink to the bottom of the sea. It is a sight no feeling person should have to witness.

Afterwards I could not sleep. Most nights I cannot sleep.

'Nine days,' I say to Seamus.

'It is strange beyond reckoning.'

'What am I supposed to learn? What can we do to halt the hallucinations, call up the wind and get us back in motion?'

He has no answer, just places a draught on the table.

A sour steam slides over the waters. We are always wet with sweat.

The body of the ship is feverish too, its bones damp, hollowed out of men. The sails droop like pale spectres. We keep up with our watches as best we can, marking time with the bells. The crew looks to me for guidance, so I remind them that the wind is fickle, gone without warning, and certain to return just as suddenly.

To Seamus, I confess. 'I have seen my father out there. His ghostly hand waves to me from the waters.'

'Aye?' His hand to my forehead, thermometer under my tongue. 'It is merely the heat, Tom.'

I see your mother, Catherine, waiting for me in my cabin when the stars come out. Memory is a cave I enter, searching the walls for signs.

You too must have thought me a ghost at times, my own son. I do not blame you.

We are all wraiths here.

'The fever hits at night,' Seamus explains.

'I see. Those in its grip must be restrained so as not to cause themselves harm.'

He does not waver at my command. He tends to the afflicted with pragmatism as much as tenderness. He is hoping to put them back together again.

*

After my breakfast, I am summoned. A seaman has fought the fever and grown lucid. Charlie cups his head and holds a beaker to his lips. Seamus has the man's wrist pincered between fingers and thumb and looks off to the side, counting.

'Good,' Seamus says, and signals to Charlie.

They come to me, confiding in low voices.

Seamus leans in. 'He speaks of deep moist grass, as far as he could see.'

'There is nothing but ocean out there and miles of it,' Charlie whispers.

'You're right,' I agree. 'There's no land in sight.'

'Which is likely part of the cause.' The doctor hesitates. 'There is an explanation for such confusion. I had thought it an old superstition, but have heard of a fever that brings on melancholy for home, and for the land.'

He pauses to search my eyes. I can only nod uncertainly for him to continue.

'Cases where a sailor has stepped off the ship because he believes he is no longer at sea. He thinks he is ashore. There are stories of men who see the fields of their youth, stretched out before them like grassy plains. Scotland, Ireland, New Zealand, wherever: the sea becomes the land of their past. It calls them home.'

'And they yield to that call, of course.' I glance at the ailing seamen, ten or more now.

'What, they are homesick?' Charlie asks.

'It's true. They long for it, but it is a treacherous melancholy,' Seamus confirms.

'So that's what we have here?'

'Aye, Tom. It's the only explanation I have. Calenture. A delusional state brought on by extended exposure to humidity, the heat, this relentless stagnation in the midst of the ocean. A longing for land; a fear of never reaching it.'

'And are we all at risk?'

'Every single one of us.'

As dusk illuminates above the masts I follow Seamus's instruction, ordering the remaining twenty-odd men and boys to gather their kit from the decks and return below. The uproar is too furious. It's true – it is foul underneath. And so reluctantly, in a devil's bind, I allow them to continue to sleep atop, directly under the stars, but with the instruction that they must be vigilant. They're to restrain anyone who appears affected.

And so the night skulks around us, shifting in nimbus-black formations. Alone in the cabin, the windows opened to stern, my eyelids have slipped to half-closed and I am limp on my bed with my forehead tight, and my mind too languid and unmoored to defend against feverish destruction.

I float over past seas, gathering them together to show you, my son. So many paths taken and not taken.

Enough. I rise again.

Even at this hour Seamus unrolls his leather kit, and the blades and hammers and pincer-like implements gleam. Charlie mixes powders and administers liquids as the doctor instructs. Fifteen men to tend now. Seamus and Charlie hook the stethoscope into their ears, studying the sounds of hearts and lungs, as each have taken turns to study my own.

On the raised quarterdeck, I look out over the boards. The view of a ship's master is expansive. Everything rolls out before us. I watch the crew move like shades of black against black, variations of darkness. Black that looks blue. Black that looks grey. Our lamplights cast a lemon haze. The water is a reflection at our feet.

I have seen paintings like this, by an Italian in particular, Canaletto, who showed Venice in such tones, and like the Turner that hung in your late grandfather's study, which I remember so well. The hue may be similar but on our deck those imperilled fishermen are ailing merchant sailors and the storm a flat menace.

I lift your letters from my jacket pocket, unfold and fold them again, a signal to all my ghosts to rise. Tonight I console myself with the thought that Catherine would understand I did what I did out of love. I have always feared she would hate me for my choice, for she was defiant, and could not know what it looked like to live shaken with grief, to cower without privilege. I knew such an existence well. And your uncle, the man you came to call Father, understood that I did.

He may have begrudged me and my assumption of a role in his family, but he loved you from the outset.

57

Now I will confess: Charlie is my son, though he is not of my blood. This makes him your brother.

Tonight, he is unnerved. His forehead beads with sweat and his eyes are puffy. I suppose a mirror might tell me the same. I have a tri-fold mirror still, which I brought back from Calcutta as a gift for your mother before we were married. It has become mottled with age and salt. It distorts a man's image. Still I cannot part with it. Once it showed both a splitting and a gathering together of parts, urging me to lay my contradictions to rest in a new life.

Another of my crew was lost to the illusory fields last night. Just a boy. Fifteen years old. Drowned by melancholy.

Charlie sits and stares out beyond our stern. I will not force conversation upon him. It's easy for us to share companionable silence.

Eventually, he says, 'I'm afraid to sleep. They all talk of fields. Rolling pastures. They don't see the sea any longer.' Charlie searches the dark, shaking his head. 'They are tired of these flat, heated waters. We all are. But they see green, and they simply . . . jump.'

'I know, Charlie.' I sigh and reach for the whisky.

'What, you see it too? God help us!'

'No, Charlie. I have no need to jump.'

'If only we could all be so certain of ourselves.'

I pour us each a glass. 'Why don't you write to Kiti?'

'I've done so already. But when will it be possible to send it? That's the question.'

'Write again anyway. Share this with her, even if it's after the fact.'

'Perhaps you're right. And I've made up my mind. I'll ask her on my return, if you agree, sir.'

'I do. I think you'll be very happy together.'

'I've been thinking also, if we ever make it out of this sea swamp, I should train properly. As a medical man. Seamus will help me,' he says. 'It's not that I don't appreciate—'

'You have a bright future back in New Zealand, Charlie.' I smile at him with what I hope he will see is pride.

'Should we make it.'

'Of course we'll make it.' I hear my response: too sharp, too certain, too fast, and as Charlie's eyes meet mine I wonder what he supposes. It's clear what we fear. Some more of the crew won't make it, and how can we know we two won't be among that number?

'Has Seamus checked you?'

Charlie nods. 'There is no fever.' Nevertheless, he touches a palm to his forehead.

Then he moves to one of the paintings I have hung at the end of my cabin, opposite the stern windows and above the table. 'It is a lovely town, isn't it? You've captured it well.'

Port Chalmers, he means. It's observed in a tranquil lemon-violet light, one of those rare days when the harbour lay unruffled and the sky could be viewed within its bright depths. I painted the two of us along with Seamus into the longboat in the foreground. The hills behind were patched pink and white with houses, and the bay was an array of resting ships with canvas furled, crews at work and passengers taking air above decks. What it could not capture: the bone-chill of the frequent southerly winds, and the redolence of the air in winter, its clarity cut through with wood smoke.

'I miss those skies already, sir. Especially from the hilltops, which have always felt to me like mountains.'

His longing for home is hard to hear, and not because of the fever.

'Easily provoked,' I say. 'Changeable in a moment. That's how I've always thought of a Port Chalmers sky.'

'You were right to withhold this one from sale, though it might have fetched a good amount. And this one next to it – *Caribou*. The closer I look, the more I am certain it is you on deck, reaching out your hand to the woman in the white gloves. Is it true? She is not closely detailed, but you've succeeded, I suppose.'

'Succeeded?'

'No more dabbling on broken tiles, at least.' Smiling then, his cheek has returned. 'Do you know, I haven't thought of that in the longest time. Do you still have some, sir?'

Shaking my head, I wonder if the remaining portrait of Catherine still gazes out from the windowsill at Alma Road. I am glad I did not keep any of the pieces. It is a story for another day, my son. To capture the intellect and energy of your mother in a flat portrait was an impossible challenge for me. I attempted it only out of grief, after I had lost you as well. I cannot now say why. They were never meant to last.

'Well,' he continues, 'I never suspected I was in the acquaintance of a famous artist when I found you in the laneway.'

'You weren't. And I found you.'

'Oh? Let's agree we found each other.'

58

Cecilia is right: I did return. I came for you. High on the winds of colonial opportunity. Foolishly confident. As we beat across the seas, I imagined you already beside me, sailing south to our future. I imagined the miniature oils I had sent to you, wondering if they were in your hands and what you thought of them. I could not wait to see your face.

I would spend the next decade and more wondering without hope of an answer. It is only with your recent words that I learn you have received my gifts, and how long after the fact it was that they came to you.

That day is still a wound. I can see it, smell it, recall it all. It's just at my ear. The clip of hooves on cobblestones, the disturbance of the path underfoot. The air seemed to crouch as I approached the house, as if observing me, hushed and without movement. The house too was quiet, lying in wait, hand covering mouth.

Almost four years I lived there with your mother, and almost as long with you. That place clawed me with memories. I moved through the wide hall and shivered past pale sculptures on plinths, a tableau of impassive faces.

I grasped Cecilia's thin hands and felt the veins under her skin, like the shallow roots of gum trees spreading beneath the Melbourne soil. Dear Cecilia, how I had missed her too.

Quickly I saw I had allowed hope to smudge the true outline of circumstance. It had seemed straightforward as I set out from Melbourne. I had coins heavy in my purse, options for secure and regular postings, a growing reputation as an artist. I had packed my bag in a solitary St Kilda room and thought it enough for us.

How badly I had forgotten.

Was it an hour that I waited for you, James? Two? Stopped short across town outside an iron gate. In my mind I moved up the path, through the door and there you were, your head bent over a wooden desk. You were working on a mathematical equation, or writing in neat, looped handwriting, learning by rote the words of a famous poem. You were learning paints and colour, or even points of the compass. You would emerge and run to me, and I would gather you in my arms, take you away from there.

I remember it exactly as if it were happening now: your face, when I saw it, burned like the sun. You called, but so quickly I lost you. I dashed across the road just to see your feet disappearing into the carriage. With the sound of the whip against the horses' hard bodies, you were gone too fast. Or I was too slow. I've never been sure which.

Father.

You had called not to me but to your uncle. You were not to blame. In your voice I heard you were happy.

I knew then, although I fought it, that I would have to let you go.

Did Cecilia say how, in the end, she persuaded me to turn away from the house? You should know she did so to protect you. I returned to Melbourne, after some years at sea, with just a stolen painting that she'd handed to me at the docks. Stolen, because she would not have been permitted to remove it had she first asked; stolen, although it was painted by me, and embellished by your mother's hand. All the disappointment I imagined your mother would have felt, and all my guilt glimmered in that oil paint.

I was certain you would have opportunities and choices that I had never had. And however much I resented the bargain your uncle had forced upon me, there was never a doubt that he loved you as a son.

I swear I tried. But in the end, how could I disturb your peaceful existence? I felt such shame. I knew the pain of losing a father and what it was to live with that absence, and still I thought: my son is better off without me.

When I wake it is with an open mouth, parched, capturing air. Everything is dark. A series of bangs on the cabin door and a long groan, which I mistake for the sound of my own body. I am conscious of a motion beneath me, quickening tread above, the shouts of men, the heavy dropping of a sail and the creak of the lines hauled tight. These are sounds I know like the rumble of my own stomach. I feel it at my neck, wet with heat. A breeze swims through the window. More banging. They call my name again, and I smile, but my head spins and I find I am unable to move.

It is beginning. The clipper will soon sing from its sails.

One day I will be enshrouded in sailcloth, weighted with lead. But not just yet. Not yet. Instead my mind is adrift, wandering the hillside of my youth, the green fields of Richmond, capturing memory in oil and brushstroke.

59

'Feel it, sir! How extraordinary it is!'

I roll my head to one side, nearer the voice, but my eyes remain closed.

My breath is easy and regular.

I open my eyes to the light.

'We're on our way!' Charlie's face is as ecstatic as his voice.

'And I am pleased to say you will be joining us for the final leg.' Seamus hovers, preparing to shuffle the stethoscope yet again beneath my shirt.

A breeze glides through the window. The ship moves beneath me. I imagine the men all around us, on deck, upon the masts, deep in the forecastle hold. I cannot speak.

'The mate and helmsman have it under control,' Seamus pre-empts. 'The fever is breaking as the air cools and circulates. Most of the infirm are up from their beds already. Activity and a changing horizon will be the best medicine from now. But you, my friend, are under doctor's orders to rest a little longer.'

I close my eyes again and wait for each footfall.

So we have motion again. Soon, with luck, we will find the north-east trade winds and make a direct course to Yokohama. We move towards you, my son.

I am left alone again to steep in sweat and contradiction.

At times I have been too fond of absence. Too familiar with loneliness. This I know of life and can tell you: we play out what we know, what we learn from an early age, no matter if it is any good for us. Grief remains a kernel at our centre, and all else grows from it. But when we allow it, that shadowed heart can bloom into something more beautiful than we could have imagined: a life, a love, an expression rich not in spite of but because of its origins.

After two days I emerge, greeted with a cheer from the men who have mustered before the quarterdeck. Grog. They shall have plenty of it tonight. I urge them to find as much speed as they can to move us across the wide Pacific. We have many days and many miles to recover.

For now they will remain under the command of Mr Rehu, who is willing and ready to succeed.

Before us, far across the decks, the spray conquers the bowsprit and falls like diamonds over the rails. I grasp the brass at stern, bracing against the swell while Charlie balances casually against the side. The wind lifts his hair as we cut through the sea. Everyone is relieved. In less than three weeks we should make landfall. The crew laugh and sing again, nimble and revived, their sweat-soaked shirts billowing. They could not be more in love with wind and sail.

Relieved of my duties, I am an invalid on deck, a tartan blanket at my shoulders. I did not expect a sea fever to fell me so.

Catherine is watching for the shore. Her smile gathers like a curling wave. Her hand is at my shoulder. When I see you, I will see her too, and hold you both in a delayed embrace. You will hold up the cairngorm and it will catch the light. Her sketchbook will tell her story. I will do all I can to fill in the gaps. One day I hope to see her canvases on display in a London gallery, as you have planned. It was a dream she could not manage in her too-short life.

> *I am not so interested in what a biologist or chemist might say a thing is, but in what a thing implies. How perspective is simply that: a point of view, an awareness of ourselves and what lies beyond our simple eyes. A way of seeing that can be altered, expanded, reinvented.*
>
> *I wish to hold what is fleeting and ephemeral, feel it sifting through my hands. Like Elizabeth Barrett, I shall build a house of clouds for all my dreams. Hide them from society, hide them from heaven. They belong nowhere but in nature, Tom. Nowhere but in my heart and yours.*

I have read these lines so many times, they have become a living memory.

Now her dreams live in her son's heart too.

Charlie's eyes are steady, turning from the horizon to my face as if they are the same.

Smiling, but with the barest lift of his mouth, he appears to be waiting.

'Catherine,' he prompts, leaning in.

How does he know my thoughts?

'Tell me, how will you describe her to James?'

'Catherine,' I begin, and the green, grassy hill spreads before me as I move back in time to the start, to the middle, to the ending, which now seem all the same point to me.

*

We each sleep on the past. To me it's a pillow I can finally rest my head upon.

You wondered if I have a new family and it is true. It is a family built not of blood but mutual consolation.

But blood is thick. I know I will recognise your face when we draw in to Yokohama.

The Pacific dissolves beneath our hull as we leave the Line far in our wake. Our instruments once again provide certain position and we make a confident trajectory. North we plough and then, at last, we reset to the west.

Charlie is at my side as the clipper hits speed. Like you, he has all the future laid out before him. Unaware of what he will face, and how he will handle it.

Seamus brings my paintbox like it is medicine, dosing me in pigment. If he were to diagnose my state, he might describe this feeling in simple terms: optimism, of a kind that is both aware and unstraining.

We move through pure colour now: the viridian sea and ultramarine sky, the lemon sun, the many colours of the men's skin, the boards a shade of freshly dug earth, straight, parallel, running up to the bowsprit, silvered with spray, pointing us to your shores. Colour that is living. It beats like a heart, full of hope. If I have not told my story well in words, I can always tell it in paint.

And when I see that shadow of land emerging, I know it is no hallucination. The wind presses at my face. When I stand into it, my breath is taken from me.

Yokohama.

The closer we move to the coastline, the more I inhabit a space between the two faces of my life. I stand here on the deck with Charlie and Seamus but my eyes take me to the horizon. The land reveals its pattern best from the distance. It's strange: with the dissolving of each mile, the less distinct the coast becomes. I see instead a scattering of colour, dots and lines. I move from stern to bow, eager to take up my brush. I will mix my paint as the harbour opens up to receive us like a widening jaw, search the port for a figure waving his arms in greeting, and lay the first wash as the space between ship and land grows ever smaller.

Author's note

Thomas Rutherford is a fictional character inspired by the art and seamanship of my great-great-great grandfather, Captain Thomas Robertson, a master mariner and maritime artist. I have taken the liberty of gifting my character with various details drawn from the life of my relative. Additionally, a number of the works painted by Tom Rutherford are directly inspired by those created by Captain Thomas Robertson. The life story of Tom Rutherford, however, is imaginary. The character of Catherine Ogilvie shares a name with my great-great-great grandmother, but nothing more.

Captain Thomas Robertson was born in Borrowstoness (Bo'ness), Scotland, in 1819. The son of a shipmaster, he married Catherine Ogilvie Lumsden of Edinburgh. They had three children: Ann (who died as a child), David Ogilvie Robertson and Marion Robertson – my maternal great-great grandmother. Catherine died young, and Thomas Robertson emigrated to Melbourne in 1853 with his children, David and Marion, and a relative to care for them. In Melbourne he resided at Alma Street, St Kilda, and made a living as both a seaman and an artist. His works were shown in the 1853 exhibition of the short-lived Victoria Fine Arts' Society, of which he was a committee member, and in the inaugural exhibition of the Victorian Society of Fine Arts in 1857. He captained the steamship *Lady Bird* between Melbourne and Launceston, and *Pirate* on the mail run between Melbourne and Port Chalmers, New Zealand. From the early 1860s he resided in Port Chalmers, where he built a house on Magnetic Street. He worked as Inspector of Steamers and continued to paint and exhibit to acclaim. In 1871 he sailed with his son, who was also an artist, to Yokohama, Japan. Thomas Robertson died in Yokohama in 1873. To my knowledge he is buried there in the foreigners' cemetery.

Captain Thomas Robertson's paintings can be found in museums, galleries and libraries around Australia and New Zealand, including the National Gallery of Victoria (NGV) and State Library Victoria (SLV) in Melbourne; the Australian National Maritime Museum and State Library of New South Wales, Sydney; Toitū Otago Settlers Museum and the Hocken Collections, Dunedin, New Zealand; and Museum of New Zealand Te Papa Tongarewa, Wellington, New Zealand. His sextant was donated to the Port Chalmers Maritime Museum by my great-aunt Helen McIntyre Elliot.

Though I have taken care in my use of historical detail throughout this book, imaginative flight has been a vital and necessary guide. I've adjusted dates and timelines where necessary for the fictional story.

Liberty has been taken with the placement of two JMW Turner paintings: *Fishermen at Sea* (1796), purchased by the Tate Gallery in 1972, which I have hung in Lord Ogilvie's study; and *Snow Storm – Steam-Boat off a Harbour's Mouth* (1842), first exhibited at the Royal Academy Exhibition in 1842 and gifted to the National Gallery as part of the Turner Bequest in 1856, which I have allowed Tom and Catherine to view on a visit to the gallery in 1847.

The *Aurora* and *Majestic* are fictional ships, as is the mention of the *Icarus*, though the telling of the latter's demise off the Barbary Coast is based on a true event of the time. The *Lightning, Lady Bird* and *Pirate* were real ships, captained by my relative during his career.

In all accounts of history, sailing, art and setting, any errors are my own. I've drawn upon numerous resources, including historical texts, academic texts, journals, memoir, family histories, paintings and photographs, newspaper extracts and archives (including Trove, Papers Past and the British Newspaper Archive), historical and digital maps of land and ocean, sailing manuals, blogs specialising in sailing and in the Victorian era, YouTube videos, television documentaries, podcasts, and poetry and novels written by seamen. There are too many fascinating and informative resources to mention, but the following were especially invaluable: *Two Years Before the Mast* and *A Seaman's Manual* by Richard Dana; *Victorian Women* by Joan Perkin; *Victorian Women Artists* by Deborah Cherry; *JMW Turner* by Michael Bockenmühl; *1835* by Richard Boyce; *Aboriginal Victorians* by Richard Broom; *Black Gold* by Fred Cahir; *Melbourne Dreaming* by Meyer Eidelson; *The Face of Nature: An Environmental History of the Otago Peninsula* by Jonathan West; *Port Chalmers and its People* by Ian Church; and content on the websites of Te Rūnanga o Ngāi Tahu (ngaitahu.iwi.nz) and Te Rūnaka o Ōtākou (otakourunaka.co.nz).

The quote beloved of Catherine, '*Thy firmness makes my circle just, And makes me end where I begun*', is taken from John Donne's poem 'A Valediction: Forbidding Mourning'.

Acknowledgements

While the writing of this novel was an act of solitary creativity, it would not have found its current form nor its way into print without the generous community of supporters who kept me going over many years, who shared expertise and feedback when I needed it most, took my ambitions seriously, and sustained me through the highs and lows of drafting and redrafting.

Huge gratitude and thanks to my intrepid agent, Melanie Ostell, for making it all happen. My incredible publishers at Simon & Schuster Australia – Fiona Henderson, who prompted me to unlock something deeper and finer, and Anthea Bariamis, who picked up the baton with love and ran wholeheartedly to the finish line with me. Thanks to Lizzie King for her diligence and Victorian-era obsession, Libby Turner for astute suggestions and care, and Katherine Ring for the final touches. Thanks to Anna O'Grady for the energy and ideas to support my wee (big) project, and all the rest of the wonderful team.

This achievement would have been so much more difficult without the early assistance of both a Varuna Residential Fellowship and a Glenfern Fellowship, which gave me time and space to write, and truly fuelled my journey.

Sincerest thanks to readers of various early drafts and chapters: Christopher Miles, Kate Whitfield, Janine Mikosza, Anne Myers, Alicia Coram, Amanda Benson, Christopher Raja and Ian Britain. Particular thanks to Janine Mikosza and Anne Myers, whose support formed the bedrock of this novel. Thanks to Antoni Jach and Antoni's masterclass participants, who shared their thoughts on my work over the years.

A huge thank you to Angela Findlay, who held my hand through varied research challenges and always had an authoritative resource or lead to recommend.

To Sue Casey, Peter van Leeuwen and, in particular, Jeffrey Mellefont for their generous and expert advice on sea and sail. Any errors in this novel are apologetically my own. To Tricia Dearborn, Janine Flew and Justine McGill for putting me in touch with each of them.

Many thanks to Dale Wandin for reading and for the yarn, and the kind assistance of Charley Woolmore at the Wurundjeri Woi Wurrung Cultural Heritage Aboriginal Corporation.

In Ōtepoti Dunedin, thanks to Beth Rees at Toitū Otago Settlers Museum and Sarah Snelling at the Hocken Library for showing me the works of Captain Thomas Robertson held in their collections. I'm grateful to Bill Dacker for the careful and insightful comments on local and Kāi Tahu history and Seán Brosnahan at Toitū for facilitating Bill's reading. Thanks to Te Rūnaka o Ōtākou for dialectic advice.

To all my family and dearest friends, thank you for your interest, support and forbearance, and lots of love to my mum, Kate, for the use of her spare bedroom as a writing studio and her home in Ōtepoti Dunedin as a makeshift international residency on more than one occasion.

To anyone else who was ever interested enough to ask about my writing: thank you. Sincerely.

The majority of this book was written in Naarm/Melbourne on the unceded lands of the Wurundjeri and Boon Wurrung peoples of the Kulin Nation. I wish to acknowledge and pay my deepest respects to Elders past, present and emerging for this privilege.

Book club questions

1. Art is intrinsic to Tom's journey to find his place in the world, to express himself, to heal from grief and to love. Do you think it's the practice of creating art or the final result that has the most impact on Tom, and on artists in general?

2. There are many types of loss in *Where Light Meets Water*: loss of a parent, a child, or a loved one – but also the loss of one's freedom, homeland, identity and aspirations. Which kinds of loss make us stronger? Which are hardest to recover from?

3. Travel can awaken the senses to new possibilities, experiences and ideas. How do you think Tom's travels changed him as a person? How have your own experiences of travel changed you?

4. Catherine finds the strict social, moral and even artistic codes of Victorian England restrictive and oppressive. How much have things improved since the 1800s? What has remained the same?

5. Tom, James and Charlie all suffer in different ways because of the father figures in their lives. How do these relationships shape them as people? What does it mean to be a father?

6. Passion can take many forms. Passionate love, passion for art or one's vocation, passion for the natural world. Which kind of passion is the strongest? Which is the most long-lasting?

About the author

Susan Paterson is a writer and editor from Aotearoa New Zealand. Her debut novel, *Where Light Meets Water*, was shortlisted in an earlier version for the 2019 Michael Gifkins Prize for an Unpublished Novel and written with the assistance of a Varuna Fellowship. Her poetry and short stories have appeared in various publications including *Meanjin*, *Going Down Swinging*, *Etchings*, *Wet Ink* and *Poetry NZ*. She lives in Naarm/Melbourne.